DARK TRUTHS

A.J. CROSS

BLACKTHORN

This paperback edition published in Great Britain, the USA and Canada in 2021
by Black Thorn, an imprint of Canongate Books Ltd,
14 High Street, Edinburgh EH1 1TE

Distributed in the USA by Publishers Group West
and in Canada by Publishers Group Canada

First published in 2019 by Severn House Publishers Ltd,
Eardley House, 4 Uxbridge Street, London W8 7SY

blackthornbooks.com

1

British Library Cataloguing-in-Publication Data
A catalogue record for this book is available on
request from the British Library

ISBN 978 1 83885 394 5

Print   .A.

ONE

The sports car turned into the entrance and came to a stop. Its lights went out. The young woman in the passenger seat gazed around. 'Why here?'

'Because you said you wanted us to get away, be out of doors, in the dark.' He glanced down at her, grinning. 'Why didn't you change into something less . . . "pure"?'

She pushed open the door. 'I wanted to keep it on.'

'And I'll have you out of it in the next twenty seconds.' Out of the car, they gazed at each other across its roof.

Her brows rose. '*You* sound confident.'

He came around the car towards her, a travel rug under one arm. 'I am.'

Her face glowing, she laughed, started running. He went after her along the black tarmac, followed as she veered from it to the grassy sloping field below them, lost her balance and went down in a pool of pale light. He came to her, put out his hand. She took it, removed her shoes, then watched as he spread the rug on the grass, held out his hands and bowed low from the waist.

'*Madame* said she fancied it al fresco.'

1

She came to him, took his hands in hers. 'I want us to be on our own.' She pointed down the hill. 'Look. There are some houses down there.'

He reached for her, pulled her gently down, whispered, 'Let's give them something to talk about.'

After a few minutes she tensed, sat up.

He touched her bare shoulder. 'What's wrong?'

She held up her hand. '*Sssshh!* Did you hear that?'

'Hear what?'

'The voice,' she whispered. 'There's someone here. Up there. People.'

He looked in the direction she was pointing. 'How do you know it's people?' He reached for her. 'Oh, come *on*, Lucy—'

'No.' She got to her feet, gathering up her skirt. 'I'm not staying here with some angry, menacing person hanging around.'

'I didn't hear anything.'

'Your ears are full of champagne.'

'I think it's the champagne that's getting to you.'

'I *heard* it, Hugo, and I don't want to be here. Come on.'

He watched her walk carefully up the slope and on to the tarmac. Folding the rug, reaching for her shoes, he followed, quickening his pace, his tone low and teasing. 'Here I co-*ome*. Coming to *get* you . . . in a weirdly menacing way . . .'

Squealing with laughter, she took off in the direction of the car park.

Monday 15 August. Six forty-five a.m.

THE ATHLETIC LOOKING BLONDE MOVED along the trail, ponytail flipping from side to side, the sun strong on her thumping head. Her date the previous evening had let her drive his car. She'd got it up to seventy, immediately pulling it back to forty as headlights appeared behind them. The car had followed them for a couple of agonizing minutes before pulling around and away. Her date had laughed as she'd given the police car the finger.

Now, she sped along the familiar tarmac, ignoring the headache, revelling in her own fitness, savouring the softness of the white vest against her skin, well worth its hundred-plus price tag. In another eight minutes she reached her usual turnaround spot and headed back, getting the familiar endorphin rush. Runner's high. Exhilarated, she upped her speed, picking up a distant, steady rhythm some distance behind her. She grinned, increased her speed again. Within seconds the footfalls were gaining on her. She increased her speed some more, flying now. He passed her on a blast of displaced air, causing her to flinch, almost stumble. Regaining her balance, she shouted, 'Too damn close, moronic *idiot!*' The car park was directly ahead. If he was still there when she reached it, she would tell him there was an etiquette to running. She ran on, reached it, chest heaving. It was deserted. She checked her fitness watch, smiled. Despite the moron, she had reduced her time by five whole seconds. She went to her car without a glance for another parked on the opposite side. She took out a water bottle and drank from it, eyes on the heavy tree-cover just ahead. Tensing at a soft movement, she half-turned, felt breath on her cheek, in her hair, thumps to her chest. She sank, still looking at trees, letting go of the day and her life as the soft white vest grew red.

TWO

Monday 15 August. Nine thirty a.m.

Detective Inspector Bernard Watts squirmed on the wooden seat, his shirt sticking to him. He took a fifth glance at his watch in as many minutes, picking up the ping of a phone. Organ music swelled, the sizeable crowd got to its feet and turned. Watts did the same, followed it to the door and out into the hot morning sun. He joined those walking past the floral tributes laid along the edge of the wide path because he couldn't think of anything else to do. He gazed down at them, stopped at the large wreath bearing the West Midlands police logo, muted comments from fellow officers drifting to him. He looked back at the church. Acting Chief Inspector James Brophy from Thames Valley, in full dress uniform, was emerging. Watts' thoughts drifted to his own father's funeral years before. His view of life while he still had some had been straightforward: life was about class. That was class with an *a*, not an *ar*. He'd extolled Birmingham's car industry as the place to work. As well he might, with seven kids to support, even if he hated the mindless work. 'And people will always want cars, our kid. British cars.' Even in the mid-seventies, there were signs that his father had got it wrong. In the years that followed, Watts had learned that education was

5

what life was really about. He'd made sure his own daughter knew it. It had got her to Oxford.

He looked up, smiled. Pathologist Connie Chong was coming towards him. 'Wherever you are, it's miles away.'

'True.'

'Weather like this is enough to remind us that it's good to be alive.'

'Too hot for me.'

Her eyes drifted over him. 'Why aren't you looking pleased with yourself? Twenty-nine pounds takes a lot of getting rid of.'

He followed her gaze to the church and the large coffin emerging from it. 'You know I haven't got a face that does "pleased".' They watched Brophy stop to talk to Maurice Gander's widow. Watts imagined the sentiments being expressed, suspected that Brophy was good at that kind of thing. On a series of soothing nods, Brophy shook Mrs Gander's hand then headed quickly in their direction.

'That went well, wouldn't you say?'

Chong expressed agreement. Watts said nothing, thinking that as funerals go, it had gone. Brophy took his arm and steered him away from the other mourners.

'This concerns you too, Dr Chong. Police in the south of the city have a situation. An attack on a woman early this morning. I don't have the details but I've agreed for headquarters to assume overall responsibility for the investigation. SOCOs and forensics are already on their way to the scene, plus uniformed officers.' He looked at Watts. 'I know there's four days of your leave still outstanding, Bernard, but I want you on it now, as senior investigative officer. Here.' Watts took the location details from him.

It had been a while since he'd been part of a large, ongoing investigation, let alone running one. For the last five or so years he'd headed the cold case unit at headquarters with just two colleagues. Brophy turned to Chong. 'You're also needed as soon as possible' – his mouth crimped – 'because of the heat.' And to Watts, 'Take PC Judd with you.'

Memory supplied Watts with a hazy picture of a newly qualified constable with spiky blonde hair who looked about fifteen. 'Judd? She's just out of training. She's raw. Knows next to nothing—'

'And I've got six officers already working a murder, another four on beaches hundreds of miles away and Judd needs the investigative experience. She's now part of this investigation under your guidance. You'll find her in the squad room.' Brophy looked at him through heavy-framed glasses. 'Police Constable Judd doesn't share your summation, by the way. In her opinion, she's destined for great things in this force. You can tell me who's right.'

WATTS WENT DIRECTLY TO the squad room, picking up the tension among the few remaining officers getting ready to leave. She was sitting in a corner, frowning at her phone, thumbs in a frenzy. 'Judd!'

Her head came up. She sprang to her feet, pocketing the phone. 'Sir!'

He hooked a finger. 'Officers here get by with "Sarge". Car park. Now.'

Edging between desks, ignoring colleagues' glances, she

followed Watts down the stairs and out to a black BMW X5. They got inside. Judd gave it a quick once-over. 'Nice. One of headquarters' sneakers?'

'Mine,' he snapped, his attention snagged by a small tattoo on the inside of her left arm: a bird trailing barbed wire in the direction of her wrist. He looked again, the wire morphing into a single word: Free.

She was looking at him. 'Where are we going?'

'Why the question?'

'I don't like surprises.'

He drove across the car park, between the tall brick pillars and out, wanting to get the measure of her. 'What's your investigative experience so far?'

'In the four months I've been here I've attended several domestics, helped arrest a violent drunk, attended a suicide where—'

'I said, "investigative".'

She gazed at the scene rushing past her window. 'Nada. I've put in a complaint to Brophy about it.'

He gave her a sideways glance. 'That'll be Acting Chief Inspector Brophy.' His eyes went back to the road. 'You the stroppy type, Judd?'

Her head spun to him. '*No*, sir, Sarge. All I want is a chance to do some real police work. What's happened?'

'Violence, is all I know.' He jabbed the CD player. Following a soothing couple of minutes of Karl Jenkins, he frowned, picking up a repetitive *tk-tk-tk*. He glanced at Judd. Her head was repetitively nodding, earbuds in, phone clutched in her hand. Aware of his attention, she pulled out the earbuds, and dropped them and the phone into her bag. Jenkins prevailed. For Watts, whatever problems and pressures he had, there was nothing like being out of reach for a few minutes, listening to—

'Got any hip-hop?'

He felt heat rising to his face. 'Do I *look* as though I have!'

Twenty more minutes of Jenkins and they entered Blackfoot Lane, narrow, sloping steeply downwards, official vehicles parked nose to tail close to a high brick wall on their left. Watts shot another quick glance at Judd in profile. He knew next to nothing about her but his instincts were already working overtime: she was trouble. Whatever was waiting for him, he could do without a loose cannon. 'All I want from you is that you do exactly as I tell you. What you don't do is get creative. Got it?'

'*Sir.*'

Watts sighed. After a week with his daughter and son-in-law in Amsterdam, which had been OK until he'd realized that he didn't have a lot in common with either of them and all the sights had been seen, he'd been more than ready to get back to work. What he hadn't anticipated was the chief, Maurice Gander, dying from a stroke, being handed a case for which he was SIO with zero briefing by a temporary boss he didn't rate *and* being stuck with a rookie on a mission to prove herself. Maybe he should ease up on her. 'Where are you from, Judd?'

Her head spun to him. 'What do you mean?'

'I can tell you're not from around here. Down south, somewhere?'

She looked away, out of the window. 'No.'

So much for sociability. He slowed as he reached a wide entrance, blue-and-white tape strung across it. A uniformed officer appeared in front of them, hand raised. Watts activated his window. The officer came to it looking overheated. 'Morning, Sarge. Hot enough for you? If you hang on here, there'll be a parking space in a tick.'

Watts waited, eyeing a young, red-faced constable some distance away talking to a woman next to a yellow Boxster, two small dogs bouncing and yipping inside it. Her voice carried on the heavy air. 'Now *you* listen to me. This is a right of way. You cannot refuse me access and—'

'Pain in the arse,' murmured the officer.

Tuning out the woman's voice, Watts looked beyond her. 'When did they arrive?'

The officer turned to look at the knot of reporters standing some distance away behind a barrier. 'Not long after us.'

'Tell everybody out here to keep it zipped.'

'Sarge.' The young officer hurried to the entrance, released one end of the tape and sent a signal inside. An official vehicle nosed its way out, turned and drove down the hill. The officer motioned Watts forward, the woman's voice drifting through his open window as he drove inside.

'So, why are you letting *him* in?'

The car park was crammed, a large white forensic tent taking up much of one tree-lined corner. Among the squad cars was a van marked 'Forensic Services', a black estate car next to it. Chong was here. Sliding into the available space, he and Judd got out into intense heat. He glanced at her uniform trousers. 'While you're on this investigation and the weather's like this, wear something light.' He headed for the tent, Judd at his heels. At its entrance a young officer wrote down their names, time of arrival and handed them plastic coveralls. They shrugged their way into them, Judd looking ultra-casual, like it was something she did every day. The constable held open the mouth of the tent. The heat inside was oppressive. Judd's nose wrinkled. A sickly, metallic smell was riding the heavy air. Watts felt his head tighten and perspiration surge on to his face. He eyed the small red car, its driver's door wide open, below it a glazed red-brown patch. Hearing movement, he headed to its passenger side. In the narrow space between car and trees, a small figure in white coveralls was crouched over tanned limbs.

'Anything to tell us?'

Chong looked up at him, pulled away her mask. 'Only the basics from a five-minute examination.' Her eyes moved to Judd.

Watts waved his big hand. 'PC Chloe Judd, this is Dr Connie Chong, headquarters' pathologist. When she speaks, we listen.'

Chong stood, nodded to Judd. 'Thanks for the build-up. I'll tell you what I know so far. A call was received by local police at nine a.m. from a Julia Prentiss, reporting concerns about her daughter, Zoe Roberts. Apparently, the daughter's employer had contacted her to tell her that Zoe hadn't arrived at work for an early meeting and hadn't phoned to say why she was delayed.'

Watts frowned. 'Why was the mother so quick off the mark to report it?'

'From what I've been told, Zoe Roberts was regarded by her family, her employers and her colleagues as highly organized and competent, to the point where they considered her non-arrival for what was an important meeting extremely out of character.'

'Any sign of the victim's phone?'

'Her mother has it. She tried to ring her this morning, got

voicemail, then found it where Zoe left it the previous evening when she visited. According to her, Zoe runs here once a week.' She laid her latex-covered hand on the car. 'And she owns a red VW with the same licence plate details as this one. I'm confident that the remains are hers. A low-loader is on its way to transport the car to headquarters for examination.' She pointed at what was lying on the ground. 'Come closer.' They did, Watts picking up Judd's quick intake of breath as they looked down at red fading to rust, a pale green pathology sheet covering the body from the shoulders up. Chong pointed to the blood-covered area below the sheet. 'Six stab wounds to the torso, each of them deep into the chest. See the marks on the vest around each of them? The weapon used had a hilt. The blood on the ground below the driver's door is a likely indication of where the attack began.'

'Any sign of the weapon?'

'Not according to SOCOs.'

Watts' eyes were fixed on her. 'Something else I should know?'

Chong gave him the look she generally used when he pushed. 'You'll have to wait. Right now, I want her out of this heat and back to headquarters so I can start her post.'

He looked down at the body again, then back to Chong. 'At least we've got an early cause of death.' He looked to Judd. 'That can be a big help in a homicide.'

'That would depend on whether the stab wounds killed her,' murmured Chong.

He looked back at her. 'Six, straight into the chest? Where's the mystery?'

'As I said, you need to wait.' She lowered her voice further. 'Unless you can find PC Judd something to do elsewhere?'

Judd looked from her to Watts. 'Hang on! Brophy has assigned me to this investigation. Which means I'm party to the crime scene and *all* the information pertaining to it. If we're talking head injuries here, I'm already very familiar with a wide range.' She itemized them on her fingers, her face flushed. 'I've attended RTAs, seen the results of domestic beatings, plus a jumper from a multi-storey. I don't want special consideration. I don't need it.'

Getting a nod from Watts, Chong turned to the body, knelt, reached for the green sheet and gently lifted it away. Watts' mouth twisted downwards, eyes narrowing against a mess of cut flesh, white bone and protruding pasta-pale ligaments. His morning toast gave his diaphragm a swift nudge. Swallowing, he picked up Chong's words.

'Not the neatest decapitation, I have to say.'

Hearing a soft sigh and feeling a sudden weight against his side, he caught Judd as she slumped. Lowering her to the ground, he looked a question at Chong.

She shook her head. 'SOCOs and forensic officers have done a search of her car, plus the immediate area beneath. It isn't here. Ask them about the blood spots they've found.'

He stared at her. 'You're saying it's gone? He *took* it?'

'In the absence of an alternative explanation, yes.' She replaced the sheet. Igor, her assistant, came inside the tent carrying a folded stretcher, a constable in tow.

Watts moved aside, crouched next to Judd, still lying on the ground.

'How's she doing?' asked Chong.

He tapped Judd's cheek. She gazed up at him, eyes drifting. 'Sleeping on the job already, Judd?'

She batted away his hand. 'Fine. I'm . . . fine.' Moving on to her side, she paused, got to her feet and stood, wavering. Watts held out his arm. She hesitated, reached for it.

He tracked an officer leaving the tent and heading towards the line of close-parked vehicles. 'Where's he going?'

'Headquarters,' said Chong.

'He can take Judd back with him—'

'*No.*' Judd pushed away from him, took a couple of shaky breaths, started dusting off her uniform trousers. 'What's next? What do we do?'

Giving her a quick once-over, he headed outside. She followed him to two officers, the backs of their navy jumpsuits inscribed 'Forensic Services' in large white letters. They turned.

'Morning, Sarge. Nice day for it,' said one.

Watts grunted. 'I hear you've got some blood.' He followed one of them a few metres to a small yellow marker.

The officer pointed. 'See? There and . . . there. Blood droplets.' His finger moved on. 'They continue to the trail over there, along the tarmac, then divert to the field on the right beyond the hedge.'

As the officers moved away, Chong emerged, hood pushed back, her short black hair damp to her head. Sipping water from a plastic cup, she came over to Watts. 'I've had a look at those droplets,' she murmured. 'I'm no blood pattern expert but I've seen it in enough contexts to have an opinion, for what it's worth.'

'Which is?'

'He carried it by the hair.'

Judd at his side, Watts walked the tarmac, following yellow

markers, eyes fixed on dry-looking splotches. Had some madman been hanging around here early this morning, done what they'd just seen inside the tent? He shook his head. A few years back, it wouldn't have been a question. More, an assumption. But that was before he'd been put in charge of headquarters' Unsolved Crime Unit and learned a thing or two about psychology and madness. That it was rarely the simple explanation for extreme violence he and a lot of others expected or wanted it to be. They continued on to where several white-suited SOCOs were methodically searching the ground running alongside the tarmac. Seeing Watts, one of them pointed at the hedge to the right. 'See that gap there, Sarge? That's where he forced his way through and into the field. The blood stops just inside.' They carried on to the thick hedge.

Judd looked as though she'd recovered, her head turning this way and that. 'This is crazy.'

Watts glanced at her. Her colour was back. She was looking vexed.

'No *way* would I run here.'

'What's your problem with it?'

She jabbed her finger. 'Too many trees. Too many places where somebody might hide. Plus, it's got a feel to it, an atmosphere I don't like.'

His eyes moved over their surroundings which in normal circumstances he might have judged pleasant. If you liked that rural kind of thing. Which he didn't. 'I've checked. This is a popular place for runners and walkers.'

Judd looked dismissive. 'They're welcome to it. I run on the roads where I live. Plenty of people around.'

'You take your chance with traffic fumes and being run over. As for atmosphere, I didn't have you down as the fanciful type.'

'I'm not. It looks all right, but it feels . . . desolate.'

Watts glanced around at wild flowers and vegetation lining the trail, much of it now dried by the recent weeks of unflagging sun. 'I see what you're getting at.' He didn't but a bit of agreement this early never went amiss. She wasn't finished.

'I'm a realist. In any physical confrontation with males, most females come off worst. I do martial arts.'

He looked down at her. She was no bigger than Chong. He thought she had a point. He went through the hedge, holding back thorny branches. She followed him into the field, more a meadow, of tall bleached-looking grass mixed with wild flowers, poppies bowing their heads.

She pointed to two tall yellow flags. 'How did they find blood evidence here?'

'People who go into forensics have an obsession for detail. Probably the same for all police work.' The sun bearing down on them, they headed in the direction of several officers on hands and knees, shoulder-to-shoulder, eyes downcast, moving slowly across a cordoned-off section of field. 'How's it going?' he called.

He got a shouted response. 'We're doing a whole-field search, quadrant by quadrant, starting this side. Zero blood in this area so far and no weapon.'

Watts and Judd continued on. 'This is looking better than I expected,' he said. 'Yes, it's a big area, but it's a contained scene, plus, these specialist officers know their stuff. Best of all, the public is excluded so . . .' He turned to her, seeing himself reflected in large, mirrored sunglasses. 'What do you think *this* is, *C.S.I.*? I want to see that you're absorbing all of this. Take 'em off!' Hot and irritated, he walked on. He thought about the victim and her early morning run. What he needed was another live-for-ever type who'd been here early this morning and had seen or heard something. His first job back at headquarters would be to get Brophy to sanction a witness appeal. Recalling Brophy's opinion of Judd, he asked, 'Got any ideas on this homicide?'

'Yes, Sarge.'

'Thought you might. Let's have 'em.'

She pointed back the way they'd come. 'Whoever killed her forced his way through that hedge, carrying . . . it, which means he's strong but also very confident. Which tells me he knows this area well. I think we should pull in all the locals with form for sexual violence, starting with those out on licence or who are known to have a connection to this particular area.'

'Do you now,' he murmured. What she'd said about this being a sexually motivated homicide chimed with his own thinking so far, but that was all. He pointed at the scene around them. 'What you just said about him knowing the area. Take a look.'

She did.

'Whoever killed Zoe Roberts wouldn't necessarily have needed local knowledge. This is typical countryside. See? Right of way from the car park to an exit at its other end. Hedges both sides, plus fields. If he's as familiar with it as you say, he'd know that Blackfoot Trail is a public path. That somebody might come along it at any minute.'

She nodded. 'Exactly. Like I said, confident.'

He walked on. 'There's something more urgent to do before we get into stuff like that. A visit to Zoe Roberts' family.' Sensing that he was walking alone, he turned. Judd was standing, arms folded, her face set. He frowned. 'What's up with you?'

'I just *got* it. The reason I'm here at all. To do the emotional stuff. The stuff I've been doing since I finished training and arrived at headquarters. Commiserating. Supporting. Being understanding and sympathetic to people in trouble.' She flushed. 'I'm bored of it! That isn't what I joined the force to do.'

He started towards her, his eyes fixed on hers. 'Now, you listen to me. I've got thirty-plus years on the job and I've got no problem "commiserating" where needed. You think you're special, Judd? That that aspect of the job doesn't apply to you?'

'No, I don't, but—'

'I'm glad we got that sorted. If that's all that's aggravating you, forget it. Zoe Roberts' family already has a liaison officer. Our purpose in seeing them is to get information about their daughter which just might tell us why she ended up here in the state we've just seen.' He stared down at her closed face. 'Keep your complaints and dissatisfactions to yourself while we work this case. I don't want to hear them and I don't want you following me about with prima donna antics. *Got* it?'

Her eyes were fixed on the ground between them. 'Sir.'

He frowned at her. 'You've got a lot to learn, Judd, and the way you do that is by working alongside other officers and not being an opinionated pain in the . . . You keep your mouth *shut*. You *watch*. You *listen*. You take in all you can from colleagues who've got years of experience doing this kind of work, most dating back to before you started infants' school.' He paused. He'd learned plenty about her in the last hour or so. She was full of attitude. Something else he knew about her. She wasn't what he wanted on this investigation. Or any other for that matter. He looked down at the set young face beneath the short blonde spikes. 'Any more ideas about this case?'

'Only what I've said. That there has to be a sex angle.'

'Because?'

'Lone woman, vest, shorts. It's obvious.'

'You don't say? What would you expect her to wear for a run in this weather? A greatcoat?'

She frowned up at him. 'A what?' She shook her head, impatient. 'I'm pulling all the relevant factors together as I see them: the surroundings, her physical presentation, what was done to her. You can bet your pension the pathologist will confirm it's sexually motivated. Zoe Roberts' killer was waiting here early this morning for her to start her run. He saw her as easy prey. It's very likely he stalked her.'

He walked on. 'All of which gets you a gold star for conclusion-jumping.' If he'd had similar thoughts about the victim's physical appearance, he'd have thought twice about saying so and risk a huffy response about females' rights to go wherever they want, whenever they want, however they want. He didn't need that kind of politically correct palaver. But she'd gone straight to it and never mind anybody else's opinions. 'For somebody of your years, Judd, you sound like you've got a low opinion of males. Anything else?'

'Yes. A suspect age range of twenty-five to forty.'

'Which lets me and a few others working this case off the hook.' He raised his head, picking up the hum of steady traffic. 'Hear that?' He looked around. 'Where's it coming from?'

She listened, pointed ahead. 'See that steep incline over there? I reckon the M42 is on the other side of it.'

He looked to where she was pointing, saw Adam Jenner, head of forensics, a few yards ahead of them, in conversation with a lanky thirtyish male Watts recognized from a cold case investigation twelve or so months before: Jake Petrie, geoscientist from the University of Birmingham. He headed for them, Judd following.

'Jake's giving us a hand again,' said Adam, pointing to the small drone sitting on the grass nearby.

Petrie held out his laptop to Watts. 'I've got some good aerial shots of the immediate area for you, DI Watts. Take a look.' Watts did, seeing the field they were in, the snaking black tarmac of the trail, a few distant houses on its other side. He passed the laptop back to Petrie, his attention caught by several SOCOs working the field's perimeter. Adam looked in the same direction, eyes narrowed against brightness. 'They're searching for the weapon. It's taking them a while because of the vegetation.'

Watts looked around. 'It looks like it's running wild.'

'The landowner says he's paid to leave the margins around the fields to wildlife, and the same for the rest of this field, which he's happy to do, given the way it rises on either side.' Adam pulled out his phone, studied the screen. 'Text from Dr Chong confirming that wedding and engagement rings on the deceased's finger match the mother's description of those worn by daughter Zoe Roberts.'

Judd sent Watts a look of suppressed excitement. 'No indication of robbery, Sarge. Like I said, this is sex.'

Watts glanced at Adam, stone-faced. 'PC Judd is bringing her extensive homicide experience to this investigation. She'll have it wrapped up for us by lunchtime.'

She flushed. 'I'm only saying—'

'And we only heard.' He pointed at the steep rise directly ahead. 'Judd thinks the M42 is on the other side of that.'

Adam looked across at it. 'She's right. It is.'

Watts headed towards it. 'I want to have a look, pinpoint exactly where we are in relation to the motorway.'

Judd was at his heels again. 'Sarge, how about this: he came off the motorway, looking for a victim. Question: if he was in his own vehicle, where did he leave it? Second question: why didn't he take her body with him? Answer: he didn't think he needed to. Why? Because he's not aware of Exchange Theory. I'm talking *all* forensics here, not just the obvious, like DNA. That lack of awareness is telling me that this is his first homicide.'

Watts stopped, turned to her, his face flushed. 'I get that you're keen, but I can do without your rattle and your questions, to which none of us has answers right now. We're in the "let's-have-a-look" stage, so let's have a *look*.' Mouth set, she followed him to the foot of the incline where he paused, listened to traffic noise. It was louder now. If there was a junction close by, one of the first things he would be wanting was a check of motorway CCTV for vehicles passing here early this morning. Make that during the whole of the previous night . . .

'Sarge?'

'Yeah.'

'Dr Chong said that Roberts ran here every week.'

Watts trudged on, the ground ahead of them getting steeper. 'So?'

'Just hear me out. Like I said, this probably started as a stalking case, her killer waiting, watching her run, getting to know her routine, getting to know her. How about I go and ask Dr Chong about the condition of Roberts' fingernails? If they're damaged, the odds are he's a total stranger. That she fought him. If it's a no, we need to consider that she knew her killer, which actually fits with her jewellery not being robbed because . . .' She stopped, eyeing Watts.

'Have you got a hearing problem, or just one with listening? It's already topping eighty degrees, you're not the only one with a head full of questions and no answers and . . .' He was about to add that he wouldn't see fifty again, but he didn't hand out ammunition like that to anybody, not even a rookie like her. 'Leave Dr Chong to do her job while we do ours.' He pointed upwards. 'Stop rattling and come *on.*'

They walked the steep incline in silence, traffic noise increasing as they went, bone-dry earth shifting under their feet. After a couple of minutes Watts stopped, perspiration coursing down his face. Judd passed him effortlessly, continued on. Frowning after her, he followed, reached the top of the incline and stood next to her. They gazed down at dusty saplings, a low retaining wall, a metal barrier and three lanes of roaring, surging traffic, pumping out a miasma of fumes. A glance across the motorway to an area of vast, numbered buildings opposite told Watts their exact location: The National Exhibition Centre. Chong would be starting Roberts' post-mortem in the next few hours. If they got really lucky, there might be a quick resolution from DNA identification. Which would go some way to easing her family's heartache and Judd would be back to her domestics and whatever else she didn't like.

He reached out, grasped a slender tree limb and leant to look further along the motorway, seeing an arrowed sign, another some way off for an upcoming exit. Straightening, Watts nudged Judd, pointing the way they'd come. He moved downwards with cautious steps, his feet sliding over powder-dry earth and meagre grass. A third of the way down his spirits rose: a quick wrap-up of this case was exactly what he needed. A signal to the brass that he had what it took to direct a big, current case and . . . His feet lost all traction. Arms flailing, he over-corrected, dislodging more loose earth. Briefly airborne, he hit the ground on his back, arms flung wide. He lay, winded, looking up at a sagging canopy of leaves, time sliding away. Hearing feet rushing towards him, he tried to sit up. 'No, Sarge, don't move! Stay still.'

He closed his eyes. *Jesus Mary mother of* . . . 'Stop going on . . . I'm OK.'

Judd's face appeared above his, her eyes huge, fixed on something to his right. 'Stay where you are, but have a look to your right. You have to see it, Sarge.'

Following the direction of her gaze, he slowly turned his head to his outstretched hand lying between two neat rows of tiny, white stones, wondering why she was getting so steamed up. Realization slamming his head, he snatched away his hand, putting quick distance between himself and it.

Judd whispered, 'What do we do, Sarge?'

'Get Dr Chong. *Now.*' He heard her moving quickly down the incline, soon picking up the rhythmic swish of plastic cover-alls. Chong appeared at his side with Adam, who planted a yellow marker. A forensic photographer arrived, began firing off multiple shots from various angles. Chong put her hand on Watts' shoulder. 'Are you all right?'

'Yeah.' He got to his feet, rubbing his back, his eyes fixed on what was beside the yellow marker. Having examined her efforts, the photographer gave them a cheerful nod and headed away down the incline. He and Judd watched as Chong knelt to examine the partly exposed skull. Watts glanced down at his hand, his face creasing in disgust.

Chong looked up at him. 'Brophy will be totally thrilled that you've increased this investigation one hundred per cent.' Reaching inside her forensic suit she took out a brush and a small plastic implement, knelt closer to the skull and began gently brushing where bone met dry earth. Watts watched her place her gloved hands either side of it, test it for movement, his head in overdrive: one just-murdered, headless victim, one skull that had to have been here for . . . how long?

'What's she doing?' He whirled on Judd. 'Don't do that!'

'Do what?'

'Creep up on me when I'm focused!'

Chong gently eased the skull from its resting place and raised it in both hands, its empty sockets now contemplating the high, blue sky. She studied it then turned to him. 'It's undamaged, see?'

He looked at it, feeling he was part of some cosmic joke. Judd looked at both of them. 'What happens now?'

He watched SOCOs steadily moving up the incline towards them. 'We give other investigators room to work. There's a lot of waiting about involved in investigations. Now's your chance to get used to it.' They headed down to the field, Watts flapping his hand at a ponderous bee, picking up birdsong for the first time.

'I've never seen so many wild flowers,' murmured Judd. Watts said nothing. For him, this whole area was blighted. He knew things Judd didn't. The long hours of painstaking investigation heading their way, the heartache for two families. She glanced up at him. 'Never mind, Sarge. Dr Chong seems to know what she's doing. Are you two mates?'

He sent her a repressive look. 'Dr Chong is first class at her job, which you might be in twenty-plus years, if you keep focused and stop with the yacking and the questions.'

THREE

Following several hours at the scene, Watts was inside Brophy's office. 'Dr Chong has confirmed the homicide victim as Zoe Roberts, sir. Liaison officers from the local force have broken the news to the family, but not yet the full details of what was done to her. You know about the other find?'

Brophy nodded, looking like a man with a lot on his mind. 'The skull, yes. I'm assuming you think it's connected to the Roberts killing?'

'Yes, given the location, plus the likelihood of decapitation.'

Brophy shook his head. 'This is a bad business, Bernard. Keep the press in the dark for as long as you can.'

'I've already briefed officers on that, sir.'

'How did PC Judd cope with seeing the body?'

'She was fine.'

Brophy's eyes were on him. 'You realize what this means, don't you?'

Watts knew what was coming. A term he had zero use for. The serial-killer label which served only to ratchet up the emotional heat, excite the press and unnerve the local populace. 'A repeat offender, sir.'

Brophy's eyes were fixed on him. 'Let's get one thing clear

between us from the off: I can't spare any more officers. All forces are stretched and West Midlands is no exception. I know about the cold case unit you managed and what happened to it, so you don't need any explanation from me about finances and priorities.' Watts didn't. He'd become familiar with both over the years. Money, followed by no money. Urgent priorities followed by changes to priorities. Priorities abandoned. Most decisions dependent on whatever hot issues the media and the government were pushing. Or so it seemed to Watts. The decision to close down the Unsolved Crime Unit still stuck in his throat. He looked up to find Brophy regarding him. 'As SIO, what are your immediate plans?'

'Given the proximity of the scene to the motorway network, I want a televised appeal on both local and national news. We need potential witnesses who were in the vicinity of Blackfoot Trail during yesterday and early this morning and it needs doing fast, while it's still fresh in people's minds.' He gave Brophy a direct look. 'You've spoken to the Roberts' family, sir?'

Brophy nodded.

'How likely is it that they can put somebody up to attend an appeal? I'm thinking Zoe Roberts' husband.'

Brophy looked doubtful. 'From what I've heard, they're separated and it might be a bit soon for any of them to handle it. I'll get on to family liaison to establish the current situation. I'll also contact Internal Communications to set up the appeal for say eleven a.m. tomorrow.' Watts was surprised by Brophy's quick response. He wasn't done. 'You'll be divulging news of the other remains?'

'No, sir, not yet. I want to keep the public focus on the Roberts murder. That skull has been there several years. The immediate area where it was found is still being processed. I'll hold off any reference to it till that's done and we have an ID. Best keep it simple.'

Brophy stood. Watts did the same. 'Bernard, I know you're doing all you can with limited resources on what is obviously a far more complex matter than we anticipated.' He walked with him to the door. 'I'm following up an idea to get you some specialist help, not more officers, but one specialist. How is PC Judd shaping up, generally?'

'*Very* keen, sir.'

WATTS LEFT HEADQUARTERS AND drove back to the scene. Leaving the BMW on the narrow lane, he walked down the steep hill to the car park, headed for the trail then on to the field and the incline, all of it still an area of intense activity despite the failing light. He passed officers moving portable lights into position. He'd known most of these headquarters-based officers for several years, knew their calibre, their meticulousness. If there was anything here which belonged to the skull, anything relevant to the Roberts homicide, they would find it. He did a quick calculation of costs so far, got an eye-watering guesstimate. They needed progress and soon. He looked ahead, raised his hand. '*Adam*. A quick word.' Adam came towards him, tiredness etched on his face, which had caught the sun. 'Anything to report since I was here earlier?'

Adam shook his head. 'Still no weapon. We'll have to wait till tomorrow to do a coordinated fingertip search of the whole area. We'll continue processing the area where the skull was located. If we find anything, you'll be the first to know. I've asked Petrie to bring back the drone tomorrow.'

Watts nodded. 'If you do turn up anything phone me, regardless of the time.' Leaving Adam, he headed to the incline, carefully tracing his earlier steps to halfway then turning to gaze down at the forensic activity in various areas. From here he could see the curve of Blackfoot Trail, the field on its other side, the houses he'd seen on the aerial photographs. In the next day or so, he'd send a couple of officers to knock on their doors. The light was failing fast now. As a murder scene it was starting to look endless. Tired, frustrated, knowing it was time to pack it in, he headed down the incline and back to where he'd left his vehicle.

THIRTY MINUTES LATER, HE came on to his drive, parked and headed to his house, a series of tiny jingles starting up behind him. Pushing his key into the lock, he looked down at the small black animal waiting patiently next to his feet. He'd inherited it from a colleague who had left several months before. 'Just a reminder that I had a pricey cat flap put in round the back for you. Why won't you use it?' Shaking his head, he went inside and headed for the kitchen, the cat following. Filling a bowl with biscuits, another with cold water, he left the cat to it and switched on the kettle. He reached for instant coffee and was pushing paracetamols out of their packaging when his phone rang. Seeing Chong's name, he picked it up. 'Know anything?'

'Zoe Roberts' cause of death. It was the six stab wounds to the upper chest. Removal of the head was post-mortem.'

'Glad to hear it,' he murmured, shelving the coffee, dropping a teabag into a mug.

Chong continued, 'I'm exhausted and guessing you're the same. All I want is a cool shower and an end to this day.' There was a brief pause. 'How about you?'

'The same. What's on your agenda tomorrow?'

'I'll finish the Roberts post-mortem, then start my examination of the skull. Or, I might go a little crazy and reverse the order. I like to surprise myself, occasionally.'

He grinned into the phone. 'I'll get over to the scene early to check how Adam and his team are doing. See you at headquarters some time?'

'You will. Where else would I be?'

THE COMBINATION OF RELENTLESS heat and the cat's snoring was making sleep impossible. On the point of dropping off for the nth time, Watts came upright, scattering images of grinning, chattering rows of teeth. A recollection of something he'd seen when he'd stood at the top of the incline looking along the motorway, brought him out of bed. Showered, dressed, he spent a few minutes examining the aerial photographs Petrie had supplied, one in particular snagging his interest.

Leaving the house with it, he drove along dark, almost deserted suburban roads and joined the motorway. Within a minute of passing the crime scene he saw the arrowed junction sign, another soon after: WORKS UNIT ONLY. He entered the narrow tree-lined access road, followed it past the white-on-red STOP sign and on to an open area and a sturdy, metres-high chain-link fence. He stopped, turned off the engine, reached for the photograph. The drone had captured all of it: fenced compound, road repair equipment and two prefabricated buildings inside. He looked across at them. There was a dull glow of light inside one of them. Getting out to the *whoosh* of passing traffic, he went to the compound's gate, lifted the hefty padlock hanging from it by a chain, looked up at the dull glow. It disappeared, appeared again, so quickly he could easily have missed it. What he'd thought was merely a security light was evidence of movement inside. Somebody was here. He went back to his vehicle, turned on the ignition, hit the horn twice and waited. No movement from the building. No movement anywhere. He followed the fence along, searching the area beyond it. In the darkness it was impossible to see all that was there. He went back to the gate, his eyes on the small light beyond the window. Seizing the chain-link with both hands, he pulled it back and forth, setting metal squealing and jangling.

'Police! . . . *Police!* Open up! *Now!*' His words reverberated then died, leaving only silence, interspersed with traffic noise. Returning to his vehicle, he hit the horn again, once, twice, three times, his eyes fixed on the building. The third blast faded to nothing. All was quiet. He couldn't get into that compound and nobody was coming out of it. Frustrated, he got inside his vehicle, started the engine. Reversing, he drove slowly down the access road, his eyes fixed on his rear-view mirror, the compound slowly growing smaller, soon lost to him. Re-joining the motorway, he thought of the proximity of that compound to Blackfoot Trail.

He'd be back to find out who was inside that building and why whoever it was had chosen not to show himself. He took the junction exit which led home, thinking about the trail, the area around it and Judd and her atmospherics. She was wrong in her criticism of Roberts for running there. Zoe Roberts' decision had been a lethal misjudgement, based on incomplete knowledge. She couldn't have known she was running through a cemetery. He came on to his drive as his phone pinged. A text from Adam: *Nothing more found after you left. Search continuing with an early start this a.m.*

FOUR

Tuesday 16 August. Seven a.m.

Watts was looking out of his lounge window, his mind on the events of the previous day. His eyes moved over the houses opposite, exactly like this one, except for different coloured paint and porch design. Small bids for individuality. He turned away, thinking about what he wanted from today. A name for the skull would be a start. He patted his trouser pockets, nodding to Mrs Donovan who was vigorously dusting and talking. 'Mr Watts, I'm ever so sorry to disturb you this early but I'm leaving at midday. The council's sending the pest control man to my house.' Watts lifted a cushion, then another, letting them drop. 'I daren't miss him. I tell you, I was knocked on my heels when I got my second-best mac out of the cupboard the other day and found he'd chewed his way around the collar.'

Watts stopped, looked at her. 'The pest control bloke?'

'The *mouse*.' She took keys from her pocket. 'Would these be what you're wanting?'

THE EXTRACTOR FAN WAS emitting a low hum as Igor let Watts inside the post-mortem suite. 'Is she in?' Following Igor's finger-point, he found Chong sitting at her desk, eyes on her screen. 'You're an early bird.'

'Brophy wants to see me at eight to tell me about some specialist help he's lined up and at eleven I'm fronting a news appeal.'

'So I hear. I'm guessing you'd like a conducted tour of your skull find?'

He followed her to the examination table and the rounded shape sitting at its centre covered by a thin, green sheet. She removed the sheet. He gave the stained, pinkish-brownish dome a once-over, no more pleased to see it than he had been the previous day. Pulling on white gloves, Chong lifted and rotated it.

'See? It's undamaged.' She carefully separated the jaws, held them towards him. 'Teeth well-maintained. Only two tiny fillings, indicative of her being born post-fluoride.'

'Her?'

Chong nodded. 'I did a comparison with MISPER dental records and got a perfect hit.' She held up the skull. 'Annette Mary Barlow, single, twenty-eight years old at the time she disappeared a decade ago, manager of The City Wine Boutique off Colmore Row, which she left at six p.m. on Saturday, the ninth of September 2006 and reportedly was not seen nor heard of thereafter.'

Watts thought of his wife's fight to live which had ended around that time. He sat on the edge of Chong's desk, arms folded. 'I was on reduced hours, but I remember it. That investigation dragged on for weeks without a result.' Chong was holding a file towards him. 'This is the overview. There's more information in the basement.'

'I bet. I'll have it brought up.' She watched him leaf through the few pages. 'I'm hoping to finish the Roberts post-mortem sometime this morning.'

'Anything you find is welcome. All I've got for her murder so far is a load of questions.' He pointed at the skull on the table. 'My worry is that some sex type has been on the loose in that area for a decade.'

She replaced the sheet. 'A reasonable hypothesis.'

'I went back to the scene at around three a.m.'

She gave him a quick glance. 'It's early days. You might consider pacing yourself in this heat.'

'I couldn't sleep because of it, plus the cat making a bloody racket. I wanted to check something I saw from the top of the incline. There's a motorway works road just past the scene. I drove along it last night. The whole place was deserted, but there was a light inside one of the prefab buildings there. Somebody was inside. I shouted. Announced I was police. Still no response.'

'Sounds like somebody was actively avoiding you.'

'I'll be back there, first chance I get.' He headed for the door, the cases he'd investigated during the past five years surging into his head. Cold cases. Good colleagues. 'You trained in America, didn't you?'

'Yes. San Diego.'

'Ever get to Boston?'

'No, but I heard it's a great city.' She watched him reach the door. 'You still miss them, don't you?'

He stopped, his back to her. He knew who she meant: one-time colleagues Kate Hanson and Joe Corrigan. 'Situations change. You get used to things in time.'

Leaving the PM suite, he quickly covered the two flights of stairs, pausing at the top to slow his breathing. He was in good shape compared to the start of the year, but he could do without Brophy or anybody else drawing negative conclusions, particularly given his own recent observation that the average age of officers here looked to be around thirty. Coming into the squad room he saw Judd at her computer screen, the buzz of talk from fellow officers flowing around her.

'Judd! Brophy's waiting.'

She stood, wearing light, loose-fitting trousers. He led the way to Brophy's office, knocked, looked down at her.

'Say nothing unless he specifically asks you a question.' Hearing Brophy's voice, Watts opened the door and they went inside.

'Have seats,' said Brophy, sending a quizzical look in Judd's direction.

'PC Judd should be part of our discussion, sir, seeing as she's part of the investigation.'

Judd straightened, chin up, making herself as tall as possible. The chief gave him a direct look. 'Dr Chong has an ID for the skull found yesterday. You're confident in your view that there's a link between it and the Roberts homicide?'

'Yes. I don't go for two killers choosing more or less the same dump site.'

'Any thoughts on how you'll proceed? With the personnel you've already got, of course.'

'As far as any media address is concerned, the focus of this investigation is the Roberts homicide. All we've got on Barlow is ID. We don't know where she was killed or the location of her other remains, so it stays under wraps for now.'

'Got any investigative theories regarding the two?'

Watts kept a grip on his irritation. 'I'm going with both cases being likely sexual homicides. We'll check out both women's lives, see if we can establish any kind of link between them. In the absence of an established link, I'm anticipating an investigation of both as random homicide by stranger.' Watts decided to give Brophy what else he knew. 'There's a service road off the motorway, leading to a works compound. It's hardly any distance from Blackfoot Trail.' He felt Judd's eyes on him. 'It's an angle we'll be following up. The killer could be local, but given the scene's proximity to the M42 there's a possibility he travelled to it by motorway, accessed it via that service road, left his vehicle at the compound there, continued on foot, killed Roberts and left by the same route. The same could equally apply to the Barlow skull.'

Brophy frowned at him. 'At this time of the year it's light from around five o'clock. If you're right, he's no cautious killer.'

Watts nodded. 'I'm hoping the media appeal will identify potential witnesses at Blackfoot Trail on the morning Roberts was killed and I'll be checking everybody who works at that compound. I want motorway CCTV footage for the early hours prior to the Roberts killing. It might be an idea to raise it with the motorway surveillance unit as soon as possible, sir.'

Brophy gave a brief nod. 'I'll get on to them.' Watts waited. Brophy clearly had something on his mind. He looked at Watts. 'Remember the help I said I might have for you? We're in luck. The chief constable has suggested a name. Somebody he personally rates. A criminologist.' Brophy pushed stapled A4s across the desk towards him. 'Have a look at his CV.'

Watts reached for it, read the name on the topmost sheet, returned it to the desk. 'I'm not happy about having him on the investigation, sir.'

Brophy sat forward, face reddening. 'This isn't a situation where you can be choosy. It's too high-profile.' He pointed to the CV. 'You recognize his name because he's an expert in the area of violent crime. He analyses it, measures it, but he's not just an academic if that's what you're thinking.'

'It isn't.'

The chief continued as if Watts hadn't spoken. 'He's worked on some of the most challenging homicide investigations we've had in the UK over the last fifteen years. He's got a wealth of criminological theory, plus analytical skills, *plus* a lot of direct experience of offenders and their behaviour, all of which means he's able to take their perspective. Think like them. Be a step ahead. What's more, he knows the law, so he can be trusted to follow the rules and not be compromised by the media.'

Watts' eyes were on the CV. To date, he hadn't heard Brophy talk with such vigour and in such detail on any issue. 'I know about William Traynor. So does the media.'

'In that case, judge the man, not the talk,' snapped Brophy. His eyes were fixed on Watts. 'I've already agreed Dr Traynor's involvement in this case with the chief constable. As I said, he rates him.'

Feeling Judd's eyes on him, Watts decided against a response. A silence grew between them. Brophy made some conciliatory hand movements. 'Bernard, I hear your concerns, but what I said about Traynor still holds. You've got a hell of a case here and his skills are exactly what's needed.' He pushed the CV back towards Watts, not looking at him. 'According to the chief constable, Dr Traynor is available and willing to come on board. Think about it. It could be like old times for you. The specialist help you had from the forensic psychologist when you headed the Unsolved Crime Unit worked very well, from what I've heard.'

Watts suspected that Brophy's persuasive tone owed much to his reluctance to go back to the chief constable and tell him that the help he'd suggested hadn't been welcomed. Watts gave a mental shrug, knowing that his reservations wouldn't cut much ice.

'I've heard that Traynor knows his stuff, that he gets results. I've also heard that he can be difficult to work with. The Zoe Roberts homicide is a high-profile homicide, sir, without the media knowing about the Barlow skull. Yes, we could use specialist help but it has to be from somebody who's able to be part of the team.'

Brophy stood, held out the CV. 'Dr Traynor's expecting you to contact him. Ring him this morning. Go and see him as soon as possible. Take PC Judd with you. Show her how profession-alism operates in today's force.'

Watts took the CV. 'I'll see him at his office.'

Brophy sat, moving papers around his desk. 'He works mainly from his home. You've got his contact details and address. Let me know that you've agreed his involvement.'

Watts came out of the office knowing he'd been stitched up. Bypassing the squad room, he headed downstairs, Judd trailing him.

'Sir, Sarge? Who's this criminologist? Why don't you want him on our case?' She followed him through a door and into a large, silent room, its blinds half down. After the friction with Brophy, Watts needed to be here. Preferably, on his own. Judd pointed up at scripted words high on one wall. '"Let justice roll down." Hey, cool! A mission statement. *Like* it.' She turned, stared at the massive screen of the wall-mounted Smartboard. 'Look at *that*. What goes on in here?'

'Nothing. It used to be the Unsolved Crime Unit where I worked until the start of this year.' Judd was at the Smartboard, had located its on-button. The huge screen radiated sudden light. 'This is *some* kit.' She glanced at him. 'What happened to this unit you're on about?'

'Stop messing with the technology and I might tell you.'

She switched it off, came to the big worktable.

He avoided her gaze. 'We sorted a lot of unsolved homicides here but one good colleague left, another did the same and the brass decided to close it down.'

She sat on the table. 'Happens all the time, Sarge. People come. People go. I'll be moving on in a couple of years. Hopefully, sooner. To get promotion.' She raised her hands, fingers hooked. 'Ker-*ching*.'

He closed his eyes, adding another irritation to a growing list: too brash by half. He headed for the door, her voice following him. 'These two mates you're on about, Sarge, where did they go?'

'America.'

She got off the table, hurried after him, face lit up. 'Go *on*! You're saying they got jobs there? How did they—'

'That's enough Memory Lane. I've got a press conference in half an hour and a phone call to make first.'

'Who to?'

He headed down the corridor. 'Dr William Bloody Traynor.'

FACING SCRIBBLING JOURNALISTS, THEIR phones and cameras, Watts brought the appeal to a conclusion with a statement he knew they wouldn't like. 'For investigative reasons, I'm not releasing any details of the Zoe Roberts homicide at this stage.' Ignoring the dissatisfaction on the faces, he spoke above the clamour of voices, indicating the man in his mid-thirties seated next to him at the table, his face drawn, eyes downcast. 'We're very grateful to Mr Alec Prentiss for being here today. He's going to say a few words about his sister, Zoe.'

Watts turned to Prentiss, who had grey shadows under his eyes, starting to doubt that he would manage to get through the brief sentiments about his sister which he had been persuaded to say. The press watched in anticipation as Prentiss unfolded a single sheet of paper with quivering fingers and got to his feet, despite Watts' advice to remain seated. He held up the large photograph he had also brought with him. It shook in his hand. 'This is . . . my sister, Zoe . . . Actually, her hair was blonder than you can see . . .' He swallowed. 'Our family is shocked and devastated that anyone could do this terrible thing. Zoe was funny and clever and . . . she didn't deserve . . .' His control wavered. 'If anyone thinks they might have seen her at Blackfoot Trail yesterday, sometime between six thirty a.m. and seven forty-five, or any other day, *please,* contact the police.'

He sat heavily as Watts stood. A hand shot up. 'DI Watts, do you have a statement yet from the victim's husband?'

The press had obviously got on to that aspect of Zoe Roberts' life. He sidestepped. 'We'll release more details as appropriate. West Midlands Police is committed to apprehending whoever committed this violent act which resulted in Zoe Roberts' death.' Alec Prentiss bowed his head. Watts spoke direct to camera. 'This is an appeal to *anybody* who was in the vicinity of Blackfoot Trail early on the morning of Monday the fifteenth of August, from say five a.m. onwards, to contact headquarters on the number at the bottom of the screen. We would also welcome information from anyone in that area during the previous seven days, no matter how insignificant that information might seem.' He turned, gave a quick nod to Prentiss who got to his feet. They and the family liaison worker went to the door and out, shouted questions following them.

JUDD STARED OUT OF the window at greenness rushing past. 'Are we going to this service road you mentioned to Brophy?'

Watts' eyes were on the satnav's screen, which he tolerated as long as he didn't have to listen to it. 'No. The criminologist is expecting us and I want to get it over with.' He felt her eyes on him. 'Whatever I do or don't agree with him, I want you to note down the details, along with anything else that's said.' Watts had already decided that he wouldn't be leaving this meeting without details he might need in the future to make a case against Traynor's involvement in the investigation. Seeing an indication of a left-hand turn, he slowed.

She looked up at him. 'You know what, Sarge? That name rings a bell.'

'Whose name?'

'Dr Traynor's.'

'That, I doubt, but cast your mind back a decade or so. Which in your case, Judd, is probably of no help, as you'd have been about ten, tops.'

'Depends what was happening then.'

'Try three homicides in different parts of the country, all three linked by the motorway network and committed inside the victims' homes.'

She smacked her hands together. 'Got it! I remember them.' Seeing Watts' disbelief, she said, 'I *do*. I decided I wanted to be a police officer when I was six, so I started reading crime reports in the papers.'

He stared at the road ahead. If he'd learned anything about Judd during the last couple of days, it was that she wasn't like anybody else he'd ever met. And he'd met plenty. She was tiring, irritating, opinionated and now he was having trouble believing what she was telling him. 'You're having me on.'

'No.'

He took another left, deciding to go along with her. 'Remember any details of those three homicides?'

She nodded, itemizing them on her fingers. 'The first in York, the second, Oxford . . . and lastly, some place in Surrey.'

'Guildford.' Details came into his own head, including the theory the police worked to at the time that the killer was a lorry driver. He glanced across at her. 'You're telling me that at ten, you were interested in homicides?'

She gazed at him. 'No. Way before that. I remember one when I was about seven. A really scary one. While he was on the loose, I slept with my hands like this.' He looked, saw her hands folded around her own neck. 'Because he was a strangler, somewhere in London.' She grinned at Watts. 'I was convinced he was on the prowl where I was. No way was I taking any chances.' She saw his face change. 'What's wrong with that?'

Wondering where to start, he chose his words. 'Anybody ever tell you back then that you had unusual interests for your age?'

'The woman at our local library.'

He gave her a sideways look. 'I thought your generation was born complete with a CD-ROM.'

She gave him a bright-eyed look. 'Those three linked cases were *really* interesting, Sarge. Too bad, Dr Traynor and the police couldn't catch the killer.' Watts slowed, entered a steep drive and followed it to where it opened on to a large area of land surrounded by sturdy trees, in the middle of it a rambling stone and tile house. He switched off the ignition, ignoring Judd's finger-point. '*Look* at that. This criminologist must be well rich to have a place like this.'

He looked across at the house. 'Your memory for that triple homicide case is disturbingly on the money in every respect, Judd, except one.' They got out of the vehicle and Watts headed for the big house.

Judd followed. 'But he was involved in it, like he will be with us?'

Watts headed across the expanse of yellowing, otherwise immaculate grass. That massive police investigation had been worked by the combined York, Oxford and Guildford forces. He recalled chaos borne of desperation to find the killer of three women and a lack of evidence culminating in its demise.

Suppressing irritation at a nudge from Judd, he glanced at the silver-grey, fifteen-plus-years-old Aston Martin parked next to the house. They walked towards the house, up shallow steps to the wide front door. Looking for a bell, not finding one, Watts pounded glass. They waited. He pounded again, seeing movement deep within, a shadow approaching the door. It was opened by a tall, slender, fair-haired man in his early forties, rimless glasses giving his face a cool, bookish air. Despite the passage of a decade or so, Watts immediately recognized him. He showed ID. 'Detective Inspector Bernard Watts, Dr Traynor. We spoke earlier.'

Traynor gave a brisk nod, opening the door wider. 'Come inside. The chief constable contacted me yesterday and outlined your case.' Traynor's gaze was direct, his voice deep, well-modulated. He held out his hand to Watts, his handshake firm.

'This is PC Chloe Judd,' said Watts.

Traynor held out his hand to her. 'PC Judd.'

She took it, blushed. They followed him into a huge, square, high-ceilinged room of glowing wood floor, bookshelves and pale, immaculate walls, its wide windows looking out on to a small lake several metres away. Traynor indicated for them to sit. Whatever Watts had heard about him during the last decade, this tanned man wasn't the twitchy, rumpled individual he'd been anticipating. His eyes drifted over a pristine white linen shirt, black jeans, burnished leather boots. Traynor looked like an academic. Which was exactly what he was. Watts had read his CV. Eight years ago, Traynor had left the Oxford college where he worked and was now Researcher in Criminology at one of Birmingham's central universities. Watts also knew that somewhere beneath the crisp white linen was scar tissue. He'd come here anticipating a lot beneath the surface where William Traynor was concerned. It looked like he might have got it wrong.

He got down to the reason for their visit, outlining the murder of Zoe Roberts, its location and the finding of the skull in a nearby field. 'That's not yet been released to the press, by the way. If it was solely the Roberts murder, I wouldn't be here, but this case is now bigger, more complex than we anticipated. Which is why our acting chief spoke to the chief constable about you joining our investigation.'

Traynor gave him a cool, direct look. 'As a criminologist, I routinely follow the city's homicide investigations in the press. My understanding is that you already have the services of a forensic psychologist. A Professor Hanson.'

Watts kept it brief. 'Not any longer. Right now, I'm heading a team of eighteen officers, plus in-house SOCOs and forensic experts.' He glanced at Judd; the words 'green', 'inexperienced' and 'annoying' surging into his head. 'PC Judd has joined the investigation as part of her training and she's bringing keenness and ideas to it.' He looked directly at Traynor. 'Your university job allows you time for investigative work?'

'With my agreement, yes. It's a quid pro quo. In exchange for my skills my department adds to its research knowledge and development. I teach two days per week. The remainder of the week I work from here, contacting my post-grad researchers via email. I select the best, so they know what's required of them and they do it.'

Watts looked towards the wide windows and the rural scene beyond, then back. 'Sounds like a convenient arrangement.'

Traynor was on his feet. 'Unfortunately, I have very little time to talk this morning so, if you don't mind, we need to continue our discussion whilst I get on with some preparations.'

Watts stared up at him, wrong-footed by Traynor's sudden change of focus. Finishing what she was writing, Judd tracked Traynor as he walked away from them across the room, her words following him. 'You'll find working at headquarters a big change, Dr Traynor! No chance of anybody being lonely there.' She caught Watts' look, returned an irritated one of her own.

'*What?*' Traynor had disappeared inside a room off the one they were in.

Watts raised his voice. 'We need your skills, your research knowledge on our case. Starting now. Today.' Beyond the open door of the room, he saw part of a wall covered in maps, charts, notes, labels, all linked by tape of various colours.

Traynor reappeared, carrying a leather backpack. 'I'm not fully available until probably the end of next week at the earliest, but until then I'll provide whatever advice I can.' He reached for his keys. 'To do that, I'll need whatever case data you have so far. Courier it to me here and I'll email you my initial responses.'

Watts was on his feet, his eyes fixed on Traynor's face. 'I haven't come here for "advice". I've got two homicides and sky-high media interest. I need you at headquarters. At the scene. Working with us, *now.*'

Traynor was looking preoccupied. 'Detective Inspector, I've just told you I can't do that. I already have a case. Let me have copies of all you have on the crime scenes, plus biographical information on the victims' – Judd was furiously writing – 'their daily lives, employment history, criminal history if any, family relationships, interests, friendships, plus all the available forensic information, pathology reports and photographs, crime scene photographs, including aerial if you have them—'

'We have,' said Judd.

'I also want time-of-death estimates where possible, types of weapons used, maps of the area.'

Watts stared at him, raised his hands. '*Just* . . . hang on a minute. We've barely made a start. Come with us to headquarters now. Be part of it. I'll give you copies of all we've got so far and we can agree a schedule of investigative actions and—'

'Detective Inspector, as I've just explained, I cannot do that. Certainly not this week.'

Silence grew between them. Watts gave him a long look. 'Sounds to me, regardless of what the chief constable thinks he knows, you're not available, full stop.' The look on Traynor's face, in his eyes, told Watts he was keyed up, more than ready to leave. Whatever Traynor had planned today, wherever he was going, inside his head he was already on his way.

Traynor spoke. 'I already have a responsibility to a case. There's a lead I must follow up. Contact me in a week or so but for now you must excuse me.'

Watts watched him lift the backpack and head for the front door. Traynor opened it, waited. Anger climbing, Watts started towards it. Clutching her pen, notes and bag, Judd got to her feet and followed. Watts was already through the door, down the steps, heading away as Traynor locked the door. Heading for the Aston Martin, he got inside and quickly reversed. It purred its way down the drive and disappeared from view. Watts climbed inside the BMW, slammed the door and gripped the steering wheel, getting his breathing under control.

Judd glanced at him as she sat. 'If he's as good as Brophy says, it's no surprise he's got another case. And it's only a few days.'

Watts turned to look at her, saw for probably the twentieth time since Brophy had put her on this case how young she was. 'You asked me a question earlier. About how Traynor came to be involved in the York-Oxford-Guildford homicide investigation.' She waited. 'He wasn't the criminologist. His wife was the Oxford victim.'

She stared at him, silent, eyes wide.

He started the BMW. 'I'm sympathetic to anybody who's been victimized like his family has, but right now I feel the same about the Roberts and Barlow families.' He glanced back at the house, shook his head. 'Those two families will eventually have a place to visit, mourn their loss. Traynor's problem is that he hasn't got that.'

'What do you mean?'

He glanced across at her. 'His wife's body was removed from the scene and never found.' He turned the key in the ignition, deciding not to add that as the investigation of the case grew more desperate, the focus had very briefly turned on Traynor himself, due to investigators discovering that his wife had significant financial means. 'But we've got our own problems. The Roberts and Barlow murders. They're our priority and we'll do it without his help.'

'But, Sarge, if he's got a responsibility for another case like he said—'

'You *still* don't get it, do you? There *is* no "current case". What we've just seen is Traynor doing what he does whenever he sees a chance of locating evidence on his wife's murder. He can't let it go.' Judd was looking in the direction the Aston Martin had gone, her face unreadable. Watts had known all along that approaching Traynor for help had been a mistake. He was as unstable as the rumours he'd heard about him. Brophy had made another mistake assigning Judd to this case. Too young. Too raw. He reversed and they headed down the drive. 'Traynor's good at what he does but it depends entirely on where his head and his thinking are at.'

'So, where does that leave us?'

'Without any specialist help because Dr William Traynor, criminologist and obsessive, is a non-starter.'

They drove towards headquarters in silence. Judd broke it after several minutes. 'He must have loved her a lot. I thought he was nice.'

'How does "nice" help us, exactly?'

'It doesn't. I'm just saying. And look what he said about the information he wants. He knows what he's about, Sarge, but if you don't like him, that's that.'

Watts waited for a gap in the traffic. 'Judd, this isn't about "nice" and it isn't about "liking". It's about having somebody reliable, who'll *be* there. Not somebody who's so driven that if he sees any possibility, no matter how remote, of finding his wife's remains and identifying her killer, he's on to it and never mind anything else. His every thought, every action is still geared to compulsively following it up, and that's after the combined efforts of trained officers from *three* forces couldn't get a result.'

He breathed. 'And, right now, the neck on the line in our case is mine. I don't need that kind of complication.'

'But anybody in his situation would want the same. To get somebody done for what happened.'

Watts sighed. 'He hasn't managed it in the last decade. All it's done is get in the way of his leading a normal life and affected his mental health.' He glanced at Judd. 'Here's what I know about that case: the family had a German shepherd they adopted after it was retired as a police dog. On the day of his wife's murder, Traynor was still at his Oxford college. His wife and nine-year-old daughter were at home. According to the daughter, the wife called the dog to come inside. It didn't come, so she went out to look for it, found it in the garden, dead from neck injuries. She comes back to the house, locks the door and a couple of minutes later there are sounds of somebody inside the house. She quickly hides the daughter in a cupboard, where she stayed throughout the attack on her mother. When Traynor arrived home, he was attacked. The police came. There was plenty of blood evidence, I heard the place was awash with it, but no sign of his wife's body. They found the daughter traumatized, still inside the cupboard.' He looked at Judd. 'You didn't read any of that back then?'

She looked away. 'No.'

'Glad to hear it.'

'What happened to his daughter?'

'She went to live with the maternal grandparents. She needed a lot of help. Traynor had had a breakdown and was in no fit state to look after her. Or himself, for that matter. Which probably added a shedload of guilt to his other problems. I know a few officers who've worked cases with him since then. He knows his stuff, he gets results, but having him as part of an investigation can cause big problems. He's no team player.'

'Why not?'

Watts felt a surge of irritation. 'There's no ending a topic with you, is there, Judd? You saw what just happened at his house. He's obsessed. He'll drop whatever case he's on if he gets what he thinks is a lead on his wife's murder. Every officer I know is convinced that whoever committed those three homicides is either dead or already in prison for something else.' Watts increased his speed, changed lanes. 'Forget Traynor. We've got two homicides of our own and I want to see what leads have come in following the media appeal. I also need to see the pathologist some time, so put a sock in it.'

'Can I come to the pathology suite?'

'Jesus *wept*.'

FIVE

Tuesday 16 August. Two ten p.m.

The Aston Martin moved quietly along Oxford's St Aldate's, turned left, followed the road, took another left and entered the car park at the rear of the police station. Entering a parking space, Traynor placed his visitor's permit beneath the wind-screen and got out, raising his hand against the brightness of the day, his eyes fixed on the imposing honey-coloured building. He'd felt tense during the journey. Seeing the place again, his tension spiked. Taking his backpack from the boot, he headed for the building's rear entrance and the officer waiting for him. Reaching it, he took John Heritage's outstretched hand in both of his. Heritage's gaze moved slowly over Traynor's face.

'Good to see you again, Will. You look well.'

'You too, John.'

Heritage led the way inside the building. Traynor had spent hours here in the early part of the last decade. Whenever he returned, he was welcomed, if not given what he wanted or hoped for. They walked along corridors, Traynor drawing glances and nods of recognition from some officers, others looking uncertain, trying to place him. Heritage pushed open a door and they went inside a hot, nondescript room.

'Have a seat, Will, while I open a couple of windows. How's work?'

Traynor reached into his backpack, took out a file and laid it square on the table. 'Busy. It's been suggested I consult on a current Birmingham case.'

Heritage sat opposite him. 'Anybody I know?'

'Detective Inspector Bernard Watts.'

Heritage smiled. 'Ignore the bluffness and you'll soon realize that you've got yourself a diamond. What have you brought this time?'

Traynor removed papers from the file, placed them in front of Heritage. 'Information on an arrest made by your officers here four days ago.' He pointed at the topmost sheet. 'Forty-year-old male. Lorry driver. Suspect in the homicides of five women. Two of those women were killed in this city, one six months before Claire, the other ten months after.'

Heritage gave him a direct look. 'You're referring to Dennis Sloan. After we arrested him, I did consider emailing you. You know that whenever we get a serial case we go straight to our "unsolveds" to check for links. Claire's file was the first I pulled out. If we'd known back then that Sloan was already operating in this area, we would probably have linked him ourselves.'

Traynor clasped his hands at his mouth to steady them. 'You're saying that you think this Sloan is a potential suspect for Claire?'

Heritage was no longer looking Traynor in the eye. He shook his head. 'No, Will. We've interviewed him over several hours. He's now charged with the five homicides for which he was arrested. Partly because of my direct involvement with

Claire's case, I led the interviews with him. He's denied any involvement in the Oxford, York and Guildford cases—'

'Of *course* he has!' Traynor raised his hands. 'Sorry, John. Where are you right now, with this Sloan?' He watched Heritage gather together the papers he'd brought with him.

'I know what you're asking, Will: do we believe Sloan killed Claire? If I'd been asked that same question four days ago, I would probably have said that Sloan was a person of interest. He uses motorways on a daily basis and he's admitted making deliveries in York and Oxford and ten plus other locations during the time the homicides occurred.' He looked directly at Traynor. 'I understand, Will. I know you've lived with this for the last decade. You know that if there was ever a chance of identifying who killed Claire, I'd be the first in the queue to make the arrest.' He paused. 'We can place Sloan in close proximity to each of the five homicides we've charged him with. We've matched his DNA to them. We know his MO.' He paused. 'We got no DNA from the scene inside your house and the same applies to the York and Guildford cases.' The colour had left Traynor's face. 'But we're getting better at isolating and developing trace DNA samples with every year that passes. As soon as we had Sloan in custody, we pulled out those three cases . . . sorry to use the word "case" where Claire is concerned. We got out all the blood samples, sent them back to the lab for retesting.' He paused again. 'Sloan didn't kill Claire or the other two women in that series, Will.'

Traynor stared at him. 'How can you be so sure?'

'There's no trace of Sloan's DNA, nor any other physical evidence to link him to them, plus the pattern of behaviour during the homicides he's now charged with bears zero resemblance to what occurred at your house. There isn't a single fact, shred of evidence or circumstantial tie-in of Sloan to Claire's murder.' Seeing Traynor struggling for composure, he tapped the papers he'd been holding into alignment, reached for the file, opened it, placed them inside and closed it. 'I'm sorry, Will.'

Traynor wanted out of the hot, silent room. 'Not having facts or evidence isn't the same as saying that this Sloan didn't kill Claire.'

Heritage looked at him, his gaze unwavering. 'That's how it works, Will. You know that. I wish I could give you the news you want, but I can't.' He paused. 'Sloan didn't murder your wife, and I've known you long enough to say this to you: let it go.'

Traynor was on his feet. 'I appreciate your and your team's efforts, John.'

Heritage stood, looked at his watch. 'Stay and have a late lunch with me.'

Traynor shook his head. 'Thanks, but I think I'll walk around the city for a while.'

Heritage eyed him, aware that each time Traynor returned to Oxford after leaving it eight years before, he went to the house he'd shared with his wife and daughter to look at it from the outside.

Traynor caught the look, held out his hand. 'Don't look so worried, John. I just need to walk.' They left the room and headed to the front entrance of the building where Heritage gripped Traynor's hand in his.

'We'll keep in touch, yes?'

56

'We always have, John. Thanks for your time.' Traynor went down the steps and began walking the hot city pavements. He would stop only when he reached the point of exhaustion. It was what he did whenever he came here.

SIX

Back at headquarters, Watts and Judd went directly to the squad room to collect the tip sheet responses to the televised appeal. Watts took the thick file from one of the officers who had handled the calls.

'We've hit a lull, Sarge, but there's over fifty so far.'

Judd looked elated. '*Fifty*. Sarge, we're motoring.'

'Anything of particular interest?' he asked.

The officer shook his head. 'The usual crazies. Nothing that stands out.'

Watts peered into the file as he headed for the door. 'Keep at it for now. Let me know when the call rate looks to be dropping.' They went downstairs to the room they'd been inside earlier. Watts dropped the file on to the table and opened it. 'It's quiet in here. Let's have a look through them.' Sliding the tip sheets on to the big table, he pushed around a third of them towards Judd, keeping the remainder for himself.

'What are we looking for, Sarge?'

'Anything which suggests the caller has something sensible to offer, plus any which get our attention for any other reason.'

Judd scanned the tips in front of her. 'Why did you ask for people who were at the scene a week before the murder to come forward? What's the point?'

'Because we work back from the actual crime to see if there's any indication or evidence of it being set up.'

Judd looked uncertain. 'Like?'

'Anybody seen loitering who might fit the role of stalker.'

They were engrossed in evaluating the tips when the door opened and Jones appeared, tip sheet in hand. 'This just came in, Sarge, and I thought I'd bring it down.'

Watts took it from him, read the details, looked up at him. 'Did she sound yampy?'

'No. Sensible and confident.'

Watts stood. 'Come on, Judd.'

She stared up at him, pointing at the tips on the table. 'What about these?'

'We'll finish them when we get back.'

'Where are we going?'

'To see a Miss Dorothea Banner who reckons she's got something interesting to tell us about Blackfoot Trail.'

WATTS HAD BEEN UNSUCCESSFUL in deflecting Banner's offer of hospitality. Frustrated, he watched as she poured tea into flowered china. 'I don't know about you, Detective Inspector, but I cannot *abide* tea in mugs.' He declined the fig rolls she was offering. Judd took one. Banner smiled. 'Take two, dear.'

Opening his notebook in a bid to get things moving, Watts glanced at her. Had to be at least eighty. 'First of all, Miss Banner, we're very grateful to you for phoning in response to the televised appeal—'

'You looked as though you needed help so I was pleased to do so.'

He nodded. 'How about you tell us, in your own time, what you saw?'

Miss Banner put down her cup. 'I don't see the relevance of my time. The question is, are *you* ready?' He straightened, early memories of school surfacing. 'It was last Saturday, the thirteenth; the time, nine ten in the evening.'

He looked up at her. 'That's two days prior to the case I appealed on.'

She smiled at him. 'You did say that you were interested in the seven days prior, Detective Inspector. Where was I? Ah, yes. I was in here, watching a recorded episode of *Botched*.'

Seeing Watts frown, Judd said, 'It's a programme about cosmetic surgery, Sarge.'

Banner sent her a nod. 'Exactly so. It's *unbelievable* what young women, and others who should have more sense, will allow people to do to them and mostly by male doctors, I have to say.' She gave Judd a benevolent glance. 'You're very young but I hope you'll never subject yourself to such *grotesque* violence.'

Judd grinned, shook her head. 'No way—'

'Getting back to that Saturday evening, Miss Banner, you were watching television. How did that lead to you seeing something at Blackfoot Trail?'

Dorothea Banner sat forward, her manner earnest. 'I'm glad you asked. The woman who'd already been cut to ribbons at least once by this so-called "surgeon" was being incredibly stupid and I decided to treat myself to a cup of hot chocolate. When you reach my age, you'll realize that one tends to feel a little cool, despite the weather. I went to the kitchen.' She clasped her hands together. '*That's* when I saw it!'

Watts' patience was running thin. 'Saw what?'

'*It.*'

'It?'

She nodded. 'I caught a first glimpse of it and then I went out through the side gate and stood watching.'

Watts pictured the table in his office, stacked with files still unread, tips to check, actions to action, calls to . . . 'Can you be more specific?'

'Of course I can.' She stood, gesturing them towards the room's large rear window. They followed her. From it, they had an uninterrupted view of the field as it rose, Blackfoot Trail running along the top. She pointed. 'It appeared from the direction of the trail car park. You're familiar with that area?' He nodded, mouth set. 'It moved along the trail, then left it for the grassy slope which runs down to the back of this house. I can tell you, Detective Inspector, I was *gripped.*'

'You said this was at around nine, Miss Banner.'

She turned to him. 'Nine ten, possibly twenty past and I know what you're thinking: that it was too dark for me to see it clearly. You're wrong. As I said, it appeared and started moving. *Drifting,* would be a more accurate description. I would go so far as to say *floating.*' She looked at both of them.

Watts was well past having had enough. 'Describe what this individual was wearing, please.'

Banner eyed him. 'Did I say it was a person? I couldn't see any detail but what I can tell you is that *it* was covered in white.' She waved both hands around herself, her voice dropping to a whisper. 'A billowing drifting miasma.' She looked from Judd to Watts and breathed. 'It was apparitional. A *spectre*.'

Watts closed his notebook. 'Thanks very much for your time, Miss Banner. We appreciate—'

'Oh, but I haven't told you all of it. It was being *chased*.'

'Chased?'

'Yes. As it appeared from the right, I saw more movement. A man. At least, I think it was a man. He followed it on to the grass.'

'And?'

Banner shook her head. 'That's when I lost sight of it. Them.'

'What do you make of that, Sarge?' asked Judd, once they were outside. 'Creepy or what?'

Watts headed for the BMW. 'I'm saving my energy for the tips still waiting for us.'

AN HOUR LATER, THEY had a selection of dispiritingly few tips of any use. Most had been provided by individuals who clearly wanted to help the investigation but had either not been at the trail on the day Zoe Roberts was murdered, or were but had seen nothing. Watts frowned at two in his hand. 'These are from people reporting that they were in the area and saw a male with his arm in a sling. Each sighting is dated more than three weeks prior to the time frame we're interested in.' He looked across at Judd. 'That's the problem with appeals. People want to help, but they don't have anything for the relevant time.' He pointed to several tips he'd pushed away. 'All appeals attract attention-seekers. One or two of these I recognize by name because they always respond to requests for information. That one's from a woman who was in the area on the day of the Roberts murder and rang to complain because she was stopped from walking her dogs on the trail. No guesses who *she* was.' He reached for one he'd separated from the others. 'This is from a male caller who advised that we work to the theory that Zoe Roberts, and I quote: "got what she deserved".'

Judd stared up at him, aghast. 'Have him done, Sarge! And the others, the time-wasters.'

'He didn't give any contact details and I'm not wasting investigative time giving any of the others more attention. Got anything remotely sensible?'

Judd indicated a small pile of tip sheets. 'Each of these reported being at the trail on the days prior to the murder, but it's the same story as yours: none of them saw anything.'

'Depending on how desperate we get, I might send somebody to check on all of them. That it?'

She held up a tip sheet, eyes shining. 'I saved this one for last. It's from a caller who says he was at Blackfoot Trail on the *day* of the murder and saw a woman running.'

'Name?'

She narrowed her eyes at a printed box containing hand-written details, plus two exclamation marks added by the officer who took the call. 'It looks like . . . I. Dunnette.'

Reddening, she threw it on to the table. '*Creep.* How can people be like that? Make a joke of somebody's tragedy and pain!'

Gathering them together, Watts pushed them back inside the file. 'Once I hear that the calls have slowed right down, I'll keep one line open for another few days. We still might get something.'

'Don't forget Miss Banner.'

'I'm still trying. It's time we talked to Dr Chong.'

They took the stairs down to the PM suite. Igor let them inside. It looked deserted. 'Where is she?'

The door swung open and Chong appeared behind them. 'Here, picking up evidence of tetchiness. If it's the Roberts' PM results you're after, it's almost finished.' They followed her to her desk, waited as she tapped computer keys, pointed at the screen. 'Here's what I can confirm. Roberts was a healthy thirty-year-old female in excellent physical shape. Death was due to six deep stab wounds to the chest. Removal of head was post-mortem, which you already know.' She looked up at him. 'I found zero indication of sexual assault.'

He wanted to ask if she was sure but he knew from experience that she didn't respond well to that kind of question. Pointless, anyway. She was thorough.

'There is something I'd like you to look at, but' – she looked at Judd – 'before I get the photograph on to the screen, it's very graphic. Are you OK with that?'

Judd gave a quick nod. Chong tapped computer keys. The high resolution, full-colour image of Zoe Roberts' body lying on one of the suite's steel examination tables filled the screen. Chong clicked on it, homed in on the frontal aspect of what remained of the neck, Judd and Watts gave involuntary winces as the cursor moved.

'See? The head was excised very close to the jawline . . . but, look at this on the frontal aspect of the neck.' The cursor moved in a small circular motion. 'See?' Watts leant towards the screen, following the cursor. 'That long, narrow mark is a bruise. My hypothesis is that at some stage Roberts' killer had his arm around her neck, her back to him, possibly to render her compliant whilst he delivered the stab wounds, possibly to limit staining to his own clothes, although that's conjecture.' They watched the cursor track the length of the bruise.

'Any ideas as to what caused it?' asked Watts.

'I'm hypothesizing a right-handed killer with his left arm against her throat as he stabbed her.' The cursor jiggled. 'I suspect that mark was left by something similar to a metal bracelet or watchband.' She looked up at him. 'It's unfortunate that it's only a bruise. If the skin had been scratched, we might have got DNA.' The silence in the suite was broken only by the quiet, regular thrum of the large, compartmented refrigerator unit where Zoe Roberts' remains were now lying.

Weary, despite it being barely late afternoon, Watts turned away. Chong looked up at him. 'You'll want to know what else I have.' She went to a nearby microscope. They followed. 'I collected several fibres from the back of her vest. Take a look.'

Watts did, seeing a pattern of wavy lines with an odd glow. 'What are they?' he asked, standing back for Judd.

'I'm not sure, but Adam has found similar ones inside her car.' Chong carefully removed the glass slide. 'I'll send this plus the vest to forensics. See what they make of them.'

'Could those fibres be from her killer?'

'All's possible. For now, it's a wait-and-see.' She returned to the computer, changed the screen. 'I found something else. Take a look at these.' They did: at four dark, short lengths of something. 'They're cut sections of hair,' she said.

Watts looked up at her. 'Not hers?'

'No. They're brown head hairs. Roberts' own hair was expertly processed blonde. I'll send them to the lab for DNA testing.'

Watts frowned at them. 'There's no roots.'

'They'll still be subject to all of the processing available, because' – she pointed – 'these three here were stuck to her vest by blood. This one was inside one of the chest wounds. Pushed there by the knife.' She looked up at him. 'Don't look at me like you're starving and I'm holding the only burger in town. I can't tell you any more until they've been examined. I'll be requesting expert analysis.'

'Judd has a question for you about Roberts.'

Chong gave her an encouraging look.

'I was just wondering,' said Judd, 'if you could say anything about the condition of Roberts' hands and fingernails?'

'Well-kempt and undamaged from my initial examination at the scene. After I've done a second and final check of the body, my remaining task is to remove the bags from them and examine them fully. If I find anything of interest, DI Watts will be the first to know.'

He and Judd left the PM suite and headed upstairs, picking up voices drifting down from the squad room on the first floor. 'What do you think about what Dr Chong told us, Sarge?'

'I know what you think. That undamaged fingernails equals Zoe Roberts knew her killer.' He looked in the direction of Reception, saw PC Sharma waving to him. Diverting to the desk, he took from her the weighty ten-year-old investigation file labelled in large black print: ANNETTE BARLOW. 'Thanks, Rita. Back with us, again?'

She grinned. 'Can't keep away, Sarge. I'll be doing some liaison work on your case.'

'Glad to hear it.'

They headed for the ground floor room they'd been inside earlier. 'Who's she?' asked Judd.

'Rita Sharma. Just back from maternity leave and carrying a bit of extra timber which suits her.' He caught Judd's eye-roll. 'Her real name's Rit, but here, she's Rita. She's sound. You could learn a lot from her.' He pushed open the door. 'From tomorrow, I'll be doing early morning briefings in the squad room to the whole team which includes you, after which I'll be working down here.' He glanced around. 'In my office.' It still felt like a home of sorts and right now it was ideal. The investigation team, including Judd, would be one floor up and he'd be down here in peace and quiet, getting to grips with the case.

Judd was looking around it, her face animated. 'This is great, Sarge. I'll bring my computer down here.' She pointed across the room. 'And when we really get started, we can use Big Boy on the wall.' He watched her head to the door. 'Back in a minute.'

Tight-lipped, he decided he'd have a word with her when she came back. Opening the Barlow file, his eyes slid over sheet after sheet of inquiries which ten years ago had yielded nothing. The door opened. Judd was back, holding a hefty-looking plastic box. He pushed half of the sheets across to her. 'We'll start getting together a list of details for Annette Barlow's family members, employers, work colleagues, friends—'

'You want a victimology.'

'What I want is a link between Barlow and Zoe Roberts and I don't care how tenuous it is, but before we make a start, I need to sort out something with you about this room—' Hearing a sharp click, he looked up. Judd was holding an open lunchbox towards him. He looked at white bread sandwiches, crisps, two muffins, one chocolate, the other something else, each wrapped in clingfilm, two tangerines and two small cartons of juice; part of his mind wondered how Judd managed to chomp her way through this lot every day and look the way she did. He knew the answer. Youth. 'What's on the sandwiches?'

'One's cheddar and pickle. The other's ham and mustard.' She shook the box at him. 'Go on, Sarge.' He took the cheddar. She took the other, bit into it, chewed, swallowed. 'What did you want to sort out, Sarge?'

'I was just thinking that investigations like this involve long days. That's not a problem for your family, is it?'

'No, Sarge.'

Six p.m.

JUDD SAT BACK, STRETCHED, then pushed a short list across the table towards him. 'That's all the key details I've found on Annette Barlow from what I've read. Given what we know about the kind of work Roberts did and where she lived, even indirect contact between her and Barlow looks very unlikely to me.'

Watts reached for the neat list, looked at it. His search of the available information had told him much the same: no discernible link between the two women. 'Once we get more information on Barlow it might help.' He glanced at Judd. She was a nuisance a lot of the time, but she'd kept up well today.

He dropped her list on to his own. 'It's early days, but if we don't find any link between the two victims, this case will be worked on the basis that both homicides were the work of an opportunistic sex type who didn't know either of them.' Hearing his own words, he frowned.

'What's up, Sarge?'

He wasn't about to get into what was bothering him but why would anybody kill two women a decade apart then spend time decapitating them? He checked his watch, looked up at Judd. There were shadows under her eyes. 'It's late. We'll pack it in now but be here at nine in the morning. Zoe Roberts' family is expecting us at eleven.' He gave her a second look. 'Your nose has caught the sun. We'll be out there again tomorrow, so best put something on it when you get home.' He caught the dismissive look. 'Your mom or dad will probably tell you the same.' She headed for the bin, dropping empty drinks cartons and peel into it, snapped closed the lunchbox, pushed it into her bag. He watched her head for the door. 'Oh, and say thanks to whoever puts your lunches together.'

She raised a hand, thumb up. The door closed on her.

He looked at another list she'd made, the one listing the data Traynor had demanded. Traynor was still on the treadmill he'd built for himself following his wife's murder, a tragedy however you looked at it, but right now Watts had his own problems. He gathered the papers together. Earlier, he'd phoned the Oxford police and been told that the three-homicide case of which Claire Traynor was a part was 'the subject of periodic review'. Watts knew what that meant. Inactive. Putting the Barlow file inside the filing cabinet, he switched off the lights.

Minutes later, he passed the road which would take him home, heading instead for the motorway. In fading light, the WORKS UNIT ONLY sign came into view. Leaving the motorway, he drove up the narrow approach road, came to a stop and switched off his engine. The buildings behind the chain-link fence looked the same as they had the previous night, with one exception. Both were now in complete darkness. He got out, listened. Other than the sound of traffic from the motorway, nothing. Nobody here. He headed towards the chain-link fence, veered left, followed the land sloping steeply upwards. It took him a couple of minutes to reach the top. He looked down at the compound, then towards the incline from where Annette Barlow's skull had been recovered. Beyond it lay Blackfoot Trail curving its way past tall trees to the car park where Zoe Roberts had died. From here to that compound was walkable. Had Roberts' killer parked his vehicle down there? He took out his phone, tapped out a text to Adam, head of forensics.

LETTING HIMSELF INTO HIS house half an hour later, Watts quietly placed his keys on the hall table and headed for the kitchen. Switching on the kettle, he leant against one of the cabinets, arms folded, watching the cat stand in its basket, arch, then pad towards him. 'Don't bother, lad. I'm out of energy and not feeling that sociable.' He watched it circle his ankles, put its front paws against one of his legs, giving him a yellow stare. Sighing, he leant down, rubbed the soft fur between its ears, picking up quiet movement on the stairs. He dropped a teabag into a mug as the kitchen door opened. 'Sorry. I should have phoned to say I'd be late,' he said to the small, slender woman in yellow pyjamas standing there. 'Hope you didn't wait up.'

'I did, but it's OK. Would you like something to eat?' She came to him, put her hands against his chest. He covered them with his, looked down at her face, thinking how he never tired of looking at it. No one they knew was aware of their relationship. That's how it was. How it would stay.

'No, thanks. I'll have a quick shower then come to bed.'

A PING FROM HIS phone dragged Watts from sleep, its clock telling him it was three a.m. Chong sat up. 'What's *that*?'

He read it. 'A text. From William Traynor. He's ready to work with us, starting tomorrow morning. Make that today. He's coming into headquarters.'

'Why is he telling you at *this* hour?'

Watts stared into darkness. 'Because he marches to his own beat. Which about sums up his problem. And probably mine, now.' Another text announced itself. 'From Adam. I told him earlier that the steep hill from the compound to the high ground is walkable. He's confirmed he'll have officers examine it all.'

Chong fell back on to her pillows. 'Is anybody on this case *sleeping*?'

SEVEN

Watts set the mug down on the big worktable. 'Your lead didn't pan out?'

'No.'

Watts took the chair opposite, giving Traynor a quick once-over. He looked wasted, like he hadn't slept in days. Watts' eyes went from the shadowed, unshaven face to the clothes. The same ones he'd had on the previous day, the linen shirt badly creased, marked around the collar. Traynor was here but Watts was seeing nothing which said he was fully functioning. He recalled Traynor's upbeat, driven demeanour at his house, wondering where the balanced Traynor was. Maybe there wasn't one. Watts had informed Brophy of the meeting he and Traynor had had and stated to Brophy that collaboration between them was not an option. Brophy's line was typical: they had to deal with him carefully. Having started the process of asking Traynor to join the investigation, it was possible to Brophy's way of thinking that Traynor might lodge a complaint with the chief constable about a change of plan. They needed to tread sensitively. So here Watts was, facing Traynor, still under pressure to accept him into his investigative team. But there was one thing on which he was immovable and Brophy knew it. If he got so much as a whiff of alcohol, Traynor was history. More seconds ticked by. He watched Traynor lift the mug, sip, set it down, his face shut off.

Watts kept his voice low. 'PC Judd's not in yet, so I can be straight with you.' He leant forward, emphasizing each word with a finger jab on the table. 'You look like shit.'

Traynor reached for the mug again, a tremor in his hand. 'I'm here to work on your case.'

Watts shook his head. 'Not until you and me have an understanding. I know your situation. I get it. But what's at the top of my agenda right now is the Roberts family and what they're going through, plus the family of another victim which hasn't got its bad news yet.' He paused. 'I don't doubt your skills, but if you're going to be part of this investigation, I need consistency of commitment.' He paused. 'From what I've seen and heard, that's a problem for you.' He waited for Traynor to speak. Traynor didn't. 'This case has to come before any demands from your personal life. PC Judd's just finished her probationary training but she gets it. If you can't give us that, I'm telling you, you won't be part of it, regardless of what the chief constable or anybody else has to say about it.' More silence. He pointed to Judd's list of Traynor's demands made when they saw him at his house. 'That's not how it's going to be. We need your skills, your expertise, we need *you*, reliable, focused, gathering, sharing and interpreting data alongside the team, not "out there", working on the periphery, fitting it in with whatever else you've got going on.' He paused. 'If you can't do that, say so now.'

'I understand. I'm here.'

Watts still had doubts. Traynor understanding what was

required of him was one thing, delivering it was something else. 'What about commitment to our case over time?' He looked across the big table. 'Well?'

'I accept your summation of the situation. I'm in.'

Watts slow-nodded, still not convinced but deciding to leave it there. Seeing Traynor's face, the look in his eyes, to say any more felt too much like a gratuitous kicking. Early this morning, he'd looked through information the force had on him. Eight-point-five years ago William Traynor, criminologist, had been diagnosed with severe post-traumatic stress. It looked to Watts like not much had changed. 'In an hour or so I'm on my way to see Zoe Roberts' family to get information from them, which means anything and everything they feel able to give us at this stage. Stuff they might not even know they know, which could give us an angle on what happened to their daughter and why. I've read your CV. It says you've written articles and a book on interviewing people and how best to get information out of them.' He gave Traynor a level look. 'That's been my job for years, but I'm open to anybody with specialist skills. I want you there to meet Roberts' family. We'll keep it low-key, but to my way of thinking, with us working together, we'll maximize the information we get.'

The wall clock ticked off several seconds before Traynor spoke. 'I'm sure you're adept at achieving that, DI Watts. I need to get home, shower and change, after which my priority is to examine the crime scene.'

Watts' head tightened at what amounted to a refusal of his first request. He looked across at Traynor. He had a point about smartening himself up. He glanced at the clock. Time to decide which way he was going with this: accept Traynor on to the case, or inform Brophy that collaboration with him was still an issue. He got up, went to the wide-open window, breathed slowly and deeply, looked out at the small houses beyond headquarters' railings. The low optimism he'd had since Traynor arrived dipped further as a possibility occurred to him: Traynor's research work probably kept him from a lot of direct contact with the bereaved. His expressed preference for a crime scene visit could well be avoidance of the family's grief. Because it was too close to his own. How could they work together on the case with Traynor hampered by problems like that? He went back to the table. 'Get yourself sorted, then go to the scene. Forensics and SOCOs are there. Introduce yourself to Adam Jenner. He's the head of both. He'll fill you in on what they're doing, what they've already got.'

He held out his hand. Traynor stood, took it in a firm grasp, walked to the door and out.

WATTS BROUGHT THE BMW to a halt outside a wide-fronted, detached house set back from the road, surrounded by gardens as orderly as a newly laid table, three cars parked on the wide drive behind ornate metal gates. He'd already noticed several people standing some yards away with a couple of uniformed officers from headquarters, all now looking in their direction. He turned to Judd. 'Remember what I said before we left headquarters?'

'Yes, Sarge: we're here to get information about Zoe Roberts. We don't get into details of what was done to her. We listen to what they tell us. I write it all down.'

He pushed open his car door, looked back at her, keeping his voice low. 'See that lot hanging about down there?'

She nodded.

'They're press. We go straight to the house without looking at them.'

They headed for it, the gates drifting open as they approached. They walked up to the house. Watts rang the bell. The door was opened almost immediately by a man they both recognized. Alec Prentiss. He looked worse than he had at the appeal, if it were possible.

'Something's happened?' he asked. 'There's some news?'

'No, Alec, but I'm glad you're here because this concerns you as much as your parents.'

Prentiss stepped back to allow them inside, led them across the wide hall and into a large room, thickly carpeted, its heavy curtains drawn against the road. It felt suffocating. Prentiss briefly introduced his parents sitting side by side on a long sofa, then went and sat some distance away on the arm of a chair, gazing out of a window overlooking a rear garden. Watts' attention was caught by multiple family photographs on a nearby wall. A record of two childhoods. Zoe and Alec swimming, Zoe and Alec playing tennis, horse-riding, another of them in deep snow with other children, posing for their respective graduation pictures, laughing with friends in some kind of am-dram production, Alec at the wheel of a small sports car, Zoe on skis, her face flushed, vital.

'My name's Bernard Watts. I'm Senior Investigating Officer. This is Police Constable Chloe Judd.'

Judd nodded at Zoe Roberts' parents.

Mrs Prentiss's hair and make-up were just so, but both parents looked tense, beyond tired. Watts' eyes went to a photograph on the wall behind them: Roberts in her wedding dress, taken in this room, standing beside a tall, dark-haired, smiling man. Christian Roberts? Had to be. Watts looked away to Rita Sharma, family liaison officer, unobtrusive in a corner of the room. They exchanged minimal nods. He knew she had prepared the family for this visit. He looked back to the parents.

'Please accept our sincere sympathies and those of everybody at headquarters, plus our assurances that we'll do all that's possible to establish what happened to Zoe and who is responsible.' He paused. 'We're very grateful to you for seeing us at such a difficult time.'

The parents nodded. Alec Prentiss stared out of the window. 'Thank you, Detective Inspector,' said Mr Prentiss.

'Would you like some tea? Or coffee?' Mrs Prentiss stood. Watts gave Sharma a quick look, knowing from long experience that practical tasks were latched on to like lifelines by the newly bereaved. He wanted both parents in this room, thinking, talking as much as they were able right now.

Sharma got up and went to Mrs Prentiss, placing a gentle hand on her arm. 'I'll take care of it.' She left the room, Mrs Prentiss sat and both parents turned their attention back to Watts. Situations like this were an aspect of the job Watts particularly disliked.

'We're here because we need you to tell us about Zoe.'

'We understand,' said Mrs Prentiss, 'although Alec won't be able to tell you much. He was in London. He didn't get home until late that evening.'

Watts nodded. 'That's not a problem, Mrs Prentiss. What we actually need is general information about Zoe's life. I know that's going to be difficult but it's essential at this early stage that we get a sense of her as a person. I'll start by asking you about her phone.'

Mrs Prentiss immediately stood, walked across the room to a low chest, opened a drawer and returned with a gold-coloured phone which she placed inside the evidence bag Watts had pulled from his pocket. She went back to the sofa, her face pale and set.

Watts addressed his first question to all three family members. 'Had Zoe mentioned having any problems recently, any concerns, no matter how trivial they might have seemed?' He got headshakes from both parents, nothing from Alec Prentiss. He sent each of them a direct look. 'I'll be a bit more specific. Do either of you recall Zoe saying that she was uneasy about anybody or anything?' More headshakes. 'Did she mention any concerns relating to men?'

'No, never,' said Mrs Prentiss.

'Did she ever express any worries about running in the Blackfoot Trail area?'

'Never. If she had any such concerns, she would have told us. Zoe was confident but she was no fool, Detective Inspector. If there had been anything of that nature, she certainly wouldn't have continued going there.'

Watts glanced at Judd's pen speeding along. 'What about you, Mr Prentiss? Alec?'

Alec shook his head.

His father said, 'Detective Inspector, our daughter was an

open book. If there had been anything troubling her, we wouldn't have needed to ask. She would have told us.'

Watts glanced at Alec, still staring out of the window. He looked cut off, like he was still in shock. 'Have you got anything to add to what your parents have said, Alec?'

He turned to Watts. 'Sorry?'

'Are you aware that Zoe had any worries about anything?'

He shook his head. 'I'm not the best person to ask. I live in Bentley Heath. Zoe and I didn't see each other that often.'

'We're a close family and a very busy one,' said Mrs Prentiss. 'Alec works with his father and me in the family business so we see more of him than we did Zoe.'

Watts nodded. 'What kind of business is that?'

'Clothing manufacture. My husband and Alec deal with the production side. I deal with the marketing aspects.'

Watts waited for a response from Alec Prentiss. None came. 'Was Zoe involved in the business at all?'

'Of course not. She had a first-class law degree and worked for a firm in Solihull. She'd been there for over five years. She was anticipating being made a partner in the foreseeable future.' Hearing the pride in her voice, Watts guessed that she was still at that stage of bereavement where it was possible to lose sight of reality for a few merciful seconds.

He nodded. 'We'll need details of her colleagues there, Mrs Prentiss.'

She frowned, looked at her husband. 'Zoe didn't discuss her work with us, did she, Peter? We can't tell you anything about her colleagues. She rarely mentioned them and we never met them.'

'No worries. To your knowledge, did Zoe have any difficulties of any kind with, say, neighbours where she lived, or problems with friends or anybody else, again no matter how trivial?'

Mrs Prentiss stared at him. 'No. Nothing like that. Her friends are nice, well-brought-up young women, like Zoe.'

'I'm sure they are, Mrs Prentiss, but we'll be wanting to contact them and everyone else in Zoe's life. It does happen that daughters and sons share information with their friends which they might choose not to share with immediate family members.'

Mrs Prentiss's face hardened. 'Not Zoe. As my husband said, she was an open book. If there had been anything worrying her, she would have said. Her colleagues' names are on the firm's website.' As PC Sharma returned carrying a tray and began dispensing drinks, Mrs Prentiss went to the drawer from which she had retrieved the phone, took out a small book and brought it back with her. 'I can give you details of Zoe's main friends. They knew each other since schooldays.' She gave three names plus contact details. Judd noted them down.

'They maintained regular contact with each other?' asked Watts.

'As often as work and other demands on them allowed.'

'Are you aware of anyone Zoe might have recently befriended?'

Mrs Prentiss clasped her hands tight on her lap, emotionality starting to surface. 'Detective Inspector, our daughter was a young, professional woman. She worked long hours. She had limited time for socializing. When she wasn't working, she ran, either close to where she lived or . . . that awful place. There was nothing in her life that was worrying her, or could have led to this . . . *nightmare*.'

Watts pushed on before emotion took hold. 'Zoe was happy at work and with her life generally?'

Mrs Prentiss sat forward, giving him an intent gaze. 'I know you have your job to do, but looking for something in Zoe's life as an explanation for what's happened is all *wrong*.' She moved away from her husband's restraining hand. 'Zoe was a decent, caring young woman. Whoever did this to her is a *monster*.' She pressed her hand to her mouth. 'I can hardly bear to speak about him. I want him caught. *Punished*. Zoe isn't to blame for what's happened but your questions are making me think that that's what the police believe.'

'Not at all, Mrs—'

'Zoe was a beautiful, happy, hard-working and successful professional woman. She didn't deserve . . .' She stopped, pressed her lips together.

Mr Prentiss put his hand on her arm again, looked at Watts. 'I agree with what my wife is saying.' Alec Prentiss was staring at the carpet.

Watts allowed the silence to grow. 'Have you got anything to add, Alec?'

He shook his head. 'My parents have said it all.'

Watts quickly reviewed what he'd heard so far. Zoe Roberts was a happy woman whose life was without problems or social difficulties, her murder an inexplicable tragedy, leaving her family and all who knew her reeling. In this kind of situation there never was a good time to push but there was something large and grey lurking in the corner of this suffocating room which no one in this family had yet referred to.

'What can you tell us about Christian Roberts, Zoe's husband?'

Mrs Prentiss's face flared. 'That's a *personal* matter for this family!'

Watts shook his head. 'I'm sorry, Mrs Prentiss, but there can't be any personal matters in a murder investigation. Have you had any communication with Mr Roberts during the last few days?'

Mrs Prentiss looked away. 'No. I'm sure that you're already aware that he's a partner at the same legal practice as Zoe but he isn't based there. He works from an office in Brussels. The situation between him and Zoe is . . . *was* amicable.'

Watts nodded. It might explain why Roberts was still wearing her engagement and wedding rings when she was killed.

Alec Prentiss was staring at his mother. 'What's the point in dressing it up? They were planning to get divorced.'

His father gave him a look. '*Alec*. We don't know that for certain. The police want facts.' And to Watts, he added, 'Zoe didn't confide in us about that aspect of her life, so we're unable to comment on it.'

Watts decided to leave it for now. He'd give it a day or two and ring Alec Prentiss. 'Have you heard from or seen Mr Roberts since what happened to Zoe?'

'No. We haven't spoken with him for several months.'

'Do you know his current whereabouts?'

'As my wife said, he has an office in Brussels.'

Watts looked at each of them. 'But Mr Roberts does know what's happened to Zoe?'

'I attempted to contact him as soon as we knew,' said Mrs Prentiss. 'I rang twice, left a message both times to contact us, indicating that something very serious had occurred. He would have been in no doubt that there was a problem concerning Zoe, but we've heard nothing from him.'

'What do you make of that?' asked Watts, addressing the question to both of them.

Mrs Prentiss's chin rose. 'We don't make anything of it.'

'We need Mr Roberts' contact numbers.'

She reached for an expensive-looking handbag on a nearby chair, took out her phone, tapped it and handed it to Judd who copied the numbers.

Her husband frowned at Watts. 'Those calls my wife made to him were the first I can remember in months. Since Zoe and he separated, there wasn't a need.'

Watts looked across to Alec Prentiss. 'Can you tell us anything about Mr Roberts, Alec?'

He shrugged. 'Like my mother said, he works for the same law firm. That's how they met. Christian was already a partner there when Zoe joined. She would have seen him as a good catch.'

His mother stared at him, a dark wash of colour rising on to her neck. She looked at Watts. 'Christian impressed us all as a solid, hard-working professional. He's a few years older than Zoe but that never caused any difficulties as far as we're aware. Since he and Zoe separated, there's been no contact between us. We think he may be in Edinburgh.'

Watts waited. 'What makes you think he might be there?'

'Zoe mentioned it when she phoned me on the evening prior to . . .' Her eyes grew bright. She put her fingers to her lips. 'Detective Inspector Watts, I don't know if you have children, but . . . our daughter isn't simply a photograph on the television news or just another victim of the kind you are probably used to.'

'That's not what she is for West Midlands police, Mrs Prentiss. That's not how we work.'

'I'll tell you about Zoe. She never caused us a single moment's worry.' She turned to her husband. 'Did she, Peter? She was all we ever wanted in a daughter.' Her face softened. 'From when she was a little girl, she was quick and clever, yet she still worked hard all the way through school and university. She wanted to excel and she did. She joined the Solihull legal practice and proved her worth. We couldn't have wanted for a better daughter. Zoe was kind, she was thoughtful, she was caring and . . . I can't make sense of what's happened.' Her voice shook. 'I feel like I'm going mad. Whoever did this, it has to be a madman. I want you to find him and lock him up so he can't do this to any other family.' She clasped her hand to her mouth. Her husband put his arm around her. Their son stared out of the window.

Mr Prentiss looked across at Watts. 'If there's anything else you need to ask, could we do it at another time?'

Watts and Judd stood. He walked them from the room, across the spacious hallway to the front door. Watts turned to him. 'We're very grateful to you for allowing us into your home at a time like this, Mr Prentiss. We'll be contacting the people you've named, including Mr Roberts. Hopefully, they'll give us details of other associates of Zoe's we might speak to. One more thing: we need a recent full-face photograph of Zoe as a matter of urgency.'

Prentiss kept his voice low. 'Of course. I'll scan one to headquarters as soon as you leave.' He paused. 'I didn't want to raise this in front of my wife and I feel uncomfortable doing so now, but I got an impression from Zoe a few weeks ago that Christian was involved in something, I don't know how to put it . . . questionable.'

Watts waited. 'Such as?'

'She didn't say. Perhaps I should have pressed her for details, but I was very reluctant to do so. I didn't want to add to the situation between her and Christian.'

'I understand, Mr Prentiss. Did Zoe say if this "questionable" issue related to his work?'

'She didn't, and I'd rather it wasn't mentioned to him directly.'

'When we do talk to Mr Roberts, we'll be careful how we raise it with him. Finally, can you confirm your daughter's use of Blackfoot Trail?'

'You mean her running? She went there each week, same day, same time. Zoe was a very busy person. She thrived on routine. It helped her stay efficient.'

'Who, apart from the family, knew that that was her routine?'

Prentiss thought about it. 'I imagine Christian, her friends, everyone at her office would have known.' As Watts turned to leave, Prentiss said, 'Detective Inspector? A brief word about the young woman you've sent here to support us—'

'Dad!' They turned to Alec Prentiss walking towards them. Prentiss senior's eyes slid away from Watts.

'All I was going to say is that she's very supportive. I want you to know that we appreciate it.' Watts suspected that he'd had been about to say something very different. The fact that he'd bottled it strengthened the suspicion.

'You're welcome.'

'Mom needs you.' Alec watched his father walk back across the hall to the sitting room, go inside and close the door, then he turned to Watts. 'You need help if you're going to get whoever's done this to Zoe and you've probably realized you won't get it from him or Mom but I couldn't say so in there. They're upset enough as it is.'

Watts looked at him, nodded. 'Can you help us out?'

Alec Prentiss lowered his voice, eyes fixed on the floor. 'My sister was full of life . . . very full-on. She did what she wanted. It surprised me that she settled down to her law studies but' – he shrugged – 'she was clever and always knew what she wanted.'

Watts waited. 'What did Zoe want?'

Prentiss looked at him. 'Money. Things.' He paused. 'This is going to shock you but . . . I didn't much like my sister. I was five years older but she had the upper hand with me right from the start. She took my stuff, money. I never said anything to Mom or Dad. No point really. By the time I reached twelve, thirteen, I'd learned how to deal with her and things got better between us.' He sighed, ran his fingers through his hair. 'I realized it was possible to dislike somebody but still admire them.' He smiled. 'Know what my mom always said about us? Zoe was more the son, and I . . . anyway, you get the picture.'

'We're grateful to you for telling us,' said Watts.

Prentiss nodded. 'I had to, because it's what she was like and you need to know if you're going to find whoever did this to her.'

'We will, Alec.'

'He has to be caught, punished for what he's done.'

'He will be.'

*   *   *

THEY WERE BACK INSIDE the BMW, Watts thinking that Zoe Roberts' efficiency, her love of routine had contributed to her death, and of all the people who were aware of her once-weekly run at Blackfoot Trail, her estranged husband fit two categories: family of a sort and work colleague, also of a sort. He thought of what the mother had said about her daughter's death, that she'd crossed paths with a madman. Not a million miles away from what he'd anticipated from the parents, despite their not knowing about the remains of another woman found close by. He started the vehicle, glanced at Judd staring straight ahead. As much as her keenness got on his nerves, the distant look on her face was unsettling.

'All right?'

She turned to him. 'If Christian Roberts is on the take, it might explain why he's making himself scarce. We need to track him down, get him into headquarters so we can hear what he's got to say about it.'

Watts navigated his way through slow traffic. 'If he is "on the take", as you put it, are you also saying he attacked his estranged wife and cut off her head?'

'You never know with people. She might have found out what he was up to and threatened him. She might have been narky about the direction their relationship was taking and he knew that if she opened her mouth he would be ruined.'

'With you on the force, Judd, we can consider ourselves lucky there's no capital punishment.'

She looked at him. 'What did you make of what the mother said about Zoe?'

'A natural response to the situation they've found them-selves in.'

Judd rolled her eyes. 'It's a good job the brother opened his mouth to us because all we got from her was that Zoe Roberts walked on water!' He gave her a quick glance, saw the flush on her face. 'He's thirty-something yet they talk to him like he's fifteen—'

'Thirty-five.'

'What?'

'Alec Prentiss is thirty-five. If you simmer down, I've got some advice about situations like the one we were just in. We accept what we get from the bereaved at face value until we know different and we don't go straight to being arsy and suspicious.'

'I'm not arsy—'

'A bit more advice. It was obvious from your face when Christian Roberts' name came up that you couldn't wait to get into it. Don't show people that something's got your interest. Keep it casual.' He watched her take out a pen. 'What are you doing?'

She pulled out her notes. 'Writing down what you just said.'

He looked away, thinking she was a bloody odd mix: impulsive, yet cautious and a lot more besides. She was looking at him again. 'Got any ideas about this "questionable" thing Christian Roberts might have been into?'

'None.'

She frowned at what she'd written. 'Did you notice that they didn't mention any friends Zoe made as an adult?'

'They're *upset*.' Shaking his head, he drove on, trying to get a grip on why Mrs Prentiss's description of her daughter had so annoyed Judd. 'Annoyed' wasn't the right word. He frowned, searched for another. If it wasn't ridiculous, if right now Roberts wasn't lying in one of the refrigerated drawers inside the pathology suite at headquarters, a word he might have applied to her response was 'jealous'.

Her voice came again. 'They didn't ask what was done to her, did they?'

He focused on making it across a busy junction. 'Familial responses vary. Some demand to know everything, others avoid the specifics at this stage, partly because they're in shock, partly because they think they can't handle it. Mr Prentiss is no fool. My guess is he's put two and two together but is protecting his family by not saying so. They'll have seen press coverage about her being "attacked" and they're going with that for now.' He drove on. 'The brother was open in telling us about his relationship with his sister, but what we need is information about her life beyond the family. I'll give it a few days then ask him to come into headquarters for a chat. When he does, it could be a job for you.'

'Just tell me when. Where are we going now?'

'To headquarters to look at some tips that have come in.' They'd be back at the scene later. They needed progress. Watts also wanted to know how Traynor was getting on.

EIGHT

SOCOs and forensic officers were much in evidence as they walked the trail. Catching sight of two tall figures standing in the field next to it, Watts upped his speed, hoping for progress which the tips hadn't yielded. Traynor turned as they approached, looking in a lot better shape than he had earlier. He'd changed into a fresh white shirt and khaki combats, an iPad in a red case at his side.

Watts nodded to him, then: 'How's it going, Adam?'

'No more finds, but I've been showing Dr Traynor the crime scene and its surroundings, plus the location of the skull.'

Watts held out the evidence bag to Adam. 'Zoe Roberts' phone for processing.' He looked at Traynor. 'We need to talk motive. Without Annette Barlow's body there's no determining exactly what happened to her, but so far Dr Chong is saying there's zero evidence of sexual activity on Roberts' remains.'

Traynor's eyes were fixed on the incline. 'At this stage, sexual homicide is the motivation that's a best fit. It's possible that Roberts was subjected to sexual activity which left zero evidence.'

Watts knew this to be reasonable, based on what they had so far. 'Got any observations from examining the scene?'

Traynor flipped the iPad cover, tapped the screen, tone brisk.

'I've walked the whole area from the specific scene in the car park to the incline where the skull was located. I've followed the likely route Roberts' killer took until the bloodspots ended. I've viewed the aerial photographs. Based on all of that, I've got some preliminary observations on Roberts' killer, although they may well change, depending on new information becoming available. Those observations are limited by unknowns and uncertainties.'

Watts sensed Judd on high alert. 'Give us the "knowns",' he said.

Traynor pointed in the direction of Blackfoot Trail. 'Physical evidence indicates that having removed Roberts' head, her killer took it and exited the car park, followed the trail, forced his way through the robust hedge running alongside and entered this field. His actions, so far as they can be determined from the limited physical evidence available, indicate to me that he was purposeful, fully in control of himself and his actions. He felt comfortable here. I doubt he was under the influence of any substances.'

Watts eyed him. Far from being the driven individual he'd seen at their first meeting, followed by what looked to be the wreck of a person he'd talked to that morning, this third re-incarnation was a masterclass of astute analysis and cool critical thinking. 'What you're saying is, he isn't some local nutter.'

'At this stage, very unlikely. If we factor in the lack of defence injuries to the victim's hands and arms, there is a possibility that he may have been known to Roberts.' Watts ignored the elated look arriving on Judd's face. 'However, it's equally possible that he was a stranger who presented as socially competent, whose general appearance and demeanour were such that he was able to approach her in these somewhat isolated surroundings without causing her immediate alarm or distress.'

Watts waited. 'And?'

'Indications of competence and self-control suggest that he's an individual with the ability to plan his actions, which in turn suggests he's of at least average intellect.' Traynor gave the small screen a tap. 'The timing of the murder, so early in the morning, could be an indication that he's in employment.'

Listening to the cool, unemotional delivery, seeing Traynor's attention fixed on the iPad, it occurred to Watts that some of what he'd said about Roberts' killer could easily apply to Traynor. He told himself to ease up. What Traynor had just said was encouraging, more than Watts had dared hope for this early, but he had an issue with one aspect of it. 'I've assumed that the timing of the murder was set by Zoe Roberts herself. She chose to be here at that hour because she had work afterwards. The fact that her killer was here might have nothing to do with his having a job or not. Unless you're suggesting that he was somehow able to influence the time Roberts chose to run because he knew her, which isn't backed up by anything her family has told us.'

Traynor looked unfazed. 'I'm considering all possibilities. We don't know that she always ran alone. It's possible her killer saw her at the trail for the first time that day and it was an impulsive act on his part, although the fact that he had a weapon makes it more likely that he was in the area at that early hour with attack in mind. The indications of planning suggest the possibility that he had a specific interest in Zoe Roberts, that he'd observed her over a period of time, got to know her routine, maybe got to know her, but at this stage we should avoid developing any assumptions about him in relation to her. There are, of course, no guarantees in anything I'm suggesting.'

Watts glanced at Judd, her face perky, eyes shining. He eyed Traynor. 'I'm leaning towards his having stalked her, but what you're telling us, that he maintained his cool, his control, while stabbing Roberts to death and decapitating her, would take some doing. Unless he's somebody whose feet aren't too closely attached to the planet.'

'From what I've already said, it should be clear that this is a male who is well-integrated and on the planet.'

Their eyes locked.

'OK,' said Watts. 'I get it. He's no idiot, probably works, he might have stalked Roberts, he might even have got to know her. What else?'

'If this was a situation where he had no prior knowledge of her, he wouldn't have been able to predict how she might respond when she first saw him. By observing her prior to the attack he would have acquired data about the kind of individual she was, her likely responses.' He frowned. '"Stalked" is a value-laden word, DI Watts. I prefer "observed". Less emotive, wouldn't you say?'

Watts said nothing. He'd already got plenty of 'emotive' images from this case, starting with the six knife-thrusts into Roberts' chest and her killer walking away, her blonde ponytail grasped tight in one bloodied hand. He let his eyes drift over fields, hedges and trees. They were starting to look more familiar to him than his own desiccated patch of lawn. 'Judd suggested a stalking element so I checked the PNC: no arrests or complaints relating to stalking in the area over the last two years.'

'Do you want to hear what else I have?'

'Carry on.'

'If he took the murder weapon away with him, it's a further indication of control and that he's forensically aware.' Seeing Watts about to respond, he nodded. 'Only those who don't care or, as you said earlier, are not on this planet, disregard forensics.' His eyes returned to the screen. 'He didn't transport the victim's body from the scene but left it more or less in full view.' He frowned, stared ahead. 'A single indicator of disorganization.'

'Which tells us what?'

'That we have a predominantly organized crime scene, except for one significant, disorganized feature. It might denote that he's subject to variable moods.'

Watts was now slot-rattling between accepting much of what Traynor had offered so far and thinking that it sounded exactly like what Traynor had said it was: a lot of possibilities. He reminded himself that the forensic psychologist he used to work with had had a good line in robust pronouncements. He hadn't liked a lot of those either. 'So, what do we need to firm up, or otherwise, what you've said?'

'More evidence.'

'The team's looking for it. It's possible there might not be any.'

Traynor looked up from the small screen. 'Let's hope there is. What I've outlined is this killer's likely behaviour around and towards Roberts. The skull at the incline and the Roberts homicide are geographically linked. Both were subjected to decapitation.

Not a common behavioural feature of repeat homicides, by the way. Plus, it was risky. It took time. It tells us that it was an activity this killer considered hugely important.'

Watts stared down at thick dust marking his suede shoes. 'We're agreed that Roberts and Barlow were both victims of the same killer?'

Traynor nodded. 'It's the likeliest theory. By the way, removal of heads, post-mortem, is ritualistic. The value in identifying a ritualistic sexual motive is that repeat killers tend to demonstrate a victim-preference in terms of age, physical appearance, lifestyle and so on. It could tell us something about how he regarded them, possibly where he first saw them. Unfortunately, given the absence of a body for one of these cases, and a head for the other, we'll be reliant on photographs of both victims, plus biographical information from Annette Barlow's family to help us establish any possible victim preference this killer has. We need the photographs as a matter of urgency.'

Watts took out his phone, jabbed a number. His call rang out briefly inside the squad room. 'Have we received the recent photo of Zoe Roberts her family said they'd send over? Good. Get it blown up, put it on the whiteboard, send a copy to my phone and another to the Smartboard downstairs in my office, plus one to Dr Traynor's phone. What about a photo of Annette Barlow? . . . Right. Tell them to get a move on. We need to be talking to her family, pronto.' He cut the call. 'The lads are still trying to contact Annette Barlow's family.'

Traynor pointed in the direction of the car park. 'One current homicide there, head taken, body left in situ, and' – he pointed towards the incline – 'one skull found there, whereabouts of body unknown. Question: why those differences?' He took a few steps, his eyes focused on the specific area. 'Right now, I doubt we're seeing his whole homicidal career.'

Watts stared at him. This was too close to his own worst thinking. Something he didn't want to hear, let alone consider. 'You're saying there could be more victims?'

'A possibility to be aware of, is what I'm saying.'

Watts turned to Adam. 'When do you think you'll be ready to examine that whole incline?'

Adam looked at it. 'Given the finding of the skull, we need to be ultra-careful to avoid destroying any further evidence if it's there. When that's done it's going to be a case of systematic search and excavation.' He turned to Watts. 'I can't give a time estimate because of the heat my officers are working in.'

Watts' eyes were fixed on the ground, the sun searing his own head. He looked up at Traynor. 'We are agreed that a lack of evidence of sexual behaviour so far for the Roberts homicide isn't significant in terms of a sexual motive?'

'It isn't significant, given other indicators we have, such as place, time and what was done to her.'

Traynor tapped the screen. 'I've just sent you a copy of the main points of what I've said. Would a short, verbal summary help?'

'Go on.'

'Intelligent, largely organized killer, socially adept on first contact, self-controlled during homicidal activity. A planner. If he lacks a victim preference, he's highly dangerous.'

'Which means what, exactly, for this investigation?'

'If there is no victim preference and he's attacking at random, you need to issue a public warning that he's operating in this area of the city. I'd go so far as to say a warning should be given, regardless.'

Watts stared at him. 'And risk panic and all sorts of idiots coming out of the woodwork to confess or claim they know who he is, naming an ex-partner or relative they've got a gripe against and us spending valuable investigative hours we can't spare, checking them out and wasting time?' He took a breath. Traynor's cool delivery was getting to him. 'Is that what you're saying?'

Traynor flipped the iPad cover. 'Advising. I see your difficulty.'

Watts took more deep breaths. 'We've got your overall take on this killer, which more or less fits with what I've been thinking. My priority now is getting information from people who knew Roberts and Barlow well. *Random* homicide is my least preferred option. If there's the slightest link between Roberts and Barlow, I want it. It might tell us something about their killer, the sorts of places he hangs out, where he first saw them. We've talked to Roberts' immediate family. They're knocked sideways by what's happened and don't seem to have anything to offer us in terms of a suspect, although I wouldn't be surprised if they're wondering on the quiet if the son-in-law, Christian Roberts, was somehow involved. What do you say, Judd?'

She nodded. 'Agreed.'

He gazed across the open space ahead of them. 'He's not been in touch with them or us since the news of Zoe Roberts' murder broke, which in my book is bloody odd.'

Traynor sent him a cool look. 'Christian Roberts is relevant because of his relationship with one of the victims. We need to maintain a focus on both. I'm sure we can agree that the key investigative questions right now are where, how and why their killer selected them.'

Watts nodded agreement. Recalling the route he'd walked late the previous evening from the compound to the high ground nearby, he looked to Adam and pointed. 'I got your text about sending a couple of officers up there to examine that area. Any progress?'

'Let's ask.'

Traynor remained where he was as Watts and Judd followed Adam. Judd moved closer to Watts, her voice low. 'Now we've heard Dr Traynor's ideas, what do you think of him?' She didn't wait for a response. 'We had some criminology lectures during training. He knows his stuff, Sarge. Everything he's just told us sounds like good analysis and—'

'Judd.'

'Sarge?'

'Put a lid on it.' They continued on, Traynor now following, to where forensic officers were kneeling on the ground. Watts pointed out the compound to him. 'See that? I think it's very possible that Roberts' killer approached this area from the motorway, drove up that access road, parked his vehicle down there, came up here on foot, carried on to Blackfoot Trail where he killed Roberts, then left by the same route.'

One of the forensic officers looked up. 'Adam? Take a look at this.' They went to him. He pointed at three hard-baked, sharply defined shoeprints among sparse vegetation. 'I'm about to take impressions.' They watched him position rectangles of robust card around each print, reach inside a box and take out a plastic bag, two-thirds filled with thick white powder, a layer of clear liquid above it. Kneading it for several seconds, he opened it and carefully poured its contents on to each print. They watched them disappear under a thick layer of white. He glanced at his watch. 'I'll leave it to harden off then lift the casts and take them back to headquarters for matching. They look like trainer prints to me, which means we're in luck as far as identification goes. The downside is who doesn't wear trainers?'

'Me,' snapped Watts. 'Anybody remember when it last rained here?'

Traynor consulted his iPad. 'Five twelve a.m. on the day of the Roberts' homicide. A short, heavy downpour. The only rain in the last five weeks.' He looked at the sloping ground. 'From that compound to here might be driveable.'

Judd gave Watts a bright-eyed look, her nose pink, starting to peel. 'Those footprints. It's *him*, Sarge. He came up here, like you said, then went to the trail to lie in wait for Roberts.'

As Watts walked away, she made to follow him. 'Stay there.' He headed down the steep slope and continued on to the chain-link fence and its gate. The padlock was hanging loose on its chain. Somebody was here. He pushed open the gate. It whined on its hinges. Whoever was in one of these prefab buildings a couple of nights back, if he was here now, Watts wanted a few words. He was halfway between gate and buildings when he picked up movement. A male in work clothes and boots was coming in his direction, a thick, plaited lead wound around one hand, on the other end a large dog with the look of a Rottweiler straining forward.

'I hope you've got a licence for that,' said Watts.

'Who are you?'

Watts reached for his inside pocket. 'Detective Inspector Bernard Watts, West Midlands Police. Lock him up and bring me details of who works here and when.'

The man eyed Watts for several seconds, the muscles of his forearms bulging as he pulled the animal towards him. 'Titan! Come on, boy. Job done.'

Watts watched man and dog walk away then disappear inside one of the buildings. The door closed on them. Watts started a slow count. If he wasn't back here in . . . The door opened. The man came out alone, walked back to Watts, a clipboard in hand.

'Can't be too careful out here on my own.' He jabbed a thumb at the machinery behind him. 'That's expensive kit. What did you say you wanted?'

'Details of who works here and when, starting with you. Name.'

'Shaw. Bill Shaw.'

Watts waited. Shaw reached into a back pocket, took out a wallet, pulled out a driving licence. Watts looked at it. 'What are your hours of work here, Mr Shaw?'

'I'm daytime security from seven a.m. to five p.m.'

'What happens then?'

'The night security worker arrives. There'll be fulltime security when the new road works start.'

'A constant, in my experience. You've worked here every day during the last week?'

'Yeah.'

'I want details of who worked each of those nights.'

Shaw consulted lists attached to the clipboard. 'This is the current rota. It's always me in the day and two possible workers for the night shift. As soon as one arrives, I leave. Which date are you interested in?' Watts told him. Shaw ran a finger down a short list. 'Gerry Williams worked the last seven nights.' He held out the sheet.

Watts looked at it. 'Tell me about him.'

'Like I said—'

'If you're daytime security, there'll be some kind of handover between the two of you. What's this Williams like?'

Shaw looked away, shrugged. 'Big chap. Late thirties, I'd say. Bit of an accent. Bristol, or something. He arrives. I leave. The only reason there's security here at all is that there's been a couple of break-ins at other sites along this motorway.'

'What about the dog?'

'Titan's mine. He goes home with me.'

'Does Williams bring a dog to work?'

'Not that I've seen.'

'So, he's all on his lonesome here?'

'Far as I know.'

Watts turned from him then back. 'Seeing as though you and Williams have nothing to say to each other and no time to say it, I'm expecting you'll forget this visit as soon as I'm gone.'

'What visit?'

Watts nodded, his eyes moving slowly over the compound. 'Where's your vehicle?'

'What?'

'You drove here. Where is it?'

Watts looked to where he was pointing, at a dark grey car. 'Stay there.' He went to the beat-up Vauxhall, walked around it, wrote down the registration, got down, checked its tyres. He came back to Shaw, whose eyes were fixed on the ground. 'You know what I'm going to say. That thing's a menace. Wait here.' He left Shaw, sent a text and watched a uniformed constable separate from the group at the top of the hill and start down the slope. When he arrived, Watts pointed at Shaw standing where he'd left him. 'Check his vehicle registration and sort out his violations.'

Phone to his ear, he headed back up the hill. 'Adam, I need the search for shoeprints extended down this slope.' Watts went to Traynor, whose eyes were fixed on the compound. 'I've already requested Automatic Number Plate data. Once we've got CCTV footage, I'll have a couple of the team examine it all for vehicles passing along this stretch of motorway prior to the time Roberts arrived for her run. What they'll be looking for in particular is any vehicle which turned into that access road or took the motorway exit a mile or so ahead.' He looked at Traynor. 'What you said about timing earlier. I'm hoping it works to our advantage. Whoever killed Roberts had to be here, ready and waiting, before she arrived. Like you said, it's possible he watched her more than once.'

'Let's hope it gives us something.'

Watts studied him. Sympathetic as he was because of what he'd seen of him these last couple of days, Traynor had to know that this investigation wasn't going to be an easy ride for anybody. 'I'm one hundred per cent on this investigation. I expect the same from everybody.'

'I hadn't anticipated otherwise.'

'How confident are you that she was stalked, observed?'

'It makes logical sense.'

Watts thought about it. 'Given what the family told us about her routine, he could have watched her here for weeks.'

Traynor's eyes were still on the compound. 'All's possible. He may have observed her elsewhere, but that's another "unknown".'

A sudden shout made them all turn to the uniformed officer coming towards them. 'Sarge! We've got a situation at the car park. Some workmen have arrived, demanding access. We've told them no but they're refusing to leave until they've spoken to whoever's in charge. One's a right motormouth.'

Watts went with him, Judd and Traynor following. They arrived to see a truck parked across the entrance, four workmen inside the car park, one getting into the face of one of the officers responsible for guarding it.

'*Hey*,' shouted Watts. 'What's going on?'

'I'm the boss of this crew,' snapped Motormouth, shoving a printed sheet at him. 'This'll spell it out for you. The council has sanctioned urgent work here, starting today.'

Watts shoved the sheet back at him. 'Tell the council to forget it. This is a crime scene. Nobody comes in here, except for investigative officers.'

Motormouth squared up to Watts. 'Who are you?'

Traynor arrived at Watts' side.

'Detective Inspector Watts, Senior Investigative Officer, and you're not coming in here to start any work.'

Motormouth's eyes flicked to Traynor, back to Watts. 'Now I've got your name, I'm phoning the office to tell them we're being prevented from carrying out essential work.'

'Don't waste time phoning. You're not doing anything here.'

Motormouth's face reddened. He raised his arm, pointing across the car park. 'See that wall? *That's* what we're here to sort out.'

Traynor left them and headed for it.

'The council's surveyor has deemed it unsound and we're here to rectify it. If you prevent us from carrying out legitimate reparations and it falls down and brains somebody, it'll be *your* responsibility.'

'And I'll tell you again, you're not starting any work here.'

The face-off continued. Traynor was back. 'The buttressing this side of the wall looks sufficiently robust to support that wall for a while.'

Motormouth turned on him. 'Who the hell are *you*? A civil engineering expert?'

Traynor gazed down at him. 'Somebody who believes in treating others with respect and anticipates getting the same in return.'

Motormouth's eyes slid away from Traynor. He gestured to his three workmates. 'Come on. We've wasted enough time here. We'll get the buildings inspector out to this.'

Watts and Traynor watched them get into the truck and screech away. 'I'm assuming that a police investigation takes precedence,' said Traynor.

'Exactly. He can bring the Pope with him next time, for all I care. They still don't get in.'

Traynor grinned.

Watts turned to the two constables to reinforce the 'No Access' line, then back to Traynor. 'I've got an update to put together for Brophy first thing tomorrow so I'll leave you to it.'

He and Judd climbed inside his vehicle. 'Got a job for you, Judd. No, you don't need to write it down. Let every officer involved in the investigation know that there's a full briefing in the squad room tomorrow morning at eight.'

'Sarge.'

'I'll be going over the evidence we've got so far but I also want them to know that this is a team undertaking, not just a slog in eighty-plus degrees.' Judd looked unimpressed. His phone pinged. He read the email, unsure if it pleased him or not. On balance, he decided not. 'Dr Chong's found a partial palm print on Roberts' body.'

Judd raised her fist. '*Yes.*'

'And, contrary to your early theorizing, she's now confirmed zero evidence of sexual activity on Roberts' remains.'

'*Damn!* . . . Hang on, though. Dr Traynor said that that didn't matter.'

Rolling his eyes, Watts started the engine.

NINE

Thursday 18 August. Seven a.m.

Watts was being economical on what he knew. 'Dr Traynor's fully on board, sir. I've called a full briefing in an hour when I'll introduce him to the team and update all of them on what I've just told you about the shoeprints, plus the fibre and hair evidence found on Roberts' body. I'll keep you updated as and when there's more to report.'

Brophy nodded. 'You're confident that the area where the shoeprints were found and the crime scene are accessible from this road-repair compound?'

In the brief time Watts had known Brophy, he'd formed the impression that the less he was told, the better. Give him detail and he'd go straight to micro-managing mode. 'It's early stages, sir, one of a number of aspects we'll be exploring. I'm waiting for an ident on the worker who does nights there. Dr Chong has provided identification for the skull found close to the Roberts' homicide: Annette Barlow. Her family took a bit of tracking down. It's just the father, apparently. I haven't released any details to him yet. I want family liaison involved before I do.'

'Has Dr Traynor got any ideas on the way forward?'

'He's suggested several lines of inquiry.' Reluctant as he was to tell him, Brophy needed to know. 'He's got a theory that if there's any physical similarities between Roberts and Barlow, their killer could be highly dangerous.'

Brophy's eyebrows shot up. 'Most killers are risky. Why is he upping the ante on this one?'

Excising the phrase 'bloody obvious' hurtling inside his head, Watts selected other words. 'It's the possibility of decapitation of both victims, sir, plus the long timeframe from the Barlow skull burial to the Roberts homicide. It looks like whoever this killer is, he's sticking at it. Enjoying what he does. What we've seen so far might not be his whole story.' He watched the horrified look surface on Brophy's face. 'Traynor's advice is that we put out a city-wide warning so people know that current risk exists in that area and can make informed choices.'

Brophy drummed his fingers on the desk. 'On the basis of one homicide a decade ago and one recently? I've got misgivings about that. There's too much press interest as it is without adding warnings.' He looked at Watts. 'What do *you* think?'

'If we do issue a warning, we risk attracting a load of types who want to "confess" or tell us they know the killer and we could be wasting valuable investigative time checking them out—'

'Exactly my thinking!'

'But I also get what Dr Traynor is saying. That people, particularly those in the south of the city, need to be warned so they can decide what they do and where.'

Brophy looked away from him to the open windows. Watts waited for him to show the authority which went with his rank and pay grade. Brophy looked back at him. 'We're barely a couple of days into this investigation. There's no need to rush to a decision like that, but don't tell Dr Traynor it's an outright "no". Just . . . put him off.'

Watts' impression of Traynor so far was that he wasn't easily put off. He had half-hoped that as senior officer, Brophy would make the strong choice in favour of a warning, but only half. This was a chief who preferred to avoid decisive action wherever he could. Watts stood. 'If that's all, sir, I've got a briefing to start. One other thing. Has anybody from the council contacted you about work planned at Blackfoot Trail?'

'Yes. I told them no until further notice.'

Leaving the chief's office, he got a call from Chong. 'How's your new colleague?' she asked.

'Self-contained and cool about covers it.'

'Sounds a little austere.'

'That as well. Where are you?'

'At the scene and, boy, is it hot!'

The noise in the squad room stopped as Watts finished his call and came inside. The floor-standing fans he'd requested to support the flagging air con were up and working, books, lunch-boxes and other belongings keeping papers desk-bound. His eyes moved over the assembled officers. Judd was in her usual corner seat. Traynor was also here.

'OK. Let's get on with it. First, you'll have noticed a new presence.' He raised his hand. 'Dr William Traynor, criminologist from Central University. If you're unsure what a criminologist does, ask him, but only one of you. He doesn't need asking fifteen-plus times.' He glanced at his notes. 'We've got a potential development on the Roberts homicide. Dr Chong has finished the post-mortem.' The room was silent, all eyes fixed on him. 'The cause of death we already know: six stab wounds to the chest. Indications are that initial control over the victim was achieved by the killer standing behind her and placing his arm around her neck. We know that because it left a bruise. According to Dr Chong, a likely cause is the metal bracelet of a watch. She's also located fibres on the back of the victim's vest which supports the theory that she was held from behind. Forensics have both the vest and the fibres, but it'll take a while before they're fully examined, given all else they're doing. Dr Chong has now confirmed zero evidence of sexual assault.' He picked up muted groans. 'I know. It doesn't look like we'll have a DNA "gotcha" from semen, but it's not all bad news. She's also found four sections of head hair on the remains. There are no roots, so she's sending them for expert analysis, which is going to take a while.' He looked at the rows of faces, most already frustrated. 'More potential good news: a partial handprint.' Seeing glances being exchanged, he pointed at his own upper chest. 'It's in this area of Roberts' body, just above her vest top. A partial palm-heel combination. Dr Chong's theory is that the killer steadied the body with his left hand, prior to removing her head. It confirms a right-handed killer which isn't much help but we've got the print so we'll be looking for a match.' He looked around the silent room. 'Where are you, Jones?'

'Over here, Sarge!'

'You like a rummage in IDENT1. Let Dr Chong know that you'll be needing that partial. Let me know the minute you find what looks like a match.' Watts' eyes moved over the whole room. 'You know that forensics have found shoeprints on an area of high ground overlooking the Works Unit Only compound. They suggest that Roberts' killer parked his vehicle at that compound and walked up to it some time prior to Roberts being killed. Forensics are looking for a match but we're talking trainers here so it could take a while and not yield anything useful. As soon as I know more, so will you.' He took another glance at his list. 'You've all been to the crime scene so you know how close it is to the M42. I've requested CCTV footage for the relevant date. I'm hoping for identification of a likely vehicle travelling along the motorway and possibly leaving it at the junction a quarter of a mile further on, or even better, going up the Works Unit Only approach road just prior to it. We're expecting that footage any time. When it arrives, it'll be another "rummage" opportunity for you, Jones. Who else would you like on it with you?'

Jones pointed. 'Kumar, sir.'

'That suit you, Kumar?'

'Yes, Sarge!'

'I'll let you know as soon as it's available.' Watts scanned the officers. 'Results of the witness appeal indicate a lot of local keenness, although they're poor in terms of usefulness but it's early days. Where's Connors?' A hand rose. 'You and Anson stick with the phones for the next forty-eight hours. Any general questions or comments from anybody about what I've said, or anything else?' He waited out the short silence. 'Next item: I want a records check against a name.' Several hands shot up, one belonging to a mature female PC. Watts looked at her. Here was somebody who might guide and nurture Judd, who was restlessly eyeing her watch. 'Thanks, Miller. The name's Gerry or Gerald Williams. Age range: thirty to forty-five, possibly from the Bristol area. Employment associated with but not confined to motorway repair and/or security. I want to know ASAP if you find anything. While you're at it, do a search against Christian Roberts, our victim's estranged husband, a lawyer, in his forties. Oh, and if I ask any one of you to talk to individuals associated with Zoe Roberts, I want you to make a point of establishing with each of them what they knew about her running routine, how familiar they were with it, but be subtle.' He watched as they wrote. 'That's it. If you're out there, stay well-watered. I don't want notes from your mothers complaining about sunstroke.'

Watts pulled his papers together, his peripheral vision on Traynor talking to a couple of officers. Any sign, no matter how small, that he was starting to integrate was welcome. Seeing Traynor raise a hand to him, he waited.

'There looks to be progress,' Traynor said.

Watts nodded. 'Some. Better than nothing.'

'You're focusing on the Roberts' homicide?'

'Yes, until Barlow's father has been spoken to.' He looked at Traynor. 'How about you go and see him?' He tapped his phone. 'I've sent you his address.'

Traynor nodded, walked away as Watts' phone rang. It was Chong again. He listened to her brief words. 'I'm on my way.' Ending the call, keeping his face neutral, he turned, almost knocking down Judd immediately behind him.

'What about me? What do you want me to do, Sarge?'

On the move, he opened his file, searched sheets, extracted one and handed it to her. 'Here. Location details for the city centre wine shop Annette Barlow managed, prior to her disappearance. It's still there. Current manager, a Harry Josephs. He's worked there for over ten years and he's expecting somebody today. You OK going on your own?'

She took the details, giving him a sideways look. '*Not* a problem.'

'Josephs worked with Barlow so he should be a good source of information about her if you pitch your questions right.'

'How about I go with Dr Traynor first, to see Annette Barlow's father?' She watched him head down the stairs. 'Where are you going?'

'Off my bloody head, if you keep on. Get over to that wine shop. *Now.*'

She followed him out of headquarters and over to her car.

WATTS WALKED THE FIELD, passing officers intent on their tasks, getting none of the usual hand-raises or acknowledgements. The atmosphere had changed. Watts knew why. His eyes fixed on the incline, he headed towards it. Jake Petrie, the geoscientist, was back, in what looked to be deep discussion with Adam. Reaching them, he looked at the drone sitting on the grass, close to a rectangle of bare, dry earth, a shallow depression at its centre.

Chong came to him. 'You're not going to like it but you need to see it.'

He followed her to a deep plastic container, something shadowy inside. She removed the lid and they crouched either side. He looked down at a dome-shaped bone, looked up at her, opened his mouth, managing the few words at his third attempt. 'I'm inside my own nightmare.'

Chong reached inside the box, lifted out the item, voice subdued. 'Skull number two. Carefully placed, like the first and sufficiently shallow-buried to be accessible to the elements, animals, birds and insects, hence the lack of tissue and hair.'

Watts eyed it, looked away, letting his eyes roam over the incline. When Zoe Roberts came here, she'd had no idea that she was running through a killing field. He found his voice. 'A sick bastard with some kind of grudge against women has turned this place into his own personal graveyard.' He looked up at Chong. 'How long's this one been here?'

'Adam and I are agreed on an estimate of around a decade. For anything more specific we'll be relying on identification.' She paused. 'There's a surprise element.' Watts recalled Judd's comment about not liking surprises. Chong held the skull closer to him and pointed. 'See the brow ridge here? It's more pronounced than that of the Barlow skull.' She turned it on its side, pointing at the jawbone. 'And this curve to the mandible? That's further confirmation.'

'Of what?'

She met his gaze. 'It's male.'

He stared at her in disbelief, then at the skull. She returned it to its box. 'Sorry if this is messing up any investigative theories you have.'

Watts looked down at it. 'It's a total broadside to the only one we've got: a homicidal psycho on the loose, with a thing against women.'

'Better now than later.'

Watts looked at Petrie. 'You found it?' Petrie pointed at the drone straddling the grass. Watts eyed it. 'It's been over this whole area?'

Petrie shook his head. 'No. I sent it up once and it located what you've got there almost immediately.'

Watts took out his phone, tapped a number, waited for the deep-voiced response. 'News for you, Traynor. I'm at the incline. There's a second skull here and it's male.'

'I see.'

'Where does that leave us if this isn't some sex type with a grudge against females?'

Traynor's voice flowed into his ear. 'Not necessarily rejecting the theory of sexual homicide. Victims of both genders does not preclude a sexual motivation. Neither does the absence of evidence of sexual activity. We'll talk more about that, but what it does suggest is a seriously aberrant individual. What I said about warning residents of a high risk still stands.'

Watts gazed at open countryside shrouded in heat haze. 'I hear you.' He didn't add that it was even more unlikely now that Brophy would agree to a warning.

TEN

Thursday 18 August. Ten fifteen a.m.

Judd pushed open the door of the city centre wine shop and went inside. It looked deserted. Glad to be out of the heat, she walked slowly along a shelf of bottles, eyes drifting over coloured labels. Wine was something she rarely drank and knew nothing about. One bottle on a low shelf, a flash of blue on its label, got her attention. She crouched, reached for it, touched its smooth coldness.

'Can I help you?' Her hand jerked, causing the bottle to teeter on its shelf. Flustered, she steadied it, looked up in the direction of the voice to a man who had appeared from nowhere. '*Sorry,* I've got it.'

He smiled down at her. He was tall, looked to be in his early thirties with a full beard, heavy-framed glasses, his hair styled and swept back from his face. 'My fault entirely. I startled you. Do you need some help?'

She straightened. 'Yes, but not with wine. I'm Police Constable Chloe Judd. Hang on.' She dug into a pocket, pulled out identification. 'I'm here to speak with Mr Josephs, the manager.'

He nodded, smiled again. 'That's me, apparently not conveying the gravitas I thought I was.'

'Mr Josephs, is there somewhere we can talk?'

He looked around the empty shop. 'It's always like this in the morning. How about we go over to the counter?' He reached down for the bottle Judd had almost upended and led the way across the shop to the polished wood counter. She stopped as he went behind it, indicating two high stools. 'Come on. Have a seat. You might as well be comfortable while you're here. If customers come in, we'll stop while I deal with them.'

She joined him behind the counter, took the stool he was pushing towards her and sat, pleased that her first solo contact in this case was with somebody who was pleasant and might have useful information about their second victim. 'Thank you. Mr Josephs, I'm here to talk to you about a colleague of yours from around a decade ago. Annette Barlow.'

He stared at her, saying nothing.

Judd returned his gaze. 'She was the manager here prior to her disappearance?'

Josephs ran a hand through his hair. It rippled back into place. 'Yes . . . Sorry, PC Judd, I did get a call from an officer wanting to talk to me but I didn't link that call with you. I do apologize.'

'No problem.' She waited as he took a couple of deep breaths.

'Actually, it was a bit of a shock when you mentioned Annette's name. How can I help?'

'Did you know Ms Barlow well?'

He paused, giving the question some thought. 'It depends what you mean by "well", I suppose. On balance, I'd say, pretty well, given the disparity in our ages back then.'

'When did you start work here?'

'Around twelve years ago. I was nineteen. I'd dropped out of university and I knew less than nothing about wine, but I answered an advertisement for a trainee.' He smiled at her. 'This is a nationwide company so when Annette took me on, I was really grateful.'

Judd nodded, writing quickly. 'You must have impressed her.'

'I don't know about that, but she gave me my start, sent me on courses and to wine shows.' His gaze moved to the shop windows and the street beyond. 'We worked here together until she disappeared, which was about two years later.' He looked at her. 'Why are the police interested now?'

She sidestepped his question. 'Back then, you were working full time here?'

'Yes.'

'So, long enough to get to know Annette as a colleague?'

He shrugged. 'I suppose so. Like I said, the difference in our ages meant we weren't exactly friends. Not that I'm saying there was a problem,' he said quickly. 'If there had been, Annette wouldn't have given the company such good reports about me. I stepped in as acting manager after she disappeared and a year later they made me manager. The youngest they had at the time.' He looked at her. 'You're writing all of this down?'

'Yes. Is that all right?' She cursed herself. If it wasn't all right, she would still have to do it.

He shrugged again. 'I suppose so.'

'So, Mr Josephs—'

'Harry.'

'Harry. You were working here on the day Ms Barlow disappeared?'

'Yes, I was.'

'I need you to tell me as much as you can about that day.

I understand from information obtained at the time that Miss Barlow left work late that Saturday afternoon.'

'Yes. Around six o'clock, as far as I recall. She usually left at about four on a Saturday.'

Judd wrote quickly, anticipating that he would move smoothly into an account of that day. She looked up. He was waiting, his eyes on her. 'Why was she late leaving that Saturday?' she prompted.

'She stayed on because it was really busy here and there was a late delivery.'

'Where was she going when she finally left at six p.m.?'

'I don't know.'

Judd looked up at him. 'She didn't say?'

'No.'

Judd searched the questions she'd brought with her. 'I want you to talk me through that Saturday, from when you arrived at work . . .'

Josephs shrugged. 'I'm not sure what I can tell you about it. It was just an ordinary day, like any other. I got here at about eight thirty. I would have sorted out the post, checked the shelves for spaces, all the things I usually do, ready to open at ten o'clock.'

Judd nodded. 'What time did Ms Barlow arrive that morning?'

Josephs gave this some thought. 'I'm not sure. Fifteen minutes after I'd opened?'

'You've described the shop as busy later that day. Tell me about it.'

Josephs frowned. 'I'm not sure what you mean.'

'Well, did anything happen that was unexpected or unusual?'

His face cleared. 'Oh. I see. No. It was a normal Saturday. A lot of customers. The delivery I mentioned.'

'Did Miss Barlow mention to you in passing that she had plans for that evening?'

Josephs looked doubtful. 'Ten years is a long time. I'll need to think about it. I need to get it right, don't I?'

Judd waited. Surely the police who spoke to him at the time had asked him the same question? But he was right. It was a long time ago. She looked up at him. His eyes moved to a point beyond her right shoulder.

'Let's see . . . Annette had a phone call that morning. At around ten thirty I think. I don't know who it was from, she didn't say, but afterwards she seemed excited – no, not "excited". Her mood improved. Maybe she did have plans.'

Judd looked up at him. 'Are you saying that Ms Barlow's mood was low, prior to that call?'

He smiled at her. 'You're good at picking up nuances, aren't you? I wouldn't say low, exactly. I probably thought she'd fixed up a date or something with whoever called her, but she didn't actually tell me that. I suppose like most kids of my age back then, I was pretty clueless, but I don't think she was very happy, you know.'

Judd looked up at him. 'Oh? Was there a reason that you were aware of?' She watched him choose his words.

'She was in her late twenties and I don't think she liked being single.'

'Did she actually tell you that?'

'Not in so many words, but she'd joined a couple of dating agencies.'

'How do you know?'

He smiled. 'There you go again with the nuances.' He raised

both arms, linking his hands behind his head. 'She just mentioned in passing that she'd registered with them and that she'd been to a speed-dating evening run by one. I think it was a new thing, back then. She didn't tell me anything about it, just that she'd been.'

'Did Miss Barlow tell you anything else about her private life?'

'Not really, but there were times when she had a lot of phone calls. I assumed they were from contacts she'd made through the agencies I mentioned.'

Judd felt her interest quicken. 'Did she ever talk about those callers to you?'

Josephs let his arms drop. 'In passing.'

'Did she mention any names?'

'No, never.'

'What did she say about them?'

He lowered his voice, leant towards her. 'She described one as "mad for sex", her words, that he wouldn't leave her alone. Another one she mentioned sounded fairly similar.'

Judd gave him a direct look. 'The police came here and spoke to you after Ms Barlow disappeared, didn't they?'

'Yes, very briefly. They asked me one or two questions.'

An earlier quick look through the Barlow file had shown no reference to the two men Josephs had just described, nor any dating agencies. 'Where did the police actually talk to you?'

Josephs pointed towards the back of the shop. 'Staff room. Through that door. Come on, I'll show you.'

'No, that's OK. I was just wondering if you told those officers what you've just told me?'

Josephs frowned, looking distracted. 'You mean about those two guys being mad for sex? I'm not sure whether I did or not.

As I said, I was a kid back then and there was no indication that anything bad had happened to Annette. I just assumed she would surface in a few days. If she had and she got to know that I'd given out personal stuff like that to anybody, she wouldn't have been very pleased, I can tell you.' He grinned at Judd. 'Annette had quite a mouth, when she chose to use it.'

Judd eyed him. 'It wasn't exactly "anybody" who was requesting that information, Mr Josephs. It was the police.' Judd had worked out that at the time Annette Barlow disappeared he would have been around twenty-one, older than Judd, yet no way would she refer to herself as a 'kid'. 'If the police were concerned enough about Miss Barlow's welfare to come here and ask you about her, didn't it occur to you that they needed to know about those men?'

Josephs was looking very uneasy. 'Oh dear. Now that you put it like that, I think I assumed that the police would talk to other people who knew her better than I did.' He ran a hand through his hair again. 'You've started me thinking. I should have told them, but I'd had no contact with the police before that. I was a bit naive.' He looked downcast. 'I'm thinking about how nice Annette was, how good to me . . . Excuse me.'

He stood, turned his back to her. Thinking that her questions had touched a nerve, Judd waited, picking up the soft, steady glug of liquid being poured. He turned back to her, a filled glass in each hand.

She shook her head. 'Not for me, thanks. I'm on duty and I don't . . .'

He placed the glass next to her. 'It's as weak as water. I'm finding all this talk about Annette a bit upsetting, to be honest and I don't like drinking alone.' He sat. Judd looked at the small glass. This was the first job DI Watts had given her to do. He was under a lot of pressure and she wanted something worthwhile to take back to him. She reached for the glass. Josephs raised his to his lips. She did the same but didn't drink, merely swallowed for effect. He nodded. 'See? Like I said, weak as water.'

Judd looked at her notes. 'Do you know if there were other men in Ms Barlow's life, not connected to dating agencies?'

'She never mentioned any. Annette was a private kind of person, actually. A little aloof at times. I put that down to my being so much younger.'

Judd wrote. 'From what you've said, it sounds like she was a very good manager to you.'

He sighed, sipped more wine. 'She was. Isn't it sad, how things turn out? She gave me my start, and all these years later it's still quite upsetting for me thinking about her.'

She looked up at him. He did look upset. 'Mr Josephs, how about we take a short break? I'll come back in about half an—'

He was on his feet. 'Sorry, that's the phone ringing in the back. I won't be a minute.' Judd was thinking that the call had come at a good time. She recalled a criticism levelled at her during training, that her attitude to others tended at times to be 'cavalier', which she'd learned meant offhand, dismissive. Had she been too direct in her approach to Josephs? If so, a short break whilst he took the call would hopefully give him a chance to relax and she would go easy with the remainder of her questions. She stayed where she was, noting down a couple more as he walked away from her to the back of the shop.

After a minute or so, she looked up. He was waving to her

from the doorway. 'Come on, Detective Judd! I can see you don't like the wine. The kettle's on. How about I make us some coffee?'

Grimacing at the wine, wanting whatever information she might get from him, she got up and walked towards the back of the shop. Coming into the room, she found him organizing mugs and instant coffee. 'That was a quick phone call.'

He nodded. 'Wrong number.' He brought boiling water to the table, gestured to a chair. 'Have a seat. Milk?'

'No, thanks.' She sat, glanced at her watch.

'Are you in a hurry?' he asked.

'Well, I do need to move this interview on.'

He grinned down at her. 'You know, I've never been interviewed by a policewoman before.'

'Getting back to Ms Barlow, after she disappeared and the police came here to talk to you, like I'm doing—'

'They weren't anywhere near as attractive as you.'

She looked up at his smiling face, then away to her list of unanswered questions. 'I'm interested in hearing whatever you told them about her.'

'Not a lot, actually. I told them that Annette was something of a mentor to me but that I didn't know much about her outside of work. That I didn't know where she was going when she left here that Saturday.' He fell silent. She looked up to find him still smiling at her. 'Don't take this the wrong way, but you're very young to be doing this kind of work.' She opened her mouth. Before she could say anything, he leant towards her, whispered, 'Actually, I think you're really cute.'

'Mr Josephs, I—'

'Hang on a minute. Somebody has come into the shop. I'll deal with them and be right back.' He stood, left the room.

She tracked him to the street door, watched as he talked to a youth in a baseball cap. She looked over her notes, wondering why anybody with the intelligence to go to university hadn't thought it relevant to tell police officers searching for a missing woman about two men whom the woman had, in her own words, described as 'mad for sex'. Another glance at her watch, another to see what was happening in the shop and her heart skipped. The young male had gone. Josephs was still at the door, one hand on the lock, the other turning the sign to *Closed*. On her feet, she watched him coming back, their whole conversation running fast inside her head. He came into the room, pushed the door behind him, leant against it.

'Relax. Sit down. Give me a few more minutes to search my memories of Annette. You never know, I might come up with something really helpful.'

She reached for her bag. 'Thanks, but I've got everything I need.'

He was still at the door, still smiling at her. 'Now, *that* doesn't sound very friendly.'

She stared at him, the cues she'd had from him since she'd arrived rushing into her head. Seemingly insignificant cues she'd missed, so intent had she been on getting as much information as she could. His eyes were now locked on hers, his smile gone. Her heart banging her ribs, she realized how tall he was. Six-one to her five-three.

Keeping her voice low she said, 'Mr Josephs, I'll tell you just once: move away from the door.'

He gazed down at her. 'You sound upset, Detective. What's wrong?' He came slowly towards her. 'I've moved, see?'

She backed a couple of steps. 'Stay away from me.'

He raised his arms, doing jazz hands. 'Still moving.' His face was now high above hers, so close she could make out the individual hairs at the edge of his beard, smell the musky odour of him. He touched her hair. She flinched.

'Get away from me.'

He gave her a surprised look. 'Hey, come on. What's your problem? We were getting along great.' He reached for her.

On autopilot, Judd stepped back, one hand grabbing his genitals in a hard squeeze, the outer edge of the other making direct contact with his throat. She saw his face contort, his eyes roll. He sank to the floor, groaning, clutching himself, his voice hoarse. 'You . . . *bitch.*'

Grabbing her notes and bag, she ran to the door, flung it open, ran through the shop, fumbled with the lock of the street door, picking up movement behind her. She threw it wide, stumbled out into fierce heat, her feet pounding the pavement, sun bearing down on her. She ran to where she'd parked her car. Reaching it, she unlocked it, got inside, slammed the door, hit central locking, sweating, breath sobbing in her throat, rubbing the side of her hand, railing at herself for being *so bloody stupid*! His teasing tone, his references to himself as a kid as he played her, laying the groundwork, introducing sex into the conversation, alcohol, luring her into that room. She pressed herself against the seat, eyes squeezed closed, brushed wetness from her face. She of all people, with all that she'd learned about life and plenty of other stuff, to be taken in like *that*. She struck the steering wheel with both hands, hard enough to cause more pain. She stared ahead, furious now. When she got back to headquarters, she'd report what just happened. As a serving police officer, she'd make sure he regretted every word he'd said, every intent he'd had inside his head and any other part of his lousy body, the *bastard*. She closed her eyes. She wouldn't do it. Couldn't do it. If she did, it would mean DI Watts knowing all that had just happened. Josephs would doubtless deny everything. Another thought occurred to her. He might accuse *her* of assault. Which would mean the end of her involvement in the investigation. The end of her career. Panic spiralled inside her chest. She loved her job. She *needed* it. Couldn't risk losing it. It took her three attempts to get the key into the ignition. She started the engine, causing it to roar. Several people turned to look as she drove away.

JUDD PARKED THE CAR, walked up to the house, let herself into the big shared entrance hall and on to the two rooms she rented. She couldn't go to headquarters looking and feeling like this. Unlocking her door, she picked up the envelope the postman had pushed under it, went into her bedroom and sat on the edge of the narrow bed. Opening the envelope, she pulled out her credit card statement, her eyes drifting over the litany of careful living to the amount due. One she could just about afford. She recalled her drive back here, the occasional hesitancy of her car's engine which she'd noticed a couple of times recently. She had no idea what was causing it and no one to ask. It sounded like it might be expensive. She fell back on the bed and stared at the ceiling.

ELEVEN

Friday 19 August. Seven forty-five a.m.

Watts put down the phone as the door to his office swung open and Traynor came inside, followed soon by Judd. Watts pointed at the phone. 'Dr Chong's identified our third victim. His photo and details are coming any minute, plus' – he looked at Judd – 'you all right?'

She walked past, not looking at him. 'Yes.'

'To bring you up to speed, Judd, a second skull has been located at the scene.'

'Dr Traynor just told me.' Watts went to the Smartboard, feeling along its lower edge for the 'On' control. Sighing, Judd came over, switched it on.

Watts gave her another glance. 'You look like your tail's dragging. What's up?'

An electronic bleep issued from the Smartboard. She tapped its screen. It lit up, displaying three faces, each with a name and brief details beneath. One they hadn't seen before: Daniel Broughton, dark-haired, shadow of stubble.

Traynor read aloud the details. 'Age thirty-eight at time of disappearance. Property developer. Resident of Edgbaston area of city. No family members identified during the initial missing persons investigation. Sub-contractors he employed reported him missing. They were questioned. No information gained as to a reason for his disappearance. Financial status checked. Broughton solvent at the time. Last known sighting: a bookshop approximately one mile from his home. Visited by officers. Nothing gained. Location details of shop supplied.'

Watts was searching all three photographs for something, anything, which might hint at the reason they were destroyed, guessing his two colleagues were doing the same. His eyes drifted over Zoe Roberts' more recent photograph: smooth blonde hair, large, grey-blue eyes set in an attractive, open face. His gaze shifted to Annette Barlow looking away from her photographer, her dark hair hanging like a curtain either side of her face, its expression . . . He decided on 'distant'. Both women of similar age. Barlow looked older. He turned to Judd. 'How did your first witness interview go at the wine shop yesterday?'

'No problem, why?'

'Get anything of interest?'

She shook her head.

'I still want a detailed write-up of it, soon as you can.' He pointed at the Smartboard. 'How about a bit more interview experience. Give this bookshop a ring and—'

'No.' They looked at her, exchanged glances. She went to the table and sat, head down.

'What's up?' asked Watts.

'I don't feel very well.'

'Why didn't you say so when you came in? You don't look the full ticket. Get yourself off home—'

'*No.* I want to be at the briefing.'

Still eyeing her, Watts went to the table, looked down at the data lying on it. 'I've skimmed the victims' files and the only link I've come up with so far is that Barlow and Roberts were of similar age. Which shows how desperate I am.' He looked at Traynor. 'What did Barlow's father have to say?'

'PC Sharma informed me that he was unwell. I'm waiting to hear whether he's recovered.'

Watts nodded. 'By the way, a few of the lads on the team have asked me what you do as a criminologist and what they might expect from you during this investigation. Only Jones and Kumar have prior experience of repeat homicide and that was minimal. Contrary to what most people think, homicides like we've got here are a rarity so the whole team is feeling edgy, but they're all good officers. Quick learners. If you could find the time to knock a few notes together for them, I'd appreciate it.'

'How about I talk to them directly, as a group?'

'Even better. Any idea when?'

'Yes. Now.'

'You mean, this morning?'

Traynor nodded. 'Following the briefing.'

Watts looked at his watch. '*Blimey!* Come on.' He reached for one of the files. 'Don't you need to get your ideas together first?'

'No.'

The buzz of talk faded as they came inside the squad room. Watts dropped the file on the desk. 'Eight twenty and not a babby in the place washed. Let's get started. We've got ID for the second skull: property developer by the name of Daniel Broughton.' He went to the whiteboard, securing Broughton's picture and details next to those of Barlow and Roberts. 'Dr Chong has offered an observation on the burial of the two skulls. Both "shallow-buried and carefully placed" on that incline. The only reason they lay there for so long is because the chap who farms the land lets it rest. This is now a three-homicide investigation. The chief has agreed to issue a public warning to residents in the area, so expect more press presence, around which we all keep it zipped, clear?' They nodded. 'If any of you has any ideas on what we know so far, I want to hear them now.'

A tentative hand rose. 'If this killer treated the skulls "carefully" like the pathologist says, is it possible he was showing them some kind of . . . well . . . respect? Or maybe he's somebody with a religious thing?'

Amid a quick buzz of talk, Watts sent Traynor a quick glance. Traynor spoke. 'That's a reasonable theory to bear in mind at this early stage.' In the heavy silence Watts' eyes moved over the faces in front of him. 'I'm still waiting for news on a match to the shoeprints found at the scene. The search of Roberts' car should be finished today. All trace evidence from it will be processed, as will the fibres and hair found on Roberts which you already know about, but don't anticipate quick results, particularly for the hair.' He caught a few subdued murmurs. 'Don't blame the messenger. It's holiday time. Forensics are short-staffed and the lab which is analysing the fibres and hair is inundated. CCTV motorway footage should be with us soon.' He searched faces, found Miller. 'Anything to report on Gerry Williams, the night-time security guard?'

Miller pointed to the computer next to her. 'I'm on to it, following the briefing, Sarge.'

'Quick as you can.' He looked at each of them. 'I know some of you are already feeling on the back foot with this investigation. One or two of you have asked me about Dr Traynor's work and the kind of help he might give us. In the next fifteen minutes, he's going to tell you.' Watts turned to him. 'All yours.'

Traynor stood facing them in the heavy silence. 'Criminology involves research, the use of sociological and psychological theory to develop an understanding of certain types of criminal behaviour and offences.'

Watts eyed his officers, feeling sudden misgivings at the resistance he was already picking up in response to Traynor's cool words about theory. Over two-thirds of them were graduates but he knew they responded best to demands for action. Traynor was talking again.

'That covers what I do. A good use of the remaining thirteen minutes is for you to ask me any questions you have about the type of individual we're looking for in this investigation.'

Watts' eyes moved back to the team, looking for signs of engagement, not seeing any. Eventually, a hand rose. Traynor pointed.

'Ask.'

'Three linked homicides, two female, one male. No complete body. No evidence of sexual behaviour towards the first victim. Are we still investigating these homicides as having a sexual motivation?'

'Yes, in the absence of any contra-indications. Sexual expression takes many forms. The majority of repeat killers target either males or females but there are exceptions. One example you may be aware of is a series of homicides of hitchhikers in

Australia in the late eighties, early nineties which involved sexual assault of victims of both genders.' His eyes moved over the officers looking back at him. 'We'll stay receptive to other possibilities. Not all repeat homicides are sexually motivated.'

Another hand rose. 'How do we establish a non-sexual reason if we need to?'

'We might not be able to do so until an arrest is made.' Some of the faces in front of him looked downbeat. 'I give forces I work with the truth as I see it. I don't have any quick-fix answers for you. There aren't any.'

His questioner slow-nodded. 'OK. Say this killer crops up in the course of our investigation, would it be easy for us to suss him?'

'What you're asking is, can you expect him to stand out in some way, for example, present as socially isolated, a misfit?' There was a low murmur of voices. Traynor shook his head. 'Probably not. Research indicates that a significant proportion of offenders who commit repeat offences such as rape and homicide lead otherwise productive lives. They're able to blend. It's one of the reasons they're hard to stop.' He saw looks being exchanged. 'Repeat offender as odd-loner-misfit appeals because it offers the promise of that quick fix. It's a Hollywood-style myth. There are one or two other myths I can talk about, if you wish?' This got several nods. Traynor paused. The silence lengthened.

Watts felt a quick ripple of anxiety, saw officers exchanging looks. Was the talk of repeat homicide getting to Traynor? He berated himself for not insisting on his doing this via notes. He looked up as Traynor's voice came again, strong, authoritative.

'Let's start with the myth that repeat offenders are so driven to kill that they can't stop. The finding of Annette Barlow's and Daniel Broughton's remains after a decade and Zoe Roberts' murder just days ago is telling us they can and do stop. But then they're back. Worldwide research confirms such behaviour. We can't discount the possibility of other victims during those ten years, earlier even.'

'So, why do they stop temporarily?' asked Kumar.

Traynor paced. 'Consider why we might choose to stop doing something which is rewarding and is working for us.' He looked at them. 'Maybe our circumstances have changed. We're working harder, longer hours. Or, we've started a new relationship more satisfying than a previous one. Or, life in general is more relaxed, more rewarding.'

Most officers were now taking notes. Jones raised his hand. 'I get it. What I want to know about this bloke is, is he MENSA-clever or one stop past Barking?'

Several officers grinned, Traynor along with them. 'Yet another myth: repeat killer as brilliant adversary. In reality, the intellectual capabilities of such killers reflect those of the general population, ranging from above to below average. Some are highly disturbed. They tend to be apprehended relatively quickly.' He looked at the faces in front of him. 'My advice is avoid developing expectations of who or what he is.'

Jones raised his hand again. 'I read a book once . . .' Amid colleagues' quick cheers, he pressed on. 'It said that repeat killers actually want to get caught. Is that true?'

Traynor shook his head. 'That's a misreading of the research evidence. Think of the "career" of any offender. At the outset he's lacking in experience. He's unsure of himself and what he must do to satisfy his needs but also avoid arrest. He commits his first offence. He gets away with it. Now, he wants to repeat the experience. What does he need to do now?'

'Get better at it?' said Jones.

Traynor nodded. 'Well said. Like most people who begin a new activity, he learns what he needs to do by *doing*, by planning his attacks, covering his tracks, avoiding arrest. Time passes. He's getting better and better. Now he's an expert. He isn't getting caught.' The room was silent. 'What happens now?'

'He gets cocky and thinks he never will be,' said Watts.

'Exactly. Once he feels invincible, he starts taking chances, which gradually increases the likelihood that he will be caught. That's what gives rise to the myth that they want to be stopped. They never do. They want to continue doing what they want to do. What they enjoy.'

Watts looked up. Within the quick buzz of talk, he'd picked up what sounded like one or two muted references to Traynor's own family. He looked at him. If he'd heard them, it wasn't showing. His eyes were fixed on his audience.

'So, what does all of this mean for this team?'

They quietened.

'Whoever this killer is, he has a life. He may be a husband, a partner, a father, an employee, an employer, able to present himself in an acceptable way, confident in what he's doing, including when he's actively involved in selecting a victim.'

Watts glanced across at Judd. She looked better than she had an hour ago, her eyes fixed on Traynor.

'He's careful. He's likely to have a good level of intellect.

He may take time off from killing but he's not invincible. He can be stopped.' He looked at each of the faces gazing back at him. 'His confidence will be his undoing.'

Judd raised her hand.

Traynor looked at her. 'PC Judd?'

'Can you say anything about this killer's motivation?'

Traynor took a few slow steps in her direction, his eyes fixed on the floor. 'As I said, motive can be a really complex issue so your question isn't an easy one to answer. What we do know is that most repeat offenders are motivated by sex, plus the thrill of duping another person, doing what they do in the midst of people who know them, who would never, ever believe them capable of such acts.'

Hearing this, Judd thought of Josephs.

'As I said, a non-sexual motive is likely to emerge very late in the day. At this stage, it's reasonable to anticipate that these three homicides were sexually motivated and the inclusion of a male victim does not rule it out. It's telling us that this investigation is much more complex than anticipated, that whoever killed all three victims is an extremely deviant opponent. DI Watts and I are agreed on the sexual angle but we'll remain flexible as the investigation progresses. What I can say is that, whatever his motivation, this killer is feeling superior to you. To us.' He looked at Judd. 'Probably not quite the answer you wanted, but it's the best I can offer right now.'

She nodded. 'It's all interesting, and I can see how the organized-disorganized categorization of these killers fits with a lot of what you've said.'

He looked at her. 'Would you like to say something about that?'

Watts eyed her as she stood, small and intense-looking.

'Well, those with a good level of intelligence, the planners, the careful killers who don't leave evidence, they're the "organized" ones. They're the kind to stalk or observe a victim prior to striking, which is what we're considering for the Roberts case.'

Traynor nodded. 'And the disorganized type?'

'They're the other side of the coin. What they do tends to be careless or less focused. They risk getting caught more easily.'

'A good summation, PC Judd. Do you have a theory about a killer who displays predominantly organized but also a disorganized trait?'

'Well, it suggests impulsivity to me.'

Traynor nodded, looked at his audience. 'Our offender is demonstrating that, careful as he is, he can act without foresight. Let's hope so, but given his predominant offending behaviour, what type of killer do we have here?'

Watts started at the single-word chorus. '*Organized.*'

'Exactly,' said Traynor quietly. 'There's no need for anyone here to feel overwhelmed. Yes, there's pressure, but these are early days. We already have a very basic idea of the kind of person we're looking for. We have a crime scene and two disposal sites from which forensics will extract every scrap of information and meaning. DI Watts has established regular briefings. When he knows something, you'll know it. If you have questions, don't hold on to them. Come and talk to us.' He paused, gave each officer direct eye-contact. 'We will find this killer.'

Watts started again at the sudden wave of spontaneous applause.

*   *   *

WATTS CAME INTO HIS office feeling buoyant for the first time in days. Traynor had laid it out for them straight, told them it wasn't going to be easy but that they had what it took. 'That was exactly what they needed. You gave them a lot to think about, challenged what they thought they knew and reminded them that they're part of a team.' He glanced at Judd. 'And you've perked up a bit.'

She looked away from him. 'This "part-of-a-team" business is something I've heard a million times since I joined the force. What's so great about it?'

Watts deep-breathed, pointed at the list he'd added to the Smartboard.

'For the sake of my blood pressure, we'll look at next actions.' He turned to Traynor. 'Heard anything about Annette Barlow's father?'

'A text from PC Sharma saying he's recovered. I'm leaving in ten minutes to see him.'

'In that case, I'll get over to that bookshop Daniel Broughton is known to have visited shortly before he disappeared.' He turned to Judd. 'How about you pop over to Zoe Roberts' law firm in Solihull?'

'OK.'

'Hang on, though. It might be better if I went there, given what we know about Roberts' husband.'

Colour washed over her face. 'You just asked *me* to do it!'

'All right, calm down. Go, but be careful about the topics you raise. Take a "tell me whatever you want" approach.' He opened a file, removed a sheet of A4, pushed it towards her. 'The person to see is Damien Blunt, senior partner. Talk to him about Roberts, ask to speak to other employees.' He waited as Judd quickly wrote. 'You're after all the info you can get about her, the kind of work she did, other employees she worked alongside, particularly any she was mates with, what they knew about her social life, whether she had any anxieties, you know the kind of thing. See what emerges on Christian Roberts, including what they know about his current whereabouts and when they last had contact with him.'

Judd reached for her bag, stowed pen and notebook in it and headed for the door. Watts' eyes tracked her. 'Phone ahead to let them know you're coming. When you come back, I want a report on what you found, plus the one on that wine shop visit!' Watching the door close, he shook his head, glanced at Traynor. 'If you come up with any theories about *that* one, I'll be interested to hear them.'

TWELVE

Friday 19 August. Midday.

Judd was sitting in the smart reception area of Blunt, Webb & Roberts, where she'd been for the last forty minutes. Long enough to realize that, rather than lending her authority, the full summer uniform she'd decided on hadn't made so much as a dent in the workings of this busy law firm. Plus, she should have phoned ahead. Feeling the receptionist's eyes on her, she looked up.

'Mr Blunt has found a small space in his diary, PC Judd. I'll show you to his room.'

Judd stood, followed her through a code-protected door and along a corridor, breathing in perfume which smelled pricey, wondering how she tolerated the sheer tights, soaring heels and savagely tailored dress in this weather. Aware of the weight of her uniform trousers, Judd decided that their jobs weren't so different. It was all about image. The woman stopped at a door bearing Damien Blunt's name, knocked softly, opened it and moved aside. Judd stepped into the large corner office, its blinds almost down. The door closed smoothly, silently behind her. A quick glance around and Judd's eyes settled on a middle-aged man seated behind a large desk. He was beckoning to her. Stifling a quick rush of unease, she went further into the room, sat on the edge of the chair he was indicating without missing a beat of his telephone conversation.

'I know, but company law doesn't allow them that freedom.' He nodded. 'Yes. See you there.' He put down the phone, looked across at Judd. 'You're here about Zoe Roberts.'

'Yes, I—'

'This entire practice is absolutely appalled at what has happened to her. I'm going into a meeting in a few minutes, but I'll give you a quick rundown of what I can tell you about her.'

Pen poised, Judd studied the neat dark hair, the crisp white shirt, the striped tie. Her lip curled. Probably old-school.

'Zoe was a much valued, hard-working member of this firm. She joined us approximately seven years ago, following a short stint at a Birmingham practice after she qualified. She settled extremely well here and was a valued member of our team.'

Judd made quick notes, thinking that it all sounded like a standard bio any employer might offer about some faceless employee looking to new horizons, not one who had just been savagely killed. 'What kind of law did she work on?'

'Zoe specialized in tax and insurance law.'

She waited. 'You mean, like car accidents?'

Blunt's face creased into a smile. 'A little more upmarket, a little more complex than that. Zoe's specialism was tax law and regulations.'

Judd wrote quickly. 'Would that be likely to make her any enemies?'

This time he laughed outright. 'Not at all.'

'Do you know the area where she was murdered?'

Blunt's smile disappeared. 'I don't.'

'Did you know that she ran there regularly?'

'I knew only that she ran. We all knew.'

'Did she have a particular friend among the staff here?'

Blunt looked dismissive. 'Zoe was extremely driven where work was concerned. It was one of her characteristics we valued. This is a hard-working practice, not a place to socialize. Fiona Webb was probably the nearest I would describe as a friend of Zoe's.'

Judd looked up. 'She's like, a partner here?'

Blunt turned on his chair, glanced down at papers on his desk. 'No. Her husband is, *like*, the partner.'

Judd nodded, wrote. 'And Christian Roberts is also a partner, not Zoe?'

Blunt sent her an evaluative look. 'In case your questions have an agenda, both Julian Webb and Christian Roberts are very skilled lawyers, each with years of experience.'

Aware that the exchange between them wasn't offering her anything relevant to Zoe Roberts' death, Judd took a direct approach. 'Zoe and her husband were separated.'

'Yes, but what that has to do with what happened—'

'Was there friction between them during the time they worked in this office?'

'They didn't. At least, not for the last five or so years. Christian is not based here.'

She looked up at him. 'Yes, we know. Did they previously work here together?'

'My understanding is that you're here to ask questions about Zoe.'

'Yes, and as she and Mr Roberts were still married at the time she was killed, questions relating to him are relevant, particularly as he's failed to contact his in-laws and the police about what's happened to her. He must be aware that there's a problem.' She waited. 'When was the last time you had contact with him?'

'About five days ago.'

'What did you talk about with him?'

She saw Blunt's face harden.

'That was before what happened to Zoe and is of no concern to the police.'

'We don't know that, do we? It might be relevant.' She waited. 'Does it bother you that he hasn't contacted the police? What do you think about that?'

Blunt stood. She was on her feet, heart rate quickening as he came from behind his desk. 'I cannot discuss Christian with you until I've spoken directly with him.'

'Are you saying you're as much in the dark about his behaviour as the police?'

'I've said all that I'm prepared to say about Christian.'

She looked him in the eye. 'Mr Blunt, this is a murder investigation involving two of your employees. I would have thought as a lawyer you'd see the need for questions like those I'm asking you.'

He gave her a cold look. 'I don't need *you* to tell me what this situation requires.'

'Aren't you at all concerned that he hasn't been in touch? Is Mr Roberts a concern for this firm?'

'I don't like your tone—'

'Are you aware of Zoe Roberts having a problem with anyone, either professionally or socially?'

'I am not. She was a very competent, valued member of this practice. I know nothing about her social life, although Zoe always appeared to me to exude a certain' – he gave Judd a slow up-down look – '*d'esprit heureux.*'

She watched him go to the door, thinking what a supercilious twat he was. 'So, to the best of your knowledge, you're not aware of Zoe Roberts having any problems of any kind?'

Blunt now had the door open. 'I did not know Zoe that well.'

'You didn't know her socially?'

'No.' Blunt turned away from Judd as a woman walked past. '*Fiona!* Can you spare a couple of minutes to speak with PC . . .?'

'Judd.'

The woman reappeared, gave Judd a friendly glance. Blunt was already on the move with a curt nod for Judd, and to Fiona, 'Don't forget our meeting.'

Judd watched him go then followed the woman to a small, pleasant office. 'Have a seat,' the woman said. 'Would you like some coffee? Or a cold drink?'

'No, thank you.'

The woman gave her a kindly look. 'Damien didn't introduce us properly. My name is Fiona Webb, one of the practice lawyers. How can I help?'

Judd turned to a fresh page of her notebook. 'I'm part of the investigation into Zoe Roberts' homicide.'

Webb's eyes widened. 'I'm sorry, I should have realized, but . . . you're so *young*. That's not a criticism, by the way, just a little unexpected.'

'I'd like you to tell me all you know about Zoe Roberts.'

Webb looked thoughtful. 'Zoe and I didn't do the same kind of work, and we didn't socialize out of office hours, but I helped her find her feet when she first arrived here. I found her very pleasant.' Aware of Judd waiting, she added, 'I don't know what more I can tell you, except to say that what's happened to her is absolutely hideous. Her family must be totally devastated. We're all devastated here.'

Judd wrote, thinking that during her brief meeting with Blunt, she hadn't seen or heard any evidence of devastation. She was also thinking that this woman and Christian Roberts had been colleagues long before Zoe Roberts joined the firm. 'Did Zoe ever talk to you about herself, her personal life?'

'Not really. Zoe was rather reserved when it came to sharing that kind of information.'

'She never mentioned that she was having problems of any kind, such as difficulties with males?'

Webb's eyes widened. 'No. Never.'

'Did she ever talk to you about problems in her marriage?'

Webb stared at her. 'No. She didn't.'

Judd nodded. 'I suppose she might have chosen not to do that, given that you and Mr Roberts were colleagues, perhaps friends, prior to when she started here?'

Webb gave Judd a cool look. 'I don't see the relevance of what you're saying. I need to get something straight here. We were all aware of Zoe's and Christian's decision to separate a long time ago and, more recently, that they were planning to divorce.'

Judd looked up. 'Mr Blunt didn't mention that.'

'We're lawyers, PC Judd. Circumspection goes with the

territory. Maybe he chose not to talk about Christian, given that he is a partner of this firm.'

'How come Mr Roberts doesn't work here?'

'His specialism is European law. It made sense for him to relocate to Brussels.' There was a brief silence. 'Like everyone else in the firm, my contact with Christian is minimal so I don't see how I can help you.'

Judd was aware that what had started out as a relatively easy conversation now had a careful feel to it. 'As a colleague of Mr Roberts, you probably know him well.'

Webb looked across at her. 'PC Judd, varying the way you ask certain questions won't help if I don't have the kind of information you appear to want. Christian was a pleasant colleague when he worked here but since he's been working in Brussels, I, we, see very little of him.'

Judd nodded, wrote. 'Getting back to Zoe, what can you tell me about her social contacts outside of work, her interests?'

'All I know is that she was into fitness. A keen runner. She said it helped her to manage stress.'

Judd looked up. 'Zoe was stressed?'

Webb sighed, shook her head. 'Only to the degree any corporate lawyer is these days.'

'Do you know much about her fitness routine?'

Webb looked doubtful. 'Not really. I know she was careful with her diet, that she ran regularly, but that's about it.'

'Are you aware of the area where her body was found?'

Webb nodded. 'I know the general area. It's dreadful that women aren't safe to pursue their interests wherever they please.'

Judd nodded agreement. 'Was she stressed about the situation between herself and her husband?'

Webb studied her. 'As I already said, I can't speak about or for Christian. Zoe didn't take me into her confidence on that issue, but my impression was that she was living her life, on her own, and no, I don't know any details, but I doubt she was still upset about the situation.'

'So, she was upset in the past?'

Webb was looking impatient. 'It's a reasonable assumption. Most people would be, wouldn't they?'

Judd considered this. 'I suppose it would depend on what her life was like before and whether she did or didn't want to live alone, wouldn't it?'

Webb glanced at her watch, got up from her chair. 'I'm due at a meeting. I'm sorry, but I don't think there's any more I can tell you.'

'How has Mr Roberts been getting on with his life since the separation?'

Webb turned to her, looking weary. 'PC Judd, how many times do I need to say it? I can't and won't speak about Christian Roberts. No doubt he'll be in touch with the police at some point and speak on his own behalf.'

Webb walked her to the door. Judd wasn't done. 'Do you know that he will? Zoe was murdered four days ago. There's been a televised appeal about her murder. Don't you think it's very odd that so far he hasn't contacted the police or anyone here?'

Webb gazed at her. 'You're very direct, PC Judd.'

'I know. It gets me into trouble.'

'I imagine it does.' Webb had the door open. 'All I can tell you is that both Zoe and Christian were moving on with their lives.'

Judd looked up at her, widened her eyes. 'Actually, this is my first investigation. I told my DI that I'd do my best to find out where Mr Roberts is right now.'

Webb sighed. 'I heard a comment in the office that he was taking a few days' leave, possibly in Scotland, but that's all I know.' With an air of finality, she walked out of the office. Judd followed her to the secure door she had come through earlier.

Webb opened it. 'Goodbye, PC Judd.'

The door firmly closing on her, Judd glanced at the woman behind the reception desk. Not savagely tailored, this one. An older woman who looked approachable. Straightening her shoulders, Judd headed for her. 'Excuse me.'

The woman looked up, smiled. 'Yes?'

'I've just been speaking to Fiona about some leave she took in the last ten days or so. She said that you could confirm details of dates and destination.'

The woman nodded, reached for a file, opened it and studied its contents. 'Yes, here it is. One three-day period of leave for Ms Webb six days ago.' She gave the dates. 'Destination, Edinburgh. Is that it?'

Judd nodded. 'Exactly. Thank you very much.'

Judd came out of the building, her spirits high. Her phone rang. She flinched at her caller's name: DI Watts. Surely that bastard Josephs hadn't been on to him already? She answered it, picking up traffic sounds, wavering reception. Watts was on the move.

'Get anything useful?' he asked.

She glanced back at the smart, modern office building. 'The response I got to what's happened to Roberts was generally, "Oh, how appalling!" but they weren't any real help. Blunt, the main partner, didn't tell me anything useful about her, refused to talk about Christian Roberts at all, then passed me on to a woman named Fiona Webb. She and Zoe Roberts were work colleagues but according to Webb, Zoe didn't share with her what was going on in her life. Know what I think, Sarge? Roberts probably didn't like sharing her husband with Fiona Webb.'

'Come again?'

'They were having it off, Sarge. Fiona Webb and Christian Roberts. Probably for years. They worked together before Roberts joined the firm. I've got evidence that they were both in Edinburgh around a week ago.'

'This woman you spoke to admitted it?'

'Sort of.' She navigated her way across the busy road. 'I'm not getting good vibes about Christian Roberts and his hotshot job in Brussels, sodding off to Edinburgh with a female colleague, and so what if he and Zoe Roberts were separated and hadn't had much contact for months? What's that got to do with him not being arsed to get on the phone to us about his wife's murder, which he must know about?'

'All right, turn down the heat.'

'It just annoys me when people act like they don't care in situations where they should!'

'Yeah, I can tell. Did Blunt say anything specific about Zoe Roberts?'

'He described her as a "happy spirit".' She glanced back at

the gleaming office block. 'Supercilious bastard. My French is as good as his any day. Probably better.'

Watts' voice came again. 'I've arrived at the bookshop so we'll leave it there, but remind me to have a chat with you about chips on shoulders. As soon as you get back to headquarters, start writing up today's visit and the one for the wine shop . . . Judd?'

'Gotta go.'

THIRTEEN

Ending his call to Judd, Watts drove along the quiet road, eyeing pricey homes within landscaped and meticulously maintained surroundings. Finding a parking space, he stopped the engine, looked across at a row of speciality businesses: restaurant, classy-looking dress shop, a pet grooming service, a bespoke men's tailor and, snug in the middle of the row, the last place Daniel Broughton, property developer, was reportedly seen prior to his disappearance ten or so years ago. Watts had already visited the shop's extensive website, seen a photograph of the man he was here to talk to: Edward Arnold, proprietor, Member of Rotary. Founder of the area's Neighbourhood Watch. A regular pillar. Leaving his vehicle, he headed for it, eyeing the suits in the tailor's window as he passed. An absence of price tags told him all he needed to know. Pushing open the bookshop door, prompting a brief ring, he went inside, recognizing the tall, well-built man behind the counter.

Watts waited as he served a customer, the sleeves of his formal, striped shirt pulled back from a shiny bracelet watch, his words drifting across to him, 'I think you'll enjoy this, Hetty. Let me know what you think when you're next in.' He slipped the slim volume inside a paper bag, handed it to the customer, beamed at the next one. Thinking he'd stepped into a time-warp, Watts strolled further into the shop. It was unexpectedly large, well-stocked. He edged his way along a shelf of books on fishing, heard the shop door open, followed by a female voice sharp enough to engrave glass demand some bestseller. Moving along the shelves he came to an open area, two women sitting on a leather chesterfield, reading, coffee cups in hand. His eyes moved to a large, pricey-looking red and chrome coffee machine on a nearby shelf. No time-warp, this. Arnold's set-up was consumer-savvy. Watts wandered back along the laden shelves, his way obstructed by a youth sitting on the floor, leaning against text-books on economics, his legs stretched. Stepping over them, Watts recalled a book Chong had mentioned a while ago about somebody's years in Tibet. Seventeen? Seventy? He looked up at the sound of the bell and the door closing. The two women were still sitting, still reading. The customer with the glasscutter voice had gone. Watts went to Arnold, holding up identification. Arnold looked at it.

'Detective Inspector Watts. We spoke briefly on the phone. Sorry to have kept you waiting. No rest for the wicked, eh? Actually, I was a little surprised when you rang.'

'Is there somewhere we can talk without being overheard?'

'That's difficult, Detective Inspector. There's just me here most of the time, so I need to maintain a presence.' He mouthed the word 'theft'. 'I'm considering getting CCTV installed but this is a very local business and I know most of my customers so I'm loath to do it.' He indicated a window seat behind him. 'Is that all right? Unless you prefer to come back after closing time?'

Watts followed him to the sun-filled window and sat, his temperature zooming. He'd make it snappy. 'Busy place you've got here.'

Arnold nodded, keeping his voice down. 'It takes a lot of effort. You're aware of the parlous state of the retail industry? When people come into a bookshop these days, they don't want just books. They want a welcoming atmosphere, comfort, a place to sit and read, or just relax.' He leant sideways, pointed. 'See those two ladies? They often come in here. Both widows, you know.'

'Do they ever buy anything?'

'Oh, yes.' He waited. 'Is there something specific I can do for you, Detective Inspector?'

'Tell me about Daniel Broughton.'

'Good heavens. That was *years* ago. I thought it was all done and dusted as far as the police were concerned.' He saw Watts' eyes narrow. 'No criticism intended. It's the way the world is for all of us: too much to do and not enough time to do it.'

Watts nodded, thinking it wasn't often that he met somebody who matched him for height. 'The police contacted you about Daniel Broughton at the time he disappeared.'

'Actually, they didn't. It was on the news and the police were appealing for information. I phoned them.'

Watts reached into his shirt pocket for his notebook. 'Wish we had more public-spirited people like you, Mr Arnold. What did you tell them?'

Arnold repositioned himself on the window seat. 'Well, it was in the January. A couple of days after New Year. I keep holidays to a minimum. You have to in this business. If I'm closed, any customers I might get would soon find their way to the high street chains, or worse . . .'

'Broughton came in here.'

'Yes. In the afternoon. I can't be exact on time, I'm afraid, but it was late-ish. The shop was very busy. You know, people exchanging books they'd been given for Christmas, that kind of thing. He came in and went to the back of the shop. I assumed he had a specific book in mind.'

'Did he speak to you?'

Arnold frowned. 'I haven't thought about this in ages.'

'Mr Arnold, you're a potential witness in the disappearance of Daniel Broughton.'

He looked shocked. 'I am? My goodness.'

'Think back to that afternoon, picture it from the time Mr Broughton arrived.'

Arnold's eyes moved to the door of the shop. He pointed to the counter. 'I was right there, sorting out some post I hadn't had a chance to look at. Broughton came in. He'd never done that before, although I knew him to speak to because he was local. He continued on to the back of the shop.'

'What was he looking for?'

'He didn't say, but after I'd sorted the post I went and asked if he needed any help. He said he was looking for a particular book on property improvements, that he'd had an inquiry for something really special from a very demanding client. Or, words to that effect. I directed him to where I knew there were several books of the spin-off variety.' Watts' brows came together. Arnold smiled. 'From the TV shows. People buy a barn with no roof and one wall standing and turn it into something unrecognizable, which looks totally out of place for its surroundings.'

'I'll take your word for it. What happened then?'

'Well, that's the funny thing. A couple came in. I recall books more easily than the people who ask for them. She was after a Brontë . . .' Seeing Watts' facial expression, he hurried on. 'I showed them the biography section and went to see how Mr Broughton was getting on.'

'And?'

'He wasn't there. He'd gone.'

Seeing Watts' eyes drift to the door of the shop, Arnold wagged a finger. 'Why didn't I notice him leave? Back then, the bell on that door didn't always ring. I've had the whole shop rewired since then. You wouldn't *believe* the level of pilfering that—'

'So, you don't know exactly when Mr Broughton left?'

Arnold shook his head. 'No. Which is what I told the police at the time.'

Watts stood. 'Show me where you last saw him.' He followed Arnold to the rear of the shop. 'Those are the kind of books Broughton was after.'

Watts went to them, took one down, leafed through photographs of homes he couldn't afford and wouldn't want if he could. He replaced it and moved on to more shelves, mostly legal and tax-related books. He pointed to a door set within a wall of shelving. 'What's through there?'

'Storage.'

'I'd like to see it.' He watched Arnold take keys from his pocket, select one and insert it. It turned easily.

'Open, Sesame!'

Watts followed him inside the hot, stuffy room, his eyes moving over a large trestle table supporting neat stacks of books, more in boxes on the floor. 'Where's the rear door to these premises?'

Arnold headed out of the room. 'This way.' Fussing with the keys to the store room, checking several times that it was secure, he led the way through another door into a small kitchen, an external door at its end, a key in its lock. Unlocking and opening it, Arnold stood to one side. Watts stepped out into harsh sun, squinted down at a small gravelled area, bright geraniums in terracotta pots, a narrow road running past. Watts walked to it, saw that it gave rear access to the shops either side and continued on in both directions. He came back to where Broughton was waiting. After ten years, there was no way of establishing which way Broughton had left, but this rear door looked to be a strong contender. Why, was the question.

He pointed. 'Is the key routinely left in the door?'

'Yes, but it's always locked so that nobody can come in from outside.'

Watts eyed the small area. Broughton could have parked out here, come into the shop by the street door, then left taking a shortcut through the kitchen back to his car. He said so.

Arnold shrugged. 'I don't recollect seeing his car, but it's possible. He was the kind of person who pleased himself what he did and never mind anyone else's . . . Oh, my *Lord.*' He pointed to the geraniums. 'I said I'd water these, first thing.' He headed back inside.

Watts watched him take a large jug, place it under the tap. 'A job from your wife?'

Arnold came outside, carrying the jug. 'My experience of marriage is water under an almost two-decade-old bridge.'

'Did you know Broughton well?'

'Well enough for an occasional exchange of "Good morning" if I saw him out and about. A little brash for my taste.'

Watts gave an encouraging nod. 'Sharp suit and fat wallet?'

Arnold shook his head, letting the last water droplets fall. 'He wasn't like that at all. He dressed casually but well.'

Watts followed him inside, watched as he relocked the rear door. 'You never had business dealings with him?'

Arnold gave him a surprised glance. 'No. Like I said, he was into house make-overs. He bought houses, improved them, at least to his way of thinking, and sold them on at vast profit.'

'He lived near here.' Watts had brought with him two addresses from a decade before, had driven past Arnold's modest home where he still lived and followed the road to the sprawling, relatively modern brick construction with numerous elevations behind wrought-iron gates which had once been home to Daniel Broughton.

'Yes,' said Arnold. 'In an utter monstrosity of a house he built himself. *That* caused some fur to fly, I can tell you.'

Watts now had the measure of Arnold. Well-informed local gossip. Potentially useful. 'Go on.'

'Well, the owners of the houses either side of Broughton's, plus the one at the back of it, were livid when they saw his house plans. They argued that what he was proposing was ugly and tasteless and that some of its windows on the planned third floor would overlook their properties. It didn't bother me. I can't see it from my house. Their objections failed. This is going back fifteen years or more.'

'Broughton wasn't married?'

Arnold's mouth tightened. 'No, but from what I heard, he didn't lack female companionship.'

'Give me the names of these neighbours who objected to his plans.'

Arnold stared at him. 'Detective Inspector, we're talking well over a decade ago and all three were a good age then. Two have since died. The other one moved to a care home, but don't ask me where.'

'Did Broughton do any of his gentrification work in this area?'

'Not as far as I'm aware. I heard that most of his work was in the south of the city.'

'What about this rebuilding of barns? Did he do much of that?'

'I've no idea. They would be in areas well away from the city, wouldn't they?'

Watts was now overheated, ready to call it a day. Arnold was either unaware of Zoe Roberts' murder or he knew nothing about the area where it occurred. Or both. 'So, you had no dealings with Broughton beyond his being a customer?'

Arnold's mouth turned downwards. 'I don't think his one visit that day merits "customer". He didn't buy anything. The only other contact I had with him was through our local Neighbourhood Watch.'

'He joined, did he?'

Arnold looked scornful. 'Not him. We had friction with him.'

'Oh, yes?'

Arnold gave a series of quick nods. 'Our committee decided that false activations of burglar alarms should incur an agreed fine.'

'There always seems to be one going off where I live. Very annoying. Particularly when it's late.'

'Exactly. This is going back some years. Another resident named Mountjoy and I were the Neighbourhood Watch organizers back then. We hand-delivered a questionnaire which got an overwhelmingly positive response against false alarms following which we devised a residents' agreement that it shouldn't happen and that a system of very modest fines would be imposed if it did, the money to be donated to charity.'

'Sounds reasonable. How did that go down with Broughton?'

'It didn't. I was at a book fair in London, so Mountjoy delivered the agreements. Guess what Broughton did with his.'

'Tell me, it's quicker.'

'He came after poor old Mountjoy, tore the agreement into small pieces and stuffed them into the breast pocket of his blazer. I said that that constituted assault.'

Watts turned a page in his notebook. 'Give me this Mountjoy's address.'

'Somewhere in Poole is all I know. *If* he's still alive. Which I doubt. I really need to get back to the shop.'

Watts followed him. 'Have you heard about the murder of a young woman runner to the south of the city?'

'I heard something about it on the local news. Shocking.'

'Do you know that area at all?'

'I have no connection with it, so no.'

Watts quit writing, flipped his notebook closed. 'Thanks for your time, Mr Arnold. If you think of anything which might relate to Daniel Broughton's disappearance, give us a bell at police headquarters.' He searched his pockets, drew out a card, handed it to him.

Arnold looked at it. 'If I do, I'll certainly let you know, Detective Inspector.'

Leaving the bookshop, Watts walked to his vehicle, aware of a slight sense of dissatisfaction, hitting on a likely reason: he hadn't eaten since five thirty that morning.

FOURTEEN

The atmosphere inside the small room was leaden. Traynor looked across to PC Sharma. She shook her head. He had arrived over fifteen minutes ago, yet beyond a cursory nod when Sharma introduced them, the man slumped on the sofa hadn't responded to Traynor's words of sympathy on behalf of the force. Pete Barlow looked clammy, unwell. His hand shook as he lifted his cigarette. Traynor gave the room a quick glance, not finding what he was expecting to see. He stood. 'Mr Barlow, we understand that this is a very difficult time for you so I'll keep what I need to ask you for another day.'

Barlow looked up, making eye contact for the first time. 'I want to tell you about my daughter, Annette.'

Traynor sat, waited for Barlow to speak.

'She had everything going for her when she was young, you know.' His face darkened. 'Not like her two brothers. Never any damn good, either of them. Drinking, pinching cars, driving like maniacs, police chasing 'em all over.' He looked at Traynor. 'I haven't seen either of them in years. They could be dead for all I know. Or care. Annette was too good for the likes of them. Trouble is, she was loyal. She told me that one time she was in a car with them and they had an accident. What does Annette do? She says *she* was the driver, because Dale, the one that was driving, was already banned. I went barmy at her. Told her to keep away from both of 'em.' He shook his head. 'Annette was a good kid. Good at her school books. She used to help me on the stall.' He squinted up at Traynor, his eyes wavering. 'I had my own business. In the Bull Ring. Fancy goods. You should have heard her drum up the punters, even though she was only a kid. She took no messing. *"C'mon, you lot. Get your money out!"'* Traynor waited out another lengthy silence. 'Then, she turned fifteen, sixteen and she changed. Got secretive, wanting to do what she wanted to do, messing with lads who were a waste of time, getting into trouble. I couldn't control her. The wife had died by then and I . . . lost my business.' He shrugged. 'That's it.'

Traynor recognized the lack of chronology in what Barlow had said so far but he wanted more. 'Mr Barlow, are you able to tell me about Annette's adult years, her employment, her friends, the relationships she had? That's the kind of information which could help our investigation into her disappearance and what subsequently happened to her.'

Barlow looked away. 'Looks obvious to me. Some mad bastard who's into rough sex.'

Traynor glanced at Sharma, then back. 'Why would you think that, Mr Barlow?'

'. . . Dunno. Just an idea.' It was evident to Traynor that the man slouched opposite him was struggling with daily life in addition to the news about his daughter, but he couldn't leave it there.

'Did Annette ever complain to you about having problems with men?'

Barlow avoided his gaze. 'She never was one to tell me much of what she was up to and I never asked. She seemed to settle down once she hit twenty, started doing shop work, clothes and that. She got a job managing a posh wine place in town. She moved out of here, got herself a bedsit.'

Traynor had seen reports of police visits to the small bedsit where Annette Barlow had been living at the time she disappeared. They had come away with little which told them about her life.

Barlow was talking, a trace of pride in his voice. 'Annette could put herself over well. Dress the part. Put on the right voice. She never said so, but I think she liked that job at the wine shop. From how she was as a youngster, I was pleased that she'd managed to sort herself out. She'd give me a few quid occasionally.'

'It sounds like Annette turned her life around.' Barlow looked up at him then away. Traynor studied him. 'Mr Barlow, if you have any information about Annette which you didn't give to the original investigation, maybe because it was difficult for you to do that, you need to tell us.'

Barlow gave him an up-down look. 'What does somebody like you know about "difficult"? Life's easy for people like you. I dare say you don't have trouble with your kids, if you've got any.'

Traynor didn't respond.

'All right. You asked. Around the time I'm talking about, I found out what she was really up to from somebody who knew me from the market. "Hey, Barlow," he says, "did you know that girl of yours is working in 'customer services'?" He didn't have to spell it out. He said he had a mate who was into that kind of thing and recognized Annette, *my* daughter. A bloody slapper!'

'It must have been a shock to hear that.'

'"Shock" don't cover it.' Barlow looked up at him. 'Have you got any kids?'

Traynor gave an almost imperceptible nod. 'Then you'll know how it felt.'

Traynor studied him. He still looked unwell, his face putty-coloured, slick with sweat. 'If you have any other information about Annette's life, we need it, Mr Barlow.'

Traynor watched him reach for a cigarette. 'There isn't anything else.'

'Did Annette ever mention a boyfriend?'

Barlow's face reddened. 'You mean apart from the Tom, Dick or Harrys who were paying her?' He shook his head. 'I can't remember. Fact is, I never asked. I didn't want to hear about what she was up to on that side.' Hands shaking, he managed to light the cigarette. 'One time she came here, she mentioned somebody who had offered her a better-paid job.'

Traynor waited. 'When was this?'

Barlow shrugged. 'Can't remember.'

'What did she say about that?'

Barlow looked at him, his eyes vague.

Traynor sat forward. 'Mr Barlow, what did Annette tell you about this person who offered her this better-paid job?'

'All she said was that he had people working for him and that he could find a big-paying job for her.' He stubbed out the cigarette. 'I thought, Yeah, right, I *bet* you can.'

'You can't recall when Annette told you that?'

Anger flashed in Barlow's eyes. 'I've *told* you, no. He was just some bloke, out for what he could get. I didn't want to hear that kind of stuff from my own daughter!' His tone turned maudlin. His eyes swam. 'A great kid, she was, but after her mother died . . .' His head dropped back. His eyes closed.

Sharma stood, walked quietly across the room, pointing in the direction of the hall. Traynor followed. 'This is my second day here,' she whispered. 'No prizes for guessing he's alcohol-dependent.'

'I looked for it but didn't see any.'

She peered through the narrow gap in the door to the sitting room. 'He's careful to keep it where it's not visible, yet easily available. If nobody can see it, it's not a problem, right? I checked against his name before I left headquarters. It's a grim read. A long history of domestics between him and his wife. She died of liver failure. The two sons are known for twocking and driving offences, plus other types of theft. I doubt he's seen them in years and hasn't got a clue where they are.'

Traynor turned to the front door.

She followed him out. 'We don't get many happy families, do we, Dr Traynor?'

He headed to his car. 'Whoever takes over from you, please ask them to let me know when he's more focused.'

'I will. It might be a long wait.'

FIFTEEN

Watts stared at Judd. 'What the bloody *hell* did you think you were doing at that law firm yesterday?'

She held his gaze. 'What do you mean?'

'You *know* what I mean! I had Damian Blunt on the phone at half-eight, accusing you of obtaining information by deception!'

'He *would,* the supercilious b—. While I was talking to Fiona Webb, I just knew that something had to have gone on between her and Christian Roberts before Zoe Roberts started working there. I was right. I tracked down the hotel they both stayed at in Scotland.'

'So what?' He got up, paced, hands in his pockets. 'You would have been warned during your training about the kind of thing you've just done.'

She was on her feet. 'Webb wasn't going to admit it. It was the only way! Now we know what they were up to. *Are* up to. It puts Christian Roberts smack in the frame for—'

'Again, so *what?*' He glared at her. 'You can't just ignore the rules because you're chasing a lead, even if you're right!' He turned away from her, then back. 'I'll tell you what *I* know, shall I? If we ever present this case for court, including *that* information, the CPS won't touch it with a long stick because *you* decided to ignore rules of evidence at a firm full of bloody lawyers!' He ran his hands over his hair, rubbed his face, let them drop. 'Don't you *get* it? Because of the way you got that information the whole case would be tainted. Dead in the water.'

Face flushed, she glared back at him. '*You* would have suspected the same if—'

'That's not the point! *Jesus H* . . . You don't listen, do you? I can imagine what Brophy will say about this.'

She looked aghast. 'You're going to tell him?'

He watched every vestige of colour leave her face. 'I don't see I've got much choice.'

She turned away from him, went and sat, stared down at the table. 'OK. It was wrong.'

Watts sighed, shook his head. 'Go home.'

She looked up at him, her eyes huge. '*No* . . .'

'Go on. It's the weekend. Spend the rest of the day writing up that visit you made to the wine shop, plus this bloody mess at the law practice.' He watched her stand, walk out of the room then turned away. Hearing the door open again, he looked up. It was Traynor. 'Anything useful from Barlow's father?'

Traynor nodded. 'According to him, Annette Barlow was involved in prostitution at the time she managed the wine shop, plus there was an unidentified male hanging around, offering her a well-paid job.'

'Did the father give any details?'

'I doubt he ever knew any.'

Watts added the information to the Smartboard. 'This sideline she had never cropped up during the investigation into her disappearance.'

Traynor came to it, his eyes moving over the words Watts had written. 'Getting a coherent account of family life from Barlow wasn't easy, but then his children weren't easy either.' He told Watts what Barlow had said about one of them driving whilst banned.

Watts added it to the Smartboard. 'Toe rags.'

'Did PC Judd's talk with the manager of the wine shop establish that Annette's life had another side to it?'

Watts rolled his eyes. 'You might well ask. Right now, you know as much about that as I do.' He paced, thinking about what they knew of Annette Barlow. 'If it was a client who killed her there's zero chance of us tracking him down now.' He looked at Traynor. 'Did her father specifically confirm she was into prostitution at the time she disappeared?'

'Mr Barlow isn't too good on sequences of past events, but my impression is she was.'

'A pimp might have killed her, of course, if she had one, but there's no chance of establishing that after ten years.' He leant against the wall, head down. 'So, why was her skull buried alongside Broughton's? Was he connected at all to her lifestyle? In which case, what connects him and Barlow who've both been dead for years to Zoe Roberts?' He looked up. 'I'll level with you, Traynor. I don't have a clue where this case is going.'

'Nor have I. What I do know thus far is that we need to maintain the focus on all three victims. There has to be a connection. We have to find it.' He glanced at Watts. 'Knowing that Annette Barlow was following a high-risk lifestyle is information the original investigation didn't have. That says progress to me.'

'I appreciate your optimism.' They looked up as Judd came into the room, fetched her bag, turned and went out. Watts eyed the closing door. 'Judd's been to Zoe Roberts' place of work. She's found out that Christian Roberts is in a relationship with a female colleague. Which gives him a possible motive for his wife's murder. It could be why he's avoiding us and her family.'

'Any proof of that relationship?'

'Oh yes. Judd spoke to a female colleague of Roberts' who confirmed that he's been on leave in Scotland recently. Then she got confirmation that that colleague also spent some days' leave in Edinburgh during that same time frame.'

'She did well to get that.'

'Think again. Judd's take on the job is that ends justify means. She got hold of the information by conning some receptionist. And this at an office full of bloody *lawyers*.' He breathed out, pointed at the desk phone. 'Every time that rings, I keep thinking it's Blunt, the main partner, wanting to have another go about it.'

'Ah.'

'As you say, Traynor. I suppose we've all pulled stunts when we were as green as she is, but I've had to give her a warning.'

'What do you think about the information itself?'

Watts flipped open his notebook. 'I emailed the Edinburgh police to check Roberts' whereabouts. I'm still waiting on it.' He flicked pages. 'I've talked to Edward Arnold, the owner of the bookshop which as far as we know is the last place Broughton was seen. He supplied some background on Broughton, who was into property development. According to Arnold, it was Broughton's only visit to his shop and it looks like he might have left by a back way. He couldn't come up with a reason why Broughton would do that. I'll get him to do a list of all the people who were in his shop that day around the time Broughton was there, which the original investigation never thought to ask for.' He shook his head. 'Arnold seems to have a good memory, but after ten years it's a long shot.' He dropped on to a chair, frowning up at the board. 'I don't know about you, but each time I talk to somebody about this case, get details about one of the victims, it's as though I'm dragged further away from all three being linked.'

'Details are what we need at this early stage. Details provide links, build a picture which could tell us why all three died.'

Watts looked at him. 'Did you say "early stage"? I feel I've been on this case for ever.' He gave his face a brisk rub, reached for his phone. 'Maybe Adam's got some news. I'll give him a—'

They looked up as the door opened. 'Your ears must be on fire.'

'I've got something for you,' said Adam, 'but it's not good.'

'We're used to "not good". Let's have it.'

'I've just checked with the officers searching CCTV footage from the motorway. The recordings are poor quality, very grainy due to the low spec of the cameras. Plus, the poor light of the very early timings didn't help.'

'Anything that looks even slightly hopeful?'

'One motorbike recorded at three ten a.m., leaving the motorway for the service road, then re-joining it about an hour later. No number plate or other identifying details.'

'Anything on the footprints?'

'Yes. They were made by a designer trainer, size ten, Walk 'n' Dior, to be exact, which retail for around six hundred pounds.'

Watts brows shot up. 'You *what?*' He looked from Adam to Traynor. 'There can't be many idiots about who'd pay that much for what's basically a pair of pumps.'

Adam and Traynor exchanged glances. 'You're wrong, there,' said Adam. 'I've checked the UK sales for this year: in the thousands. If any were purchased here in Birmingham, the Midlands, we'll follow up the details.'

Watts stood. 'I'll tell you now, there won't be any. We've got more sense here.'

Adam grinned. 'We'll also check online orders as soon as we can, but it's a big job. It could take a while.'

'Thanks, Adam. Appreciate it. Come to think of it, those trainers have got my interest. It looks like one of our victims was a sex worker and I've met a fair few types in my time who make a lot of money out of women, and most of them are into designer stuff.' He headed for the door. 'I'm going to the squad room to see if Miller's found anything on Gerry Williams who works nights at that compound.'

Adam held out an evidence bag to him. 'Roberts' phone. It's been processed.'

Watts took it, glanced at Traynor. 'What's in this phone could give us the details we need about Roberts' life, plus some clues as to her connection to the other victims.' He looked back to Adam. 'What did you find?'

'She had two calls, one at eight, the other at eight fifteen on the morning she was killed.'

'From?'

'Her office. Presumably wanting to know where she was for her early meeting.'

'What about the texts, emails?'

'There aren't any. Just those two calls.'

Watts stared at him, then at the phone. 'The family never said it was new.'

'It wasn't. It looks like she wiped her iCloud storage. Everything on it, prior to those two calls, has been deleted. That's not all. We used data software to access historic texts and emails. Still nothing. She, or somebody, had it restored to factory setting.'

Watts stared at him. 'This is a thirty-year-old professional woman we're talking about. Why would she do that?'

Traynor came to them, his eyes on the phone. 'It looks like Zoe Roberts had something she wanted to conceal.'

'Like what?'

Traynor shrugged. 'Maybe she was a secretive person, or maybe there was a man, a plan, a scheme or a big problem.'

Watts seized the desk phone, jabbed an internal number and waited. 'Any more calls to the tip line?' He replaced the phone, looked at them. 'Nothing. I'm going upstairs to see what Miller's found on Gerry Williams.'

Miller headed across the squad room to Watts, the results of a PNC name check in her hand. 'Here you go, Sarge. Nothing for Christian Roberts so far, but the details you gave me for Gerry Williams, night security worker at the compound, match a Gerald Williams for age and employment history.'

Watts took them. 'Why's he on our records?'

'Prolific shoplifter.'

He grimaced. 'I was hoping for something with a hard edge. GBH. GHB. Either would have done it for me.'

'His last shoplifting conviction was over twenty-four months ago.'

Watts read the details. 'This makes no sense to me. He's got an extensive record going back years, he's working nights for minimum wage, his days are free for his "retailing" activities, yet his last arrest was two years ago.' He looked at Miller. 'That make sense to you?'

'No, Sarge. Unless, like Dr Traynor said, Williams has got better at it? Or, he's earning more now.'

Watts' brows rose. 'Not as a security guard, he isn't. No mention of driving offences involving a motorbike?'

Miller shook her head. 'What you've got is what there is.'

Watts studied it. 'I'll pay him a surprise visit.'

The door swung open and one of the reception officers leant inside. 'Been looking for you, Sarge.'

'You've found me. On my way out.'

'There's somebody downstairs wanting to speak to you.' Watts went past him and through the door. 'He asked for you specifically, Sarge. He says it's about the Blackfoot Trail murder. He runs there.' Watts stopped, turned. 'He's sitting in reception, looking dead nervy.'

Watts was halfway down the stairs. 'Get back there. Put him in the informal interview room. *Don't* let him leave.'

'He doesn't look too happy to be here, Sarge.'

'Him and me, both.' He went into his office and stopped. Judd was sitting at the table, reading through a file.

She looked up at him. 'OK, I'm going. I just started looking through this and got—'

'Where's Traynor?'

She looked up at him, her face pale, dark smudges under her eyes. 'He said he had somewhere to go.'

'Drop what you're doing and come with me.'

'Where to?'

'For once in your life, Judd, do as I say without following it with a question.' Watts spoke briefly to an officer on the reception desk who nodded towards the small room, a male figure just visible through the glass. He headed for it, smoothing his hair, dragging a genial expression on to his face and opened the door. 'Mr Lee Townsend?'

The man shot to his feet. 'Yes?'

Watts came inside, held out his hand. 'Thanks for coming in, Mr Townsend. I'm Detective Inspector Bernard Watts. I'm in charge of the investigation at Blackfoot Trail. This is PC Chloe Judd. Sorry about the heat in here. How about a cold drink?'

Townsend pointed to a sports water bottle on the table, shook his head. He was built like a greyhound, except for the well-developed calf muscles below his to-the-knee shorts. Watts absorbed the close-cut hair, his attention dropping to the inscription on his T-shirt: *Run for your life!* Townsend was just the type he'd been hoping for since this case started. What had been a dead-loss day so far looked like it might be coming good.

He sent him an encouraging smile. 'Have a seat, Mr Townsend. We understand you've got something to tell us.'

Townsend looked from him to Judd, then back. 'I saw the appeal on the television. It's probably nothing.'

'That's for us to decide, so don't you worry about it.'

Townsend gave him a nervous glance. 'I wasn't going to come at all. It's hardly anything.'

Watts' smile was now fixed. 'How about you tell us and we'll see?'

Townsend gave the table between them a worried look. 'I was there. At the trail. When that woman was there.'

Sensing a start from Judd, Watts said, 'Which woman would that be?'

'The one you were on television about. The one that was murdered.'

Watts slow-nodded, wanted every single thing Townsend thought he had, but first there was a bottom line which needed checking. 'What did this woman you saw look like?'

'I didn't see her face.'

'Tell us what you did see.'

'She was blonde. Her hair was tied up at the back and she was wearing a white top and running shorts. Black, I think, maybe navy, with a horizontal silver stripe running across the back.' He pointed to a stripe on his own shorts. 'Like that. All decent sports gear has them. I can tell you about her trainers. Black Nike Downshifter Sevens.' He looked at Watts. 'I know my trainers.'

Chong's schedule of clothing removed from Roberts' body zoomed into Watts' head: white vest, black shorts, silver stripe. Downshifter Sevens. 'What time was this, exactly?'

Townsend reached for the gym bag on the floor between his feet, lifted it on to his lap and brought out a hardcover notebook. 'This is my training regime. I can tell you exactly.' He flipped it open, turned pages, pointed. 'Monday the fifteenth of August. I was at the trail from six thirty-five a.m. until seven twelve. I ran the whole length of it.'

Resisting a strong urge to wrest the notebook from Townsend's hand and clap him soundly on the back, Watts said, 'Talk us through everything you saw.'

Townsend sat back, looking marginally more relaxed. 'I was running in the same direction as her. That's why I didn't see her face. That trail has some long curves. I first saw her some way ahead of me. I soon passed her and ran on.'

'Where did you finish your run?'

'The car park.'

Watts waited. 'That's where you were parked?'

Townsend shook his head. 'I didn't drive there. I still had five miles of road running to do after I finished at the trail. I do marathons. I ran straight out.'

Watts kept his tone light. 'Notice anything in the car park as you ran through it?'

'Only the two cars.'

'Just to be certain what you're telling us, Mr Townsend, you saw these vehicles as you were leaving the trail?'

'Yes. I started my run from the other end.'

'Describe both cars.'

'One was a dark colour, very dusty. It might have been an Audi but I'm not sure.'

'Did you notice a registration number?'

'No.'

'Tell us about the other car,' said Watts.

'A red Volkswagen. I'm not much into cars but everybody recognizes a Volkswagen Bug, don't they?' He gave Judd an uncertain look.

Under the table, Watts gave her foot a nudge. 'That's very helpful, Mr Townsend. Is there anything else you want to say?'

Townsend looked at Watts. 'No. Not unless you want to know about the man. But I can't see how he's useful to you.'

Watts eyed him, heart rate picking up. 'Everybody at that trail on that day is of interest to us. Describe him.'

Townsend appeared to give it some thought. 'I'd say he was older. I mean older than me. Say, thirty-plus. He didn't look very fit.'

'What gave you that idea?'

Townsend shrugged. 'Just the way he was standing, his general build, but it can't have been him who killed that woman.'

'What makes you say that?'

'He was injured.'

'What do you mean? How?'

'He had his arm in a sling.'

Watts stared at him. 'A sling.'

'Yes. Beige-coloured, looped around his neck, supporting his arm.'

'Which arm?'

Townsend thought about it. 'His left. I had a similar one myself once when I fell and hurt my shoulder and—'

'Did he speak? Say "Good morning" or something as you ran past?'

Townsend shrugged again. 'If he did, I wouldn't have heard

him. I wear earbuds so I can listen to music on my phone as I run.'

Watts was on his feet. Townsend gave him a startled look. 'We're very grateful to you for coming in, Mr Townsend.'

Townsend smiled. 'Well, I hope what I've said is a help—'

'I'll leave you to give a detailed statement to PC Judd.'

Townsend's smile disappeared.

'Don't worry. Just a formality. She'll take you through it.' With a glance at Judd, who had pulled a Witness Statement form from the back of her notebook, he sent Townsend a reassuring glance. 'While you're here, we'd appreciate you providing a description of this man to our e-fit expert.' Seeing Townsend's mouth open, he said, 'He'll talk you through the process, see what you manage to recall.' Watts headed for the door, his genial facial expression disappearing as soon as he was out of the room. He took out his phone. He didn't care who it was Townsend had seen at the trail that morning. Whoever he was, this individual was a potential witness.

THIRTY MINUTES LATER, JUDD came into the office and placed Townsend's statement on the table next to Watts. He picked it up. 'Townsend struck me as the timid type, so I thought it might be easier on him if you did it. How was he?'

She sat opposite. 'Fine. Quite a talker, actually.'

'Do you think he's a reliable witness?'

'I'd say so. I think he did pretty well, considering he was on the move when he saw what he saw.'

'Fair point. Did he add anything to what he said when I was there?'

'No. I used all the usual how-what-when-where-why-who triggers but his statement is basically what you heard.'

Watts looked through it. She'd been very thorough. 'So, what we've got here is one unidentified male with an arm injury, plus one possible Audi, that's possibly his. It could be worse. Did you tell Townsend we might be in touch?'

'Yes. I took all of his contact details.' She looked away. 'Sorry about what happened at Roberts' office, Sarge.'

He regarded her steadily. There was a lot about her that got on his nerves but he knew there was a bigger picture. She was quick, she worked hard and she was committed to the job. Maybe too committed. 'Think of it as an early lesson. Ends don't justify means in this game. Don't do it again.' He pointed at the board. 'That note you've written about your wine shop visit is too short. I want details and I want it on paper.'

'Yes, Sarge.'

'Where's Traynor?'

'Not here, is all I know.' The door opened and one of the forensic officers came in holding an A4.

'How did Townsend do?' asked Watts.

'Pretty good,' the officer replied as he handed Watts the piece of paper.

Watts stared down at the e-fit produced from Townsend's description. 'Let's hope this is accurate enough and detailed enough to ring some bells. Give it to Communications for immediate release. I want it on the six o'clock news.' He hesitated, e-fit still in his hand, wondering whether to include a reference to the second vehicle Townsend had described. Information could be gold in these situations but that depended on how reliable it was. There had been no indication from him that the car and the man with the sling were connected. He handed the e-fit to the officer. 'Quick as you can.' The officer left. Watts stood, eyeing Judd. 'I'm on my way to the squad room to put basic details of Roberts' homicide into PNC. See if there's anything remotely similar in the unsolved database.'

Subdued, she nodded, watched him go to the door.

He turned. 'Move yourself, Judd!'

She leapt to her feet.

TRAYNOR RAISED THE HIGH-SPEC digital camera and took two wide-angle shots of the car park, then another two of the area in the corner close to the trees where Zoe Roberts' body had been found. He continued on to the trail. Reaching the hedge and its widened access he took another two shots. Going through it he walked the dried-out field, stopped at the incline, camera raised and took several more. Heading quickly up the incline to halfway he turned, raised it to the field sloping away on the other side of the trail.

'Hey, Will!' He turned to the voice, saw Adam coming down towards him.

'You're not satisfied with our two hundred-plus efforts?'

Traynor smiled. 'How's it going?'

Adam pointed across to the other area of high ground where the footprints had been found. 'We've finished a comprehensive search of that area. No more found, but you're welcome to take a look.'

They headed downwards, across the field and up to where a

dozen or more officers were packing away equipment. Traynor watched them. 'You're throwing everything you have at this, Adam.'

'Yes, and getting nothing. No footprints, other than the ones you know about. No anything.'

Shielding his eyes, Traynor looked down at the Works Unit Only compound where he'd parked an hour before, then at the ground immediately in front of him sloping down to it. 'You said that all of this area has been processed?'

'Yes.'

He started down the hill towards the compound. SOCOs and forensic officers watched, faces rapt, as Traynor got into the Aston Martin, heard it thrum to life, its sleek shape moving past the compound and starting its ascent of the steep hillside, its engine deep-throated as it came steadily upwards. They watched it crest the slope on another roar of powerful engine and pass close to where they were standing. On a final wheel turn, Traynor brought it to a halt, engine idling then falling silent. The driver's door opened and he got out to whoops, hand claps, and a shouted, 'Va-va-*voom*.'

He walked to Adam, pointed at the steep ground he'd just driven up. 'Blackfoot Trail is accessible from the motorway. Roberts' killer could have driven up here.' He pointed to the Aston Martin. 'That's almost sixteen years old. It didn't break sweat. Any good quality, modern car could do the same.'

Adam gazed down the incline. 'You've convinced me.' He frowned. 'Who's that, do you think?'

Traynor followed his eyes to the compound, a male figure moving across it. 'Probably Shaw, the day security worker DI

Watts spoke to. Given the motorbike recorded leaving the motorway and driving up that service road, anybody around that place is a potential witness. I want to talk to him. I've got an idea I want to follow up with your help, Adam. Got a blood kit with you?'

'Never go anywhere without, plus a lot more.'

'Good. Give me a few minutes and I'll ring you.'

Adam reached out his hand, his eyes fixed on the scene below. '*Wait,* Will.'

'I see it.' Traynor started down the slope. Reaching the chain-link fence, he followed it along to the open gate. Some four metres inside the compound a heavy-set, black-brown dog was moving restlessly back and forth. Seeing Traynor, it stopped, raised its massive head, fixed its eyes on him. A low rumble started up deep inside its compact chest.

A man some feet away, less vigilant than the dog, turned, saw Traynor and pointed. 'Hey, you! Get the fuck out of here, *now.*'

Traynor remained where he was, the big animal coming slowly towards him, head lowered, flanks quivering. 'You heard me! He's off his leash. You shouldn't be here.' Traynor's eyes stayed fixed on the dog. The man moved towards it, his face agitated. 'Easy, Titan! Stay, boy.' The dog gave a low, lingering growl, its eyes locked on Traynor.

'You need to stay quiet and calm,' Traynor said to the man.

The man stared at him. 'You'll be "quiet and calm" when he rips your head off!'

'Sshhh.'

The dog was still on the move, its head raised now, teeth exposed, coming towards Traynor . . . closer . . . three metres

. . . two . . . one . . . Traynor looked down as it raised its head to his hand hanging loose at his side, ears twitching at his low words. 'Hey, boy . . . good boy . . .'

The man's voice was barely audible. 'Are you mental, or what?'

The dog sniffed Traynor's hand, opened its mouth . . . and licked. Traynor slowly raised his hand, gently rubbed the black-brown fur. The man came slowly towards them, reached for the dog's thick leather collar. Hands shaking, he clipped a heavy-duty plaited lead on to it. 'I don't know who you are or how you managed that but you're one lucky bastard is all I can say. Now, clear off or I phone the police.'

Traynor ran his hand over the dog's head and nose, his face turned to the distant high ground. 'No need. You are Bill Shaw?'

The man looked up at the line of officers gazing down from the top of the hill. 'Yeah. What of it?'

'Do you own a motorbike, Mr Shaw?'

'*Piss* off.'

Traynor watched as Shaw led the dog in the direction of the prefabricated buildings, then took out his phone, looking up at the waiting officers. 'Bring it all, Adam.' He cut the call, his eyes back on the buildings. If Zoe Roberts' killer was familiar with this place, there would be evidence of it.

FRUSTRATED, JUDD FELL BACK against her chair. 'We've been at this for nearly an hour, Sarge. There's nothing that remotely links with the Roberts case.' She hit a key, sending on-screen details flying upwards. 'Only five decapitations listed in the last two decades. They look as though they were done for the killers' own convenience, as a way of concealing or transporting the body or possibly in an effort to slow identification.' She pointed. 'See those two? Both cases included a history of domestics, and . . . those three were homicides linked to organized crime.'

Watts reached out and switched on a nearby fan. 'Blimey, it's hot in here.'

Her hands propped either side of her face, Judd stared at the screen. 'What other questions can we ask the database?'

Watts started gathering papers. 'We've finished.'

She looked up at him. 'Why?'

'Because whatever we ask would be guesswork.' He pointed at the computer. 'Put guesses into that and we'll get enough "might be's" to keep us busy from now till Christmas.'

'What if we interrogate for abductions?'

'Zoe Roberts wasn't abducted. As for the others, we don't know how they ended up at the scene.' He headed out of the squad room and down the stairs, Judd following. 'Heard anything from Traynor?'

'No, Sarge.'

SIXTEEN

Saturday 20 August. Twelve fifteen p.m.

His eyes fixed on Shaw, Traynor pointed to forensic officers approaching. 'They're bringing test equipment for both of these prefabricated buildings. They're ready to search for all kinds of evidence.'

Shaw gave a quick shrug. 'What's that to do with me?'

'I don't know, Mr Shaw. Is Gerry Williams the night security guard a friend of yours?'

'No. I told that other officer, the older one, I don't have nothing to do with Williams.'

'You're not benefitting from anything he might be into?'

Shaw's face darkened. 'I don't know what you're talking about. I don't get involved in anything. I've got a ten-year-old kid I don't see enough of. I don't do nothing that might be used against me where he's concerned. You're wasting your time asking me for information because I haven't got any. I do my job. I go home. That's my life, apart from my kid.'

Traynor left him with a uniformed constable and followed forensic officers to the nearest building, one of them carrying a small camcorder, another handing Traynor a white coverall. He stood at the door, pulling it on, watching the synchronized activity as Luminol was sprayed on to various surfaces. At a signal from Adam, Traynor came inside and closed the door. All of the blinds were pulled down, all internal lights extinguished. No bright, blue-green glow leapt out of the darkness.

Adam switched on the lights. 'No blood,' he said.

Traynor pointed at the two large tables. 'How about testing for something else?'

'Got anything specific in mind?'

Traynor's eyes moved over the surfaces of each table. 'I'm thinking motorway access, rural location, a private place and a motorbike picked up by CCTV in the small hours, plus a night security worker who didn't respond to a police order.' He looked up at Adam. 'What that's telling me is drug distribution.'

'Put like that, you're not the only one.' Adam nodded to his officers. Snapping open metal cases, they got busy. Traynor watched them wipe each of the tables with small squares of what looked to be plain paper. A small tool the size of a biro released liquid on to each square. Colour bloomed on the squares. Adam pointed. 'Indications on this one of significant traces of cocaine and methamphetamine.' They moved to another table, Adam pointing to several small, liquid filled sachets. 'These indicate the presence of heroin. We'll take additional samples back to headquarters for definitive testing.' As the evidence was bagged Adam looked at him. 'Where does this get us in terms of Roberts and the other two victims?'

Traynor was silent for several seconds. 'I don't know.'

He left the building and walked across the compound to where Shaw and the uniformed officer were still standing. He pointed towards the high ground, looking Shaw in the eye. 'Any idea why police have been here these last few days?'

'I heard something on the radio that some woman got killed around here a few days back.'

Traynor removed his coveralls. 'What do you know about that?'

Shaw stared at him. 'Nothing!'

'What about your colleague who works nights? The one who's already in deep trouble?'

Shaw's eyes slid away. 'I had my suspicions he was involved in some kind of racket here, but if you're asking do I think he murdered somebody, no. A thief is what he is. Always on the lookout for an earner.'

Traynor left him, walked up the hill, oblivious to officers' eyes on him, got inside his car, drove it slowly down to the compound, followed the access road and on to the motorway.

WATTS LOOKED UP AS Traynor came into the office. 'Where've you been?'

Traynor dropped on to a chair. He looked drawn. 'Working on the case.'

'As SIO, I need to know where you are and what you're doing.' He studied him. 'You look edgy. What's up?'

'Nothing. I can tell you that it's possible to drive from the Works Unit Only compound to Blackfoot Trail. I requested Adam's team test the prefab offices for blood and drugs. No blood but they got traces of cocaine, meth and heroin. It looks like Williams the night security worker is part of a drug-running racket there. The motorbike on the CCTV recording was probably a courier. Adam has the evidence.'

Watts headed for the door. He was back within five minutes.

'Good work, Traynor. I've sent two officers to arrest Williams.' They sat in silence. 'I've been looking at the information we've got on our victims. According to Edward Arnold, Broughton told him that he had a client who wanted something special built. Barlow's father told you that an unidentified male had offered Annette a well-paid job. Both have got my interest. What do you think?'

'I hear what you're saying but as I said, Barlow can't be trusted on timings of events or the quality of his information.'

Another silence grew between them. Watts looked at Traynor, saw his jaw muscles moving beneath the skin. 'You look wired. Like I said, what's up?'

Traynor got to his feet. 'I'll give you a reality check. My reality. No sleep. Talked to a bereaved father this morning. Spent what felt like a month at the Roberts scene in thirty degrees.' He walked to the open windows, looked out. 'I know. It's the same for everybody.'

Suspecting there was a lot more going on that Traynor wasn't talking about, Watts said, 'If the case is getting to you . . .'

Traynor turned to him. 'Haven't you heard? Work is *the* best means of achieving equilibrium. That's straight from the mouths of two psychiatrists of my long acquaintance.' He came back to the table, reached for his keys.

Watts looked up at him. 'I suppose that depends on the nature of the work.'

'It's been a difficult day, is all I'm saying.'

'What about medication?'

The door opened and Judd came inside. Traynor shrugged. 'It doesn't always work.' He walked past her and out.

The phone rang. Watts snatched it up, listened. 'OK. I'll come and get it.' He replaced the phone. 'Post.'

'I'll get it,' said Judd. Halfway along the corridor she heard a sudden tumult coming from the upper floor, looked up at several officers coming down the stairs at speed. 'What's going on? What's *happened*?' she shouted above the din of voices and feet.

'Development at the scene!' shouted one.

'Like *what*? Tell me!'

They surged past her and out. Running back to the office, she flung open the door. Watts had his phone pressed to his ear, his face fixed. He cut the call, made another. 'Will? We're needed at the scene.'

HEAT HAMMERING THEIR HEADS, they walked to Adam who led them to an area of exposed earth. Chong was kneeling beside it, a red-and-white striped stake driven into the ground nearby. She gazed up at Watts, pointed at the smooth shape, its lower aspect still within the dry soil. 'You just missed Jake Petrie. He's spent two hours here, sending the drone criss-cross fashion over this whole area.' Watts' arms hung at his sides as he stared down at this latest find. 'I'm just about to lift it,' she said quietly. Reaching for it with both hands, she applied gentle side-to-side pressure. It came away easily. She turned it slowly, examined its surfaces. 'Zero indication of trauma.' She placed it inside a plastic container, pointed upwards to two more red-and-white stakes. 'As soon as the drone located it, I marked its position, plus those of the two previously found, Broughton on the left, Barlow to the right.' She looked up at Watts. 'If you can see any significance, any pattern, in the respective positions of all three, you need to tell me, because I can't.' Watts didn't respond. She squinted up at Traynor. 'See any pattern, Will?'

His eyes moved over the three stakes. He shook his head, looked down at the area of parched earth from which the third skull had just been removed. 'Was the manner of concealment similar to the other two?'

'Yes. Carefully placed. Minimally covered. I'll confirm his ID as soon as I have it.'

Watts looked up. 'Male?'

'Yes.'

He crouched next to her, staring down at the skull in its box. 'Are you OK?' she asked quietly.

He shook his head. 'This case is killing me. We're doing all we can but . . . it just never lets up.'

Glancing at Traynor and Judd now several feet away, she reached forward, gave his arm a quick squeeze. 'See you later,' she whispered.

Watts stood, walked slowly down the incline. They returned to their vehicles, Watts tracking Traynor's car as it left. They had to get together, discuss this latest development, the whole investigation. He closed his eyes, thinking of an admin job waiting for him in his office. Glancing at Judd, he said, 'The chief wants an appraisal of your general progress on the investigation. When we get back to headquarters, I'll make a start on it. You still haven't given me your report of that wine shop visit. From what Traynor's learned about Annette Barlow's lifestyle, it could be relevant to what happened to her. Once I've read what you've got, I'll go over there myself and have a chat with the manager. See if he's got anything to add.'

Judd stared out of the window. He started the engine, his attention suddenly taken by one of the officers guarding the entrance to the car park, his arms raised, barring the way to a man. Alec Prentiss.

Watts got out, walked over to them. 'I'll sort it.'

Prentiss looked like somebody had taken an eraser to every scrap of colour he'd ever had. He attempted a smile. It quickly disappeared. 'DI Watts, I hope it's OK to bring these?'

Watts looked at the flowers he was holding: white-pink lilies fashioned into a large wreath in one hand, in the other a container of small, white flowers. Prentiss raised the wreath. 'This is from our parents. They're having a bad day so I said I'd bring it.' He nodded at the small flowers mixed with dark green leaves. 'These are from me. Stephanotis. Zoe chose them for her bridal bouquet.' He swallowed. 'Actually, their scent is giving me a headache. Is it all right to leave them?'

'No problem. Come on in and decide where you want to put them.'

Prentiss came into the car park, walked to the shady corner, knelt and placed the flowers on the ground. 'They'll probably last a bit longer here.' He remained there for several seconds then stood, turned to Watts. 'Thank you.' He walked slowly away, across the car park to the entrance and disappeared from view.

Watts looked at the flowers. His own life felt like it was full of death. He returned to his vehicle, guessing that the look on Judd's face was a mirror of his own: distracted weariness.

SEVENTEEN

Monday 22 August. Six thirty a.m.

Coming into his office, Watts found Traynor already there. One glance told him that sleep problems had brought him in early.

'Dr Chong has an ID for the third skull,' said Traynor. 'Justin Rhodes. Twenty-three years old when he disappeared in October 2011.'

Watts sat opposite him. 'Which makes him the second most recent victim to Zoe Roberts. That might work to our advantage in terms of establishing a link.'

Traynor reached across the desk. 'Here's the file on Rhodes' disappearance. I had it fetched from the basement. I've gone through it. He worked as a reporter on a local newspaper. Their offices are fairly close to where Zoe Roberts was running the day she was killed.'

Watts took it from him, winnowing its contents. 'That could be the first link.' He quickly read the first few pages. 'How about we go and talk to the Rhodes family? See what they can tell us.'

Traynor was looking elsewhere. 'It might appear a little heavy-handed for both of us to go. Why not take Judd?'

Watts eyed him. He'd talked to Annette Barlow's father but Watts still suspected that Traynor was avoiding contact with bereaved family members whenever possible. Probably a wise move, given how rocky he was looking. 'I've given Judd a late start today, so I'll go and talk to the Rhodes family. How about you go and see Justin Rhodes' colleagues at this newspaper he worked for?'

As Traynor headed for the door, Watts made a phone call then went to the Smartboard, his eyes moving over the actions listed. The desk phone rang. He reached for it. 'Watts.' He paused. 'Anything?' He listened to Adam reporting zero results of a search of Walk 'n' Dior trainers purchased in the Midlands.

'It was a long shot,' said Adam. 'The ones which made the prints we found could have been purchased anywhere. Most of those we traced were bought in London and Manchester by people whose names appear to be Japanese.'

Eight a.m.

A PLEASANT-LOOKING WOMAN IN her late thirties to early forties with a mane of blonde-brown curls to her shoulders appeared in response to a phone call from the young woman behind the glass of the *Southern Times* reception area. 'Dr Traynor,' she said, smiling up at him, holding out her hand. 'Jess Meredith, the paper's owner. We spoke on the phone earlier. It's good to meet you.' Then to the young woman on reception: 'Anya, can you make us some coffee, please?'

The young woman nodded, sending Traynor a smile as he followed Meredith through a security door and into a large square office.

'Everyone else is out, but they all predate Justin's time here. Fortunately, I don't so I'm happy to help you in any way I can.'

'Thank you for agreeing to an early meeting,' said Traynor.

'No problem.' She smiled. 'The news world is known for its early starts.'

He looked around at vacant desks, each supporting a computer, then on to shelves of files. She caught his glance. 'Welcome to the paperless world, right? Except that it isn't.' She indicated a chair at one of the desks, taking another for herself. 'Although, as the proprietor, I'm glad paper in some form is holding its own. At least, for now.'

'For now?'

'My dad started this business over twenty years ago. We've had a good run, still are, but we're changing to a digital format in a year or so.' She rotated her chair to him, her face open, gaze direct. 'You're not here to talk newspaper business. When I said it was good to meet you, I wasn't being merely polite. I'll help your investigation in any way I can. Justin Rhodes was a highly valued member of our team. I liked him a lot. It's been a long time since he disappeared. Too long.'

Her directness made Traynor wish he could be as open with her, but Brophy had not yet sanctioned the release of information about any of the skulls found, beyond informing next-of-kin. Coffee arrived. Meredith handed one to Traynor, seeing his eyes move to a group of framed photographs on a nearby wall.

She pointed. 'See the one in the blue frame? The man sitting down? That's Justin.'

Traynor went to the photograph and looked at the young, dark-haired man, his mouth open in a wide smile, several people grouped around him, some with their hands at his shoulders, others with arms raised, all smiling. Off the lower edge of the picture was what looked to be a large cake. Meredith came to his side. 'I took that. It was his twenty-third birthday. Six months later, he was gone.'

'How long had Justin worked here?'

'Almost five years. He joined us when he was eighteen.'

'He was a good employee?'

'Oh, yes,' she whispered. 'One of the best.' She turned away. Traynor followed. 'Justin had the instinct, the understanding which makes a good reporter. Initially, I gave him only local interest pieces to write up but it didn't take long for me to realize how capable he was. During the time he worked here he developed from a youngster who loved the news world into a really great reporter.'

Traynor looked back at the photograph. 'He was well-liked by his colleagues?'

'Yes, he was. I'm convinced he would have gone on to do great things.' She looked up at him. 'Justin wanted to work in London. He would have done well there if he'd had the chance.' She looked away, hesitated. 'Sad person that I am, I sometimes tell myself he's in London, working and happy. There's a lot to be said for a little self-deception.' He knew what she meant. She straightened. 'How can I help you, Dr Traynor?'

He responded with a question of his own. 'What do you think happened to Justin?'

She shook her head. 'I have no idea. I was hoping that as a criminologist you might tell me.' She regarded him. 'If you're concerned about what you say to me, don't be. This is all off the record. No details will find their way into this paper. You have my word.'

Traynor went with his impression of her as an honest person. Time for some openness. 'Remains belonging to Justin have been found fairly local to here.'

Silence lengthened between them. 'Oh, my Lord,' she whispered. 'How are you involved, exactly?'

'By invitation. I give some of my university time to supporting complex police investigations. It adds to my department's research.'

She gave him a direct look. 'In the last few days, this newspaper among most others has reported on the murder of a woman at Blackfoot Trail.' When Traynor didn't respond she said, 'I understand. You'd rather not confirm a connection.'

'Can you tell me about the last time you saw Justin?'

She looked from him to the window full of sun. 'It was here, on the 31st October 2011. He'd come in early that morning. He was planning to leave at about four. I told the police this when they came.' She reached for a pen, offered it to him. 'Do you want to write down the details?'

'No, thank you. My recall for detail is . . .' He was about to say 'faultless', but he substituted. 'Pretty good.' He already knew the details she'd just given him from the Rhodes' file, had read what his family and friends had told the police following his disappearance. Justin Rhodes: good son, good friend, liked by all who knew him. He frowned. Except that somebody hadn't liked him at all. 'You said he had plans, later that day?'

'Yes. He and some friends were going out to celebrate Halloween.' She smiled. 'They'd hired outfits. They were meeting at Justin's flat, then going to another friend's house in Bentley Heath.'

Traynor had studied countless maps of the Midlands since he'd come to live here, knew that Bentley Heath was fairly close to the location where Roberts had been killed. 'How did they travel there?'

'In two cars. Justin drove his because he wanted to leave the party early without impinging on his friends' evening.' She gave Traynor a steady look. 'I gave the names and details to the officers who came here to investigate Justin's disappearance. They came back to report that their inquiries hadn't yielded anything and to ask if I could suggest any other contacts he had or places he might have gone following that party. I couldn't. I told them that Justin was planning to come into the office early the following morning. Actually, he had some leave owing and he wasn't supposed to be here but he'd told me he was planning to start a new article. I give those I trust free rein to pursue their own interests.'

'What was the article about?'

'He said he was interested in two disappearances in the Birmingham area a few years before. He didn't give me any details but he said he'd made contact with someone who was willing to help him with it.'

'He didn't say who that was, leave any notes on what he was planning to write?'

She shook her head. 'No, and I didn't find anything on his computer or in his files. From the little he said, I don't think he'd got as far as making any.'

'When you first heard that Justin was missing, did you have any ideas, any suspicions as to what might have happened to him?'

She shook her head. 'None at all. I was totally shocked. We all were. As time went on it didn't get any easier because none of us could think of a reason.'

'You never came up with any possibilities?'

'No.'

'He liked the work here?'

'Very much. One of Justin's strengths was his attention to detail. I used to give him crime stories to cover and I did briefly wonder if his perfectionism had led him to overwork.' She gave Traynor a direct look. 'I'm not trying to absolve myself of responsibility when I say that I didn't think that for long.'

'You don't believe that his crime reporting had anything to do with his disappearance?'

'No, I don't. This newspaper looks after its staff. It has a policy which protects all who work on it. If there's a concern, a problem, an incident of any kind which makes staff feel uneasy, there's a procedure we follow: report it immediately and verbally to me, followed by a written report, and I decide whether any action is required.' She shook her head. 'Justin never reported anything of that nature to me.' She looked away. 'As I said, he had a great capacity for detail. I think you'd have got along with him.' She paused. 'Our crime correspondent. Sounds grand, doesn't it, for somebody who still spent some of his time covering local fêtes and road-building protests. That's how it works in a small setup like this.' She reached for a folder. 'After you phoned, I had Anya pull together some of the articles Justin wrote. We don't rely on rehashing what's in the big dailies.' She held out the folder to Traynor. 'Here. Take them with you. They will show you the calibre of his work.'

He took the folder from her, opened it. Meredith pointed to the first article. 'That's about a dog-fighting ring Justin followed up. Those involved were arrested and taken to court.'

Traynor looked at the date of the article: August 2005, then up at her. 'There are some pretty unpleasant people involved in that kind of activity. I've met some of them. They're violent, diverse in terms of their criminality and they have long memories.'

'I understand what you're saying, Dr Traynor, but if you're suggesting that those involved targeted Justin because of what he wrote, I seriously doubt it. They all received lengthy prison sentences, not just for the dog-fighting but numerous other offences. Two are still inside. Another two were deported on release.'

Traynor turned the page to a second article, read the first few lines. Meredith was right. Justin Rhodes had been good at what he did. Clear and incisive. She leant forward, pointed at it. 'Now, that case is the one which shows Justin's determination to get to the truth. It won him an award. A hit-and-run which killed an elderly couple. He kept on with it, pushing, talking to people, maintaining its high profile. When he decided he had enough information, he turned it over to the police. As a result, the driver was identified, convicted and questions were asked of the probation service about its management and supervision of young offenders with a history of dangerous driving.' She sat back. 'The families of those two victims were very appreciative.'

Traynor looked at her. 'My impression is that Justin was someone who did what he thought was right.'

She nodded. 'Exactly.'

He turned the article over, looked at the one beneath: a large, front-page picture of himself, a decade younger: *Dr William Traynor, husband of tragic victim Claire Traynor . . .*

His immediate surroundings receded, Meredith's voice coming to him from a long way off. '*Oh!* Dr Traynor, I'm *terribly* sorry. I thought your name was familiar but I didn't make the connection. I should have checked those articles before you arrived. The responsibility for what I've given you is all mine. I'm truly sorry.'

He looked up at her flushed face. 'No apology needed. These things happen.' He knew he had to leave, but there was a question clamouring to be asked. 'Did Justin develop any theories about those three murders? Come to any conclusions?'

Meredith looked at him, her face still troubled. 'He wrote two features on the York-Oxford-Guildford cases. His view was that all three were . . . destined to be an abiding mystery. I'm sorry.'

Traynor was pulling air into his chest, chill perspiration on his forehead. 'Can you say anything about Justin's personal life?'

'He had a very close family but he didn't have much of a social life. There were one or two girls, women, but they didn't last because he would break arrangements with them due to work. I tried to encourage him to extend his social life, but his focus was on what he did here.'

'He had no personal problems as far as you know?'

'None. Justin was a great talker. If he'd had any problems, I believe he would have told his family and me. He was very open. Which is why it's so hard even now to make any sense of what happened.'

Traynor stood. He had to be outside. They left the room, came into the sunlit reception area.

'If you need to come back, you're very welcome. I'll open our archive for you.'

'Thank you. One last thing. Did Justin take his phone with him that evening?'

Meredith shook her head. 'As far as I recall, he'd lost it a couple of days before.' She held out her hand. 'Goodbye, Dr Traynor. I think you're probably very good at what you do, which makes me feel that Justin is in safe hands . . . and I'm truly sorry for what happened earlier.'

'There's no need. Thank you for your time.'

Traynor drove through country lanes towards the motorway, the folder next to him on the passenger seat, his eyes fixed on the road, scenes of Claire's murder running on a loop inside his head. Nauseous, he touched his face, felt sweat running. He tried to swallow. Couldn't. Self-deception. Self-lies. He'd used them for years: *Claire wasn't dead. She was waiting somewhere for him to find her. If she had died, she hadn't suffered* . . . His foot jerked involuntarily to the brake as a sudden, full-colour image of Claire's blood pooled on pale kitchen tiles slammed his retinas, their daughter's hysterical crying reverberating in his head, a thousand nettle stings at his side. Heart rate spiralling, sweat streaming from his hair, he turned off the road on to a small rest area. Chest in a vice, face slick, he cut the engine, pushed open his door, breath rasping his throat.

Bringing his breathing under control, he took out his phone, texted Watts to tell him that, like Broughton and Barlow, Rhodes had received some kind of offer of help from an unidentified source. He sat, rested his head back, waiting for calm. His breathing slowed. His heart gradually settled, no longer feeling like it was trying to break out of his chest. He sat up. He'd beaten it. This time he'd actually beaten it. Got back control. He got out of the car, took a couple of steps, the ground ahead suddenly morphing into a heaving ocean. He stumbled to the edge of the rest area, stared down at a mess of discarded paper coffee cups and parched grass, waiting for the familiar burning rush. It came, insistent, relentless, forcing his upper body forward, pulsing from his mouth. A brief respite. It came again. And again. Spent, he straightened, wiped his mouth with his hand, the sun splitting his head. Legs unsteady, he walked back to his car. Reaching inside for a plastic bottle, he poured water into his mouth, over his head and then slid to the dusty ground.

His phone was ringing. Brushing water from his face, he reached for it. 'Hello. Yes . . . It's great to hear your voice.' He listened some more. 'No, no, I'm fine. No, really . . . Would you like to meet?' He gazed ahead, the ache in his heart enough to break it. 'That would be wonderful,' he whispered.

His phone rang again. It was Watts, sounding out of breath. 'Where are you?'

'I'm on my way back to headquarters from the newspaper offices where Justin Rhodes worked. You've seen my text?'

'About the two disappearances Rhodes was interested in and somebody offering him help? Yes. Looks like you might have found a link.' A silence between them grew. 'You still there, Traynor?'

'Yes. I owe you an apology for yesterday. We're all working under the same conditions.'

'You don't owe me anything. Let's hope the victims told

other people about these offers they were getting so we can follow them up.'

Traynor listened to his upbeat tone. It was time he levelled with Watts about his change of thinking on the case. About the other link he had made. But now wasn't the time.

'You all right?' asked Watts.

'Yes.'

'You sound . . . a long way off,' said Watts.

'I'm fine.'

'I'm at Blackfoot Trail, following up a possible new angle. I'll keep you posted.'

EIGHTEEN

Watts ended the call, his eyes moving from the plump woman sitting in the open doorway of his vehicle, to the small tan and white terrier taking a close interest in one of his suede shoes. He moved his foot. The dog pounced. The woman pointed. 'Stop that, *naughty* dog!' She looked up at Watts. 'I'm sorry.'

'That's all right, Mrs Merriman.' He gave her a quick once-over. She'd rallied in the last half hour. 'How are you feeling now?'

'Better, thanks.' She looked up at him. 'To be honest, I'm more incensed than anything.'

'Do you feel up to talking about it?'

Merriman straightened her shoulders. 'Yes.'

He looked around the car park, saw Judd and raised his hand. She hurried towards them. 'Mrs Merriman, this is my colleague, PC Chloe Judd. We need you to fill in some detail on what you've already told us.' He flipped notebook pages. 'So far, you've described a male of stocky build, dressed in dark clothes with a small, dark-coloured backpack and his arm in a sling.' Merriman gave a confirmatory nod. 'Take your time, then tell us what happened.'

Merriman dabbed at her nose with a tissue. 'I often come here with Douglas. Nothing like this has ever happened.'

He frowned. 'Douglas?'

She pointed to the dog. 'I'd heard what happened here recently, that Blackfoot Trail was closed, so I decided we'd take the path leading off the top of the lane. I thought it would be safe with so many police in the area. We weren't going anywhere near the trail.' She sent a nervous glance in its direction.

'Mrs Merriman, how about I drive you up to that path and you show PC Judd and me the exact location where you say this assault happened?'

'Actually, I'd rather walk. I need to calm down before I see it again and it isn't far.'

Mrs Merriman got down from the BMW and they walked with her and her dog out of the car park, up the steep lane, past the line of police vehicles parked nose to tail and on to the top of the hill. After a few minutes, Merriman stopped, pointed at a narrow path. Watts sent Judd a look. She moved to Merriman's side.

'Do you think you could show us the exact route you took, Mrs Merriman?'

She looked at Judd, nodded. Flanked by both officers, she headed on to the path. After a couple of minutes, she stopped, took a shaky breath. 'We got as far as here. That's when I heard him.' She pointed. 'See those bushes over there? He was behind them. He pushed his way through them.'

Watts looked to where she was pointing. 'Was there anybody else here? Any other dog walkers?'

She shook her head. 'I didn't see anybody except him.'

Watts headed to the bushes, carefully examined the ground around them. Not finding anything, he looked towards the line of trees screening Blackfoot Trail and its car park, the incline just visible, tiny uniformed figures, others white-clad, moving over it. This woman seemed reliable. Whoever had assaulted her had to be a real chancer. He went back to her. 'Mrs Merriman, can you confirm what you've told us about this man's appearance?'

'Yes. He was dark-haired and he was wearing a dark long-sleeved shirt, I think black, but I can't be certain, dark trousers, and he was carrying a backpack. I think that was dark-coloured as well . . . and he had one arm in a sling which was light in colour, sort of beige, oh, and trainers, but I don't recall anything about them.'

Watts got on his phone, raising an eyebrow to Judd who turned to her. 'What we need now, Mrs Merriman, is a description of what happened after you first became aware of this man.'

Merriman pointed to the bushes again. 'As I said, he came through there. I didn't look directly at him, of course. You don't, do you? I just carried on walking, but I could hear him following us.'

Judd pointed at the dog. 'He didn't bark?'

'No. He isn't that kind of animal. He's very "hail-fellow-well-met", aren't you, Douglas?' The dog looked up at them, tongue lolling, tail wagging.

Watts ended his call. Judd said, 'The man started to follow you. Then, what happened?'

Merriman's face flooded with colour. 'I'm sorry, but it's rather embarrassing.'

Watts raised his hand to her. 'I'll leave you to talk to PC Judd, Mrs Merriman. When you're done, she'll ask for your contact details and arrange for somebody to take you home. We'll need a more detailed statement from you at some point.' He headed back to the lane, the dog pouncing on one of his shoes as he went.

TWENTY MINUTES LATER, JUDD came into the car park. Watts got out of his vehicle. 'How was she?'

'Fine, considering. Jones has taken her home.'

'What else did she have to say?'

Judd pulled out her notebook. 'The man started following her. After a few seconds, he spoke, said, "That's a nice dog. Is he fierce?" She didn't respond. Carried on walking. Suddenly, he's in front of her, exposing himself. She said she was surprised by his quickness because of his arm injury and that she was shocked when she got a proper look at his face. He looked much younger than she'd initially thought.'

'Townsend said he looked to be in his thirties. How old does she think he was?'

'She's got a son of twenty-four. She thinks he might be younger.'

Watts' head fell back. '*Bugger*. If she's right, we can forget him for Broughton and Barlow. He would have been at most a teenager when that graveyard started and he'd have been on the young side for Rhodes.'

'Old enough to have killed Roberts, Sarge.'

'I'm not ruling him out of anything until we find him, establish his age and a lot more besides. What else did she say?'

Judd turned pages. 'He stood in front of her . . . made comments about her build. Told her he liked well-built women.

He asked her to remove her top, that he wanted to see her . . .'
She held up her notes, pointed at the four-letter word. 'I hate
that. It's disparaging of women.'

'He "asked" her to remove her top?'

Judd nodded. 'That's what she said.'

'Then what?'

'Before she could do or say anything, he reached out, grabbed
her top. I had a quick look at it. It's made of some stretchy
material. She said he pulled it down, exposing her upper body.'

Watts reached inside his vehicle for a tissue, patted his face,
offered one to Judd. He was starting to loathe the relentless
heat and this whole area. His phone buzzed. He lifted it. 'Yeah?
. . . You *have*? Bloody hell, that was quick work. Where?' He
listened, cut the call. 'I sent Merriman's description of her
attacker to two officers down at the scene and asked them to
go and have a look for him. Looks like they've got him. He's
on his way to headquarters.'

WATTS PARKED OUTSIDE HEADQUARTERS, glancing at the
dashboard clock.

Judd eyed him. 'Can I be part of the Merriman assault
interview, Sarge?'

'That was my plan, but I've just remembered I've arranged
for Alec Prentiss to come in to tell us what he knows of his sister's
personal life. He should be here now. Remember I suggested you
talk to him?'

She brightened. 'You trust me to do it?'

He looked down at her. 'Yes. Keep it low-key, more of a chat,

so he feels comfortable. What you're after is any and all information about his sister's life, people she spent time with, anybody
taking an interest in her recently. If he mentions Christian
Roberts, you say nothing, just write down what he says.'

She nodded. 'Yes, Sarge. I will.'

She walked into reception ahead of Watts. Alec Prentiss was
there. He looked pale. Unwell. 'Mr Prentiss?'

He started, looked up at her.

'I'm PC Chloe Judd. I was at your parents' house, remember?'

He stood. 'You've got news, haven't you?'

'News? No, I'm sorry . . .'

'I could tell from the way the officer over there on the
counter looked at me when I arrived that something has
happened. It's not right to keep information from us.'

She shook her head. 'Mr Prentiss, believe me when I say that
I'm sorry but I don't have anything to tell you that relates to
your sister's murder.'

He stared at her then glanced at his watch. 'I can't stay long.
I have to get back to work.'

'Shall we make a start?' She indicated the small interview
room.

He gazed at her, uncertain. 'I'm supposed to be seeing DI
Watts. Where is he?'

'He's been detained on another matter.'

'What matter?' He pointed to the officer on the desk. 'When
I told him my name, his face gave him away. He looked like he
knows something. What's going on? Why isn't DI Watts giving
all of his time to my sister's case?'

Judd was fazed. This wasn't what she'd anticipated. She kept her voice even. 'Nothing's going on, Mr Prentiss. Your sister's murder is still a top priority here. DI Watts, Dr Traynor and a whole team of officers are working long hours on the investigation.' She led him inside the room, reminding herself of the considerable stress he and his family were under. They sat. He ran his hands through his hair, looking agitated. 'Do you feel up to talking to me?' she asked.

He nodded.

'Mr Prentiss, we need to know as much as possible about your sister Zoe's life and we think you might be able to provide that kind of information.' Judd glanced at the plastic bottle containing something green which he'd placed on the table between them. She read the label: *Kale and Strawberry Energy Rush Smoothie.* 'We know this is a very difficult time for you and your family but can you talk to me about what you know of Zoe's daily life?' She waited. 'I get that it's probably difficult for you to do that, so soon after what's happened.' Judd didn't get it. When people lost people, wasn't talking about them what they wanted to do? She let the silence drag on a bit longer, noting the constant small bouncing movements of his legs, his general restlessness. 'We need that kind of detail to have a chance of identifying what happened to Zoe and why. You understand what I'm saying?' she asked quietly.

Prentiss looked across at her then away. 'I don't know what I can tell you. I chose not to spend too much time with my sister. You can probably understand why, from what I said when you came to the house.'

'I remember what you said, but—'

'I found Zoe's personality rather overwhelming. She was an

in-your-face kind of person. She got that from our parents.' He looked up at Judd. 'I know what you're thinking. That my dad doesn't come across like that. Take my word, my parents are both straight-talking, dominant people. Zoe was the same.' He frowned. 'You'd never know it because he never says much, but Dad's totally in charge of the business. And the money.'

Judd wrote quickly to keep up with his flow of ideas. 'What about you, Mr Prentiss?'

He stared at her. 'What about me? I learned to go with the flow. Zoe was nearly five years younger than me but she was always the dominant one.' He reached for his drink. 'Would you believe, when I was about nineteen, I borrowed five pounds from the money she'd earned babysitting and all three of them went ballistic?' He shook his head. 'She took my money whenever she saw a chance. Funny, but I think she understood me better than they did. She always knew what was in my head. Sometimes before I did. She still does.'

Judd looked up at him. 'I'm sorry, Mr Prentiss, I'm struggling to get what you're telling me. Can you explain?'

He looked away. 'I'm upset. Confused about what's happened. I hardly know what I'm saying. When I think about it, Zoe must have had real problems when she was young. *God* knows what else she did.'

She frowned. She hadn't got Alec Prentiss down as a religious type. 'Mr Prentiss, I'm a bit lost here.'

He rubbed his neck. 'I'm full of tension. I shouldn't be here, talking about her. It's too confusing and upsetting.' He gave Judd a fleeting look. 'You know about the family business?'

Judd nodded.

'Mom and Dad were back there the next day. They expected me to do the same, said it would "give me something else to think about".' His face grew sullen. 'Our company offers staff discounted spa breaks, treatments, massages, the works. That's what I need but Dad refused me the time off, said he "can't spare me during the holiday period". He told me to take a day off.' Judd watched sullenness turn to resentment. 'As though a *day* would make any difference! I told him I needed a week. He said, "What for? Why a week?" I told him I needed to get away. That I was upset. Depressed.' He shook his head. 'As if it needed saying.'

'Maybe they're finding it hard to make decisions, given their own upset?'

He stared at her. 'Families must look after each other. Is going back to work like they did normal?'

'I suppose they're doing their best.' Aware that she wasn't getting much of what Watts had asked for, yet feeling she couldn't ignore Prentiss's distress, she asked, 'Could that be their way of handling their own emotions?'

'And that gives them the right to ignore *mine*?'

Judd covertly studied him, noted the casual-pricey clothing, the styled hair, its sides close-cut, the top longer, carefully tousled. Something in his manner, his appearance, stirred an unpleasant memory inside her head. Josephs.

'Zoe was always the favourite. Their great hope for the future!' He folded his arms. 'Well, she doesn't have one now, does she?' He stared at the table between them. 'I'm sorry for what happened to her, but that's how it is.'

'Tell me about Zoe's work life, her colleagues,' she prompted.

He appeared to consider this. 'She was the smart one. I don't mean the first-class law degree, her job at the legal practice, marriage to a successful lawyer. What I mean is, she *escaped*. I did an English Lit degree and ended up trapped in the family business because I couldn't think of anything else to do.' He looked beyond Judd. 'Zoe warned me. She said that if I joined it, I'd never get away. That all I'd be doing was following Dad's orders. She got that right. Dad comes across as mild. He isn't. He's totally in charge and that's how he acts. What's happened to Zoe has brought all this to a head for me. I'm not getting on with him or Mom.' He looked up, crossed two of his fingers. 'Zoe and me were like that. Two amigos.'

Judd stopped writing, looked up at him. 'I'm really confused, Mr Prentiss. I'm not sure I understand what you're telling me about Zoe and your relationship with her.'

He lowered his head. 'I don't want to talk about her any more. I'm exhausted. I feel like I'm going mad.'

Judd had to keep the conversation going, get information about his sister's life. She changed tack. 'Tell me about yourself, Mr Prentiss. Your life.'

He stared at her. 'That isn't something I'm ever asked at home.' He looked away, gave her another quick glance then leant towards her. 'What I'm about to tell you would come as a shock to Mom and Dad if they knew. I don't want them to know about it. I've decided on a complete change of career. I've decided to set up my own business.'

'That's interesting,' said Judd, encouragingly. 'Doing what?'

'Life coaching.'

'That's popular now.'

'I signed up online for information and the guy whose business it is really made sense.'

Judd nodded, wondering how much money Prentiss had paid this 'guy'. 'What does it involve?'

Prentiss's face became animated. 'There's a lot of skill to it, but basically, you get clients and you tell them how to reach their potential in business and in life. I'm exactly the type of person that people like that need.'

'Right. So, you'll run courses, teach them skills—'

'No, no. The kind of people I'll be targeting are go-getters, energetic, highly motivated. They won't have time for that kind of thing and I've got no desire to deal with the general public. It'll be done via an app. I'll be using my own negative experiences of working in the family firm. I'll just put them on the right track. Tell them what they need to do and how.'

Judd chose her next words. 'Might clients have their own ideas and not like being told?'

His enthusiasm disappeared, like a light being switched off. He stared at her, downbeat, his voice a monotone. 'No. They'll be benefiting from my direct experience. What's happened to Zoe has been a wake-up call. I'm thirty-five. I want a life. Zoe's future has gone. I still have mine.'

Determined to get him back to family relationships, Judd asked, 'Your father started the family business?'

'Years ago. Mom got on board when we were kids. Zoe never wanted to know about it.' He gazed across at Judd. 'She was always a quick learner. She really got our parents. She wanted out of the family from when she was a teenager but obviously she couldn't because she was dependent on them. They had the money. They controlled her more than they did me.' He shrugged. 'If it helps them to keep Zoe a saint, that's all right by me.'

Judd was thinking back to her and Watts' visit to the Prentiss home, the wall in the sitting room devoted to the lives and times of both Prentiss children. 'My impression of your family when I was at your parents' house is that they were very involved with you and your sister as children—'

'No. They weren't. It was Zoe and I who were close. They were always too busy, building the business.'

Already confused, Judd was now picking up what sounded like whininess. She thought of two busy parents who still made time to record and display two childhoods over so many years, wondered what it might be like to have pictures of yourself as a baby, a small child. She re-tuned to Prentiss's voice.

'When Mom and Dad went on about things when we were younger, we'd laugh behind their backs, Zoe and me. She would impersonate Mom.' He grinned. 'She was a fantastic mimic, my sister, with a bit of an edge. Over the years we created an alliance. Us against them.' He looked away. 'I talk to Zoe every day. Tell her what I'm thinking.'

Not knowing how to respond, Judd said, 'I'm starting to get the picture of Zoe as someone who was very much her own person and—'

'I'm the one who's like that. Like I told you, I'm starting along my own path.'

Feeling the beginnings of a headache, Judd asked. 'You'll finance your plan yourself?'

'What? No. I'll float it past my mom and she'll talk to Dad.'

'Getting back to Zoe, was she popular?' He looked at a loss. 'What I mean is, was she a sociable person? Did she have a lot of friends?'

He was still looking adrift. 'You mean when she was young?'

'I mean any time.' She watched him think about it.

'I wouldn't describe Zoe as popular. I suppose she was sociable, but only on her own terms. She had friends but I don't think she went out of her way to create friendships.' He looked up at Judd. 'That's the big difference between us. I'm very much the individual but having loads of mates means that if you need to be out there, doing something, and one or two of them aren't that bothered, you've got others to hang out with.'

Judd tried imagining Prentiss with his loads of mates. The picture wouldn't come. 'Did you know Zoe's friends?'

'Not really. She had three or four from way back. They met at school, stayed friends as adults. That's something I don't get. Catch me hanging around with kids I was at school with. Too much like announcing to the world that you're a bad case of arrested development, but it seemed to work for Zoe.'

Judd had had enough but Watts had asked her to get all the information she could. She wouldn't let him down. She took a quick glance at Prentiss, his styled hair, another memory of the wine shop inside her head. 'Is that how you saw Zoe?'

He stared at her. 'Of course not. Zoe was savvy and sharp.'

'As adults, did you and Zoe discuss your lives?'

'I would occasionally tell her about work, the business, but not that often. She heard it all from Mom and Dad when she visited. She would mention what she was doing but I wouldn't class it as a discussion. Occasionally, she mentioned Christian, but not so often during the last year or so. Just odd comments about him, usually work-related which didn't much interest me.'

'Did you socialize with Zoe at all?'

'No. The only interest we had in common was fitness, but I'm not into running. I lift weights. Have done since I was a weedy teen.'

Judd gave him a covert glance, now seeing shadows of well-defined muscle beneath the finely knitted top. Cashmere? Silk? 'When I came to your parents' house, you referred to your sister thinking that Christian Roberts was a good catch when they first met.'

'So? What's wrong with that?'

'Nothing. Maybe it was the way you said it which made me think that you disapproved.'

'Not at all. That was typical Zoe: "Know what you want and go for it". It was something I admired about her.'

'Is that how you'd like to be?'

He stared at her. 'I'm already doing it. I'm running the business.'

She looked back at him. 'I thought your parents did that?'

'It's me who's dragging it into the future.'

Judd quickly wrote. 'What's going to happen to it when you leave?'

'What do you mean "leave"? I'm not leaving.'

'I thought you said you were. To set up your life coaching.'

'That's . . . going to take a while.'

'I understand. Your parents probably need you around. They have a lot on their minds right now.'

'Which doesn't mean the world stops turning,' he snapped.

Judd put down her pen, gave him a direct look. 'Mr Prentiss, we don't seem to be getting to the detail of Zoe's life, do we?'

He looked away from her, both legs restlessly bouncing. 'I'm finding it . . . difficult. I can't find the words. I loved my sister, but we were brought up to be independent. We didn't live in each other's pockets. Actually, I'm feeling unwell. I need to leave.' He covered his face with both hands, whispered, 'With all that's going on, it feels like I'm losing my mind.'

Before Judd could respond, he straightened, reached for his keys. She eyed the fob. Alfa Romeo. 'I have some names for you, Mr Prentiss. I'd like you to tell me if you recognize any of them. Annette Barlow.' Judd waited, getting no flicker of recognition. 'Daniel Broughton. Justin Rhodes. Mr Prentiss?'

He stared at her. 'I don't know them. What's the meaning behind this?'

'It's a straight question, Mr Prentiss, nothing hidden. I didn't ask if you knew them. I asked if you recognized their names.'

'No.'

'Is there anything else you'd like to say about Zoe?'

'No. It's too upsetting.' He paused. 'Is Christian a suspect?'

'What makes you ask that?'

'It's what the police do, isn't it? They look at who stands to gain.' She waited for more. It didn't come. 'How might Mr Roberts gain from your sister's death?'

He shrugged. 'Not a clue. It was a general observation of Christian. He's a slick character. He gets into people's heads, takes advantage.' He jiggled his keys.

She stood. He did same. 'How's the investigation progressing?'

'We're following up lines of inquiry and Dr Traynor is bringing his skills to it.'

He gave her one of few direct looks. 'I saw him on the news recently. The cool intellectual. Is he any good?'

Ignoring the question, she led the way from the room to the main entrance, held out her hand. 'Thanks for coming in, Mr Prentiss.' He took it briefly. She walked him out of the building, watched as he got inside the sleek red sports car then drove past her without a glance.

She came into Watts' office, hugely irritated and frustrated. She'd failed to get from Prentiss what she wanted. She gave the door a hard shove against its frame. 'Of all the spoilt, self-centred, contradictory, immature . . .!' She went to the sink, ran water, filled a glass and drank. On a deep breath, she went to the computer and began word processing a detailed account of the half hour or so she'd just spent with Prentiss, the words racing across the screen. Deleting 'wanker' and 'tosser', she searched for other words. 'Contradictory' would definitely stay, as would 'immature'. Immature at thirty-five. She shook her head, added: 'Overly focused on his own physical health. One minute depressed-looking, the next angry, and the next optimistic.' Her fingers flew, except for a short pause over a particular phrase. Leaving it in, she jabbed 'Print', fetched it from the printer and placed it squarely on the table where Watts usually sat.

NINETEEN

Watts waited as the duty sergeant inside the basement custody suite painstakingly processed details grudgingly supplied by the man standing before him. Richard Conrad Nilsen. To Watts, he looked much as Merriman had described, and also familiar. Dark-haired, on the heavy side, his backpack and its contents were now spread out on the desk. Watts eyed the pale sling as the duty sergeant methodically entered all of them, then sent the details to the printer. When it lapsed into silence, he reached below the desk, lifted out the sheets and handed them to Watts. 'All yours, Sarge.'

Passing them to Traynor, Watts glanced again at Nilsen, whom he'd cautioned half an hour before, then to a duty solicitor coming into the suite. A door on its other side opened and a belligerent-looking male in jeans and vest emerged, flanked by officers.

The duty officer nodded to it. 'That interview room's all yours.'

Watts took out his phone, said a few quiet words then cut the call. He gave Nilsen's belongings another once-over. 'I need audio-visual facilities.'

'You should come down here more often. That room has both.'

Watts turned to Nilsen. 'This is Dr William Traynor. He's a criminologist and he'll be sitting in on the interview. He'll show you into the room.' Cradling his arm in his free hand, looking angry, Nilsen went with Traynor and the duty solicitor. Watts reached for an item of Nilsen's belongings, held it up to the duty sergeant. 'I'm taking this for the next ten minutes or so.' Entering the interview room, he activated the PACE machine, getting an aggrieved look from Nilsen.

'You had *no* right to take my sling away, my arm is causing me considerable pain and I wish to lodge a formal complaint against you.'

The solicitor eyed Watts. 'Any response to what Mr Nilsen has just said?'

'No,' he snapped, taking the chair next to Traynor. 'Richard Conrad Nilsen, I'm interviewing you under caution in connection with an alleged sexual assault at approximately nine fifteen this morning on a path off Blackfoot Lane.' Watts' eyes moved over the smooth face opposite. Nielson's age was no longer a mystery. From a distance his clothes, build and demeanour might suggest late thirties, early forties at a push. In fact, he was just twenty-two years old and looking increasingly irrelevant to the skulls found in the vicinity of Blackfoot Trail. Despite his agreeing with Traynor on maintaining the investigative focus on all of the victims, Watts was now considering Nilsen as a possibility for Zoe Roberts' murder. 'Is there anything you'd like to say, Mr Nilsen?'

'Yes. There is. I did *not* assault that woman.' He pointed to his arm. 'I couldn't have.'

'We know you were in the area. Did you see any females this morning, Mr Nilsen?'

'Only *her*, walking her dog where I happened to be and which I don't deny. I'd hardly admit to it if I had done what she said.' He looked at the duty solicitor. 'And which I find personally insulting.'

Watts studied Nilsen. 'Tell us about this woman.'

'There's nothing to tell,' snapped Nilsen. 'I'd gone for a walk to take my mind off the pain I'm experiencing. I saw her. Admired her dog. That was the sum total of my engagement with her. She walked on and I went back to the road. I don't understand why she would level such an accusation at me. I'm not the kind of person to assault anybody. I've never had dealings with the police. You must know that.'

'What's the problem with your arm?'

'Cervical radiculopathy.'

'Sounds painful.'

'It *is*. Extremely.'

Watts slow-nodded. 'Are you on medication?'

'Yes.'

Watts allowed a small silence to build. 'For the benefit of the visual recording, would you demonstrate the limitation of your arm, Mr Nilsen?'

Nilsen looked at the solicitor who nodded. Sighing, he produced minimal movement, winced and sagged against his chair, his face contorted. '*Don't* ask me to do that again, because I won't and you can rely on my following up this issue with your superiors.'

'That's your right, Mr Nilsen. Do you regularly walk in that area?'

Nilsen shook his head. 'I've been there a couple of times at most.'

'When?'

Nilsen looked irritated. 'I don't remember! I don't plan walks. I tend to do them on my days off.' He jabbed the table several times. 'I want it on record that I totally deny everything this woman has accused me of. It's ridiculous.'

'Where do you work?'

'Greenway College in its administration department. What's that got to do with this farce?'

'You're not at work today?'

Nilsen rolled his eyes. 'It so happens it's my day off.'

'Were you at Blackfoot Trail early on the morning of Monday, the fifteenth of August?' Watts saw sudden wariness in Nilsen's eyes.

'What's that got to do with today?'

'Just answer the question.'

Nilsen looked at the solicitor again, got another nod. 'No, I wasn't. That was the day I returned from holiday in Crete.'

'What time did you arrive back in Birmingham?'

'In the late afternoon. About five p.m.'

'You're sure about that, Mr Nilsen?'

'*Yes.*'

Watts' eyes were fixed on him. 'How did you injure your arm?'

'I tripped carrying my suitcase inside my house.'

'We'll want to see printed confirmation of your travel arrangements.'

Nilsen's eyes flicked to Traynor and back. 'Why?'

'As proof of your whereabouts on that particular day.'

Nilsen's head spun to his solicitor. 'Do I have to provide those details?'

The solicitor gazed amicably at Watts. 'Perhaps you'd outline your interest in that particular Monday, DI Watts?'

'No problem. Early on the morning of Monday the fifteenth of August, a male answering Mr Nilsen's description and wearing a light-coloured sling, was seen at Blackfoot Trail.' He regarded Nilsen for a few seconds. 'Also, that same morning, a young woman was attacked and killed there. What do you have to say about that, Mr Nilsen?'

Nilsen said nothing. He looked shocked. Watts waited,

wondering how long Nilsen would stick with his return-from-Crete story. He saw canniness arrive in the dark eyes. Not long at all, by the look of it. A phrase of Judd's came into his head. Watts was now betting his pension that Nilsen knew what had occurred at Blackfoot Trail, the hole he was digging for himself and was now weighing up two options: sexual assault charge, or sexual assault-plus-murder?

His words came quickly. 'I've confused the dates. It was the Sunday afternoon I returned from Crete.' He still looked worried. As well he might, thought Watts.

'Tell us what you were doing at Blackfoot Trail on that Monday.'

Nilsen stuck with denial. 'I was *not* there that day.'

Watts slow-nodded. 'In which case, you've got a twin. The description we've got fits you and him to a tee.' His eyes fixed on Nilsen, he knew there was zero chance of his murdering three adults, two of them male and removing their heads when he was twelve years old, but Nilsen was a sex attacker and there was an agreed sexual motive for Zoe Roberts' murder. Watts made a quick note to get Merriman in to look at a video of database images, including Nilsen's to see if she could identify him. No fan of technology, Watts made an exception for VIPER which would save Merriman the ordeal of facing her attacker. 'Let's get back to this morning. You've admitted seeing and speaking to a woman whilst walking along a path off Blackfoot Lane.'

'So, it's a criminal offence now to be pleasant to somebody? Is this a police state?'

'She says that you exposed yourself to her, made comments about her physical build and that you pulled down her top, exposing her upper body.'

Nilsen stared at him. 'I did no such thing! If she said that, she's got some kind of problem.' He tapped the solicitor's notepad. 'I hope you're getting all of this. I totally refute this woman's accusations. If I had the urge to do something like that, which I *don't*, I couldn't have. You've seen my physical limitation.' The solicitor calmly wrote. Nilsen leant to Watts, his arm held close to his chest. 'I want some water. I want to *leave*.'

There was a quiet knock on the door. It opened. Watts spoke. 'For the benefit of both recordings, PC Chloe Judd has entered the interview room.' She came to the table, placed a single sheet face down in front of Watts and left. He picked it up, turned it over, looked again at the e-fit supplied by Townsend, passed it to Traynor. Little wonder Nilsen had looked familiar. Watts was satisfied that this twenty-two-going-on-forty-something college employee had been at the trail on the morning Zoe Roberts was killed and that he had also attacked Merriman in broad daylight this morning, in an area with a strong police presence. All of which told him that Nilsen was an impulsive, opportunistic sexual offender with a raft of problems. He glanced at Nilsen's mulish face. There wasn't enough yet to charge him with Roberts' murder, but he was raising him to person of interest.

'It's hot in here. I'll get somebody to fetch you that water.' Watts stood, walked steadily across the room to the door then turned. 'Mr *Nilsen?*'

Startled, Nilsen looked up, both arms rising smoothly, his hands closing on the blue squash ball Watts had sent travelling at speed towards him. Watts came back to the table. 'Richard Nilsen, I'm charging you with the sexual assault of Alicia

Merriman . . .' Nilsen said nothing. Watts brought the interview to a close. He looked down at him. 'That's not the only trouble you're in as far as I'm concerned. I'll see that you get that water.'

THE PACE MACHINE WAS dormant, Nilsen gone. The duty solicitor watched as Watts gathered papers, glanced across at Traynor and smiled. 'A nice theatrical turn, Detective Inspector, but I'm wondering what Nilsen's solicitor will say about it when he appoints one.'

'I'll leave you to wonder about it. Nilsen sexually assaulted a woman this morning, and we have a witness who's placed him at Blackfoot Trail on the morning of Monday the fifteenth of August, the day a woman was murdered there. That's all that interests me.'

Watts and Traynor came into the office. 'What do you think?' asked Watts.

Traynor nodded. 'Nilsen assaulted Merriman.'

Watts reached for the phone, tapped the number of Nilsen's college. After a brief exchange he ended the call. 'Confirmation that Nilsen was in the UK on Monday, the fifteenth of August. He called into the college in the afternoon. Not good at constructing an alibi, is he?' Watts' hands slapped the table. 'Right. He's now a person of interest in the Zoe Roberts homicide but we need more evidence than an e-fit.'

'I cannot agree. How is he linked to the other three victims? His assault of Merriman has zero commonality with the murder of Zoe Roberts, except for its geographical proximity. That, in my view, is not enough to pursue him for the Roberts homicide.'

Watts eyed him, words that had been at the edge of his thinking for days now surfacing. 'I've got to say this to you, Traynor.

We've been searching for linkage for days and it's got us nowhere.'

'You must do what you think is right. I am saying you are wrong about Nilsen. He's an opportunistic offender against women. Whilst not in any way minimising what he did to Merriman, the extreme violence used against Zoe Roberts is of a massively different order. As a criminologist I'm saying that to link the two makes no sense.'

'I'm changing the focus of this investigation.'

Traynor regarded him for several seconds, then reached for his backpack and headed to the door and out.

Watts sat heavily, watching him go, recognising the soundness of Traynor's reasoning. He had to hear it. Now there was a case against Nilsen for the Merriman assault but not for the Zoe Roberts murder. Feeling worn out, he looked down at Judd's report of her informal interview with Alec Prentiss, pulled it towards him and was halfway through it when she came in.

'I've just seen Dr Traynor,' she said. 'He doesn't look too happy. What's happened?'

'Nothing.' He held up the report. 'What's your problem with Prentiss?'

She rolled her eyes. 'Where to start? I really tried to get him talking about his sister's life but it was like packing smoke. My opinion? He's a rich man's son, the spoiled centre of his parents' universe, although he's got zero time for them. He and his sister are enough to make anybody think twice about having kids.' She pointed at the report. 'I didn't get much of what you asked for and what is there I had to drag out of him. I just couldn't get on his wavelength. He was all over the place.' She looked at Watts. 'If you'd been there, you'd know. He's contradictory, unsympathetic to his family, too busy bleating about his own upset, *plus* his view of himself is so wrong it's laughable. He thinks he's an entrepreneur but he's never spent a day out there, earning his own living. He should try it, some time. He's your typical millennial. He thinks he's special and different and entitled and he's totally unrealistic about life, the world. He's lucky to have his parents supporting him.'

'I'll take that as a "don't like".' Watts put the report down. 'I know you've got no time for that family but as police officers we accept what people in trouble tell us and we keep our own attitudes out of it.'

She frowned, impatient. 'But some of what he told me didn't make sense.'

'Don't you think you're being a bit tough on him? He, that whole family, is under extreme stress. Maybe you had expectations of him today because of our prior visit to the family.'

She sat back, looking vexed.

'You have to stay objective, Judd. Put personal attitudes and expectations to one side.'

She reddened. 'All he did was complain about how he's treated by his parents, about their not letting him take a week off work for emotional exhaustion, and not *one* word about how they're feeling. He's a selfish bastard! I admit I wasn't keen on the mother. Now, I feel sorry for her. And the father.'

Watts pushed the report towards her. 'It's detailed and to the point, but you don't need me to tell you that you can't include phrases like "self-centred arse".' He sighed. She was exhausting in all sorts of ways and today he'd had enough. 'I've told you, lose the chip.' He reached for his keys. 'I'm off to see Justin Rhodes' family.' He saw her mouth open. 'On my own!'

TWENTY

Watts came through the small gate, raised his hand to the Rhodes family standing at their front door and walked to his vehicle, his phone to his ear. He ended the call. His third effort to contact Christian Roberts had gone straight to message, no doubt to be ignored like the other two.

He got inside his car, took a breath. It had been a tough three-quarters of an hour, but not because they'd made it that way. He was often surprised by the courage of people in their situation. Justin's sister had arrived and they had all talked freely about him, smiled during the telling of one or two anecdotes, answered all of Watts' questions as best they could. Watts reflected that for every grieving individual or family there was no predicting how they'd respond to news of the kind he'd just delivered. The Rhodes family had accepted it calmly with some tears. They would have been expecting it at some time, maybe reached that stage of grieving which allowed them some acceptance. Watts knew first-hand about accepting loss so you could drag yourself out of its pit. It was a long road, your foot slipped, but over time it got easier. He'd asked them if they knew of anyone who might have wanted to harm Justin. They'd said no. Asked if they thought his work as a reporter might have put him at risk; they'd been adamant that that wasn't the case, that Justin had never so much as hinted to them that what he did at the newspaper carried personal risk, had never styled himself as any kind of press vigilante. Finally, he had asked if Justin had mentioned receiving an offer of inform-ation or help, maybe, something to do with a new job? No, they said. Nothing like that. They had told Watts how proud they were of Justin. Neither parents nor sister had mentioned any problems he was having with colleagues or anyone else in his life and they'd spoken very positively about his boss, Jess Meredith. From them Watts had got a real sense of the living, breathing Justin. Very different from the meeting he and Judd had had with the Prentiss family, the father mostly silent, the mother effusive, the brother contributing next to nothing. Judd hadn't fared any better today where Alec Prentiss was concerned. They'd get him in again and Watts would question him.

His phone rang. It was Brophy. 'Sir.'

'Where are you?'

'I've just left the Rhodes family home. I'll be at headquarters in about twenty minutes—'

'Come straight to my office.'

WATTS ARRIVED IN RECEPTION looking and feeling overheated. The officer on duty pointed. 'Christian Roberts, Sarge.'

Watts looked at the pacing fortyish, heavyset male in a formal suit and striped tie who stopped pacing and looked back at him. Watts went to him, hand extended. 'Mr Roberts, DI Watts, SIO of your wife's murder investigation. We appreciate your coming in.'

Roberts gave a brief handshake. 'You want to talk to me about my wife's death.'

'Yes, in two minutes.' He turned to the duty officer. 'Show Mr Roberts into the small interview room. Get him whatever he wants to drink.' Leaving Roberts frowning after him, Watts headed upstairs to Brophy's office, knocked and went inside. 'Sir, Christian Roberts is waiting downstairs for me—'

'About time he made himself available. What's your thinking where he's concerned?'

'Mixed, until I talk to him about his relationship with his wife. I also want his account of his whereabouts during the last couple of weeks and why it's taken him several days to contact us. I've requested details of his movements between Brussels and the UK during the last ten days and I'll be asking him about his relationship with a work colleague.'

'Oh?'

'There's a possibility he could be involved with one of the other partner's wives.'

'Sounds hopeful, if a little late in the day.' He looked away from Watts. 'Bernard, there's something you need to know.' Watts knew from his face that whatever Brophy had on his mind, he wasn't going to like it. 'As from tomorrow, I'm giving you a maximum of one more week on this investigation. If there's no significant progress I'll be requesting the chief constable bring in somebody else to run it.'

Watts wasn't surprised. Hearing it was a shock. 'We're making progress. We've got a person of interest for Zoe Roberts.' He told the chief about Nilsen.

The chief regarded him. 'Evidence?'

'E-fit identification.'

'It's not enough.'

'If we need more, we'll get it.'

Brophy looked back at him. 'You need more.'

'What about Traynor and Judd if I have to hand over the case? They've given a lot to the investigation so far.'

'They'll continue under whoever replaces you.' There was a brief silence. 'I have no choice, Bernard. All I'm hearing is *more* remains being recovered and no real progress, the whole case a growing mayhem.'

Watts looked down at him. 'If remains are there, it's our job to locate and investigate them.'

Brophy stood. 'I *know* that. I also know that it's your job as SIO to get a grip on whatever a case throws at you. You're working long hours but I'm not seeing any results and the media knows it.'

Watts considered several possible responses clamouring to be said. He went with one of them. 'You know what we're facing. Four homicides. Four lives to explore. A hell of a lot of work for my team in this heat—'

'And *I've* got the chief constable on the phone at least twice a day, demanding results because of the sky-high press interest. Right now, he'd settle for an indication of real progress, but if you can't make that happen during the next few days, that's it, Bernard. You're finished.'

Watts left the office, went down the stairs processing Brophy's words. He'd considered asking him what he thought he and the team might do that they hadn't done so far. Or, more relevant, what anybody taking over might do to bring the case to a quick resolution. Pointless questions. Brophy hadn't got any answers. The best he could come up with was the solution of desperation.

New broom. Coming into reception, he looked towards the interview room, which was empty, then at the officer on the desk.

'Where is he? Where's Christian Roberts?'

The officer looked up. 'He said he'd be back in half an hour, Sarge.'

'Let me know as soon as he is!' Watts pounded the corridor to his office, fed up with being sidelined.

TWENTY-ONE

They watched the sleek, black Mercedes slide into a parking space and the well-dressed male get out of it. 'What do you think of Christian Roberts, Sarge?'

Watts turned away. 'What's there to think?'

Judd pointed. 'Would you say he looks like somebody whose wife was brutally murdered only days ago, because I don't. Hey, look! Dr Traynor's outside. He's giving Roberts a once-over.'

The desk phone shrilled. Watts went to it. 'Yeah, we've seen him. Dr Traynor's just arrived. Ask him to show Roberts upstairs to Interview Room Three.' He put down the phone, reached for his interview notes, aware that Judd was looking at him.

'Can I come?' she asked.

'Yes. I've got a job for you.'

Looking eager, she followed him. As they approached the interview room, he opened the door of the room next to it, showed her inside and pointed at a dull rectangle of one-way glass, a small desk below it. 'This is where you'll be.'

She looked around the room, grimaced at the observational glass, then up at Watts. 'I haven't participated in a single formal interview yet. Why can't I be part of this one?'

'Roberts is here voluntarily. It won't be recorded and I need you here, watching, listening and learning, if that's possible.' He jabbed a button below the glass. It brightened. She went to it, stared through it to the interview room next door. 'There's pads and pens here,' he said, opening a drawer of the desk.

She dragged out a chair and sat. 'All I ever hear on this case is, "Follow me, do this, don't do that, write this down".'

He headed for the door. 'And why do you think that is?'

Reddening, she looked away from him. 'You don't trust me. Maybe if I was one of "the lads", it would be different.'

He turned, pointed at her. 'Don't you lay that card on me. I didn't choose you for this investigation but you're on my team, which means I'll do all I can to help you show that you've got what it takes.'

'I *have.*'

He looked at his watch then at her. 'It's not that simple. If I let you have too much rope on a big homicide case like this, it would be unfair to you and it could jeopardize any result we get.' He eyed her. 'But we already know that, don't we?'

She flushed again.

'Watch, listen, write. That's all I want you to do.'

Movement beyond the glass alerted him to Traynor's arrival, followed by Christian Roberts. Leaving Judd to it, he headed for the room next door, took the chair next to Traynor, giving Christian Roberts a direct look. 'We met earlier, Mr Roberts. Detective Inspector Watts, SIO of your wife's murder investigation.' Roberts made no response. 'This is Dr William Traynor, criminologist, who's assisting our investigation. We appreciate you coming voluntarily to headquarters for this informal interview. You are not under arrest and you may leave at any time.'

'I know,' responded Roberts coolly. 'Ask whatever you want so that I can do that.'

Watts' eyes fixed on him. 'During the several days since your wife's murder you made no effort to contact us or her family.' He glanced at the open file in front of Traynor. 'I left three messages on your mobile phone, requesting you to contact me, Mr Roberts. Your deceased wife's family also left messages. Why didn't you respond to any of them?'

Roberts gave him a direct look. 'A couple of days prior to my wife's death I left my office in Brussels and flew to Edinburgh for a few days' leave. I've been ignoring my phone.' He reached into an inside pocket of his jacket, brought out small pieces of paper which he placed on the table. Watts looked down at Lufthansa plane tickets. 'They're proof of what I'm telling you. My being here without representation should indicate good faith on my part. There are just two things I want to say. First, I did not kill my wife. Second, I understand that an officer who is part of your investigation into my wife's murder visited my firm and obtained information about my personal life via subterfuge.'

An image of Judd's face flashed inside Watts' head. 'The officer in question lacks experience and has been spoken to. Have you got anything you want to tell us about your private life, Mr Roberts?'

'Yes, but once I've said it, I won't be answering any questions. As I've already stated, I did *not* kill my wife. We'd been separated for over twelve months. That situation was by mutual agreement. It suited both of us. As to other aspects of my personal life, I am involved with a female colleague who is aware that I have come here.' He stood. 'That's all I'm prepared to say at this point.' He reached inside his jacket again, pulled out a business card and one folded A4 sheet, placed both on the table. 'That's my position statement. If you need to speak with me again, it will be with legal representation.'

Watts stood. 'We'll take a look at what you've just made available but before you leave there are three names which we'd like you to consider. The first is Annette Barlow.' Roberts made no response. 'The second is Daniel Broughton . . . and the third, Justin Rhodes.'

'I've never heard of any of them and I'm leaving.' They watched him go, the door slowly closing on him.

THEY WERE BACK IN the office, Judd staring moodily ahead. Watts tapped the sheet left by Roberts. 'He categorically denies killing his wife. He says he likes the Prentiss family, describes them as nice people.' She rolled her eyes. 'He goes on to describe his relationship with his wife. According to him, it took him eighteen months from when they got married to realize' – he sat up – 'that it was a mistake. Listen to this, Traynor. "I left when I could no longer deal with the relationship. Zoe was bright, clever, ambitious but also extremely self-centred, moody, impatient and demanding." He says she kept pressuring him to push her progress at the firm, demanding a partnership, despite his telling her he couldn't make that happen.' Watts pointed. 'He's alleging a couple of incidents when Zoe Roberts attacked him physically, threw things at him. This is a new view of her.'

Judd sent him a sidelong glance. 'Am *I* surprised? *Not*.'

'We don't know enough about Christian Roberts to accept what he's saying,' said Traynor.

Watts was re-reading Roberts' statement. 'True. For all we

know, *he* could be the problem, a control freak who resented her being independent, made her life a misery, but he's given us a picture of her which is a million miles from what we got from her parents.' He looked up at Judd. 'I know. You said the mother was overly positive and unrealistic. Either that's how the parents actually felt about her—'

'Or, they're compensating,' said Traynor. 'Compensating for what they really knew. What else does he say?'

'That he would regret the Prentiss family becoming aware of his perceptions and experience of Zoe but that it needs to be said . . . and he goes on that he had little contact with his wife during the preceding twelve months, that the last time he saw her was about six months ago, at the Solihull office where she worked. The impression he gained at the time was that she had more money available to her than he would have anticipated.' He looked up. 'He doesn't say what his impression was based on, but it sounds to me like another line of inquiry for us.'

Hearing Christian Roberts' words, Judd said, 'Get Damian Blunt to check the firm's accounts, Sarge. She might have been helping herself.' She found herself under scrutiny. 'Just saying.'

'Judd, Blunt is a *lawyer*. If he knows half of what Roberts has told us, he's probably doing it right now.' Watts looked at Traynor. 'What's your view of Christian Roberts now we've met him and got this information?'

Traynor shook his head. 'I'm not seeing him as the killer of our other three victims, if that's what you're asking. Why would he?'

'I'm not ruling him out of anything until we know more

about him. I still don't get why the mother gave us that spiel about Zoe.'

'Because it's what families *do*,' snapped Judd. 'They say good stuff about people they want *in* the family and rubbish about those they don't.' She got up and headed for the door. 'And I was right about Christian Roberts having a thing with Fiona Webb . . . although I shouldn't have got the information the way I did.'

Watts waited until the door closed on her. 'Moving on for the sake of my sanity, this is Judd's report of a talk she had with Alec Prentiss yesterday.' He pushed it across the table. Traynor reached for it, slid it into a file, pushed the file into his backpack. Watts looked at him.

'I want a check of the Merc Roberts drove here.'

'I already did it. It's a rental car. He got it three days ago.' Watts studied him. 'Something on your mind, Traynor?' He was about to repeat his question when Traynor got to his feet, went to the board and began writing.

He tracked the words. '"What is motive?" That's not even a question as far as I'm concerned.'

'Then it needs to be. Motive is one of the reasons we're struggling with this case. We haven't identified what it is.'

Watts stared across at him. 'Yes, we have. We agreed these are most likely sexually motivated homicides—'

'I've reconsidered.'

Watts watched open-mouthed as Traynor pointed to what he'd written. 'I had no solid reason to doubt it as a motive for the Zoe Roberts and Annette Barlow homicides and I still didn't when the remains of Broughton and Rhodes came to light. I've worked on enough homicide cases to know the extremes of deviant sexual behaviour directed at both genders.'

Watts waited. 'So? What's your problem?'

'I was slow to see it.' He tapped names. 'Broughton. Barlow. Rhodes. Roberts. All found in the same geographical area, all four decapitated, three of their heads buried there.' He turned to Watts. '*Place*, plus *behaviour*. Given the huge risks involved, *both* were hugely important to whoever killed them.'

'I don't get where you're going with this.'

'These weren't random sex killings. I think their killer knew all four.'

Watts went to the Smartboard, called up data, sent it flying across the big screen. 'In case you need reminding, Traynor, have a look through this lot . . . at this . . . and *this*. We've spent hours talking to the families, other people who knew them, reading the files, looking for a common link. If what you're saying is right, why haven't we found it? I'll tell you why. There *isn't* one.'

'There is. There has to be.'

'Says *you*,' snapped Watts.

Traynor shook his head. 'No. What he did to them and where he did it, says so. He killed them and kept them together in that one place for a reason.'

Watts sat heavily. 'All the cold cases I've investigated have shown me that that's what repeaters do.'

'Did all of the victims in those cold cases differ as widely as ours? Not just in age and gender, but backgrounds, education, work, lifestyle?' Watts didn't respond. 'These victims didn't know each other but their killer had to know them, perhaps only indirectly. Which might explain why we can't find him anywhere in their lives.'

'All it's saying to me right now is that after hours of being out there in thirty degrees, following up everything we can, we've got nothing and I'm on my way out of this investigation.'

'You're wrong about us having nothing. We know how each of these victims lived their lives.' Traynor came to the table, placed his hands on it, looked down at Watts. 'Zoe Roberts: not the positive personality portrayed by her family. Selfish, demanding, money-hungry. Annette Barlow: sex worker. Daniel Broughton and his utter disregard for the rights of his neighbours.' He saw Watts' mouth open. 'I know what you're about to say: that those behaviours lack equivalence, but the victims' outlooks on life, their attitudes, the way they lived, were similar, don't you *see?*'

Watts shook his head. 'Where does Justin Rhodes fit into that? That newspaper woman you spoke to described him as a decent young bloke. A regular boy scout.'

Traynor went to the Smartboard, pulled up data, pointed. 'Jess Meredith told me that on the day he died he'd been planning to write an article on two Birmingham disappearances.' He looked at Watts. '*Two.* How many disappearances does this case have, prior to Rhodes' own? *Two.*'

Watts stared at him. 'You're expecting me to redirect the whole investigation in its final week, on the basis of a vague theory that—'

'That's exactly what I'm saying. I think it's possible somebody made a judgement about them, that they deserved to die.' Deserved. The word resonated inside Watts' head. Traynor continued. 'I think their killer has a lot of problems, not the least of which is probably a God complex. I think there could be more remains at that scene—'

Watts was on his feet. 'I don't know about any God complex but if there *are* more, I won't be investigating them.' He stared at Traynor, a ghost of a suspicion surfacing. 'You've got another victim inside your head and I know who she is! You want to look for her in that damn place!' He watched colour ebb from Traynor's face.

'While Claire was still alive, there were references in the local Oxford press to her charity work, to the fact that she was a wealthy woman. She got a couple of calls from a male she didn't know, offering her an investment opportunity. She declined. He never contacted her again.'

Exasperated, Watts said, 'That's what happens! Well-off people get targeted. What's that got to do with our case?'

Traynor came to him. 'Because we know that Annette Barlow, Daniel Broughton and Justin Rhodes each received some kind of offer. Claire was another victim in this series. You have to include her in this investigation.'

Watts shook his head. 'No. I don't. Sorry to say this, Traynor, but I think you're losing all perspective. As far as this investigation goes, I'm on borrowed time, but while I'm still in charge, I won't let what happened to your wife, your family, hijack it.'

TWENTY-TWO

Monday 22 August. Four p.m.

Watts eyed the files he'd taken out of the cabinet which were now covering the table. Files full of reports on investigative actions so far. Years-old files on each of the victims.

The door swung open and Judd came inside. She stopped. 'What's going on?'

'I'm going up to the squad room. When I come back, I want a detailed report from you of that wine shop visit waiting for me. I *won't* ask you again.' He pointed at the files. 'When you've finished it, get started on these. Start reading every page in every file and list any fact, any inference, *anything* that strikes you as something we might have missed. Something which might kickstart this investigation.'

Judd looked at the files, then at him. 'Just me? It'll take ages.'

'I'll work on them as well. I've got a week left on this case.'

She looked up at him, shocked. '*What?* Who said?'

He headed for the door. 'Get started.'

CHONG CHECKED THE LINES of post-mortem information she had just entered, hit 'Print' and stretched both arms as the printer did its thing, then headed across the PM suite to her locker.

Reaching inside for a small cosmetics bag, she raised her voice. 'Igor? I'm going upstairs for a few minutes!' Getting a muffled response, she headed out of the PM suite and one floor up to the ladies' room. Going inside, she opened the bag, took out a few items. She and Watts had a date later. Not the going-out kind. More the stay-in-I'll-cook-you-dinner kind. Which was exactly what she needed. She frowned at her face in the mirror. Mascara and lip gloss applied, she considered her reflection, took out a small hairbrush and gave her short, black hair some energetic swipes as the door opened. She glanced at the small figure standing there.

'Hi—' She dropped the brush, went quickly to the door. 'What on earth's the matter? What's wrong . . .? No, Chloe. Don't go.' She reached out, felt the tremor in the slender arm, lowered her voice. 'Whatever it is, you can tell me.'

Judd shook her head, pressing the back of her hand to her nose and mouth, tears sliding. 'Stay right there.' Chong went quickly to a cubicle, emerging with a tissue. 'Here.'

Judd took it, wiped her face. 'I'm in the worst trouble.'

'Oh?'

'DI Watts wants my notes of a visit I did. He's been asking for them for days and I don't want to give them to him because I'm already in trouble with him, but if I do, things will get really bad for me, but if I don't . . .' She bowed her head, sobbed. 'It's all a big *mess*.'

Chong picked up the cosmetics bag, placed a firm hand on Judd's arm. 'We can't talk in here. Just a minute.' Going to the door, she opened it, looked out, then gestured to Judd. 'Come on.' She quickly led her downstairs and into the PM suite where she pointed to a chair, taking one herself. 'Now, what's this about, Chloe?' She watched more large tears slide.

After a minute or two, Judd spoke, eyes averted. 'I went to this wine shop where Annette Barlow used to work. To speak to the manager. He worked there at the time she disappeared so obviously Sarge regards him as a key witness.'

Chong gave her an encouraging nod. 'It sounds like you were given an important investigative job.'

The blonde head jerked upwards. 'Has he said anything to you about it?'

'No.'

'I made a mess of things.'

Chong leant towards her. 'That's not a disaster. You're just starting out. What you do is, you tell DI Watts what the problem is and—'

Judd was on her feet. 'You don't understand! I *can't*. He's already mad at me for something else. He'll throw me off the team. Off the investigation. What happened at that wine shop is just what he's looking for to get rid of me!'

'Listen to me, Chloe. I've known DI Watts for a long time. Yes, he can come across as gruff, offhand, especially when he's under pressure, but whatever's happened, you need to tell him, not only because he's the officer in charge, but also because he's one of the kindest, fairest men I know. He'll understand. He'll do whatever he can for you, trust me.' Chong gazed at the mascara-streaked face, feeling suddenly uneasy. 'Tell me what happened at this wine shop.'

'I can't.'

'Chloe, I'm getting a strong indication that whatever's

worrying you, it's something DI Watts should know about.' Judd wept. Chong studied the young face, thinking how convenient it must be to weep with such abandon and still look good. 'Come on, Chloe. You've made a start. You might as well tell me the rest.'

Judd wiped her eyes, folded her arms tight against herself. 'The man I mentioned, the manager of the wine shop, he . . . he . . . he was threatening towards me.'

Chong's brows met. 'Threatening? How, exactly?'

'Sexually.'

Chong stopped the swift anger from registering on her face. 'Then you report him. There are procedures—'

'I can't do that.' Judd's tone was flat, uncompromising. 'OK. I'll tell you about it and you'll get what I'm saying. His name is Harry Josephs. Did I say that he manages the shop? I wanted to get as much information as I could from him, to give to DI Watts. To help our case. It took me a while to realize how Josephs kind of manipulated the situation when I was there. How thick is that? He didn't force me to go into the room at the back' – Chong's anger was climbing – 'he suggested it and . . . I went. Plus, he didn't actually touch me, because that's when I realized what was going on.'

'None of that matters, Chloe. It's irrelevant. You need to file a complaint against him—'

'I *can't.*' Tears spilled again. '*I* touched *him.* I grabbed hold of . . . him. I hit him. He could make a case for assault against *me*! If I lose my job I'll have nothing. No money. I won't be able to afford to stay in my flat . . .'

Chong reached for her hands, held them firmly. 'Chloe, listen to me. You can take this as far as you want and, in my view, you should, but it's your decision. Have you told anyone else about it? Your family?' Judd shook her head. 'It's important that you do. You need their support.'

Judd stood. 'I've got to make a start on the case files. Find something to move our case on.'

Chong watched her go to the door, her head down. 'Chloe, trust me, you'll need to do a lot of talking about this before you feel better.' She went to her, reached out her hand. 'I understand that it's difficult but confiding in your family, somebody you trust, will help. It will give you a sense of control over what's happened.' She saw the smooth forehead crease. 'Whatever you decide to do about this man, *please* don't keep what he did to yourself.'

Judd looked up at her. Her next words were heart-breaking.

WATTS TOOK THE WASHED plate from Chong. 'And Traynor and I are at loggerheads because he's changed his mind about the motive in our case. He's demanding another search of the scene.'

She passed him another plate. 'That was a really lovely dinner. Have you considered getting a dishwasher?'

'What for? There's just me here a lot of the time and on the odd occasion when there's a few things left, Mrs Donovan sees to them.'

'It sounds like you've had a hard day.'

'Yeah. Like most of them since this case started but Brophy's decided it won't be my problem for much longer.'

'Oh?'

'I've got one week max, before he replaces me with somebody out-of-city.'

She stared up at him. 'That's so unfair. Nobody could have worked harder, longer hours since it started.'

He slid plates into the cupboard. 'You're making Brophy's case for him. Hard work. No real results. I'm starting a sweep of all the files to see if we've missed anything. I put Judd on to it earlier and she's mardy as hell at having to do it. She doesn't think it's "real" police work.' He shrugged. 'I've had enough, Connie. Whoever takes over can pursue Nilsen as a suspect for the Roberts murder. Traynor's theory is that the murders are the work of somebody with a God complex who knew something about each of the victims, that sex isn't the motive. Our discussion ended on bad terms but I've had time to think and I might consider going along with the idea, during these last few days, because I can't think of any alternative.'

'How is he?'

He looked at her. 'My honest opinion? He's falling apart. Not only is he convinced his wife's murder is connected to our investigation, he believes her remains are at that scene.'

'Why would he think that?'

'This is Traynor we're talking about. He doesn't need a why where his wife's death is concerned. He's obsessed with it.'

'Have you considered that he might be right?'

'No. This investigation doesn't need two of us losing it.'

'Coffee?' she asked. He nodded, draping the tea towel over the cold radiator. Chong measured scoops into the cafetière. 'How is PC Judd getting on?'

'Don't ask, unless you want me to have indigestion all night.

This morning I told her I wanted a report which I'd already asked for umpteen times. I still haven't got it. In fact, I've hardly seen her. As soon as she arrives in the morning, I'm going to have it out with her.'

She turned to him. 'Tell me how she's doing generally.'

'She's made one or two mistakes, but she's bright, she's full of ideas and she's a hard worker.'

'Does she know that's what you think?'

'She will when I do her first appraisal with her. Her non-stop questions drive me nuts, but she probably knows that by now.'

'I saw her earlier today. In the ladies' room. She was very upset.'

He watched her pour milk into cups. 'What about?' He raised his large hands. 'Unless it's something female and not my department, thanks all the same.'

Chong leant against a worksurface waiting for water to heat. 'Leaving aside your antediluvian tendency to maintain impermeable male–female divisions, I can help you where Chloe is concerned, but first I want you to tell me what you know about her.'

He frowned. 'I just told you.'

'I mean, her background. Her life.'

He shrugged. 'She's told me she wanted to join the force since she was about six and that she followed murder cases in the press from about the same age. That's another thing. I'm not sure I believe any of it. As far as the job is concerned, she's a bit too quick with the theorizing, seeing the worst in people, but she's smart. If she listens and learns, she's got all the makings of a good officer. Like I said, she's full of ideas. The only trouble is, she never lets up. She tries too hard.'

'Would you like to know why Chloe tries so hard?'

He went to her, looked down at her face, traced his thick forefinger slowly, gently down the soft curve of her cheek. 'Go on,' he whispered.

'She's desperate to belong, Bernard.'

He frowned. 'She does belong. She's part of this investigation. For longer than I'll be, by the look of things.'

'Outside of work, Chloe has nobody to support her when times get hard. The only money she has is what she earns, so she doesn't have much, if any, security. She can't afford to lose her job.'

He frowned. 'What's all this about money, security? What about her family? She knows that if she's got a problem, she can come to me, as her SIO.'

Chong looked up at him. 'Would you like to know why Chloe has such a huge need to belong?'

'Go on.'

'She grew up in care from when she was six years old.'

He stared at her. 'What?'

'She went into foster care, a place which wasn't good for her, then to another which was better, followed by a third where she stayed. She has no contact with any of her birth family. She did extremely well at secondary school, joined the volunteer police cadets at fourteen. At eighteen she started her police training. Her last foster carer is ill now, so Chloe chooses not to take any problems she might have to her. What else? She rents two rooms in a large house converted to multi-occupancy, which she tells me is very nice.'

Watts looked at Chong. 'Poor little sod.'

She shook her head. 'Chloe Judd is a success story, Bernard. She didn't say why she came to be in care and I didn't ask, but she's got determination and she's making her way in the job she's always wanted, as part of your team. Coping on her own at just twenty, making a life for herself.' She placed her hands against his chest. 'I remember what I was like at nineteen, twenty. At university, as though it was a right, supported and surrounded by family who loved me and wanted the best for me. You come from a big family. You've told me how important that was to you. Chloe's never had what we've had. By the way, I've asked PC Jones to have a look at her car. She's worried about it.'

'Why didn't she tell me all of this?'

'Because she's fiercely independent and desperate to do well in your team.'

'I'll talk to her.'

'Before you do, there's something else you need to know. About a visit she made to a wine shop.'

'That's the report I've been chasing her for. What's the problem?' He followed her to the sitting room and the sofa. The cat leapt for his lap as soon as he sat.

'She told me about the man you asked her to go and see.'

'The manager, Harry Josephs.'

'Yes. Chloe is terrified that she'll lose her place on your team and her job if she tells you what happened to her there.' She paused. 'Harry Josephs made a sexual advance to her.'

Watts was on his feet, the cat airborne. 'He *what*?'

'Chloe hasn't told you about it because she thinks she was to blame.'

'She knows better than—'

'She's worried. She thinks Josephs might make a counter-accusation against her for physical assault.'

He stared at her. 'What did she do?'

'She grabbed his genitals, following it up with a smart chop across his throat.'

Watts paced the room. 'The *scumbag*! I'll bloody have him!'

'Bernard, listen. You don't know what Chloe wants. You need to think about that, before you say or do anything.'

He sat, his big hands bunched together, staring ahead. 'Yeah. I will.'

TWENTY-THREE

Tuesday 23 August. Ten a.m.

An enduring sense of dissatisfaction took Watts back to the bookshop the next morning. As on his previous visit, he found Edward Arnold occupied with customers. When the last had moved away, Watts walked over to him. 'Busy as ever, Mr Arnold?'

'Detective Inspector! Yes, but you won't hear me complaining.'

'I was passing and I thought I'd drop in. See if you've remembered anything since I was last here.'

Arnold looked disconcerted. 'Oh, dear. Did I say I'd think about it? I did very briefly after you left, but that was about it.'

The observations Watts had made during his previous visit here had told him something useful about the bookseller. He was a conformist, somebody who lived by the rules and had a critical eye for his neighbours. A person who judged. He glanced around. 'You've got a great business here. I can see that your customers trust you.'

Arnold looked uncertain. 'I hope so.'

Watts took a few steps away, turned. The strong sunlight streaming through the shop window glinted on Arnold's watch. 'Something's on my mind, Mr Arnold.'

'Oh?'

'What's bothering me is Daniel Broughton's visit here, shortly before he disappeared. I've got questions about it which aren't going away. Why did Broughton come in here *that* day, when he'd previously never set foot in the place? Why did he leave the way he did? I thought you might be able to help us out on that, seeing as you knew him.'

Arnold's face reddened. He shook his head. 'I *didn't* know him. Not to the degree I think you're implying.'

'I never "imply", Mr Arnold. Have you got any explanation for why Broughton was in here that day?'

'Only what he told me and I told you last time you were here, that he needed a book on house designs to show to a very demanding client.'

'I'd have thought an experienced property developer like Broughton would have plenty of that kind of stuff already.' Arnold didn't respond. 'Why did Broughton leave by the back way?'

Arnold raised his hands. 'I don't *know*. Actually, he could have left by the main door and the bell didn't ring.'

Not getting what he'd hoped for, Watts changed tack. 'Did you, the people around here, view him as trustworthy?'

Arnold appeared to give this some thought. 'His line of business was very different from mine, of course, but I'd say he was well enough regarded.'

Watts heard the careful endorsement. 'My impression is that he upset a few people around here because of the house he was building, his attitude to the Neighbourhood Watch.'

Arnold frowned at him. 'Please don't take what I said out of context, Detective Inspector. This suburb regards itself as a "village". Residents tend to stay for years and inevitably those kinds of small frictions occur.'

'There would have been speculation among residents following Broughton's disappearance? Some talk about what might have happened to him?'

'All I recall is everybody being mystified. We couldn't understand it.'

Watts lifted the cover of a book on the counter, let it drop. 'It never occurred to you or anybody else that Broughton's disappearance might be linked to something he was involved in? Somebody he'd upset?'

Arnold stared at him. 'You mean . . . something *illegal*?'

'Did any residents here have business or other dealings with him?'

The look on Arnold's face changed. 'Nothing which would have led to his being harmed, if that's what you're suggesting. He put some of his men on to a garden reconstruction for Penny Ainsworth, a near-neighbour of mine at the time, but that wasn't "business dealings" in the sense you're—'

'Tell me about it.'

Arnold shook his head. 'Detective Inspector, these are people I've known for years. What you're asking is making me uncomfortable.' Watts waited. Arnold sighed. 'Penny Ainsworth asked Broughton to remodel her garden. This would have been about twelve years ago, possibly more. She complained about cost, duration, the quality of the work. She accused Broughton of instructing his workers to dig deeper than was needed, simply to prolong the job and add to costs. That's it. That's all I can tell you. She still lives here. Ask her about it.'

'Who else didn't like Daniel Broughton?'

Arnold looked like he was doing some thinking. 'I recall he had a falling-out with another resident, David Winter. Winter was always complaining about Broughton parking his car and business vehicles on the roadside and allowing his employees to do the same, some of it opposite Winter's house. He went on about it to anyone who would listen. He suspected Broughton of doing it purposely. One day, Winter reversed out and into the side of Broughton's car. Broughton accused *him* of doing it on purpose. He was furious.'

'I dare say he was.'

Arnold was looking troubled. 'Detective Inspector, these were relatively minor fallings-out. I can't believe that an incident such as that had anything to do with Broughton's disappearance. Winter is a successful businessman and Penny Ainsworth is a small woman. How could she have done anything to . . .?' A quick ring and the door of the shop opened. Arnold's face lit up. 'Good morning, Marjorie.'

Watts turned to a shapely woman in a close-fitted, low-cut cream dress printed with red flowers. She came to them, leant on the counter and kissed Arnold on the cheek. Watts got a cloud of perfume, watched the look of embarrassed pleasure arrive on Arnold's face.

'Are you busy?' she murmured.

Arnold indicated Watts. 'This is the police officer I told you about. Detective Inspector, this is Marjorie Ellis, a friend of mine.'

The woman's brown eyes widened on Watts. 'You're here about the builder who disappeared. How *exciting*.'

'Did you know Daniel Broughton at all?'

'Sorry, no. I came here five years ago.'

'Do you know David Winter?'

'I know of him.'

'What about Penny Ainsworth?'

She grinned at Arnold. 'Oh, yes. I bought Penny's house when she downsized to a few roads away. When she showed me around the house and the garden, she went on and on about Broughton having cheated her over some landscaping work he'd carried out years before. She was still annoyed about it.' She grinned at Watts. 'I can't see Penny in the role of kidnapper or worse. Her problem is that she has great difficulty letting go of life's annoyances. Ask her ex-husband. He'll confirm it.'

'Marjorie,' murmured Arnold. 'You are talking to a police officer, you know.'

She looked back at Watts. 'Are you having any success with your case?'

'We're seeing progress.'

She looked at him, eyes shining. 'I've read about it in the newspapers, you and a criminologist investigating together. I find police work *so* interesting.' Hearing a subtle cough, she turned to Arnold. 'I know. Stop talking to the policeman and let him get on.' She leant on the counter again, looked up at him. 'Actually, I'm here with an invitation to lunch.' Seeing the wide smile arrive on Arnold's face, Watts looked away. The bookseller had got it bad. 'I'll pick you up at twelve thirty. Nice to have met you, Detective Inspector.' Arnold watched her leave.

Wanting the bookseller talking, Watts went with his gut. 'That looks serious.'

Arnold nodded. 'It is.'

'From what you said last time I was here, about being married years ago, I got the impression life suited you on your own.'

Arnold looked at him. 'Eighteen years of being alone is a long time and one divorce is enough for anybody, but then I met Marjorie.' He gave Watts a direct look. 'You want to know, so I'll tell you. My marriage was fine but there was one problem: Suzanne, my first wife, wanted children. I didn't.' He nodded. 'A big problem. We separated, got divorced, she met somebody else and they started a family.'

'So, everybody got what they wanted.'

Arnold reached for a stack of books. 'Is there anything else, Detective Inspector?'

Watts glanced at his notes. 'One last question. Did Broughton travel much?'

The shop door opened and Arnold smiled and nodded at the couple coming inside. He lowered his voice. 'I think he went to Spain fairly often, but he didn't ever talk to me about that. We weren't on those terms.'

Watts' eyes tracked the couple to shelves some way off. 'He never said anything to you in passing about any plans he had?'

Arnold shrugged. 'There was one time I recall him referring to "making himself scarce" for a while, or words like that. The impression I got was that it was something to do with a woman.'

'When was this?'

Arnold gave it some thought. 'I'd say a few months prior to his disappearance.'

'Did you tell the police at the time?'

'It never occurred to me that it was relevant. His comment

was a little "nudge-nudge". Broughton tended to brag, so I dismissed it.'

Watts headed for the door. He'd had enough of this case and Brophy could do what he liked with it. 'OK, Mr Arnold. If you think of anything else, ring me.'

'I'm as perplexed as you, Detective Inspector. It's a real mystery.'

Watts stepped outside the shop and closed the door, deep in thought at Arnold's last words. Inside his vehicle, he started the engine, his eyes fixed on the bookshop. 'I've never liked mysteries.'

HALF AN HOUR LATER, he was in the city centre, looking across the road at his destination, preoccupied with how to handle the next few minutes. He knew what he wanted to do. It could bring him a load of trouble. He'd been watching the place and the two men moving around inside it for about five minutes. It looked quiet. Crossing over, he headed to it, pushed open the door and walked the expanse of wood floor, his eyes going to the shop's high ceiling and its corners: one security camera positioned towards the door. He turned to where the two men were talking together. One was much younger than he'd expected. The one now walking away fitted the description of Harry Josephs. He glanced in Watts' direction, gave a professional smile.

'If you need any help or advice, sir, just ask Dom.'

Watts followed him the length of the long counter, blocked his exit from it. The face beneath the styled hair looked startled. 'Tell Dom to get lost.'

Josephs' brows shot upwards. 'Excuse me? I don't—' He stared at the ID.

'Does this help?' Watts waited as Josephs walked back to his young colleague, listened as he suggested the youngster take a break, watched as he returned with a self-assured smile. That brief exchange told Watts that Josephs was a swift thinker who'd used the last few seconds to do just that. The next words out of Josephs' mouth confirmed it.

'If this is about a visit here recently by a young, female police officer, there's something you should know.'

'Exactly my thinking.'

'Whatever she's said, it's all lies.'

'What do you think she's said?'

Josephs hesitated. 'I'm guessing here, but something about me giving her some wine to drink?'

Watts waited. 'Did you?'

'Not in the way you're probably thinking. She was very insistent that I talk about Annette Barlow, the previous manager here and a good friend of mine, who went missing. It upset me. I poured myself a small glass of wine and she asked for one. She had three glasses, as far as I recall. Then, she told me she didn't feel very well, what with the heat and everything. Although it's strictly against company rules, I showed her into our staffroom, made her a black coffee.' He sighed, shook his head. 'I felt rather sorry for her, but I was also shocked.'

'What about?'

'The way she started behaving when we were in the staffroom. She became very giggly and over-friendly. I can tell you I was very surprised.'

Watts nodded. 'Makes two of us.'

Josephs placed his hands together, prayer-like. 'I was really concerned about her leaving here, driving.'

'Show me this staffroom.'

'Like I said, we don't allow members of the public in there.'

Watts leant towards him. 'I'm your exception.'

Still reluctant, Josephs walked ahead of him to a door at the back of the shop, pushed it open, led the way inside. 'There's nothing to see.'

Watts came into the room, his eyes going from the youth sitting at the table, a magazine in front of him, to the high ceiling and its corners. No security. 'Dom?'

The youth didn't look up. 'Yeah?'

Watts walked to him, lowering his head to his ear. '*Beat* it!'

With a start and a harried glance at Josephs, Dom grabbed the magazine and moved quickly to the door. Watts' eyes tracked him to the street door and out. 'You were telling me what happened here between you and one of my officers. Let's have the rest of it.'

Josephs held up his hands again. 'I'm getting a really bad vibe about this so I'll say it again: whatever she told you, she's lying.'

Watts fetched his notebook from his shirt pocket. 'Any guesses as to what she told me?'

Josephs' eyes flicked sideways, words falling from his mouth. 'Well, I'm only guessing of course, but if she said anything about me coming on to her, it's an outright lie. Actually, it was the other way around, plus, I could make an allegation against her for physical assault. Right now, I'm seriously considering it.'

Watts nodded, wrote quickly, put down his notebook and

looked him in the eye. Before Josephs knew what was happening, his back was hard against shelving, bottles and glasses crashing either side of him to the floor, Watts' hands gripping his shirt, his mouth next to his ear. 'I've checked you out, you sleazy bastard,' he whispered. 'I found nothing but I'm making it a regular check as of now.' He shook Josephs, whose face was now the colour of sour milk. 'I'm really interested in you and I want to know exactly what your relationship was with Annette Barlow.' He gave him another shove. '*All right?*'

Josephs took a quick breath, pulling at his shirtfront. 'Annette . . . I had sex with her. In here. It was no big deal. I put a stop to it as soon as I realized she was a slapper and a bit too keen on the stock. I was young. No way was I putting my health or my job at risk.'

'You're a real star. Was she having any trouble with punters as far as you know?'

'I never saw them but she had a lot of phone calls here from men. She told me they were clients wanting her to talk sex. She called them "financial transactions".'

'Listen in, did you?'

Josephs smoothed his hair. 'Difficult not to. She told me one of them came here while I was on my lunchbreak. She showed me the money he gave her. Later, he rang her, talked to her, if you get what I mean.'

'No.'

'Calling her names. That was the arrangement they had. Whenever he came on the phone, she told me to mind the shop.'

'What else?'

Josephs shrugged. 'There were a couple of oddballs like him.

One of them would call, be very polite, ask for "Miss Barlow". At first, I thought he was her father or some other older relative but as soon as she got on the phone, he was off, screaming at her, calling her names. I heard them. "Jezebel! Harlot!" Annette laughed, said he was one of her regulars, an old-fashioned weirdo. She took it as one big joke.'

'What about the other one? What did he say to her?'

'I don't know. She said he liked to rage at her. She didn't seem bothered by it.'

'Got a name for him?'

Josephs gave a vigorous headshake. He sent Watts a swift, evaluative glance. 'I hope that's helpful.'

'Might be.' A final shove of Josephs against the shelving dislodged another bottle which joined its mates in pieces on the floor. 'Don't get the idea you've seen the last of me. You interest me, Josephs, given that Annette Barlow's murder is still unsolved.' Watts loosened his grip, picked up his notebook, tucked it into his shirt pocket, walked from the room into the shop and out.

Ten minutes later, he was stuck in traffic, Josephs still on his mind. He crept up to the traffic lights. They changed to red. He leant his head back, eyes drifting to several medium-sized manufacturing businesses to his left, stopped by a single name: Prentiss. He sat up, looked across at parked vehicles facing towards him: a couple of vans, three larger vehicles, also with the name Prentiss, and the one car which had snagged his attention: a dark blue-grey Audi. Getting a loud hoot from a vehicle behind him, Watts drove on.

*   *   *

HE HAD BEEN BACK at headquarters fifteen minutes when he got a call from an officer he had told to follow up Nilsen. 'I've talked to his colleagues at this college he works at, Sarge. My opinion, he wouldn't win any popularity contest there, but a woman named Eve Saunders who works in his department told me she was driving up Blackfoot Lane at around eight twenty a.m. on the Monday Roberts was murdered. She says she saw Nilsen appear from the path at the top of the lane.'

'And?'

'She says she stopped and offered him a lift because of the heat. I asked her to describe him and how he seemed. She's confirmed he was wearing dark clothes and carrying a small backpack. She also confirmed that his clothes and his hands looked clean and his behaviour was as usual.'

'Hands, plural?'

'Yes, Sarge. No sling.'

'Go to the college, talk to her and whoever else is available. Find out if she's got any reason to say what she did. She and Nilsen might be an item.'

'Doubt it, Sarge. She has to be about fifty.'

'Fifty-year-olds have their moments.'

'Yes, Sarge. I didn't mean—'

He put down the phone as Traynor walked in. 'Townsend, the runner, placed Nilsen in the general area of Blackfoot Trail on the morning Roberts was killed. Now we've got a fiftyish female colleague of his who's telling a similar story.' He shook his head at the interest quickening in Traynor's eyes. 'She stopped at the top of the lane to give Nilsen a lift. According to her, there was no blood on him. No indications of unusual behaviour or mood.' He went to the Smartboard, started writing. 'That whole area is Nilsen's go-to for watching and stalking women but his colleague's description of him that morning appears to rule him out for Roberts.' He jabbed a full stop, stared at what he'd written. 'We've got him for the Merriman assault, but that's it.'

Traynor let his backpack slide from his shoulder to the floor. 'The team asked me this morning if there was a briefing. I was noncommittal.'

Watts eyed him. If Traynor didn't refer to their discussion the previous day, neither would he. 'I should have told them, no. I had to go out. One of the places I went was the wine shop Annette Barlow managed.' He told Traynor about it, omitting facts relating to Judd. 'As part of her on-the-side earnings, Barlow took regular calls from men who paid to talk rough to her, call her names.'

Traynor looked at him. 'What kind of names?'

'Old-fashioned stuff: harlot, jezebel, that kind of thing. There was another one who "raged" at her. Our chances of tracing any of them are minus zero, but the current manager there is worth consideration.'

Traynor reached inside his backpack, took out an envelope, opened it. 'I've been back to the newspaper office where Justin Rhodes worked. I wanted to check with Jess Meredith whether she'd had any more thoughts about him and his disappearance. She said not, but she's lent me this photograph.' Watts came to look at it. Traynor pointed. 'That's Justin Rhodes.' He pointed to another figure in the photograph. 'He was a work experience student who moved with his parents to Scotland not long after this was taken. These two females were support staff on the newspaper, both married women. The older man here is Jess's father who owned the paper back then.' His finger moved along. 'Take a look at him.' Watts did, at a sandy-haired man standing apart from the others, his hands pushed into his jeans' pockets, not looking at his colleagues, his face unsmiling. 'He looks a bit of an outsider,' said Watts. 'Who is he?'

'Paul Clarke. According to Jess, he left the newspaper shortly after this photograph was taken.'

'Did she say why?'

'Yes. She didn't sack him but she told him he had no future as a reporter, that he lacked the easy manner and ability to get people to talk. He didn't take it well.' He looked at Watts. 'Jess said she suspected that Clarke felt he was being compared to Rhodes, although Rhodes' name was never mentioned. Clarke was twenty-nine when this picture was taken. She advised him to look at other kinds of work more suited to his personality.'

'That's a lot of detail, Traynor.'

'I took Jess to lunch.'

'What else did she say?'

'That Clarke left and she never saw nor heard from him again.' He paused. 'Not even requests for references.' The implications of Traynor's last words hung in the warm air between them.

Watts tapped the photograph. 'I heard the expression "bad vibe" today. It's what I'm getting now about him.'

'Same here. I'll phone Jess in a while, see if she's located any more information on him.' The door opened and Judd came in. Watts was on his feet. 'How about a cuppa?'

She pulled a face. 'I've fallen for that before. I say yes and you say "so do I".' She sat, pulling one of the several files on the table closer. 'I'm dead sick of searching these. It's taken for ever to get this far and there's nothing.' She looked up. 'Have forensics finished examining Zoe Roberts' car?'

'Yes. No prints that weren't hers.'

'What about the cars owned by the other victims?'

Watts went to the Smartboard, dragged information on to it. 'Annette Barlow owned a Mini but didn't drive into the city to work because of the hassle and expense of parking. Rhodes' car, a Renault, was found outside his apartment block. Daniel Broughton's Merc was on his drive behind locked gates when he disappeared.' He sat on the edge of the table, pointed to the old files. 'Any evidence in those that they took taxis or other types of public transport?'

Judd shook her head. 'So far, I haven't seen any.'

He looked to Traynor. 'Got any observations on that?'

'Yes. I'm revising what I said yesterday. I still doubt the victims knew him but if they each had some kind of offer of help from him, he might have offered them transport somewhere.' Traynor looked at him, keeping his voice low. 'And, in case you're wondering, that revision doesn't change what I said yesterday about Claire.'

Watts looked at him. 'I didn't think it would.'

Traynor went to the Smartboard, pointed at data. 'What Christian Roberts said about Zoe offers confirmation that each of these victims was involved in potentially illegal activity. That's a possible link.'

Watts stared at the board, the pressure inside his head growing. Avoiding Traynor's eye, he went back to the table, patted papers, lifted others. Judd reached for the paracetamol pack, held it out to him. He took it. 'Where does Rhodes fit in? Answer: he doesn't.' He sat, giving the files a once-over. 'What you said, Traynor, that whoever killed them was playing God. I want to follow up your idea that he selected the victims because they all featured at some time in newspaper reports. How about you float it past your friend Jess?'

Traynor reached for his iPad. Watts left the table, returned in a couple of minutes with mugs of instant coffee.

'Isn't there some theory about everybody knowing everybody else? Three degrees of freedom, or something.'

Traynor took one of the mugs. 'That's a statistical term. Do you mean six degrees of separation?'

'Not a clue. What is it?'

'It's a way of measuring social distance between individuals. Example: all three of us are one degree from everyone else we each know, and two degrees away from all of those individuals they know. There have been experiments involving sending letters and emails to unknown but named individuals via acquaintances. Where it works, the average length of the chains of communication is five to seven steps between them, hence, the "six degrees" theory. I don't see how it helps us.'

'Me neither,' said Watts, 'but it's got a small-world feel to it that I like. It's stopping me seeing this case in the basement, regardless of whoever they send to take over. It also reassures me that whatever the link between this killer and his victims, it's possible to find it, given time. Which I haven't got.'

The iPad beeped. Traynor reached for it and quickly read the email. 'Jess Meredith. She's found no reference to Annette Barlow or Daniel Broughton being mentioned in her newspaper and so far, she hasn't found any references to them in other papers. She also says that when Justin wrote pieces which were crime-related it was under the by-line "Just/ice". His true identity was never divulged.'

Traynor came to the table, placed his hands on it, giving Watts a direct look. 'Like I said, *place* is what all four have in common: Blackfoot Trail. One ran and died there, the other three were already there. Had been for years. Those are the factors which link all four.'

Watts guessed where Traynor was going with this: a demand for a search of the whole area.

The iPad bleeped again. Traynor said, 'Jess has located Paul Clarke's current whereabouts. I'll go and see him first thing tomorrow.'

Watts eyed him as he got ready to leave. The look on his face was the one Watts had seen when he and Judd were at his house. Focused. Intense. He gave his face a brisk rub. 'I'm going to see two neighbours of Daniel Broughton's.' He located his keys. 'I watched a programme on the telly a while ago. It was about crocodiles or alligators at this sanctuary place in Australia. Apparently, they don't eat that often. They go months without anything, but they're always there. On the lookout for prey. Waiting. There was one lurking under the water. You couldn't see it but it was there. A bloke went up a ladder above where it was, held out a chicken's foot. Nothing happened for a minute or two and *then*' – he brought his hands together – 'this massive thing *shot* out of the water like a bloody rocket, and the bloke dropped it into its mouth. Down it went into the water and disappeared, leaving hardly a ripple.'

Judd looked up from the file in front of her. 'It's bad enough having to go through all of this without listening to stuff like that. It's horrible. Scary.'

'*That*, Judd, is our killer.'

CHONG WATCHED WATTS PUSH his dinner around his plate. 'Leave it, if you don't like it.'

He put down his fork. 'It's me. I'm not hungry.'

She stood, took their plates. 'Should I ask about the case?'

'Best you don't.' They moved around his kitchen in silence. He looked at her. 'I'm thinking of quitting. I mean, completely. I've worked repeat cases before, but nothing like this. I've had enough of Brophy's carping. Enough of the scene, the grinding heat, the leads that go nowhere, the . . . everything.' He gazed at her. 'I'm done with it. I can't carry on. I can't take the pressure.'

She nodded. 'I'm guessing it's of no help to say that Brophy is motivated solely by self-interest and that whatever decisions he makes are no reflection on you?'

'I can't blame him for calling time on me as SIO. We're nowhere. I know it. He knows it.'

'You've had difficult cases before and resolved them. Why are you allowing yourself to be diminished by someone whose focus is solely on protecting his own future? Has *he* got any ideas on how to take the case forward?' She fetched milk. 'No. I didn't think so. By all means quit, if that's what you want to do, but not because you're tired and can't see your way ahead. That's doing Brophy's work for him.'

'I told you that Traynor thinks this case holds the answer to his wife's murder. He's convinced himself he's right.'

She came to him. 'Maybe he is.'

'No. It's what Traynor does when he's a bit haywire.' He gazed at her. 'The reasons I just gave for quitting. It's nothing to do with any of them. What sticks in my throat is having this case taken away from me.'

TWENTY-FOUR

Wednesday 24 August. Nine fifteen a.m.

Traynor got out of his car, his eyes moving over the neat order-liness of the low-rise technology park, current working address of Paul Clarke, one-time newspaper reporter. One-time colleague of Justin Rhodes. The location was just beyond the city's southern boundary, Solihull lying a couple of miles further on. Which made it midway between the place where Zoe Roberts had run her last run and the legal practice where she'd worked. Entering the modern building Clarke had grudgingly described on the phone, finding nothing that resembled a recep-tion area, Traynor went to one of several young males at standing workstations, headphones in place. He asked for Clarke. Not lifting his eyes from his screen, the worker pointed in the direction of a distant door. Traynor headed for it, walked inside a huge square room, boxes stacked around most of its perimeter, in its centre an island of wrap-around desk, a man slouched behind it. Late thirties to early forties, longish, sand-coloured hair mixed with grey, phone clamped to his ear, he was rotating on a black leather chair.

'Luke, *Luke,* mate, just listen, will you? Those are the terms of the contract you signed. If you want out before the two years, that's up to you, but you pay us an additional percentage . . .

Yeah, yeah. OK, let me know what you want to do.' He ended the call. *'Fuckwit!'* Dropping the phone on to papers in front of him, he looked up, frowned at Traynor. 'Who are you?'

'William Traynor, criminologist, police headquarters. We spoke on the phone yesterday and agreed a meeting here this morning.'

Clarke began sorting papers. 'I forgot. You'll have to reschedule.' Hearing Traynor's footsteps coming closer, he looked up. The phone rang again. Clarke snatched it up, his eyes fixed on Traynor. 'Yeah? Let's do lunch, discuss it. One o'clock.' He put down the phone. It rang again.

Traynor pointed at it. 'Take that call, I leave and you come to police headquarters at a time I choose.'

Clarke glared up at him. 'You want to see me. *This* is my workplace. What do you expect?'

'Basic courtesy. My time is as valuable as yours, Mr Clarke. Police headquarters, two o'clock. Don't be late.'

Clarke was on his feet. 'Just a minute! The phone's off and I can spare you ten minutes.'

'Anything we don't cover, we'll do at headquarters, like I said.'

Clarke's mouth tightened. 'Let's get on with it.'

Traynor walked across the big space, dragging a chair to the desk. 'Tell me everything you know about Justin Rhodes.' He waited out the silence, studying Clarke's face. 'That name appears to have taken away your power of speech, Mr Clarke. Why is that?'

Clarke shrugged, pushed back his hair. 'I'm trying to remember who he was.'

Traynor allowed the pause to run on. 'Was?'

'I've just remembered. He's somebody I knew from years back. What about him?'

'As I said, I want everything you know about him.'

Clarke's mouth twisted downwards, his eyes moving from Traynor's. 'We worked at the same place. Not here. Somewhere else. Why the interest?' Traynor didn't respond. Clarke's hand twitched around the switched-off phone. 'He worked for the same local paper but I can't tell you anything about him. I didn't have that much to do with him. I was a reporter. He was just a junior who knew nothing. There to learn the ropes.'

'How was he doing?'

Clarke shrugged. 'Barely mediocre, on a good day. I tried to help him, set him straight. He wouldn't have it. One of those people who knew it all.'

Traynor gazed at him. 'Sounds like he wasn't doing too well.'

Clarke's mouth twisted again. 'He wasn't but he had the owner of that paper fooled.'

Traynor went with it. 'He rated Rhodes?'

Clarke winked. '*She.* She fancied him. Gave him special interest stuff to follow up. I'd done some of that so, like I said, I tried to advise him.' He looked at Traynor. 'You want my honest opinion? Rhodes was an arrogant git. I'll give you an example: he wanted to write this article about some murder case, don't ask me which one, I don't remember the details, but he was going on about getting the public on side because nobody had been arrested for these three murders. He was hoping he'd solve it.' Clarke laughed. 'What a dreamer! I told him straight, "Don't waste your time. Why would people round here give a toss about some women murdered miles away, plus it's old news, there's no local interest, forget it".'

Traynor gazed at Clarke's face, wanting to drive his fist into it. 'Did he?'

'Not him. He'd dredged up some articles, one saying that the husband of one of the women was a potential suspect.' Traynor's face was a careful blank. 'I said to Rhodes, "See? The police know who did one of the murders and they still can't sort the other two out, so what chance have you got?"'

'What did Rhodes do?'

Clarke sat back. 'Far as I remember, he wrote something and it died a death.' He looked at Traynor, his face splitting into a grin. 'So to speak. That was around the time I left.'

'Why did you leave?'

Clarke shrugged. 'The place was a professional dead end for me. I had ideas for building up the paper, but the woman who owned it wouldn't listen. She felt threatened by me, see. I should've left sooner.' Canniness crept into Clarke's eyes. 'If you're thinking of asking her about Rhodes, I wouldn't waste your time. She'll tell you nothing. Like I said, she and Rhodes were . . . you know.'

'No.'

'Come *on*. You look like a man of the world. A player. You know what I'm saying. She was in her thirties then, nice enough looking, single. A bit desperate.' Traynor's hands gripped together. 'Next thing I hear, Rhodes has disappeared. *Pfft!* Gone. Without so much as a word. Serves her right for not listening to me.' His eyes narrowed. 'Why the interest in him?'

'How come you're working here?' asked Traynor.

Clarke gazed around his office, face smug. 'This is *my* company. The reason I quit the newspaper. Leadership is my forte. It's what I do. It isn't my first venture. I ran a pub with a friend once but we fell out and it was too much like hard work so I ditched it. After that, I bought into a coffee shop. You'd think that the mark-up on a cup of coffee would put anybody selling it on Easy Street, wouldn't you, but you'd be dead wrong. You have to sell thousands a week to make a profit. I offloaded it on to a bloke who hadn't got a clue.' He grinned. 'He went on about the changes he was going to make to it, give the punters what they wanted. I told him, "*Mate*, they want bloody coffee!"'

'Did he succeed?'

'Do I look like I care? I'm back to another of my strengths with this place: software. I started it with my dad as a sleeping partner. I've got big plans for it—'

'It must have been a big financial reach, even with a partner.'

He stared across at Traynor. 'If it's any of your business, a year after I set it up, my father passed away . . .' Traynor could hear the word 'luckily' hanging on the air. 'A terrible shock, of course, but he wanted me to make a go of this place, so I used the money he left to grow the business. It's been hard, I can tell you. It's no easy ride being the boss.'

Traynor had recognized hubris and resentment in every word falling from Clarke's mouth. He watched him consult a large wristwatch and preen. Traynor had met people like him in the course of his work, their insecurities and fault-finding antagonizing bosses and employees alike. A picture was forming inside Traynor's head of this whole set-up deserted, a large board outside saying To Let, driven into the ground by Clarke. There was a lot about him to dislike and Traynor knew a number of unpleasant people who were also killers. 'What do you think happened to Justin Rhodes?'

'Not a clue. I know he disappeared. It was in the papers, so I'm guessing the police thought something had happened to him. He was always on about going down to London, being taken on by one of the big dailies.' He grinned across at Traynor. 'Maybe he met somebody who was as big a git as he was. *Or* a bit of a psycho.' He pointed at Traynor. 'Now *there's* a lead for you, if you're looking for one.'

'Why would you think he met a psychopath?' asked Traynor quietly.

Clarke's face changed. He sat up, switched on his phone. 'Just a joke, for fuck's sake. You asked me what happened to him. I don't have a clue and care even less. You're with the police. *You* sort it.'

'We'll bear in mind how much you disliked Justin Rhodes as we do that, Mr Clarke.' Traynor went to the door, feeling Clarke's eyes on him. The phone rang, Clarke's words following him. 'No, Luke, *you* listen. I've told you how it's going to be . . . In that case, fuck you!'

EYES FIXED ON THE road ahead, Traynor's thoughts were still on Clarke. Liar. Schemer. Talentless. Envious of Justin Rhodes. It was easy to imagine him goaded into action by his own inadequacy and jealousy of Rhodes, seizing any chance to make life difficult for the young reporter who was showing the promise he himself didn't have. It was possible that those feelings had coalesced into violence. Traynor put his hand to his hot forehead.

He was doing exactly what he'd criticized Watts for doing: focusing on one victim. The feeling of unreality, of being disconnected, was back. Clarke's dismissive comments about Claire's murder had been another unexpected broadside. Is that how people thought about her? That she didn't matter any more? It suddenly occurred to him that after ten years they probably didn't think about her at all. He gripped the steering wheel, getting himself together for the young woman he was on his way to meet.

TWENTY-FIVE

Wednesday 24 August. Nine thirty a.m.

Following an early jog and a cold shower, Watts had made breakfast for Chong and himself, after which she had left for headquarters and he was now looking across at a wide brick façade.

David Winter was pointing across the road to it, his hand on Watts' arm. 'That was Broughton's place.'

Watts moved away from the hand. 'Who lives there now?'

'No idea. They don't bother me so I don't bother them.'

Watts looked beyond the black railings at two sports cars and a Range Rover Sport. He followed Winter inside his house. The quick once-over he'd already given him told Watts that this suspiciously black-haired, late-forties man who owned a business which described itself as a 'security consultancy' had a physique he worked at.

Winter was talking again. 'When Broughton was working on that place, I was on his case the whole time. It went on for months, an eyesore and a nuisance from start to finish.'

'That the only problem you had with him?' asked Watts, knowing it wasn't.

'No. Even before he started the refurb, he had a habit of

parking his vehicles on the road, letting his employees do the same. Then he started leaving one of his skips there. I told him that the road was too narrow and to keep his vehicles on his own property, away from my drive.'

'What was Broughton's response to that?'

Winter gave him a shrewd look. 'I got nowhere with him but you wouldn't have come here without checking me out. I had a Barbarian truck back then. One day I reversed out, straight into the side of his Merc . . . accidentally, of course. The Merc came off worst, I can tell you.'

Watts slow-nodded. 'It would. What happened?'

'Broughton came flying out of his house, mouthing off. I grabbed him, pushed him against his car. He called the police. They came. Questioned us both. I was cautioned for laying my hands on him. That's all it was.'

Watts had seen it on the PNC. 'Was it reported in the papers?'

'No, but everybody round here knew about it. They'd seen the build-up of months of aggravation from Broughton. Most of them supported me in what I did.'

'What did you know about Broughton?'

Winter gave it some thought. 'I heard talk about his revamping houses, charging clients way over the top. I also heard a rumour that he had some kind of "business interests" in Spain. We all know what that means.'

'Do we?'

Winter gave Watts a look. 'Come on. He was into something over there.'

'Like what?'

'I've got a couple of theories: drug-running, money laundering, maybe both.'

'Anything to back that up?'

'Common sense.'

'Can you think of any other reason why somebody might have wanted to harm Broughton?'

Winter stared at him. 'Isn't what I've said enough?'

WATTS LOOKED BACK AT Winter's house. Beyond the businessman gloss, he guessed that Winter was a thug, although he could see some justification in his complaints about Broughton. Watts finished what he was writing, looked at the last few words: *suspects Broughton was involved with drugs and/or money laundering.* Snapping his notebook closed, he looked at the house again. Had Broughton been involved with drugs? Was he caught in the eye of some illegal storm which was about to break and wreck whatever he was into? Or, had Winter lost his rag and got rid of Broughton, the irritant, for good? If he had, where was the tie-in with Zoe Roberts and the other victims? He started the engine and pulled away. Drugs had already figured in the investigation. If that's where this case was heading, each of the victims needed a second look. Prostitution and drugs. The quick surge of optimism at the two linked activities vanished. Justin Rhodes. Clean-cut. Liked by his boss. Loved by his family. How did he fit into that scenario? 'Good luck to whoever comes to sort this lot out,' he murmured, checked the next address on his itinerary, drove a short distance down the long road and pulled in again.

* * *

WATTS WAS BACK INSIDE the BMW, jabbing the air con. He'd never had much time for people who held on to grudges and Penny Ainsworth, the woman he'd just talked to, was a past master. He looked at the dashboard clock. He'd listened to a solid twenty minutes of diatribe against Daniel Broughton and the men he'd sent to remodel her garden close on fifteen years ago. The only person she'd had a positive word for was Marjorie whatsit, Edward Arnold's girlfriend. Arnold himself had come in for his share of criticism: too talkative. This from Ainsworth who seldom paused to draw breath. He started his vehicle, looked up to see Ainsworth still at her door, smiling and waving. He bared his teeth at her and pulled away.

TIRED, FED UP, JUDD closed a file, pushed it away and reached for another. She'd gone through four now and found nothing new or potentially interesting. She looked up as the door opened. 'Hey, Jonesy. You're a stranger.'

'I'm on my way to the scene but there's something for you, Chlo.' He waved a tip sheet at her.

She went to him, took it, read it. 'You spoke to this woman?'

'Yes. She said that she and Zoe Roberts worked for the same agency.'

'Agency?' She shook her head. 'Roberts was a lawyer.'

'I'm just telling you what she said. She ended the call before giving her contact details but I retrieved her number.'

Judd looked at the slip. 'Nobody at the legal practice where Zoe worked mentioned a Vivian Smith and nobody's said anything about any agency work.' Jones left and she reached for the phone, listened to the number ringing out as Watts then Traynor came into the room. She waved the tip sheet, switched to speakerphone.

'Hello?' said a female voice. Judd did a quick thumbs-up. 'Am I speaking to Vivian Smith?'

'Who's this?'

'Police Constable Chloe Judd, calling from headquarters in Harborne, Miss Smith. I have a note of a call you made to the Zoe Roberts murder tip line a short while ago.' She looked up. Her colleagues' eyes were fixed on her. 'According to the information you gave, you were a work colleague of Zoe Roberts.'

'What do you want?'

'Some details about the nature of that work?' She waited. 'Ms Smith?'

'I'd rather not get into this.'

Judd frowned into the phone. 'Ms Smith, you phoned headquarters because you thought you could help. We need your help. You told the officer that you worked for an agency, that Zoe Roberts worked for the same agency. Is that correct?'

Smith's words surged across the room. 'All I did was deal with the bookings. Keep the diary organized. I didn't know this Zoe Roberts. I never met her. I can't tell you anything about her.'

'Can you confirm the nature of the agency, please?'

'It was a service agency.'

Judd looked up at Watts. 'Can you describe the nature of those services?'

'Escort. If there was anything illegal going on, I never saw it. I was told that all the escorts were over eighteen. She was one of them.'

'Miss Smith, we would really appreciate talking to you in person—'

'Like I said, I'd rather not be involved.'

'All we want from you is what you know about Zoe Roberts' work for the agency. We can come to wherever you are or, if you prefer, you can come here to headquarters.' Silence. 'How about tomorrow morning at eight thirty?' Judd frowned at the receiver, replaced it. 'She hung up.'

Watts looked at Traynor. 'What do you think?'

'Confirmation of Roberts having another source of income has to be good for our case, *if* what the woman said is reliable. It fits with what Christian Roberts said about her appearing to have more money than he anticipated. Her family never mentioned it. Maybe they didn't know.'

'Get anything from Paul Clarke?' Watts asked.

'Clarke is a potentially dangerous mix of hubris, resentment and personal inadequacy. When he worked at the newspaper, he must have hated seeing Justin Rhodes progress, whilst his own career was going nowhere. I would anticipate that in a situation where Clarke is face-to-face with his own inadequacies, he has the potential for violence. I think he needs a closer look.'

Watts got up, went to the board, pulled information on to it. 'What you've said is just what I want to hear. I'm moving this case forward while it's still mine.' He pointed to the short list of names he'd written that morning. 'Edward Arnold. Paul Clarke. David Winter and Richard Nilsen. As of now, they're our persons of interest.'

Traynor shook his head. 'I hear what you're saying but we don't have enough evidence to raise those three to POI.'

Watts walked away from the board. 'I'll find more. No way am I waiting around to be sidelined on this case, *any* case, after thirty years' service.' He looked at Judd. 'Give us a minute, will you?' She headed for the door. It closed on her. Watts had come to a decision. He looked at Traynor. 'I know you're interested in that whole area around Blackfoot and we both know why. I've given it some thought, Will, but while I'm still running this investigation, there'll be no searches for victims of cases from other jurisdictions. We maintain our focus on the victims we've already got.' He waited out the silence.

Traynor looked at him. 'Your internalized map of the UK has Birmingham in huge capitals at its centre, every other city labelled "Somewhere Else".' He stood, headed for the door, Watts' voice following him.

'As long as you keep searching, Will, you'll never have a life!' He watched the door close then dialled reception to let them know that a Vivian Smith was expected at headquarters at eight thirty the following morning.

TWENTY-SIX

Watts and Judd had spent several hours poring through files, searching for anything that had been missed, anything to progress the persons of interest to suspects. A database search had confirmed that only Winter had previous, for his assault of Broughton.

'Winter and Broughton still interest me,' said Watts. 'I'll get on to the Spanish police. See if they've ever had cause to investigate either of them.'

Judd was looking at the Vivian Smith tip sheet. 'I wonder why she didn't come?'

'People get cold feet. Change their minds.' He headed for the door as Traynor came into the office. 'Vivian Smith, the escort agency worker, was a no-show, but I'll check with reception.'

'She probably had mixed feelings about it when she rang,' said Traynor.

Judd frowned. 'So, why bother ringing at all?'

'Escort agencies are a policing grey area. Some are above board, others not. It's possible she had doubts about the one she worked for.' He took clipped-together sheets from his backpack. 'I've got some reading to catch up on.' He leafed through them, pointing to one. 'You spoke to Alec Prentiss. Was he any help?'

Judd rolled her eyes. 'If you want my honest opinion, he's an idiot.'

Watts was back, holding several A4s. 'Have a look at these.' He laid them on the table. They stared down at the black-grey image of a dark-haired, fortyish woman, her hand extended to one of headquarters' main doors, her face tilted upwards, captured by headquarters' CCTV system. 'I had officers check the list of names who were due in by appointment. The only female expected was Smith at eight thirty. She was the only no-show.'

Judd pointed at the time printed at the lower edge of the copy image, her face animated. 'Eight twenty-six! She did come, but only as far as the door.' Judd frowned at the image, half-listening to Watts on the phone, enunciating his words.

After several minutes, he ended the call. 'No investigations of any kind by Spanish police of David Winter or Daniel Broughton. I'll release a short statement to the press that we have a possible escort link in the case.'

He looked across at Traynor. 'From tomorrow I'll start running this investigation on the basis that there's zero links among the victims, that we've got a random killer and I'll be requesting Arnold, Clarke and Winter come in for formal interviews.'

Traynor returned unread papers to his backpack. 'In which case, you'll be going in the wrong direction. Nothing about this case is random. The key to it is where they were found. That's the link. The area has been searched but not in the necessary depth.'

Hearing this, Watts knew that what he'd said to him the previous day had had no impact. Nothing would. 'Traynor, I decide the direction of this investigation because it's my neck that's on the line. You know as well as I do the hours this team and the specialist officers have spent at that scene. Forensics is still there, although not for much longer. Whether I take this case to its conclusion or they replace me, I know it's a mess but it's *my* mess and I'll do whatever it takes to sort it while I still can.' He looked down at the thick files on the table. 'This case isn't going down into the basement. Not while I'm in charge of it.'

TWENTY-SEVEN

Friday 26 August. Ten a.m.

'Sarge?' Watts looked up at a uniformed youth, his arms full of the morning's newspapers. 'The chief told me to bring these to you. He said to read them.'

'I'm busy. Drop them on the . . .' He reached for the topmost one bearing a huge, black headline:

REMAINS OF THREE OTHER VICTIMS AT BLACKFOOT TRAIL!

Judd looked at it, eyes widening. Throwing it aside, Watts stared down at the one beneath it and the one beneath that. The door opened and Traynor came inside. Watts pointed. 'We've got a bloody leak!'

An officer appeared at the door. 'Sarge?'

'*What?*'

'There's a woman in reception asking for you. She won't give her name.'

Watts was on his feet. 'That'll be Vivian Smith, having second thoughts.' He and Traynor headed for the door. Judd made to follow them. 'Stay there.'

'That's not fair!' She watched them leave, waited, then

followed. Coming into reception, she stopped. Alec Prentiss was standing at the main doors, his eyes fixed on his mother who was facing Watts, her voice shaking with anger.

'We heard it on the early news. How *dare* you release information about my daughter, saying she had a connection to some *escort* agency!'

Watts shook his head. 'That wasn't what was said—'

Her hand shot up, made sharp contact with his face. 'And *that's* for not telling us that our daughter was killed by some sick serial killer!' She spun from him, headed for the door and out, shaking off her son's hand. With a quick glance at Watts, he followed her.

Watts, Traynor and Judd returned to the office where Watts sat, a red welt visible on his face. Judd looked across at him. 'I think Mother Prentiss reacted like she did because she already had an idea Zoe was up to something.' She paused. 'Zoe Roberts was getting on a bit, so it's possible she *was* just an escort, a sophisticated date for some businessman who'd just hit the city.' Watts slowly turned to her. She bit her lip. 'Arrived in the city.'

'Judd, the worst bit of what you just said was your definition of thirty as "getting on".'

Traynor looked at him. 'Roberts definitely fits the theory that these victims were each involved in behaviours which might have attracted disapproval.'

'Rhodes wasn't,' said Watts flatly. 'You said once that without full inclusion, there is no theory.'

The door opened. One of the officers from reception came inside waving envelopes, with a quick glance at Watts' face. 'Post, Sarge.'

Judd took it from him, brought it to the table, began opening an envelope. Watts checked his watch. 'I've called a briefing. Traynor, I want you to share your information and ideas about Paul Clarke.'

Judd's eyes were fixed on the single A4 in her hand. Her eyes moved slowly to Traynor. 'Sarge, you have to see this.'

Watts looked at it, took it from her. It wasn't a letter. Less than a dozen words. He reached into his pocket, pulled out latex gloves. 'Envelope. Where is it?' She lifted it from the bin by a corner, handed it to him. Traynor came and stood next to them. Watts caught his arm as he reached for it. 'No. We all know the zero value of anonymous communications.'

Traynor's eyes locked on his. 'My wife's *name* is on it!'

Watts placed it on the table. Traynor stared down at the line of black capitalized characters:

DEATH SCORE ONE PLUS CLAIRE TRAYNOR EQUALS TWO.

It was Traynor who broke the silence. 'Whoever sent this is saying he killed my wife. It's confirmation that she and our cases are linked.'

Watts put his hand on Traynor's arm, lowered his voice. 'All it's telling us is that whoever sent it reads newspapers and knows you're working on this case. He's seen you on the news, knows what happened to your family. Whoever he is, he wants to mess with your head.' Traynor stared at it. 'It's not what you think, Will. This is from some unemployable no-hoper who drives a ten-year-old rent-a-wreck, saw your picture in the papers and has decided he doesn't like you.' He pointed at the communication. 'Trust me, it's got nothing to do with what happened to your wife. This is from an idiot who wants to play games.' Traynor was still staring at it, his hair and forehead damp. Watts clicked his fingers. 'The newspapers, where are they?'

Judd lifted them from one of the chairs. 'Here, Sarge.'

He took them, held one up, then another. '*Look*, Will. He knows nothing. He hadn't seen the news when he sent that. He didn't *know* how many victims there are. He's nobody's killer.' Traynor stood unmoved. Watts turned to Judd, held out the latex glove. 'Take the sheet and the envelope to forensics for processing. Request photocopies. Oh, and while you're up there, tell the team that the briefing is cancelled.' Judd returned with the photocopies. Watts sent Traynor a covert glance. He still had the miles-off look on his face.

Traynor broke the silence. 'When we talked about the possibility of our victims being featured in the press, I told you that Claire also featured in an article in the Oxford newspapers. So did I. I was asked for my theories about the York homicide. Claire was still alive at the time.' He looked up at Watts, his face parchment. 'I brought Claire to her killer's attention.'

'No. There's only one person responsible for what happened to your wife, and that's whoever killed her and you know it because you're a scientist, a rational thinker.'

Traynor stared at him. 'If there's even a chance that reports in newspapers are what fuels him . . .'

Watts shook his head. 'You're responding exactly as he wants. Yes, it was a shock to read that note, but you know as well as any of us that anonymous communications are irrelevant until there's reason to think otherwise. This one is worthless. It's not going to impact this investigation and neither am I going to make public that all it takes to be victimized by this killer is a mention in some newspaper report. There's two million people in this city, a good proportion of them already in fear of an unseen killer who's decided to come out of the woodwork during one of the hottest summers any of us can remember. Don't let whoever sent it mess with you, Will.'

Traynor reached for his backpack, walked to the door and out.

'Should we stop him leaving, Sarge?'

'How do you propose we do that?'

'Do you think he's OK?'

'No.' He sat on the edge of the table, eyeing the information on the board.

Judd waited. 'You don't believe that note.'

'No, I don't, but I've got an idea who sent it. Stay here in case Will comes back.'

SEARCHING NAMES ON PARKING spaces, seeing the one he was looking for, Watts slid the BMW into the space next to it. He didn't have long to wait. A sports car arrived, parked next to him, its music system heavy on the bass. Its driver got out. Watts gave him a once-over and was out of his vehicle, holding up identification. 'You! Just a minute.'

The man stopped, looked at him, turned and headed at a fast pace for the building some way ahead. Watts followed. Once inside, the man stopped, faced Watts, his arms folded. 'What do you want?'

Watts walked closer, watching his eyes shift to two or three workers nearby, their attention fixed on screens. 'I could have told you out there.'

The man looked at him. His eyes slid away. 'For all I know, that ID could be fake.'

'Detective Inspector Bernard Watts, SIO of the Zoe Roberts homicide investigation, Mr Clarke.' He saw his eyes shift again. 'Now that you know me, you can guess why I'm here.'

Clarke was on the move. 'Can I?'

Watts followed. 'It's about your communication to police headquarters, Mr Clarke.' Clarke reached a door, pushed it open, tried to close it. Watts stopped it with his big hand. 'Any more of that, and you'll find yourself in big trouble. More than you've already got.'

'I don't have one clue what you're on about.'

'Yes, you do. You had a visit from Dr Traynor two days ago.'

'So?'

Watts pointed to the desktop nearby. 'After he left, you word-processed a very brief communication, to the effect that the individual we're looking for is also responsible for murdering Dr Traynor's wife. I'm betting it's still on there somewhere for our technical officers to find.' Clarke's face flushed. Watts' eyes moved over the desk Clarke was now standing behind. 'What was *really* stupid was sticking it in an envelope printed with your company logo.' Clarke looked as though he was about to pass out. Watts moved closer, stared down at him. 'You haven't seen the last of me for this.'

Clarke reached for the desk, steadied himself, his face drained. 'You lot are good at throwing your weight about, but you can't take a bloody *joke*. That criminologist really pissed me off, telling me what to do, making insinuations.'

Watts headed for the door, pointing at Clarke. 'What pisses *me* off is people like you meddling, which is another word for perverting the course of justice. I'll be in touch.' Seeing shock on Clarke's face, he turned and walked out, got into his car and headed for the main road. There was no logo on the envelope they'd received this morning. Clarke would probably realize it, once he'd had some recovery time, but it had put the frighteners on him, given him something to think about until he got him into headquarters as a person of interest. Now all he needed was evidence.

WATTS CAME INTO HIS office, not surprised to find Traynor there. He'd already seen the Aston Martin. A couple of quick glances told him that Traynor's face was shut tight. 'All right, Will?' Getting a brief nod, Watts watched him walk to the door and out.

A minute later it opened and Judd came in. 'I've just seen Will. Is he OK?'

'You know as much as me.' Aware of being under scrutiny, he asked, 'Something else on your mind?'

She sat opposite. 'I've finished going through the files and found nothing.' She was looking keyed-up. 'But I've got a theory about our case, Sarge. I haven't got it all sorted but I think it's about the victims' ages.'

He looked at her. 'Their ages.'

She nodded. 'Just hear me out. Barlow and Rhodes were in their mid to late twenties when they were murdered. Roberts was thirty. They're part of a group.'

Traynor came in, his hair damp. 'What group is this?'

She looked up at him. 'Our victims were all millennials. I got the idea after talking to Alec Prentiss. He's a prime example.'

Watts gazed at her. 'Harry Josephs, the manager of the wine shop, is around the same age. Is he one of these millennials?'

Her eyes moved from his. 'Yes.'

'How does their being millennials help us?' asked Traynor.

'Whoever killed them hates them as a group. He considers them to be immature, entitled, demanding, cocky and snowflaky – you know, from the snowflake generation. Actually, they infuriate him. He wants to punish them. He's older, of course. We're not far wrong about newspapers being involved in this case, but not because the victims were individually featured. Millennials as a group get loads of press coverage.' She looked at her two colleagues. 'Just so you know, I'm no millennial: too young, no money and I'm no snowflake.'

Watts gave Traynor a quick glance. 'Since when has anybody killed four people because he hates them on the basis of their age? This "millennials" business is just a label. Something for newspaper columnists to gab about. I can think of any number of people working in this building who are in that age bracket and they're nothing like your description.'

Judd turned to him. 'That's another part of my theory. Their killer didn't know them personally. He saw them somewhere, made a judgement about them because of what he *thought* they were . . .' She paused. 'All three fit my theory on the basis of appearance plus age.'

'Broughton doesn't.'

She looked exasperated. 'I *know*. I'm still working on it.' She saw Traynor reach for his backpack. 'You're not taking me seriously, either of you.'

He looked at her. 'There might be something in what you're saying. This case is about time. It's about the now and the past.' To Watts, he continued, 'I'm going to the scene.'

Watts went with him to the door, looked him in the eye, his voice low. 'Paul Clarke sent that anonymous communication.'

Traynor stared at him. 'How do you know?'

'I went to see him.'

'He admitted it?'

'He said it was a joke. He's a jealous, resentful git who's decided he hates you because of who you are, what you do and what you've got. Now I want you to say to my face that that rubbish he sent here is exactly that.'

Traynor didn't reply.

'Don't turn this investigation into a personal mission, Will. That kind of thinking will do you no good and you know it.' He watched Traynor walk away then went back to the table. It was time for more plain speaking.

'Judd?'

'Sarge?'

'Tell me about Harry Josephs.'

She stared at him. 'I don't know what you mean.'

'Yes, you do.'

She stared at him in disbelief. 'Dr Chong *told* you?'

'She did.'

'She had no right to do that!'

'She had every right. As SIO, if there's a safeguarding issue I have to know about it.' He waited.

Her mouth trembled. 'Just get it over with: I'm finished here and with the force. Go on, say it!'

When he first got to know her, she was an irritant, still was at times, but he knew more about her now and not just her background. She was hard-working, keen and bright and she believed in the job. He'd do whatever it took to give her the best chance of a career in it. 'You know better than that. Or, you should do. What Josephs did was harassment at the least.'

She stared at the table between them. 'I won't make a complaint.'

'I can't make you do that.' He thought back to his own contact with Josephs. If Judd did make a complaint, Josephs would in all likelihood deny it and drag in Watts' own actions against him to support his case. Bring it on, he thought. I'm as good as finished here.

Judd looked up at him. 'I walked into that situation, Sarge. I won't make it an issue. I want to keep my job. I must. I want to be part of this team. Finish this case. I wouldn't be able to do any of that if I had proceedings hanging over me.'

He left the table, walked to the windows, reached a hand outside. The heat within the room and the temperature outside felt the same. He looked up at relentless blue sky. 'I'll support you, whatever you decide, as long as it's what you want.'

'It is.'

He came back, reached for what he'd planned to hand out at

a briefing the previous day, left the office and went up to the squad room. There were four officers there. By the look of them, they hadn't long returned from the scene. 'I've got a job for you, lads. A last push.' He held up one of the A4s. 'This is a list of every single thing I want you to find out about our four victims from the people who knew them, no matter who they are. You might not get much from Annette Barlow's father but give it all you've got with him and everybody else you speak to. I want you out there, talking to them, asking questions, following up every name *they* mention.'

One of the officers gave him a tired look. 'Are we looking for anything in particular, Sarge?'

'I know you've been there gathering information on every possible aspect of the four victims' lives: the areas in which they grew up, their families, friends, education, leisure interests, the jobs they've had, and those they wanted and didn't get.' He paused. 'I want you revisiting those sources.' He heard muted groans. 'Swap lots. Take whatever we've already got and ask again. I want to know what we've missed.' They stared at him. 'What you're after is *linkage*. Anything which links Zoe Roberts, Annette Barlow, Daniel Broughton and Justin Rhodes and right now I don't care how remote it might seem.' He dropped the A4s on to the nearest desk, pointed to them. 'It's all there. Start with the families, work up a list of names, start knocking on their doors. Get more names. Talk to them. If they're unavailable, ring them when they are. I want you back here with every single detail of these victims' lives from childhood till they died and I want it all by midday tomorrow.' He looked up as more officers came into the room. 'Just in time. These four will fill you in on what I want.' He looked at the pinned-up photographs, his eyes moving over the victims' faces, seeing only differences. He dropped more A4s on the table, pointed. 'Vivian Smith, if that's her real name, the woman who phoned the tip line to say she worked for an escort agency and knew of Zoe Roberts. While you're at it, show her picture to everybody you talk to. I'm hoping somebody will recognize her.'

WATTS WENT TO THE scene in the early afternoon. Having heard from forensics or SOCO departments that nothing remained there, he had given the order to close it all down. Judd looked up as he came back into the office, pushed word-processed sheets to him without comment. He read her report of her wine shop visit. 'I owe you some other notes, Sarge, but I decided to search PNC for all known cases of young adults between the ages of twenty and thirty-five of both genders who've been the target of violence. I was hoping for a lot of millennials. All I got was a load of individuals who don't conform to type. Attacks on that age-range are about theft of phones, money, credit cards, mainly drug or alcohol fuelled.'

She looked dispirited. 'You were right. "Millennials" is just another buzz word the media loves to play up. It means nothing.'

Watts looked up at the Smartboard. The victims stared back at him. 'I've got every officer I can spare talking to people, searching for connections among those four. Traynor is committed to their being linked in some way. I still think they're random but I can't see the sense in it.'

She eyed him. 'That's why they're called "random", Sarge. The sense is inside the killer's head.'

'Know-it-all.'

The phone rang. It was Traynor. 'I'm at the scene. How long are you planning to keep the forensic workers here?'

'They're finishing later this afternoon—' Traynor cut the call.

Judd was gazing at the victims' photographs. 'We haven't got a clue what their killer was after, have we? What it was all *for*.' She propped her face on one hand. 'We've done everything. Talked to people who knew the victims, chased down leads. I don't get any of it.'

TWENTY-EIGHT

Saturday 27 August. Midday.

Watts had spent most of the morning ensuring that the whole scene was closed down. The area was deserted now, except for a couple of officers he'd stationed at either end of the trail to log who came and went. He anticipated they wouldn't be busy, that people would stay away because of what they'd heard or read, but it wasn't unknown for killers to return to scenes.

Back at headquarters Watts made a terse internal phone call. 'Everybody back?' Getting a single word response, he headed for the door. 'Come on, Judd.'

She looked up at him. 'Where to?'

'You like detail and there should be plenty of it waiting upstairs, collected by a dozen mates of yours.'

She rubbed her hands together. 'Victimology.'

They came into the squad room. 'Where is it?' asked Watts.

Jones pointed at a stack of close-written sheets. 'Here, Sarge.'

Watts went to it, distributed them. 'We're going through every bit of data you've gathered. What I want is anything which stands out, or resonates as a potential link to two or more of the victims.' He pointed to the whiteboard. 'And, as we find it, it goes up there. Let's get started.'

* * *

TWO HOURS LATER THE atmosphere in the room was downbeat, the whiteboard unmarked. The officers had done a thorough job, even located an address for Vivian Smith which turned out to be a bare, single room without even a phone. Three other occupants of similar offices had no knowledge of her. Watts pulled sheets together. 'Thanks for your efforts, lads.'

Judd followed him downstairs to the office. Traynor was there, writing on the Smartboard. He turned to them. 'Murder is *the* ultimate crime. For the majority of killers, it requires massive psychological effort and exploration of other possibilities before the decision is made that death is the answer.' He pointed at the victims' photographs. 'Somebody made that decision for each of these four and I doubt he agonized over it.' He raised his hand, summoned more details on to the board, including photographs of the skulls, photographs of Roberts' body lying on the ground. 'He was monumentally angry at each of them. Destroyed them with controlled savagery. These were executions.' Watts and Judd exchanged looks. 'Dr Chong described the three skulls as carefully placed, all facing the same way. It suggests ritual. Intentionality. There was a specific reason for their killer doing what he did to them.'

'I've been to murder scenes where "intention" was flashing like neon,' said Watts, 'because of what some random killer did to his victims, expressed through blood and scene-setting.'

Traynor shook his head. 'What we have here is totally different. He hated all four. These killings were barbarous yet carefully managed, full of calm intent. They were personal. Judgement done. Ultimate vengeance.'

'Dr Chong would be the first to say that she wasn't commenting on intention or ritual when she said what she did about the positioning of those skulls. She was providing an observation.'

'It still fits the theory, whatever she intended.'

Watts sighed. 'I've had officers out there talking to family members, friends, colleagues, every associate of each of the victims.' He pointed at the sheets. 'We've spent two-plus hours going through all of it. There's not one single connection among the four. Nothing.'

'You're wrong,' said Traynor. 'You just haven't found it.'

Watts eyed him. He looked different. There was an odd gleam in his eyes. Reaching for the pathology folder, Watts removed photographs of the skulls in situ at the incline, spread them on the table, took out more photographs, taken from a vantage point further up from where they were found. 'OK, Traynor. You tell me what all this means. Why were they there?'

'Their killer wanted them looking at something.'

Watts stared at him. 'Such as?'

'Another burial site.'

Watts shook his head. 'No. No more searches.'

Judd was on her feet as Traynor moved towards him. 'This isn't a case of me *wanting* or *hoping* that Claire is there. I *know* she is.'

Watts' colour deepened. 'Look, I understand—'

'You don't! Give me a categorical assurance that my wife isn't somewhere at that damned place.'

'You know I can't do that. Nobody can.' He thought back to the first mention of Traynor's name at the start of the investigation. He had known that collaboration between them wouldn't work. Traynor knew his stuff but he was too messed up.

Traynor delivered his next words like measured blows. 'Get forensics back to the scene!' He stared at Watts. 'I want another search. Whoever killed them is organized, like I said days ago. Remember that one disorganized feature? It's now telling me that, organized as he is, he has episodes when his thinking is distorted. He's *dangerous*.'

THEY WERE BACK AT the incline, the air leaden. Above them the red-and-white stakes marking the skull burial places were still in position. They gazed down at what was just visible of Blackfoot Trail, at the rolling land below them, a persistent buzz, coming and going as the mosquito-like drone zipped and hovered on the hot, still air. Watts narrowed his eyes as it moved purposefully, watched it hover for a third time then quickly lose height. They headed down to the field, Traynor leading.

'Three possible search areas,' shouted Petrie, raising his hand and pointing. 'Two areas over there and' – he pointed downwards to his feet – 'one right here.'

Adam and one of his forensic officers headed towards it, a small digger following. Closing his mind to the cost implications, Watts followed Judd to the shade of a nearby tree, watched the digger scrape away grass. Traynor stood watching, waiting. To Watts, he looked like the loneliest person in the world.

JUDD WAS LYING ON the grass, face flushed, eyes heavy-lidded, Traynor pacing nearby. Watts' eyes were still fixed on the excavations. A shout from Adam brought Judd scrambling to her feet.

They waited as he came towards them, saw the decisive head-shake, his words drifting ahead of him.

'Buried timbers and brick from an old barn in those two over there and animal bones in the third.'

They watched Traynor walk away, then followed him to the car park in time to see his car disappear from view.

BACK AT HEADQUARTERS, JUDD headed for the office as Watts stopped at the reception desk. 'Anything for us?'

'No . . . Hang on, Sarge. There's a data check result here.' The officer reached for it, handed it to Watts.

He looked down at the details, then up. 'How long's *this* been sitting here?'

The officer avoided his gaze. 'Not too sure, Sarge.' He watched Watts walk away.

A fellow officer sidled up, speaking from one side of his mouth. 'If that check's been here for more than twenty-four hours, get busy developing a sudden attack of amnesia.'

Watts threw open the door of his office, walked inside, dropped the data check on to the table and pointed. 'See *that*? I requested that two days ago. It's been sitting in reception for God knows how long.'

Judd reached for it, eyes moving over the top line. 'A conviction for drink driving.' She read on, looked up at him. 'Well, wha'-d'ya-know? Princess Perfect.' She read aloud the details. 'Zoe Roberts fined for drink-driving eighteen months ago.'

Watts took it from her. 'The amount of the fine suggests she was just over the limit. What gets me on a line is that we've got enough problems without data delays.'

'I'll tell you what annoys me. Whilst her mother was busy painting a glowing picture of Zoe to us, nobody in that family, neither she, the father, nor Alec Prentiss mentioned this.'

Watts carried files from the cabinet and dropped them on to the table. 'Give me one good reason why they would.'

She looked at him. 'How about general cooperation and openness?'

'How about they were knocked sideways with grief when we saw them?'

'I think Mother Prentiss hit you because she knew Zoe had that escort sideline. Now I'm wondering what else that family knows that they haven't told us.'

He eyed her. 'Is drink-driving a hanging offence in Judd World?'

'How about we go and see them again? Ask them about it.'

'I want to move this investigation on, get David Winter and Paul Clarke in here for interview, but Traynor's right, we don't have enough evidence to move either of them to POI.'

'Just do it, Sarge, and see what we get.'

He eyed her, wondering if she'd learned anything recently. 'The lawyers they bring with them would have them out of here within five minutes.'

Judd huffed. 'I'm surprised anybody *ever* gets arrested!'

He went to the cabinet, took out a file and brought it back to the table. He flipped it open. 'I've got a job for you. Remember the three childhood friends of Zoe Roberts'?'

'Yes. You had officers visit them and take statements.'

He held up the statements.

'I want more detail.' He passed them to Judd. 'Arrange to go over and see all three sometime this afternoon.'

Judd looked at the names on each: Bethany Williams. Marcia Smith. Juanita Perez. She read the statements. They were very brief, to-the-point accounts of the friendships between the three women and Zoe Roberts from early childhood to their teens. She checked the dates of the interviews. All three statements were taken two days after Roberts had been killed. She skimmed the accounts again, a picture forming of four confident, secure young women. She shrugged, thinking, OK, I envy them, so shoot me. She reached for the phone.

JUDD WAS INSIDE MARCIA Smith's comfortable apartment, listening to the sounds of cold drinks being poured in the kitchen nearby. She turned pages of notes she'd made at Bethany Williams' home, recalling Williams' toddler daughter, chubby in pink, baby-blonde hair secured on top of her head, a tiny, bobbing palm tree. At Juanita Perez's home, a heavily pregnant Perez had talked to Judd about her friendship with Zoe Roberts. Neither woman had added to the information Judd already had and had indicated their shock on hearing about the sex work allegations. They had had no inkling that Zoe had ever had links to escort agencies. Judd sighed, rubbed her eyes, looked around Smith's comfortable modern lounge. It chimed with Judd's own life goals: independence, nice home, career, security. No children. She already had Smith's account of her friendship with Zoe Roberts. It was time to leave. She looked up at the smiling, dark-haired woman, drinks in hand, ice clinking against glass as she walked. Smith set one down on a small table beside Judd.

'I hope you like cranberry juice.'

'I do, thank you.' Judd reached for it, drank half, set the glass down. 'Is there anything else you'd like to add to what you've told me about Zoe?'

Smith shook her head. 'I can't think of anything. I've said it all. We tended to meet up about twice a year for a general catch-up. I wish we'd made more effort. Made it more regular.' She looked across at Judd, shook her head. 'Wishes are about as useful as good intentions.' She sipped her drink. 'Zoe and I actually started primary school on the same day so I knew her before Bethany and Juanita did. It's a lifetime ago, yet talking about it, it seems like no time at all. All of us working like crazy to pass our exams, get to university.' She laughed. 'All of us strung out, worrying that we wouldn't make it.' She glanced at Judd. 'That's something I'd tell my younger self: worry less. We all made it but it would have been great to know it, back then. It would have saved a lot of angst.' She looked away, her face clouding. 'Just as well Zoe didn't know what was waiting for her.'

Judd reached for her bag, ready to leave. 'I'm guessing Zoe's parents just left her to get on with exam preparations.'

Smith's reply was unexpected. 'You're totally wrong about that. Bethany's and Juanita's parents were like mine, encouraging but a bit laidback. Zoe's mom, and particularly her dad, were totally different. They had stratospheric hopes for her. They really pushed her. Kept an eye on how much work she was doing.' Smith looked at Judd. 'Don't get me wrong. I'm not saying they were horrible, not at all, but at one stage Zoe literally dropped out of circulation. I think it was because of her study regime. It might have been partly due to her having broken up with her boyfriend as well, but she didn't come out at all during that time. At least, not as far as I or Beth and Juanita knew. We were really hitting the books, but not to that extent.' She shrugged. 'We still had time to party.'

'How long did Zoe stay dropped out?'

Smith gave it some thought. 'I'd say a couple of months, maybe a bit more.'

'And during that time, you never saw her?'

'I saw her once. I was out shopping. Zoe was with her mother. Mrs Prentiss kept interrupting, saying that they were in a hurry. All Zoe and I managed was a few words.'

'How did Zoe seem?'

'Fine, a bit tired, but I remember being surprised at the change in her. She'd put on a lot of weight. I assumed it was because she was missing her boyfriend, eating and studying. Crisps were my thing at the time: snacking without looking, eyes fixed on my computer screen.' She smiled, shook her head. 'I didn't see Zoe again until the exams were finished.'

'How was she then?'

'Like her old self, slim, ready to enjoy what was left of the summer.'

Judd's mind was racing. 'Do you recall her boyfriend's name?'

Smith thought about it, shook her head. 'No, sorry.'

Judd got into her car, Marcia Smith's words reverberating inside her head. She reminded herself that there might be any number of reasons for a fifteen-year-old schoolgirl to curtail her social life over several weeks and gain significant weight. Of all of those reasons, Judd's thinking was circling around just one.

* * *

JUDD HURRIED INTO HEADQUARTERS and down the stairs, relieved to see light inside the PM suite. She knocked on the door and waited. It was opened by Dr Chong. 'Hello, Chloe. You're a welcome surprise. Does DI Watts have something for me?'

Judd spoke in a rush. 'No. I just got back from talking to three women who were at school with Zoe Roberts. One of them has told me something about her and I think it might be relevant to our case but I need help to work out whether I'm right.'

Chong led the way inside and pointed to a chair next to her desk. 'Go on.'

Judd sat, looking uncertain. 'It made a lot of sense an hour ago when I heard it. Now, I'm not so sure.'

Chong studied the young face. 'If I'm going to help, I need some facts.'

Judd raked her fingers through her hair. 'OK. One of Zoe's friends I just mentioned described her as dropping out socially around the time they were studying for exams. This is when they were around fifteen, sixteen years old. They didn't see Zoe during those two to three months, although one of them told me she saw her just once, very briefly, when she was out shopping with her mother. Mrs Prentiss kept trying to hustle Zoe away but according to what the friend told me, Zoe looked different. She was tired and she'd gained a lot of weight. The next time they saw her was when the exams had finally ended. They all got back together again and she described Zoe as looking like her usual self.'

Chong gave her a keen look. 'And?'

Judd gripped her hands together. 'I think Zoe Roberts was pregnant. I think she had a termination. It has to be relevant to our investigation, although I don't know how. She had a boyfriend

back then but she broke up with him. I don't have any information about him so the only way I can sort it out is to talk to
you about it.' She eyed Chong. 'I need you to confirm that Zoe
Roberts was pregnant at around fifteen or sixteen.' She watched
as Chong stood, walked across the PM suite then returned with
an old, buff-coloured file.

'Your keenness does you credit, Chloe. These are Zoe Roberts'
medical records from when she was born.' She turned pages,
quickly scanned them and stopped. 'This is around the time in
Zoe's life you're referring to.' She pushed the file towards Judd,
pointing at information. Judd quickly read lines of information
in varied handwriting, turned pages to more entries, some of
them printed. After a few minutes, she looked up. 'There's no
reference to Zoe Roberts ever being pregnant.'

Chong shook her head, took back the file. 'No. My post-
mortem examination showed no evidence of a past pregnancy
but I wanted you to see for yourself.'

Judd leant back, raking her hair into more spikes, looking
frustrated. 'I was so *sure*. It made sense.'

'Sorry to wreck your theory. My advice when you get home
is, get a good night's sleep. Other ideas will come to you.'

Judd looked at her, anguished. 'We're almost out of time as
a team. DI Watts is really stressed and he and Dr Traynor are
clashing. OK, I got it wrong about a pregnancy but I still think
there was something happening in Zoe's life back then. Her
friend said she changed. That she withdrew.'

Chong sent her a sympathetic smile. 'Sounds to me like the
common condition of most fifteen- to sixteen-year-olds at any
one time, plus my own personal experience.'

Judd looked surprised. 'I can't imagine you were ever like that. You're so . . . "together".'

'We all have those times, Chloe. It's what helps us find our way to "together". Sorry I can't help you with Zoe Roberts.'

Judd frowned. 'Did DI Watts tell you that she was convicted for drink-driving about eighteen months ago?'

'Yes, he did. You think it might be relevant to what happened to her?'

Judd shrugged. 'I don't have a clue, but it bothers me that her family didn't mention it.' She frowned. 'Mrs Prentiss is the type of person who really rates respectability, but Mr Prentiss didn't come across like that, so why didn't he say something?' She stood. 'Thanks for your help, Dr Chong. Sorry to take up your time. I can see you're busy. I'll go upstairs, trawl the databases and see if I can find any details on the drink-driving conviction.'

Chong went to the desktop, hit keys. 'I can see you won't follow my advice about going home, so do it from here.'

Judd came and sat, hit keys, watched information arrive on the screen. She pointed. 'There. That's it.'

Chong looked over her shoulder at the screen. 'Any help?' she asked.

'No. It says only what we already know. That Roberts' breath test produced a very low reading, that she went to the magistrates' court and got a small fine.'

'Given its non-serious nature it's possible there aren't any more details.' Chong looked at the dispirited young face. 'Like I said, go home. Eat something calorific. Things will look better tomorrow. It usually works for me.'

They looked up as the door opened and Watts came inside. 'Get anything from Roberts' mates, Judd?'

She outlined for him what she'd found out from one of Zoe Roberts' friends. 'I thought Zoe was pregnant but she wasn't.'

Watts eyed Chong. 'Well done for following it up.'

'I was thinking that the drink-driving offence sounded out of character, but given what we know about her, I don't think it was. She could have had others.'

Watts shook his head. 'Doubt it. If she had, she wouldn't have got the lenient treatment she did eighteen months ago.'

'There's nothing on the PNC, but it doesn't change my thinking about her. I'm telling you she was no saint.'

Watts came to the computer. 'I want to check something on the database.'

'You want a search of dating agencies?'

'No. They're like mushrooms and we don't have any details on the one Roberts was involved with. I'm thinking of something else, somebody else with an offence record: David Winter, one of our persons of interest.' Judd typed in the name and Watts stared over her shoulder at details moving up the screen. '*There*. David Anthony Winter. Assault and disturbing the peace.'

Judd's eyes moved over it. 'He accused Daniel Broughton of being a menace for parking his vehicles on the road but the police told him it was all legal.' She looked up at Watts. 'What if there was another incident between Broughton and Winter which was never part of any police investigation?'

'If there was, I don't see how it could have led to four people's deaths.' He saw her face change. 'Take it easy while I read this.'

He stared at the screen. 'Winter was furious with Broughton for parking his car by his property, which is what Winter told me.'

Judd pointed. 'That's only half the story, see? He also objected to Broughton's men doing the same. It wasn't just cars, Sarge. It was builders' vehicles and skips as well. Sounds like Broughton was one of these nightmare neighbours.' She looked up at him. 'But the police told him they were legal as well. Maybe this Winter didn't like Broughton and used it as an excuse to cause him problems?'

Watts shrugged. 'Having met Winter, it's possible. Unless the parking caused problems for somebody else.' He looked at her. 'What's the worst-case scenario you can think of in that kind of situation?'

She frowned at the screen. 'You mean, like, some kind of accident?'

Watts brought out his phone. 'Kumar, I want information on road traffic incidents in the south of the city around fifteen years ago. I'm particularly interested in those which involved parking obstruction.' He ended the call. 'Kumar's got more database access up there.'

'I'm having coffee,' said Chong. 'Anyone else want one?'

Watts nodded, began pacing, seeing Judd's impatience mounting.

There was a sudden beep. Judd went to the screen. 'Look, Sarge. Kumar's found twenty incidents dated around the time we're interested in.'

SEVERAL MINUTES LATER, JUDD was eyeing the nineteenth on the screen. 'I don't think this one's much help either: unnamed woman and infant reported deceased at the scene after her vehicle skidded in poor visibility then veered into the path of an oncoming vehicle . . . its three occupants unhurt in the impact. None of the other people involved are named. Weather conditions and the woman driver's speed were judged to have caused the accident. No further action taken.' She rubbed her eyes. 'I'm fed up.'

'Print them,' said Watts. She did. He collected them from the printer. 'Time to pack it in.' He turned to Chong. 'Any news on the hair samples found on Zoe Roberts?'

She shook her head.

AFTER JUDD LEFT, WATTS had phoned Mr Prentiss to ask about the vehicles used as part of his business. Prentiss had confirmed several vans plus a dark blue, eight-year-old Audi which he described as a run-about used by his employees. Hearing Watts' request for it to be forensically processed plus a list of employees, Prentiss sounded less than enthusiastic but agreed. Watts arranged for a couple of officers to collect both car and list the next day.

He was on his way out of headquarters when a voice calling his name stopped him. It was Brophy, working on a Saturday, which was a surprise. He listened as Brophy told him that his replacement was arriving at headquarters on Monday anticipating a detailed case handover. Watts would then spend the remainder of that week ensuring that his replacement was fully conversant with all aspects of the case. Whoever it was, he wished them luck. They'd need it. He walked to his vehicle, dropped the files on the passenger seat, pulled his phone from his pocket, his eyes fixed on a heavy bank of cloud as he left a message for Traynor. 'I'm going to see Mr and Mrs Prentiss tomorrow. There's a couple of things I need to talk to them about, not least their daughter's involvement with escort agency work, which will take some doing as I can't see Mrs Prentiss being very welcoming. Get back to me when you've got a minute.'

TRAYNOR WAS AT BLACKFOOT Trail. There had been no vehicles parked along one side of the lane as he'd driven down it. The whole scene was silent. He leant against his car, his head down, knowing what his psychiatrist would say if he could see him. Something on the lines of: 'If you want to be really ill again, continue doing exactly as you're doing.'

The mood inside headquarters had been sombre. He'd seen it reflected in the faces there and those of the press waiting outside. He'd seen Watts on the verge of exhaustion, his time as SIO almost finished. Traynor was on his own now. He knew Claire was here. It was up to him to find her. When he did, he could let her go. He looked up, his eyes drifting over the imme-diate surroundings. It had never made sense to him that the bodies of the three decapitated victims had been taken away, hidden elsewhere. It was high-risk behaviour to move them by road. Anything might have happened: a flat tyre, engine problems, an accident, a driving violation. He went to his car, opened the boot and reached for the spade, seeing papers related to the case which he hadn't yet read. He closed the boot on them. There was something he had to do. He took a couple of steps from the car. The ground beneath his feet heaved and dipped. He got a first subtle aroma: fresh bread. It drifted around him, growing stronger every second. Claire had baked bread the evening she was killed. The house was full of its smell as he'd stepped inside and into a nightmare. It was here now. All around him.

'Claire?'

He looked down at compacted ground, then on to where it met old wood fencing. No soft earth here which might offer concealment. No space. Continuing slowly along the car park's perimeter it was the same story. He closed his eyes, looked up. The high boundary wall was directly ahead. He recalled the workmen who had come here a lifetime ago to carry out safety work and were sent away. He walked to it, looked up at it, his eyes moving over dark brick, ivy and other vegetation covering it to a height of many feet, then down to vigorous bushes and nettles at its base. Pushing his way through and along, he came to the brick buttresses he'd looked at that day. He ran his hands over them, followed the wall along, thick tendrils and thorns pulling at him. He stopped where two of the buttresses were closer together than the others he had passed, the undergrowth around and between them particularly dense. He walked further along, not finding any others similarly placed. He came back, placed his hands against the cool brick of the two buttresses built so close together. A stand-out feature in a long, long wall. A memorable marker for something someone had left here? He dropped the spade and bent to the flourishing green undergrowth. He was here to find his wife. His life. He would use his hands.

He pulled at thick branches, tore ivy from its moorings. Quickening his pace, he seized more, cast it behind him, his breath coming in harsh gasps, sweat coursing into his eyes.

Robotic, oblivious to stings from wild roses and nettles, he watched the soft dark earth slowly revealing itself. He went to his knees, lowered his face to it, breathed in its rich loamy scent, looked at a mired stick, slender, delicate, resting against the dark brick. He reached out to it, touched it, ran his finger down its length, gently lifting away soil, an express-train roar inside his head.

It was a human radius. Hands shaking, he pulled away thorny branches and nettles. The fragile bone was a ten-year testimony to this place being the ideal burial ground for the victims in the case. For Claire. Gently, carefully, he scooped away earth. Distant thunder rolled. Rain spots, big as medals, splashed nearby leaves. Pushing his hands deep, he lifted away more earth, flung it from him, pushed again, stopped. His fingers had hooked something. He lowered his face to the earth, his eyes fixed on a small, earth-covered hoop. Breath catching in his throat, fingers gentle, he eased away the soil, looked at another next to it. He continued on, a pain in his chest the like of which he'd never felt as more small hoops appeared and a curving column of small bones. He stopped. Got to his feet. He had to call Chong. It was her domain now. She would tell him what he already knew. There was nothing more he could do for Claire except stay here and be with her. He raised his arms, damaged hands clenched into fists, let his head drop back and roared out his grief. Staggering backwards, stopped by a tree, he slid down it.

TWENTY-NINE

Sunday 28 August. Four p.m.

Brophy had told Watts to prepare the handover document. He'd done it. It was on the low table in front of him, the facts of the case still in his head: Edward Arnold, David Winter, Prentiss senior, Prentiss junior, all had worn bracelet watches. For Paul Clarke there was no confirmation. Watts thought back to his meeting with him, shook his head. He couldn't recall seeing Clarke's watch. Traynor had said that the software legend-in-his-own-lunch-hour had offloaded a previously failing business to somebody planning to give customers what they wanted. *'I told him, they want coffee!'* When he'd heard those words from Traynor they hadn't jibed with anything. They did now: Edward Arnold and his chesterfield sofa, his top-of-the-range coffee machine for his bookshop customers' comfort and convenience.

Unable to leave the case alone, even at this late stage, Watts reached for his phone, dialled the number in Traynor's notes, waited. His call was picked up. 'Mr Clarke, this is DI Watts, SIO in the Zoe Roberts murder investigation. I know it's a Sunday but I've got a question for you.' Clarke sounded more reasonable than he had previously. No doubt worried about the anonymous message he'd sent to headquarters. 'You told Dr Traynor some

days ago that you once owned a coffeeshop. Who did you sell
it to?' He wrote the name, ended the call, looked down at it. It
meant nothing. He dialled another number, waited. His call was
picked up. 'Mr Arnold? Apologies for interrupting your Sunday,
but I need to check something with you. Before you had your
bookshop, did you ever own a coffeeshop?' He ended the call.
So much for intuition. No coffeeshop. He watched his pen move
over paper, making loops within loops. Bookshop. Broughton's
last known whereabouts, prior to his disappearance. A place he'd
never visited prior to that day. He flipped more pages, found the
Prentiss's home number, dialled it. Mrs Prentiss had made her
feelings about him very clear but he needed one more shot at
getting a realistic picture of Zoe from them. He cut the call.
Nobody home. Again, he went through the accident printouts,
looked at details of the one which had claimed the lives of a
mother and infant. Telling himself that what he was doing was
beyond desperate, he searched his phone for a name. Not finding
it he got up, went to the bureau, came back with an old address
book, found what he was looking for.

He dialled, waited, grinned at the voice in his ear. 'Hello,
Dave. How's Traffic?' He listened to a few expletives, got down
to what he wanted. 'I need to know about a case with whiskers,
Dave. A mother and baby killed in an RTA in south Birmingham
fifteen years ago.' He gave him the date. 'I want details we haven't
got at headquarters. Can you track it down?' Watts waited,
doodled. His one-time colleague was soon back, giving only the
basic information Watts already had. 'Thanks anyway. It was a
long shot.' He listened to the voice in his ear. 'You do? Can I
have it?' He wrote down the phone number, 'I know. I never got

it from you.' He ended the call, tapped the number he'd been given, listened as it rang out and was picked up.

'Hello?'

'Is that Mrs Jill Woodhall?'

'Yes?'

Watts went with as few words as possible. 'This is Detective Inspector Watts, police headquarters, Harborne. I'm sorry for calling on a Sunday. If I leave it at that for now, can I come and talk to you?' Writing down her address, he ended the call. Fifteen minutes later he was ringing her doorbell, ID in hand. The door opened. 'Mrs Jill Woodhall?'

She nodded. 'Come in.' In the hallway, she gave him a direct look. 'Haven't I seen you somewhere before?'

'Possible. It's a common enough face.'

She led him into a large kitchen, its doors and windows open to the garden. 'What do you want to talk to me about?'

'A road accident which happened a few years ago.'

'Fifteen,' she said. 'It's fifteen years since my daughter was killed.'

On the lookout for signs of upset, he saw only resignation. 'I need to ask you for details of that accident, Mrs Woodhall.'

'I was anticipating you would. Don't look so worried, DI Watts. Memory is kind. It preserves the good and blurs the rest.' She got up, went to a high shelf and took down a photograph, brought it back to the table. 'This is my daughter.' She ran her finger gently over it. 'And that's her baby, Jack. He was just six months old.'

Watts looked at the photograph, then up at her. 'What happened?'

'She was taking Jack to hospital. He was ill. Convulsing. The weather was bad, around November time and obviously she was stressed about him and . . . her car struck another coming the opposite way. The police who were involved at the time were very kind. They told me she swerved, lost control, that it was a tragic accident in problematic circumstances.' She took the photograph from Watts, shook her head. 'It must happen all the time, somewhere.'

'Did the police give any details of the problematic circumstances?'

'They measured marks on the road or something and they said that she was going too fast and swerved to avoid an obstruction in the road.'

'Did they say anything about the obstruction?'

'Only that it was a skip which was clearly marked with warning signs.' She shook her head. 'Worry, speed, poor visibility all coming together.' She looked up at him. 'That's what an accident is, isn't it? It's a pity Suzanne couldn't have taken Jack to the hospital earlier.'

Suzanne. Watts looked at her, telling himself it was a common enough name. 'Why didn't she?'

'She'd gone out for a couple of hours, leaving him with a babysitter. She would have realized he was ill as soon as she arrived home.'

'Do you recall the babysitter's name?'

She shook her head. 'All I know is that she was young.'

Watts looked over the notes he'd made. 'What was your daughter's full name?'

'Her married name was Suzanne Elliot.'

He wrote it down, a tremor in his hand, another question in his head so loud he wondered that she couldn't hear it. 'Was your daughter married before, by any chance?'

She looked at him, surprised. 'Yes. She was.'

'What was her previous married name?'

'Arnold. Suzanne Arnold.'

Watts stood. She did the same. 'I've just realized why you look familiar. You were on the television recently.'

WATTS DROVE A SHORT way from the house and parked, getting his breathing under control and his thoughts in some kind of order. Having found no specific links during what felt like a lifetime on this case, he suddenly had them. Now he knew the reason why Prentiss had indicated Christian Roberts' involvement in questionable dealings. Deflection. Prentiss knew the truth. He looked down at the papers lying on the passenger seat, saw doodles he'd made an hour or so before. Flowers. His head came up. 'How did I miss that? How did he know that that's where she died?' He started his vehicle. He knew the answer.

THIRTY

Judd was home, lying on the small, lumpy sofa, spoon in hand, a small tub of Rocky Road ice cream balanced on her chest, preoccupied with Sarge's imminent replacement on the case and her own career falling apart before it had properly started. Chong had been right about Sarge. He'd shown Judd his evaluation of her, indicated his full support, despite the mistakes she'd made, which he attributed to 'a combination of zeal and lack of experience'. The evaluation was now with Brophy. She doubted he would be as kind. His eyes were too sharp, his mouth too thin. Putting the Rocky Road on the floor, she lay on her side. Sarge, Dr Traynor, she and everyone else had done all they could over long hot days, following up leads which had given them nothing. They'd followed up Broughton's neighbour difficulties, the newspaper traffic accident report which had looked promising, but wasn't. They had nothing to connect Zoe Roberts to the other three homicide victims and now Dr Traynor was ill and Sarge was finished.

She closed her eyes, feeling helpless, like she had when she was small. Pushing herself up, she reached for her notebook, leafed through it, words she'd written bringing back scene after scene. She pictured the wall at the Prentiss house, devoted to the activities and achievements of two children faithfully recorded by their parents, the adulation of two childhoods. She frowned. Was it all a bit over the top? She shrugged. Not having seen herself in any pictures before the age of six, she wasn't able to judge. Her eyes moved on, stopped at a single question. *'Is he any good?'* She recalled her surprise when Alec Prentiss asked it. Surprise, because he hadn't appeared much interested in their investigation. Self-centred idiot. She turned a page. Despite Mr Prentiss's observation about his son-in-law, they had found nothing to indicate that Christian Roberts was involved in any 'questionable dealings'. She dropped the notebook on the floor. There was no sense in any of it. She left the sofa, hearing little buffets of wind rattling her window. She went into her bedroom, came back dressed in dark joggers, a hoodie, trainers. Somebody had said to her once, 'If you don't understand, then ask.' Sarge was finished on the case, but there was still something she could do. She left her flat and the house under a turbulent sky, heading to her car.

* * *

QUIETLY CLOSING HER CAR door, Judd pulled up her hood against big raindrops and started towards the house. No visible lights, but the one car parked outside indicated that somebody was home. She walked between the open gates, up the drive to the front door, her eyes on the Jaguar's personalized plate: 100 PP. Peter Prentiss. She raised her finger to the bell, listened as it rang inside the big house, listened as soft footsteps approached the door. She straightened, made her face friendly. The door slowly opened. She looked up at him.

'Hello, Mr Prentiss.'

The door opened wider. She stepped inside.

THIRTY-ONE

Eight p.m.

Watts' phone rang as he headed to the Prentiss house. It was Chong, calling from her home. 'You asked me to let you know as soon as I had the results of the diagnostic lab's examination of the hair fragments found on Zoe Roberts' body. They just emailed them through.'

'And?'

'DNA.'

He eyed the dashboard screen. 'You're kidding! How did they manage with no roots?'

'Like I said, they're specialists. Are you ready for this? We're not talking usual nuclear DNA here, the kind yielded by semen, blood and saliva. The advantage of this kind of DNA is that it is present in thousands of copies per cell. Abundant as well as hardy.'

'Sounds like my sort of evidence. I'm hearing a downside.'

'It doesn't identify individuals. Those sections of hair were on the back of Roberts' vest, one of them pushed deep inside one of the wounds to her chest by the knife used to kill her. I suspect her killer got a haircut close to when he did it . . . but what . . . hairs have given us . . .'

'Sorry, you're breaking up, Connie.'

'. . . mitochondrial DNA. He's related to Zoe.'

Watts stared at the screen, Winter and Clarke, the suspects he was trying to develop crumbling. He made a sudden right-hand turn, getting an irritated hoot, picked up another call, this one from headquarters.

'I'm on my way there now. Send officers immediately. I'll wait for them outside the house.' He drove on through darkness. Traynor had been right all along. All of the victims were connected. Linked by a terrible accident which left a woman and child dead. Now he knew who the babysitter was all those years ago.

He parked some distance from the house, got out of his vehicle. There was one car parked on the drive. A Jaguar. He frowned at a small car he recognized parked nearby. 'Jesus *Christ.*' Reaching it, he tried the driver's door. It opened. He looked inside, closed it, went back to the BMW, called headquarters again, issued terse instructions then headed for the house. Reaching the front door, he found it open. Not fully, just a narrow gap around its edge. If Judd was inside, he had to go in. Pushing the door, he stepped quietly inside the silent house, listening, hearing nothing but his own blood thumping in his ears. He glanced inside the sitting room, moved on to other ground-floor rooms, went quietly upstairs to the landing, his eyes moving from one closed door to another.

A low, repetitive whimper coming from the nearest room, changing to a wail, pushed his heart into his throat. Throwing open the door, he saw her lying on the floor. He went to her, knelt beside her, patted her face. 'Judd? *Judd.*'

She opened her eyes, came up flailing. 'Ger'off me, you lousy—!'

He gripped her arms. 'Stop. You're all right. It's *me*. Sarge.'

She looked up at him. 'He . . . hit me. Prentiss hit me. He's gone.'

A sudden commotion outside the house, vehicle doors slamming, heavy footfalls reverberating, took Watts back to the stairs. He looked down at two officers. 'Is it just you two?'

'Yes, Sarge,' said Kumar.

Watts pulled out his phone. They listened as he requested backup. He pointed to the youth with him. 'Who's this?'

'PC Green, Sarge.'

'Up here, both of you.'

They came upstairs, followed Watts into the bedroom. 'A couple of the lads are here, Judd.' They lifted her. Watts looked down at her head, seeing red among the blonde. With Kumar's help they moved her downstairs, sat her on the bottom step.

Kumar touched her arm, whispered, 'What you been up to, Chlo, breakdancing?'

'Sod off.'

'She's got a lump on her head that'll be the size of an egg before it's finished,' said Watts. 'I want you to take her and get her checked out.'

Judd pulled herself to sitting. 'I'm part of this. I'm not going anywhere.'

'Don't give me grief, Judd.' He looked up at Green who hadn't opened his mouth so far. 'Go to the kitchen, get her some water and ice in a cloth. Go on, then!'

Green scurried away. Watts gave her head, then her face a once-over, looked into her eyes. Satisfied that she looked the best she could, he headed across the hall and into the kitchen.

'I could have been to the bloody reservoir and back in the time you're taking—' He stopped. Green was facing the big American-style fridge freezer, his hands on its handles. 'What's up with you?'

Green gave Watts a sideways look. 'Kumar's been filling me in on the investigation. You haven't found the head of that woman who was killed at the trail.' His eyes moved back to the tall double doors. 'It's got to be somewhere, right?'

Watts pushed him aside. 'You've been watching too many horror films, lad.' He reached for one of the handles. '*Hop it.*' Hearing quick footsteps leave the kitchen, Watts lifted his other hand to the freezer handle, gripped both tight, his heart climbing into his throat. If it was here, it was evidence. Tensing both arms, he started a slow count. Three. Two. One. He pulled. Hard. Both doors swung towards him. His phone rang. He reached for it. 'Yeah?'

He listened to Chong's voice. 'In case what I said about the DNA wasn't clear, it doesn't identify individuals. It indicates relationship only. It's DNA inherited from the mother. But that's not why I'm ringing. Wherever you are, you need to come to the scene. Traynor has something for you.'

His eyes on what was inside the fridge-freezer, he said, 'Yeah, OK.'

'You sound odd. What are you doing?'

'Staring at shelves of frozen peas and ready meals. I'm on my way.'

THIRTY-TWO

Watts drove quickly to the scene, Judd beside him, having refused all suggestions of medical attention. His eyes were on the dashboard clock: ten p.m. His phone rang. It was Jones, calling from the scene. 'What's happening?' Watts asked.

'We've had sightings of one male moving around the edge of the field adjoining the trail. He's gone to ground but thermal imaging equipment is arriving any minute.'

They reached the top of Blackfoot Lane, a twenty-five-minute journey which had taken fifteen. Judd sat forward, face intent. '*Look,* Sarge.'

He'd seen the red performance car parked half on the grass verge, its doors wide, white-suited officers approaching it. He drove on, down the lane and into the car park. They got out, headed for the trail. Watts called out: 'You!' The officer came at a clip. 'What's happening?'

He pointed to a line of uniformed officers moving along in the distance. 'He's somewhere over there, Sarge.'

'Thermal imaging arrived yet?'

'Not yet, Sarge.'

Taking Judd's arm, Watts headed back to the car park and on to where Chong was sitting with Traynor on the tailgate of one of the police vehicles. She stood, came towards them, hands cautioning. Watts slowed. 'What's happened?'

'He's exhausted, in all ways it's possible to be.'

He pointed to Judd. 'Can you take a look at her head?'

Judd submitted to Chong's search of her hair. 'How do you feel, Chloe? Any headache?'

'No.'

'Nausea?'

'No.' Chong looked her in the eye. 'Any visual disturbances?'

'Nothing. I'm fine. I don't like *fuss*.'

Chong looked up at Watts. 'She's OK. Come with me. I'll show you how Will got to be so exhausted.' They followed her to the high brick wall, continued along its length, pushed through thick undergrowth to a point where some serious clearance had recently occurred. Chong pointed to a small area of dark soil between two brick buttresses being worked by two white-clad SOCOs. 'Will has located human remains.'

A sudden shout brought them back to the car park. Jones was pointing in the direction of the trail. 'Movement up there, Sarge! He's heading to the incline.'

Traynor was on his feet, moving in the same direction. Watts went after him, 'Judd, you stay with Dr Chong. Will? *Wait.*'

They moved at speed towards the figure now heading up the incline. Traynor got there first, continued after it, Watts following. Gasping, he grabbed Traynor's arm. '*Easy*, Will. He could have a knife. Anything.'

Traynor's eyes were fixed on the man standing some way above them, lights now flooding the area, picking up the metallic fastenings on expensive-looking white trainers. 'I want to talk to him.' He took a couple of steps, looked up. 'Alec? Listen to me. I know what you're going through. I understand.'

Prentiss's voice drifted downwards. 'I'm tired. I have to finish it.'

'Alec, it is finished. You're having a breakdown. You need help.'

'I don't need help. I've completed my task. *I* am justice, not you.'

Traynor stared up at him. 'What does that mean, Alec? Tell me.'

'Transgressors must be punished and that punishment must continue after death. They don't deserve any release.' Prentiss appeared to be listening to something, nodded. 'I'm ready now.'

'*Wait*, Alec. We need you to tell us about it. All of it.'

As Traynor took a step forward, Prentiss raised both arms, smiled down at him and dropped out of sight.

'*Alec!*'

They rushed up the incline, hearing brakes screeching, horns blaring, the unmistakeable sound of metal on metal. They reached the top, looked down at hazard lights flashing in that deathly quiet which often follows sudden chaos. Prentiss had made it as far as the middle lane. Watts took out his phone, delivered the required information for a major incident: 'One known fatality. Individual on carriageway. Minimum of ten vehicles involved, two directly.' He added the access junction number. 'There's a Works Unit Only between the incident and that junction. Ambulance plus motorway police units required.'

'Information received. Actions imminent.'

As officers passed them on their way to assist people who had left their vehicles and were now gathering at the metal barrier, Watts and Traynor came down the incline to where Judd was waiting. 'Good job it was late, Sarge. Not so much traffic.'

He shook his head. 'It was years too late, Judd.' He took her arm and they walked on to the car park, Watts thinking how slow he had been when Alec Prentiss brought flowers here that day. He knew where to leave them. Because he knew exactly where he'd killed his sister. He glanced at Judd. 'All right?'

She gave a careful nod. 'Was he insane, Sarge?'

Watts looked at Traynor who said, 'He was experiencing reality issues. He could have been helped.'

Chong was coming towards them. 'Adam has just confirmed identities for the remains. Daniel Broughton, Annette Barlow, Justin Rhodes.' She lowered her voice. 'Come with me, please, Will.' They watched as he walked away with her, saw her stand close as she looked up at him, saw Traynor's head lower, both his hands going to his face. She came back to them. 'I've just given him the news he didn't want. His wife's remains aren't here.'

Watts was picking up some quiet sniffs. 'Come on, Judd,' he whispered. 'Buck up.'

'I'm *not* upset. It's a cold.'

THIRTY-THREE

Tuesday 30 August. Ten a.m.

Investigative officers filed into Watts' office, Adam and his colleagues following with Chong. They all looked tired but upbeat, Jones with a tray of doughnuts, Kumar and Miller bringing coffee. Watts glanced across at Traynor, recalling the first time he'd talked to the team, laid out what was facing them, telling them they could do it. Looking at their faces, Watts could see that now they knew it.

Watts got to his feet. 'In fifteen minutes, Chief Inspector Brophy wants to address all of you as a team . . .' He paused at suppressed groans. 'But before he does, Will has agreed to give an overview of the case so that we all, regardless of our roles in it, have the facts.' He sat.

Traynor stood. 'These are the facts. Alec Prentiss's early years were characterized by problems related to his relationship with his sister, a forceful personality, who bullied and took advantage of him. Prentiss senior has confirmed it and that she was never reprimanded for it. Neither was Alec Prentiss provided with help to manage his severe anxiety as he entered his teens.' He looked at them. 'Neither parent is psychologically-minded. They couldn't see that those difficulties left him vulnerable to distorted thinking about people, about situations, and culminated in his experiencing psychotic episodes. Mrs Prentiss is unwilling to acknowledge those aspects of his development because she believes it would place responsibility on to Zoe, which she cannot accept. Mr Prentiss fully acknowledges them. Those are the facts relating to Alec Prentiss. Mr Prentiss has also provided other facts which he and his wife have known for fifteen years: Zoe babysat for Suzanne Elliot on the night of the traffic accident which killed both her and her baby. Zoe spent most of that evening on the house phone to her boyfriend. When Mrs Elliot returned, it seems that she knew immediately that the baby was ill and rushed him to the hospital, with the outcome we now know. She swerved to avoid a skip, property of Daniel Broughton, and struck another vehicle coming in the opposite direction. The people in that vehicle, Annette Barlow and her drunk brothers, were unhurt. Annette told police she was driving. Traffic police took no further action. Alec Prentiss knew about that accident because he witnessed his parents' anger towards Zoe for her part in it, knew that they grounded her for many weeks afterwards.' He looked at each of the officers. 'This is where I diverge from facts. From what Mr Prentiss has said, it seems that familial concern at the time was less about Zoe's irresponsible behaviour and more to do with their fear that if she were to confide in anyone about what happened, it might impact on the family business. Alec Prentiss himself became increasingly fixated on that. His attitude to that business was one of general disinterest, yet he was very much aware of the benefits he enjoyed from it and that they stood to lose them if the truth emerged.'

Traynor sat on the edge of the big table. 'Which brings us to part of his motivation for killing Zoe: to remove the risk she still posed. But that wasn't the sole reason that Alec Prentiss killed his sister. He had a huge sense of injustice about her treatment of him during his early to mid-childhood and their parents' failure to emotionally support him. I mentioned earlier his distorted thinking and brief periods of psychosis. It was at those times that he decided that *all* of those individuals who contributed to that road traffic accident had to be punished. If the law wouldn't do it, Alec Prentiss would. He is dead so we can only guess how he tracked them down, perhaps via social media or newspaper reports. He learned about them as people, then made contact. He was the client Broughton was trying to find a book for; he offered to help Rhodes with information about the disappearances in the Birmingham area; and he offered Annette a job – a way out of sex work. But in his skewed view, they were bad. They had to die. They also had to know *why* they died. Alec Prentiss would "tell" them in death. That's the reason their skulls were buried carefully, close together, the hearing, thinking part of them an available audience for Alec Prentiss, whenever he wished.'

The big room was silent. Jones spoke. 'I saw him that day he came here. Saw his car. I looked at him and I thought, "Blimey, mate, *lucky* bastard, you've got it all".'

Watts glanced across at Judd. When Traynor had shown them the full significance of what Prentiss had told her during that visit, she had been furious with herself for not seeing it. Watts guessed from the little he knew of her life that it had been difficult for her to see in Alec Prentiss anyone other than the spoiled son of an indulgent family. It chimed with Jones' 'lucky bastard, you've got it all', comment. He glanced at her. She was still looking vexed.

'Why kill the newspaper reporter?' asked Kumar. 'He hadn't done anything.'

'No,' said Traynor, 'but Justin Rhodes was about to do something. He had a plan. He wanted to write about the disappearance of two people from this city. It seems likely that those two people were Annette Barlow and Daniel Broughton. Rhodes was a determined, meticulous researcher. He had to have found out about their involvement in that accident. Prentiss would have done his own research of Rhodes' career, learned that once he had a story, Rhodes wouldn't let it go. He had to be stopped. To protect the Prentiss family.'

Traynor glanced at Watts, looked back at them. 'That's it. Facts and likelihoods. This case needed psychological and criminological theorizing to reach a solution, but in the end it was proved by hard science: glowing fibres in the car Alec Prentiss borrowed from the company and drove to Blackfoot Trail, the footprints found there which matched the trainers he was wearing on the day he died, the mitochondrial DNA which indicated that Zoe Roberts' killer was related to her via her mother.' Traynor's eyes moved over them. 'And good teamwork.'

Miller's hand rose. 'What about Zoe Roberts' other remains? The knife? Where are they?'

Traynor stood. 'They're still "unknowns". I need to say something else. While you were all focused on this investigation . . . I sometimes wasn't.' The silence in the room was palpable. 'If I had been, I would have read PC Judd's data, seen the massive risk Alec Prentiss posed.' He looked to Watts, Judd and on to the other officers. 'I apologize.'

They all stood. Watts saw Miller approach him. 'Will? We're all going for a drink later. How about joining us?'

He saw Traynor smile. 'Thank you, Josie. Maybe another time.'

WATTS' EYES WERE FIXED on the floor, arms folded as Brophy addressed the team, trying to recall a word Chong had used to describe Brophy's voice whenever he addressed a group of officers. Portentous. He looked up. Brophy was enjoying himself.

'Alec Prentiss was clearly a man plagued by a heavy conscience. A man who valued the lives of others very little. A man who believed he had the right to pass judgement when he considered that the law had failed to do so, who took the law into his own hands, driven by his own internal demons.' Some officers had their eyes on him, most were looking elsewhere. Having located his inner psychologist, Brophy droned on: 'I consulted with Dr Traynor at some length at the conclusion of the case. Prentiss was clearly insane.'

Watts had been present when Brophy had 'consulted'. He had listened to Traynor say much of what he'd said to the team not ten minutes before. Insanity was never mentioned. Brophy was off again. 'His final act of self-destruction at the motorway was, of course, his choice and is *no* reflection on this force. In my view, it was the appropriate outcome. The warnings I've issued during this case about the press still apply, of course. There's a need to avoid casual comment which the press might overhear, misconstrue, and use against this force . . .'

Watts stared at him. Brophy's main consideration, first, second and last, was how this or any force to which he was attached could avoid all criticism. Law enforcement, justice came a long way down Brophy's list. He shook his head. With any luck, some village down south would soon realize it was missing an idiot. He stopped listening. He was back at the start of it all, many of his investigative team anticipating they were looking for a killer who was 'off the planet'. Prentiss never was. Mental health problems, yes. Insane, no. Everything he'd done was by choice, via planning, covering his tracks. He stared out of the window, retuning to Brophy, thinking that if there was ever a stick with a wrong end, it would be found in Brophy's hands. Subtlety hadn't figured large in Watts' thinking when he'd joined the force. Back then, he'd viewed the law as certain: right–wrong, sane–insane. Job done. He'd learned it wasn't that straightforward. Brophy was now ramping on about Prentiss's guilt, his madness. During the investigation he'd sat in his office, putting together self-interested ideas about the case, never visiting the scene or talking to the team.

Watts had gone to see Edward Arnold the previous evening to warn him that the death of his ex-wife was about to be news. He'd also been to see Mr and Mrs Prentiss, found Prentiss senior much preoccupied with the potential impact on his business of what was now emerging. He denied that Zoe had had any involvement in the escort industry. Watts had no idea what Mrs Prentiss thought or knew. She hadn't spoken.

Brophy's voice had stopped. He looked up at officers standing, stretching. Across the room, Traynor was on his feet. Watts went over to him, Judd following. He and Traynor hadn't talked about his wife and Watts decided not to mention her now. He held out his hand.

'Thanks for everything, Will. We wouldn't have got half of what we did without you with us.'

Traynor gripped his hand. 'You were focused at those times when I wasn't, so thank *you*.' He smiled at Judd. 'You too, Chloe.' She flushed.

Watts walked with him to the door, knowing that he couldn't leave it there. 'Will? I just want to say I'm sorry this case didn't give you what you wanted.'

Traynor looked at him. 'I'm not sure now that it was what I wanted. If Claire had been there, I would have had to accept that she's gone.' He smiled. 'I'm seeing my daughter later. I'm going to ask if she'll consider coming home, just for term breaks, see how it goes.'

Watts followed him out of the squad room, watched him go down the stairs. 'Good luck, Will!'

He turned away, running into Judd. Her face, always a pretty reliable barometer of what was going on in her head, was telling him that she had something on her mind. He thought he might know what it could be, although it was only a guess. He knew nothing about her early life beyond what Chong had told him and he was happy to keep it that way. They walked downstairs together.

'Look, Judd, what you, we, know about Prentiss . . . his story was bad from his early days . . . because of how his parents were and it never changed. Never got any better.' He glanced down at her. 'It's not your story, Judd. It's his.'

'I know.'

THIRTY-FOUR

Friday 30 September. Nine thirty a.m.

Watts headed for headquarters' main entrance, breathing air with a hint of sharpness. He spotted a small figure with spiky blonde hair just ahead of him. 'Aye-up, Judd!' She turned, grinned at him. 'How's things?' he asked.

The grin vanished. '*Dead* boring. Brophy's got me on some trauma resilience training. I told him I wasn't interested.'

'Bet you did.'

'He still insisted.'

'That's Chief Inspector Brophy doing what he ought to do, looking after your welfare, so you don't suffer work-related stress.'

She shot him a peeved glance. 'How's that work, to be forced into re-enactments of critical incidents, one of them an armed robbery where we got *paintballed*. It was really stressing, Sarge. I've still got the bruise.' She looked up at him. 'What have you got on?'

'A minor crime-wave.'

She brightened. '*Really?*'

'Not in the sense you're thinking. Fifteen burglaries committed by two twelve-year-olds.'

She sighed, shook her head. 'Bloody kids. Any chance of me being on your team again?'

'All's possible.'

'Yeah, right. I know a fobbing off when I hear one.'

He reached for the door, held it open for her. 'There's still some things of yours in my office.'

'Like what?'

'Some bags of crisps, a mascara—'

'Mascara? You sure it's mine?'

He eye-rolled. 'I've just remembered, it's mine.'

They walked the corridor to his office, went inside. She looked around. 'Have you heard from Will?'

'We met up a couple of weeks back, had dinner,' he said, leaving Chong's name out of it. 'He's all right. He's getting there.'

'Good.' Several seconds slipped by. 'Do you think you'll ever work with him again?'

'That feels like fifteen questions you've asked me in the last five minutes. The answer is, I don't know. It depends.'

'On?'

He sighed. 'I was full of energy when I arrived. All *kinds* of things. The kind of case we might get. Whether Traynor's available. Whether he's interested. Does he think he can contribute?' He handed her a small box. 'Your stuff. I seem to recall you had imminent plans to move on from here.'

She took the box, removed the packets of crisps, the mascara, dropped them into her bag. 'I'll give it a bit longer. Unless Brophy sends me on more waste-of-time courses, in which case I'll be off.' At the door she turned, giving his neat hair and smart suit a quick once-over. 'Got a date later, Sarge?'

'What's it to you?'

'Just asking. You can ask me stuff like that 'cos we're colleagues and it's sociable.'

He glanced at her. 'Anything for a quiet life: what you up to later?'

She grinned at him, pulled open the door. 'What's it to you? Say "Hi" to Dr Chong for me.'

Several hours later

IN THE DARK SQUAD room, the answering machine clicked to an automated message and a light, female voice drifting around it.

'Hello? We've just got back from honeymoon in Mauritius and . . . sorry, I'm a bit jetlagged. My name's Lucy Travis. My number is . . . I just wanted to let somebody know that Hugo and I were at that place where a woman runner was murdered. We were there fairly late on the day we got married, Saturday, the thirteenth of August. We sneaked away from our reception and . . . I just wanted to tell somebody that there was an odd man there that evening. We didn't actually *see* him but he sounded like he was in trouble, or upset, shouting at some people. He sounded really angry towards them, but we didn't see them either. He shouted some names. The only one I remember is "Justin", because it's my brother's name. That's it, really . . . We thought you ought to know . . . I hope it helps . . .'

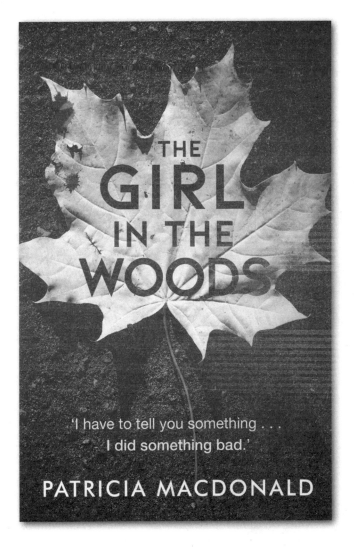

THE
GIRL
IN THE
WOODS

'I have to tell you something . . .
I did something bad.'

PATRICIA MACDONALD

'Gripping suspense'
Booklist

BLACK ❤ THORN

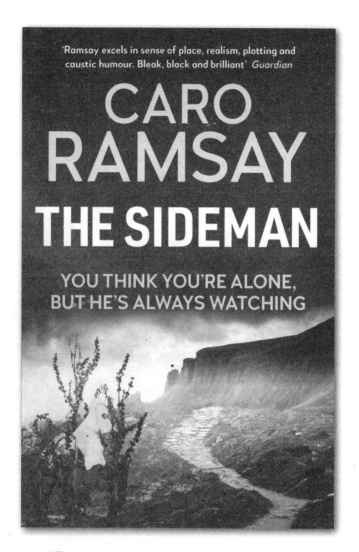

'Ramsay excels in sense of place, realism, plotting and caustic humour. Bleak, black and brilliant' *Guardian*

CARO RAMSAY

THE SIDEMAN

YOU THINK YOU'RE ALONE, BUT HE'S ALWAYS WATCHING

'Ramsay . . . continues to be one of Scotland's best'
Herald

BLACK Y THORN